How do you get a billion people through a 5-person docking bay?

> With a video camera.

How do you hear the best ideas from a billion people when they are all talking at the same time?

> With a 'castpoint.

How do you beat an alien planet-wrecker of inhuman power?

> With a video camera, a 'castpoint . . . and teamwork.

Surviving the *Shiva* will require a genius greater than Einstein, a tenacity greater than Edison, a wisdom greater than Socrates, a cunning greater than Sun Tzu. No one person could combine these abilities.

But by integrating millions of talents, embodied by **billions** of people from millions of backgrounds in thousands of different fields of expertise, we can prevent total destruction. So from Nevada to China, from the Arctic to the Equator, people of both ordinary and extraordinary skills will commit their abilities. People as diverse as a geriatric KGB agent, a teenage scam artist, a blind child, and a paraplegic ex-Marine will find solutions to small pieces of the puzzle. With a few exceptions they've never met and they never will. Yet in their billions they will work as a tight-knit team. Though the builders of the *Shivas* knew enough to use technology that borders on magic, they never dreamed they would have to face the combined intellectual might of all humankind, linked and coordinated by . . .

The EarthWeb!

laughter still in his blue

EARTHWEB

MARC STIEGLER

A Baen Books Original

Baen Publishing Enterprises
P.O. Box 1403
Riverdale, NY 10471

ISBN: 0-671-57809-X

Cover art by David Mattingly

First printing, May 1999

Distributed by Simon & Schuster
1230 Avenue of the Americas
New York, NY 10020

Typeset by Windhaven Press, Auburn, NH
Printed in the United States of America

In *Memoriam,*

This book is dedicated to Phil Salin, who recognized the remarkable consequences of electronic commerce long before there was a Web. Phil, soon the future that once you alone could see will be so commonplace, no one will believe it was not always obvious. But then, we always knew that that is how it would be, in the end, didn't we?

Acknowledgements

My heartfelt thanks go to all the following people: My wife Lynne, who told me to go ahead and quit my day job to complete this book, who also undertook every research problem with enthusiasm and charm; my daughter Shea, who gave me a break just often enough to write it; Jim Baen for a decade of encouragement to write another novel; Rosie Smith for her insightful editing comments; Fordham Otieno Wara for his help understanding the culture and character of the people of Kenya; Wilfred and Agnes Chan for their similar help with Hong Kong and Guangdong; Robin Hanson for his insights about idea futures; and all the members of the Foresight Web Enhancement Project, especially Norm Hardy, Mark S. Miller, Tanya Jones, Peter McCluskey, and Eric Dean Tribble, for their review of various aspects of the security, link, and detection features yet needed by the Web before it can achieve its true destiny. As always, any errors in this book are mine alone.

Chapter One

T minus Twenty-seven,
The End of Angel One

The Dealer stepped under the fabric canopy stretching above the alley. The delicate patter of misty raindrops rustled above him; his sneakers squished with every step. The Dealer smiled in the darkness; the rain protected him far better than even the night sky now gathering around him.

A soft hum came around the corner of the factory to his right. Lights glared, and a truck, an old white groundhugger with more than its fair share of dents and scratches, lurched into view. The Dealer tensed as it approached—the alley was too narrow, he had nowhere to dodge. It was hard to hide when you were six foot two in a country where the average height was still around five foot seven.

The vehicle jerked to a stop. The Dealer relaxed and ran slender fingers through his long black hair. Lights

1

died, the door squeaked open, and the driver jumped to the pavement, splashing in a puddle.

The Dealer peered through the fading twilight into his new customer's face. Too young to be that smart. A kid, really. An ugly one at that. The crook in the kid's nose bespoke some fighting, yet the twisted nose did not explain the twisted harshness of the kid's appearance. It was the cold anger in the eyes and around the mouth that made you want to look away from him. Such warped anger . . . The Dealer wondered momentarily if he himself looked the same. He couldn't see it in the mirror, but . . . oh, well. He was what he had made himself—a successful entrepreneur. Chan Kam Yin, the child he'd once been, had grown up to be the Dealer. In the process he had grown out of his anger, or at least into the belief that living well was the best revenge. Perhaps the kid would grow up, too. The Dealer shrugged. If the kid didn't grow out of it, he'd probably get himself killed. Either way it would work out for the best.

The kid had a truckload of high-end motherboards, the kind you'd use in the central server for a comfortable flat in Hong Kong. "Okay," the Dealer said, continuing the negotiation where they'd left off a few minutes earlier, talking on their palmtops. "I'll buy the truck too, but it better be clean."

"It's clean, all right. You have my reputation on it."

The Dealer grunted. The kid couldn't be more than fifteen years old, and new to the business. Yes, the kid had sent him email from an unforgeable identity that, when cross-referenced on the Web, turned up as the seller in half a dozen transactions. He showed all the indications of an honest burglar. Vague clauses permeated his contracts in the eMarkets, typical of the deals for illegal goods. The buyers all commended the kid on his excellent merchandise.

But half a dozen transactions, no matter how properly tricked out, didn't make for much of a reputation. The cops could have set the identity up, a ploy they tried from time to time with a modest level of success.

The Dealer would have stayed away—should have stayed away—but even in email he could tell the kid was young and earnest. The kid reminded him of himself at that age, a long time ago—a whole four years or so earlier.

The Dealer's electronic identity—the one he used for fencing operations—had almost two hundred references on the Web, most linked with glowing reports from both buyers and sellers. His reputation was worth more than gold, he'd come to realize. You just couldn't conduct business, legal or illegal, without it. His high-quality reputation—his brand—had been the means by which this kid had found him on the Web.

The Dealer continued, "Remember, you agreed to link a comment to our contract." The Dealer pointed his palmtop at the kid's system, initiating a delicate digital dance that took upwards of half a second. The kid probably didn't understand the mechanics of what was happening, but the Dealer, who'd spent more than a little time studying electronic security systems, did. The bottom line was that digital cash flowed from the Dealer through a highly reputable electronic escrow agent to his new, happy customer, while the control codes for the truck's engines flowed back to the Dealer through the same agent. At the end of the sequence, the Dealer's palmtop held new control codes. The kid's old codes, now revoked, could no longer start the truck.

Thereafter, the kid worked his palmtop, speaking softly to it from time to time. In seconds the Dealer could see the comment appear on the contract in the Wan Fen Emarket. Chalk up another notch in his brand's reputation.

"You too," the kid said.

The Dealer nodded, and a few taps made another comment appear, noting that the kid had shown up on time and delivered as promised.

The Dealer tensed—this was the moment in these transactions when risk ran high. He'd given the kid both the cash and the electronic endorsement. If the kid killed him right now, and if the kid had somehow jimmied the control code authentication system in the truck (no mean feat, but still possible), he could take his truckload of parts and sell it to another fence.

But the kid was already backing down the street. In a few seconds, he turned and started to trot.

The Dealer stood quietly for a time, trying to think of anything he might have missed that would lead someone to believe stolen goods had changed hands here. He'd bought exclusive rights to the vidcam recordings of this alley from the owner of the body repair shop next door, so no one could use that footage against him. But you never knew when some satellite would pick you out for a close look for one arcane reason or another. The canopy under which he'd completed the exchange wouldn't protect him from infrared.

He decided that he'd really done nothing suspicious or even interesting to a roving eye. A gentle tingle of anxiety in his shoulders that he hadn't even noticed till now eased off.

The Dealer wondered idly if the motherboards were all as good as the sample he'd examined. If they weren't, the kid would soon learn a bitter lesson. The Dealer's endorsement of the kid's delivery was indelibly etched on the Web—it was virtually impossible to get a comment retracted from a reputable electronic marketplace, and when working with criminals, you just had to use the most trustworthy markets—but he could always add a second comment about how the goods had turned out, upon detailed inspection, to be defective. One such comment would effectively burn such a young reputation to the ground. No sensible fence would work with him again. The Dealer hoped the kid understood the consequences.

Satisfied, Chan Kam Yin climbed into his new truck

and fired up the engine. He would have to hurry if he wanted to get home before all the Angels died. He wanted to be watching the action on his own touch-screen when his 'castpoint position paid off.

Only a handful of people ever received invitations to visit him in this room. Those invited always accepted. They rarely stayed long. Guests uniformly found the room too cold and dark for comfort. Morgan MacBride thought it was perfect.

Outside, a thick blanket of night lay softly upon the piñon pines, cedars, and scrub oaks that enveloped his isolated dwelling. Outside, the darkness finally brought cool relief from the throbbing daylight. But this room remained dusky even at sun's zenith. Morgan kept his workroom in perpetual twilight. Such darkness seemed appropriate to a place that saw so much death. The darkness had a practical purpose as well—it eliminated eyestrain while he watched his wallscreen.

The image of a sandstone corridor filled the wall. The image had traveled over a million miles to get here, yet arrived perfect, crisp, clear and life-size. The underlying screen disappeared from view for the untrained eye, building the illusion that the miles-long hallway led directly from the room.

Then the image jerked, breaking the seamless sense of continuity. The simple purity of the corridor scene jump-focused to a complex, grisly scene of dead men in spreading pools of blood.

Morgan sat transfixed by the sight. He did not move, though the heels of his large hands dug into the worn leather arms of his chrome-and-steel wheelchair. Eyes wide open, he nevertheless listened sightlessly to the sounds he had heard so many times before.

The crunch of disintegrating ceramic armor assailed Morgan's ears. Then the screaming began. The dying man did not scream in fear—he had volunteered, and had known that he would die even if he succeeded.

He did not scream in pain—a stew of pain-control chemicals coursed through the Angel's bloodstream. No, these screams filled the air with distilled rage, with frustration . . . and with apology.

Morgan spoke, his tongue thick with the effort. "Trudy, shut the wall off."

The computer responded instantly, and the image of the faraway corridor winked out. Overhead lights turned up a notch, just enough to make visible the plush maroon carpet and the navy blue velvet hangings on two walls.

Morgan bellowed in helpless fury.

Solomon, his African Gray parrot, was perched on Morgan's left shoulder. She ruffled her feathers, then whistled the first few chords of "Exodus." "No win," she observed in her trilling voice. Morgan reached across with his right hand to scratch under his companion's feathers.

"No win," Morgan agreed. For a moment it appeared Morgan would regain his composure. Then the vision of those final, fatal moments filled his mind's eye. He heaved himself out of his chair with a practiced motion and seized one of the iron rings above his head. Solomon growled and took flight as Morgan grabbed another ring, let go of the first, and hurtled across the room.

The most graceful treefolk of the world are the lemurs. With long, long arms and stubby legs, these distant relatives of humanity can swing through a forest canopy faster than a man can run. Watching Morgan MacBride swing through the room in a dizzying series of figure-eights, any lemur would have grudgingly conceded that the big primate demonstrated a certain skill. Like the lemur, the man had short stubs for legs; the truncated lower body allowed the man to achieve a rhythm of motion known only to the forest dwellers.

Solomon flew around the room at the same altitude as Morgan, crisscrossing the swinging ropes and rings in a cloverleaf pattern of her own. As man and bird swooped through the airspace, a terrible collision seemed inevitable time and again. Somehow, though, the crash never came. The two continued flying and swinging, a flowing tapestry no one else had ever seen.

The reason Morgan kept the temperature down became clear as a slick sheen of sweat covered his face. The perspiration soaked into his heavy white T-shirt, gluing the cloth to his chest, outlining the ropes of muscle that danced across his ribs and shoulders in time with his flight.

At last he dropped exhausted into his chair. The chronic dull ache in the left side of his lower back now peaked in a sharp dagger of pain, throbbing with such intensity that a sadistic masseur might contemplate it with glee. The pain and exhaustion drove the corridor images from his mind.

Silence enfolded the room, a silence that seemed to absorb every hint of sound, even Morgan's breathing. Solomon backwinged gently to land once again upon his shoulder.

A silky woman's voice with just a trace of the South penetrated the hush. Trudy, his computer, spoke. "The General's calling. Would you like to talk to him?"

Morgan's fingers dug deep into the chair arms. Of all the people Morgan didn't want to talk to, the General topped the list. "Put him through, Trudy," he growled.

A small portion of the wall came back to life, featuring a white-haired man with blue-gray eyes now hooded in sorrow. The rigid line of the General's jaw told a different story, however, a story of endurance that would yet prevail. He pursed his lips, knowing Morgan would now add to his grief. "They got pretty close this time," he offered. "They reached the previous Gate location." The voice reached for an upbeat tone, but the General hadn't fooled Morgan in over a decade.

Morgan growled. "They got nowhere close. The entrance wasn't in the same place, and they should have known it."

"Wait a minute, Morgan—the forecast was giving them sixty percent odds that they'd find the entrance."

Morgan slammed a fist into the chair. "And for *Shiva IV* and *Shiva III*, the odds were never lower than eighty-five percent. You can't just look at the numbers from a 'castpoint, Samuels . . . you've got to understand them. There were a bunch of tailriders on that one, and they were the only ones who were really certain. But tailriders aren't certain because they're smart, they're certain because they're stupid."

Samuels' eyes turned cold. "Well, it doesn't make any difference anymore." His tone softened. "You start tomorrow, Morgan."

"Yeah. Thanks for sharing." Morgan's voice dripped sarcasm as he waved his hand at one of his computer's vidcams. The General's window closed, leaving the wallscreen dark as before. Morgan sat in the crepuscular quiet for a long time. His eyelids sagged, then closed. After a while his breathing turned deep, slow, and steady.

Solomon clacked her beak twice, then in a rough, whistling voice ordered, "Trudy, lights off. Boss asleep."

The silky Southern voice replied, "Sure enough, Sol."

Solomon squawked, "Brights for seven," to set the alarm.

Trudy softly answered, "Sweet dreams."

Solomon proceeded to sing. She sang an aria that would be easily understood by other African Gray parrots, though it was wasted on her present somnolent company . . . even if he did think almost as well as a parrot. At the end of her performance she fluffed her feathers once more, tucked her head under her left wing, and went to sleep.

Chan Kam Yin sat motionless in his closet-sized apartment, thinking about facts and forecasts. The session had started so well and gone so badly.

He had come home after the evening's successful

business and sat down at his one extravagance—a black lacquered desk inlaid with mother-of-pearl in delicate garden scenes. With Singapore rice sticks in hand, he was comfortably prepared to watch the end of the *Shiva* assault. He had turned on his touchscreen, and his Factoid of the Moment had popped up with important news:

To escape the grip of a crocodile's jaws, push your thumbs into its eyeballs—it will let you go instantly.

It had seemed like a good omen indeed, a clear-cut solution to a deadly situation. So much for good omens.

Now he just stared at the mocking results on his touchscreen. He felt a moment's ironic happiness that he had decided not to purchase the bigger screen of which he dreamed. A bigger screen would have shamed him more effectively than the tiny machine he now faced.

The hideous deaths of the Angels did not upset the Dealer. He, like everyone else, had expected that result. And he had watched the videos of other assaults from the Web archives, so none of what transpired surprised him. No, his personal horror had come as the Angels broke into the hallway where the control room entrance, the Hallelujah Gate, should have been.

He still couldn't believe what had happened. This *Shiva* had suckered him as surely as it had suckered everybody else. Well, not quite everybody else. Half an hour before the Angels reached the not-entrance, while they were fighting their way past a squad of minitanks, someone had bought heavily against the forecast that the entrance lay at the end of this hall. Maybe the buyer was the mythical Predictor that gullible people around the Web speculated about. Probably not, though. Personally, Kam Yin thought the gossip ridiculous—how could anyone be that much better at guessing what lay around the next corner?—but whoever had made the massive purchase had single-handedly dropped the odds on the 'cast from eighty to sixty-five percent. Kam Yin could only draw one conclusion. Predictor or not, the guy who had bought that position had *known* that the entrance wasn't in the same place it had been on all four of the earlier *Shivas*. Whoever he was, he was either a real expert or a real fool. Kam Yin bet on the former.

The Dealer wasn't an expert, but he'd proven time and again he was a smart guy. He'd figured to pick up some easy money on the sure things. So he'd bought into the safe forecasts, like, "Would the Earth Defense Fleet destroy *Shiva V* before it got inside the asteroid belt?" Of course not; the Fleet had failed four times before. The newest weapons were remarkably advanced compared to the weapons pitted against *Shiva IV*, and they were utterly fantastic compared to the childish toys Earth had sent against *Shiva I*. *Shivas* were unthinkably powerful and deadly compared to anything ever built by humankind . . . and each new *Shiva* was more powerful and more deadly than the last. Earth Defense still had a long way to go before it could beat a *Shiva* planet destroyer with brute force.

"Would the Angel One team reach *Shiva V*'s docking bay?" Of course they would; they'd done it four times before. The Angel's *Argo* ferry craft was the stealthiest ceramic vessel in the solar system . . . even *Shiva* couldn't spot it till it was inside the dock.

"Would the Angel One team defeat the portal locks?" Once again, every Angel team had succeeded, except for Angel Three against *Shiva II*. Of course, everything about the battles with *Shiva II* had been a fiasco.

So the Dealer had bought the easy forecasts. There wasn't a lot of money in it—the ninety-eight percent odds favoring *Shiva V* against the Fleet had meant that the hundred yen he'd put down only repaid one hundred two—but he'd won reliably nevertheless.

Until now.

Kam Yin sighed. He'd have to figure out a different approach before he tried again.

He rose from the desk carefully, but to no avail—he still banged painfully into his chest of drawers, wedged against the desk at an odd angle. Rubbing his arm, he knelt on his narrow built-in bed to look out his one clean but tiny window. Bright moonlight tempted him to believe he could glimpse reflections from the ocean waves to the east. But what he *could* see straight ahead, very clearly, were the lights of Shenzhen, and beyond that, high in the sky, the pale glow of cloudlight reflected from Hong Kong's ebullient radiance.

If only he could fly into the night sky and join that reflected glory, he would see Hong Kong glittering below like a million diamonds as if in affirmation of the boundless wealth created there—wealth that had flowed and spilled from the city ever since *Shiva I* had blown Beijing to smithereens. Between the Web's history pages and the stories told on the street, he'd come to believe the destruction of that old capital had been a fabulous personal stroke of luck. He didn't really know for sure, of course. After all, it had happened before he was born.

The Dealer tapped his fingers unconsciously on the windowledge as his mind drifted back to the present, pondering *Shiva* that had just snookered him. Looking back, he was able to admit to himself that he was a tailrider: a mindless dummy who just picked the favorite forecast as if it were a sure winner. His father had educated him better than that. His father had been a bookie for cockfights, among other things. He had taught his son the tricks of his trade in between beatings. The old man had scorned the holiday customers who bet the favorites just because everyone else did. And he'd been right, because those customers were the ones who, in the long run, lost reliably.

The Dealer's father hadn't bet very often himself, but when he did he won more often than not, and often with the odds against him so he could collect big-time. His father had explained the fundamental rules of gaming to him: never bet against the house, because

the house *must and will* win; when betting against
amateurs, understand the odds; and most important,
don't bet against the top experts, because—at least in
Cantonese cockfighting—the top experts usually bet only
when the fight was fixed. In that situation, the expert
was the one who knew which way the fix was in. Watch
out when *those* experts played!

Buying forecasts on a Web 'castpoint wasn't exactly
the same as cockfighting. No one on Earth could get
in a fix on the outcome of an encounter with a *Shiva*;
the "experts" couldn't rig a surprising upset of the odds.
But important similarities existed. He'd have to ponder
those similarities. He'd have to ponder them hard. There
was just too much money on the Earth Defense prizeboards and 'castpoints for him to look away.

In the meantime, he'd have to go back to work, doing
something at which he *was* an expert. He had a ship-
ment of car parts on the docket for the following
evening. Well, at least he'd get a good day's sleep before
going back to work.

Jessica stood in the mall and stared at the screen
along with the hundreds of others who'd come here to
watch. For just a moment she dragged her eyes away
from the screen to study the people around her. Another
observer would have seen little to distinguish the people
here from the average. But people were Jessica's life.
Jessica saw no one as "average."

Few in this crowd were dressed as crisply as she,
rather unusual for this part of Cupertino. Many of them
were older, too. And most were far more quiet than
you'd expect in a bar, even in a high-class bar.

Their demographics explained their presence. The bar
had collected a crowd of lonely people without families,
people who weren't making Earthbound contributions
to the assault, people who nonetheless needed to drown
their fear in a communion with fellow human beings.

The crowd overflowed the main room of Andiamo, and

the proprietor, either through sympathy or greed, had set up a temporary wallscreen outside in the wide mall corridor. Waitresses hustled through the crowd, less efficient than usual because they, too, cared desperately about the relentless action on the display and had trouble keeping their eyes from it. When the final dash for the control room entrance began, the waitresses simply stopped serving and joined the spectating crowd, becoming individual cells in a larger organism. Everyone watched helplessly as Buzz Hikmet, leader and last Angel of the assault, died. The eyes of the crowd bulged as a Destroyer, a hulking ceramic robot of surreal strength, ripped Hikmet's arm from its socket. A collective gasp broke the silence as the Angel's lifeblood splattered on the camera lens, distorting the world through a dark red filter. The crowd started to breathe again when the Destroyer smashed the last of the Angels' cameras and the screen went momentarily blank. It cut swiftly, automatically, to a news site for the usual post-assault dissection of events. The jump-cut lent an eerie commonality to the event. All the realtime news came through the same way, be it a car accident, a heroic rescue, or the first step toward the end of the world.

Jessica knew that there would be several hundred links on the page, each running to different analysts and news teams, but Andiamo filtered out all but three. The barkeep picked one at random and a bland newscaster appeared, determinedly and desperately calm.

The crowd stirred as it too worked to appear calm. The newscaster more or less succeeded; the crowd failed. Slightly hysterical shouts for drinks filled the air. The bulk of the assembly, shrunken with horror, hurried away toward the mall exit and the parking lot.

Jessica stepped back a few paces to distance herself from the crowd, knowing that if she stayed she would share the panic. Worse, she would reflect it back and make it worse for everyone. She felt as helpless as they did, but she had developed a personal form of escapism.

She walked deeper into the mall, away from the parking lot, toward the GameZone.

The place was empty save for an emaciated pasty-skinned attendant. The kid hardly saw her—he was glued to his private touchscreen, hung beneath the registration desk, out of sight of the customers. No doubt he was watching the same thing as most of the other ten billion people on the planet. Not even pausing to smile at the guy, Jessica hurried as quickly as she could in her dress shoes—which was faster than most people could have walked in their sneakers. She came to her game's cocoon, heard the soft beep as it requested two dollars from her palmtop's cash reservoir, and okayed the request. She entered and adjusted her controls. The game began.

In general, Jessica thought video games were boring. She'd played socially a few times with friends who insisted that she try the newest and greatest. But then the Boyfriend from Hell changed all that four years earlier.

Dmitri had introduced her to *Angels' Gambit*. She'd played it off and on ever since, her play fiercely intense in the last few months since Earth Defense had detected *Shiva V* two light-days from Earth. In the last week she'd played *Gambit* every night after work. And now she understood why. Here in the cocoon she could look *Shiva* in the eye and make a difference. Tonight, she thought, she might even win.

Angels' Gambit did not lure the shoot-'em-up crowd of teenage males as much as you'd expect for a game that required so much combat. First you picked your team from an ever-changing cast of recruits, then you met the Angel Controller. That character looked remarkably like Morgan MacBride, the Angel Controller who had beaten all four of the previous *Shivas*. Seeing MacBride's avatar always gave her a chill. He was a mythical figure, and Jessica didn't believe in myths. All of the *Shivas* he'd destroyed had gotten past incredible panoplies of weapons, everything Earth Defense could throw from every spaceship and orbital platform under its command.

After reading the heroes' biographies, you interviewed them, and picked the brain of the Controller. In your interviews you looked for more than the obvious features of brains and brawn—you also looked for moral qualities . . . both the bravery that permitted you to sacrifice yourself if that was the best solution, and the wisdom beyond bravery that permitted you to *avoid* sacrificing yourself if your teammates were dying, but you had to stay alive to go ahead.

Even that was not enough—you had to look for combinations of people who complemented each other. One person had to be big and strong to carry the supplies, another quick to outmaneuver the roboguards, still another acrobatic to get behind the minitanks.

And above all, team members had to reinforce each other psychologically. Personalities were important in this game. Pessimists simply couldn't make the journey. One acidic sense of humor might work, or five might work, but three would only resonate and drive the others to murder.

In this sense the game reminded Jessica of her real work as a management consultant. Management consultants were team builders, leaders, agents of change. An Angel Controller had to be all of those things. She'd gotten into consulting accidentally, though it followed naturally from her instinctive comprehension of and fascination with people. Even in high school she had had an eerie ability to analyze and predict human behavior. She called it "playing human pinball" when joking with her closest friends. Push their buttons and people would light up, just like the bumpers in the old arcade games.

Just two weeks earlier, she and her friend Quinn had been talking about their mutual crony Christina, an ex-roommate of Jessica's who remained a close friend. Jessica had poured out what she thought would happen with

Christina and her boyfriend. Christina had asked Jessica what she thought of David, and though Jessica was not about to tell her—after all, girlfriends were there to pick up the pieces afterwards, not to poison the arrangement beforehand—she had thought about Christina and David a lot, and she had to get it off her chest.

Jessica had said, "Quinn, she and that idiot are going to split up. He's been looking at other chicks lately, and Christina has been hanging on to him as if her life depended on it . . . which she probably thinks it does. I know I would, if I were in her situation. I give them a week at the outside." She sighed. "Somebody ought to warn her."

Quinn had replied, eagerly raising her hand, "I'll do it! She's so codependent it hurts me to look at her," but Jessica had quickly scotched that. "You know how stubborn she is—that'd send her right off the deep end. Don't worry—you know Christina." Jessica had rolled her eyes.

Quinn replied, "If they break up, and I'm not sure that they will, since Christina will fight tooth and nail to keep that from happening, it'll take her a long time to recover. She's really gone on this guy."

Jessica smiled. "Nope, I'll put five dollars on it being less than a week before she finds someone new and wonderful—at least she'll think he is."

After Christina and David broke up—less than the predicted week later—Christina had spent two very depressed days agonizing over what *he* said and *she* said *ad* the *nauseum* to Jessica. Then on the morning of the third day Christina waltzed into work reborn, touting the virtues of Steve, the paragon of all that was good in the male of the species. Jessica had just blithely agreed with every ridiculous claim. It all followed formula, after all.

When Jessica had seen Quinn the next day, Quinn had just handed her a five-dollar bill and shook her head. Quinn had asked, "Why are you right so often?

Don't tell me anything about my life—I want it to be a surprise!"

Recalling it, Jessica sighed. She often felt like Cassandra when she played human pinball: the projections were uncomfortably accurate. People actually had little freedom to maneuver, given their personalities. Being able to predict future actions had almost never allowed Jessica to change them.

Perhaps that explained why she enjoyed this peculiar game so much. In *Angels' Gambit*, her ability to understand the dynamics of human relationships made a difference.

For most people, the game terminated before selecting all five members of an Angel team, because they made such a hash of matching the personalities. The teams typically blew apart during training exercises. Jessica's teams always made it through training and onto *Shiva*.

It took Jessica almost an hour of immersive play to get to the point where she loaded her team onto the *Argo* and launched them toward the bright white sphere of *Shiva*. Usually she didn't mind the foreplay, but tonight she was impatient to get to the alien ship. Tonight, even if she lost as she always had in the past, she knew she'd feel better.

When she had entered the cocoon her mind had been full of images of human beings being torn apart. Now, facing the simulated *Shiva* with her simulated Angel team, those images were being replaced by images of virtual Angels receiving the same ghastly fate. The simulated deaths were still horrible, but not as bad as the real deaths. Even if she lost, perhaps she'd still be able to sleep tonight.

But tonight she thought she just might win. Her mind was racing. She could feel her body shaking as well. The adrenaline rush should have been a disadvantage while playing the position of Angel Controller—but in its grip her mental state blended the characteristics of a bulldozer and a lightning bolt. She sent one Angel down

a corridor to hold off three roboguards, while another
stayed back to stop a team of repair mechs. A Mark II
minitank thought it was hiding around a corner, but with
her heightened senses she somehow knew it was there
and her remaining three Angels took it down with no
more loss than a broken arm. They reached the entrance
to the control room, and in the bloodbath that ensued
one of her team members survived to crawl through that
entrance. Dying but not dead, the Angel set the bomb
he carried and a white light sprang out, filling the
immersion tank, blinding Jessica momentarily.

She did it she did it she *did it*! She'd beaten the
damned thing. An electric tingle arched up her legs. She
grabbed the controls to keep from falling, she was so
weak with . . . joy, relief, *release*! Beating *Shiva* was
better than sex, she realized, uncertain whether that
meant the victory felt so good, or that her recent
experiences with men had been so uninteresting.

Her mind leaped and whirled. Just let me control
the next team, she thought in a moment of heady, foolish
joy. I'll kick the living shit out of that *Shiva*!

She blinked several times until the balls of light in
her eyes faded. At last she strode triumphantly from the
cocoon. She smiled at the attendant. He looked over,
saw her radiant expression, and tried to smile back.

Once, Jessica's friends had sent snaps of her to
Playboy as a prospective webfold girl. It had been an
utterly silly notion—Jessica had always known she was
a little plain in the appearance department. But a
charming lady photographer and her even-more-charm-
ing assistant had persuaded her to go ahead with a test
shoot. By the time they were done prepping her, Jessica
could barely recognize herself in the woman with the
billowing flame-red hair, tilted aquamarine eyes, and
inviting lips. The photographer assured her that she
would stand out even in those pages of beautiful women.
Jessica had turned them down. She still wondered if
she'd made the right decision. But she'd never doubted

the wisdom of learning to use makeup the way the photographer's assistant had shown her.

Now, when Jessica smiled at them, men—and most women—smiled back. She had naturally expected to win the attendant over for just this one moment. But the attendant was still living with the real deaths of the real Angels. He still faced the undeterred approach of the real *Shiva*. Jessica could not touch his mood. Rather, he dampened hers. She still held her head high when she reached her skycar, but inside she sagged just like the other people from Andiamo.

In twenty-six days humanity would make its last ditch stand against *Shiva V*.

Chapter 2

T minus Twenty-six:
The Month of Shiva

Years of orbital hopping had not lessened his dread of weightlessness. As the ship coasted into space and his stomach floated gently toward his throat, deep inside he just *knew* he was falling to certain death. He fought it by focusing on something else, *anything* else. Right now, he was focusing on the stars. Not a good choice. It didn't help.

Reggie Oxenford turned from the tiny porthole filled with black space and bright stars. His gaze swept the circular room, studying the other people making today's trip. Less than a quarter of the people had that "Oh-my-God-I'm-going-to-die" look that pronounced them useless for the duration of the Month of *Shiva*. It raised Reggie's spirits to see the majority of the people coping so well—after all, if the upcoming Angel Two assault failed, if this *Shiva* proceeded on the stately course of destruction set by the first one, no one on this vessel—

or anyone on the ground below, for that matter—would survive the year.

Could he work up a good news story on this topic? Reggie dimly remembered a shuttle ride similar to this one during the Battle of *Shiva II*. That time, the shuttle had been almost completely full of people who had already given up. Gross World Production had fallen by eighty percent during the thirty-six days between the Angel One and Angel Six assaults. Of course, the battle with *Shiva II* had been a ghastly screw-up from the get-go. The military bureaucrats had sent a stream of Angel teams with traditional combat training, instead of a handful of squads prepped specifically for tackling *Shiva*. Over two million men in five thousand ships had died creating the covering fire for those doomed assaults. Only after *Shiva* had fried Montreal and almost nailed San Francisco did the bureaucrats concede failure and let MacBride take control. Reggie shuddered as he thought about how close a call *that* battle had been.

The battles with *Shiva III* and *IV* had gone well in comparison. Scary and terrible though they'd been, no more cities had been turned into charnel houses. And with the defeat of every *Shiva*, the percentage of lost souls fell. People were, in a billion different and private ways, getting used to the idea that the world faced sudden and total annihilation once every five years. No one knew why the Shivas kept coming, though there were whole 'castpoints devoted to the analysis. People didn't let the uncertainty get to them, they just kept on keeping on, in a remarkable testament to the adaptability of the human mind and the resilience of the human spirit.

Gravity returned as the black sky quietly turned a deep clear blue. Reggie looked down with relief. He picked out their destination easily. Kisumu had until recently been tiny, almost primitive by Western stand-ards. Now a vast sprawl of buildings consumed the edge of Lake Victoria, marking its location. And of all the

new building complexes in Kisumu, nothing drew one's
eye faster than the drop port.

The Dover Drop Port from which he had just departed
could have fit invisibly into a corner of the Kisumu field.
Monster rotons sat on their concrete pads. Machines and
human workers alike raced to load military equipment
aboard—the rotons would lift the weapons into high orbits
in preparation for the deadly alien ship.

Over a million people had relocated to Kisumu in the
last ten years. Kisumu lay on the equator, and at an altitude of over three thousand feet it was the perfect place
from which to launch large payloads into high orbits.
Earth Defense had spotted its potential early on and had
eventually transformed the place into the heavy-lift center
for both Africa and Europe. Only the huge drop port at
Machu Pichu competed with Kisumu in scale.

The port grew rapidly in his window. Reggie stared
fixedly at the ground as it came up to meet him. His
view was scarcely altered by the commercial roton's huge
copter blades as they gained speed, whirling up to a
velocity that made them invisible.

In college, Reggie had spent a semester fascinated
by twentieth-century history. He'd studied the old-
fashioned rockets, the V-2 and the *Saturn V*. In comparison to those graceful brutes, the roton spacecraft
was almost disappointing in its simplicity. People back
then had wanted glamour and mystery in space travel,
not something that looked like it should be on your
breakfast table. Undoubtedly, people had read too many
science fiction novels where the spacecraft was gleaming
silver or deadly jet-black.

But rotons *were* simple. To make a roton, stand an
egg on its end. Attach four huge blades to the fattest
part of the egg, and attach a rocket motor to the tip
of each blade. During take-off, the rockets didn't lift
the ship—they just rotated the blades, and up you went,
just like an old-fashioned helicopter. As you rose into
ever thinner atmosphere, the blades tilted till the rocket

motors were pointing down; only then did the ship actually travel like an old-fashioned rocket.

During these takeoffs, the roton looked like a Rube Goldberg device compared to the ships invented in science fiction. Coming down, though, the roton was stranger still. He watched and listened to the descent of his own vehicle.

As always, the landing was dead-quiet. The rocket motors on the tips of the blades were shut down and silent during re-entry, since the frenetically whirling blades soaked up kinetic energy during the first stages of re-entry and didn't need more boost. By inverting the angle of the blades at the right moment, the ship used that energy to push back against the atmosphere and become an autogyro. The spinning blades contained all the power needed to make the descent smooth, gradual, and even comfortable.

A last spike of pressure accompanied the tipping of the blades to a stronger angle, and the ship settled on the ground, its journey complete. Reggie Oxenford heaved an unconscious sigh of relief.

He glanced at the sketchy map of the drop port on his palmtop, tapped for the directions to his rented skycar, and headed off.

Jessica tossed in her sleep. Work dreams hounded her tonight, as she wrestled with strategies to lure the CEO of Bigelow's Recycling into sensible action—sensible action being the course she had laid out, naturally. No strategy in the dream gave any promise. The problem gnawed at her, a virtual piranha nibbling the lobes of her mind.

Relief came only when the sound of her name interrupted her anguished slumber. She forced one eye to focus on the clock. It confirmed her worst fears. The autoperk didn't even have her caffeinated lifeblood ready this early.

"Jessica," whispered the sardonic, sensual voice of the

Boyfriend from Hell. Jessica groaned with fresh horror. Once she had thought herself clever for programming her home control unit to mimic him—his very voice raised the hair on the back of her neck, making her uncomfortable enough to ensure she got up and out. *Big* mistake. Somehow, her human pinball game always failed where she herself was concerned.

"Ugghhh," she replied, then went back to sleep.

But the Boyfriend insisted. "Jessica! Someone is at the door. He says it's urgent."

Jessica groaned. "Shut up," she told her computer. She shook her head, and once again stuck a Post-it note on her parietal lobe. She'd reprogram that computer's voice *today!*

Through half-open eyes she saw the pinkish glow of sunrise. That made her groan again. She wrapped her favorite tattered sky-blue robe around her and headed toward the door. Even her teddy bears weren't awake, she noted as she stumbled past them. She checked the monochrome display that showed the intruder; the straight-backed man in the crisp uniform did not look like a thug. Not that a thug had been likely in the first place— central computers were invariably wired to call security agencies at the first sign of trouble, and thugs knew it.

With a half-hearted jerk, she opened the door. She had planned to glare at the stranger who had awakened her at this ridiculous hour, to force him into stammering apology at the very least. Her plan suffered an abrupt change, however, after one look at her visitor.

Standing five foot eleven inches, even Jessica's friends couldn't describe her as petite. Yet she had to lean her head back to see the man's face. His snow-white hair accentuated his quiet dignity.

The cleft chin matched the chiseled lines of his face so perfectly that a biosculptor could not have done better. A biosculptor, however, would have eased out the ingrained worry lines from the forehead and temples. No, Jessica concluded, this man had always looked like a Canadian Mountie. She suspected he'd make a good dance partner—Jessica had trouble finding men tall enough who could lead properly, and he just looked like the type.

Her eyes fell to the six stars on the shoulder of his Earth Defense uniform. She wondered how long it took to acquire that many.

"Jessica Travis? I'm General Samuels. Kurt Samuels." He held out his hand.

She shook his hand automatically, feeling foolish in her faded old robe as she studied this *GQ* poster boy for the mature male. General Samuels. She'd heard that name somewhere before. If only she could remember where. She switched off her glare and gave him a small smile instead. "How can I help you?" she asked.

The General pursed his lips. "Well, that's a long story. The short version is, I need your help to destroy *Shiva VI*."

Finally his name clicked. Her eyes widened, and she came fully awake. "General Samuels! Please come in!" The Chairman of the Joint Chiefs of the Earth Defense Agency entered her two-bedroom townhouse.

"Thank you," he said as he followed her into the living room. He laughed. "I'm sorry, but you should have seen your first expression."

Jessica pointed to a chair for her guest, then sat herself on the sofa. She wrinkled her nose and replied dryly, "Perhaps it's available on the vidcam instant replay." Had another man laughed at her like that, she'd have stored the offense for later retribution. The General . . . well, he deserved a little slack. After all, he'd guarded humanity for something like fifteen years, or ten anyway—she knew he'd been Chairman during the *Shiva III* action, though she was not sure who'd been in charge against *Shiva II*. And of course, *Shiva I* hadn't been defeated by the military at all.

"You won at *Angels' Gambit* last night," he said, with laughter still in his blue eyes, the twinkling so bright she could have used it to light up her Christmas tree. Then the meaning of his words hit her.

How did he even know she played *Angels' Gambit*? How did he know she played *last night*? She stared at him.

"Did you ever wonder how *Angels' Gambit* could be so inexpensive even though it's a total-immersion game? Have you ever heard of anything like it, with a top-of-the-line cocoon, that you could play for two dollars?"

Jessica nodded thoughtfully. "I confess, I wondered how they made a profit. It was too cheap to be that real."

"Earth Defense owns *Angels' Gambit*, Jessica. We used it to find you."

Jessica tipped her head back and threw the General's laughter back at him. *Her* laughter was just a touch too loud and too wild, however, to reflect his properly. "Okay, I'll bite. Why?" she asked, knowing that he wanted her to ask.

The General's eyes searched the living room, from the Southwestern knotty-pine daybed-*cum*-sofa by the brick fireplace to the Oriental prints and undersea photos that adorned the walls. "You have a weblink in here somewhere?" He stood up and lifted her blue teddy bear off the sofa to peer under it in mock inquiry.

She laughed in spite of her tension. "Not in the living room." She waved her hand. "My office." Jessica led the General down the hall to her office, awkwardly unable to think of anything to say. Fortunately the hall was short. She flipped on the wallscreen as she entered the room, then realized with horror what a shambles her office was. Her central server stood agape in the corner, its wires streaming in wild disarray across the floor. Plug-ins stood naked on the motherboard—its case lay halfway across the room. She'd been working on a CPU upgrade the other night and hadn't gotten around to cleaning up yet. *Not* the image she wanted to present to this man. Granma would chew her down to her toes if she found out that Jessica had brought General Samuels into this wreck of a place.

Jessica rolled her spare chair over next to her desk, letting the General sit down. She grabbed the trackball and set up an anonymous connection to the Web—she wasn't going to log in with her permanent identity if she was going to turn control over to the General. She offered him the trackball.

The General cleared his throat apologetically. "Actually, Ms. Travis, it would be easier if you could slave the screen to my palmtop. I have all the information here," he explained. "Is that possible?"

"No problem. Call me 'Jessica,' by the way." She popped a window on the screen, set its capabilities so it could access the Web but not her server, and turned authority for the window over to the infrared port on the General's palmtop. A picture of another tall, handsome man appeared there, with pale skin and dark curly hair. She recognized him immediately, both from the onscreen photo and as the avatar in *Angels' Gambit*. "Morgan MacBride?"

"That's right, Jessica." The General tapped his chin with his finger. Jessica just bet women went for that cleft. "He's the best-known person on Earth today. Ten billion people recognize him at a glance. Morgan MacBride, savior of Earth, honored by more people than Jesus Christ, Buddha, or Mohammed. He's the private citizen who, after all the fleets of Earth had been destroyed, took four ex-Marine buddies, snuck a partially stealthed roton into *Shiva*'s docking bay during the fireballing of London, and blew the damn thing to kingdom come. He couldn't quite save Washington, but he saved everybody else." The General's eyes glittered suspiciously as he summarized the well-known tale. Then he blinked; the fleeting window into his soul snapped shut. He shook his head as if to clear it. "But, Jessica, there's a problem with this picture." The window split; in the second half of the window another man appeared.

Every feature of this man's appearance seemed out of sync, a complete integration of contradictions. The tan skin of his face, neck, and hands had the texture of creased and battered old shoe leather. Yet his huge—even grotesque—chest and shoulder muscles marked a physical strength seemingly impossible in a man who appeared that old. Liver spots formed an irregular pattern across his smooth bald head, another sign of age and fatigue. Yet the man's eyes burned with youthful though dark intensity. Those eyes looked familiar. She looked just at the eyes for a long moment. Then she looked back at the other picture. The eyes were the same. Her breathing stopped for a second as she stared at Kurt Samuels. "Morgan MacBride," she whispered.

The General nodded.

She looked back at the new picture. Curiously, for all his physical deficiencies, he was not unattractive. Despite the blemishes and the wrinkles he was a legend, and she could see why. He reminded her of the Beast from childhood tales, who did not even look human, but whose sheer strength and passion gave him character that the smooth-skinned twenty-something Ken—or even GI Joe—dolls she knew could never achieve. Still, he looked older than she'd expected. "I'd heard the rumors that he was dead," Jessica muttered, "But I never took them seriously. I didn't realize . . ." She thought back to her childhood memories of *Shiva I* and the aftermath. She looked again at the photo of MacBride taken just after his return to Earth. "He can't be more than fifty years old!" she exclaimed.

The General agreed. "You're a bit high . . . he just turned forty-eight. But we still have a problem." His stylus danced across the surface of his palmtop, and new information filled the window of her wallscreen.

It was a medical report. The General spoke as she read. "Morgan has a couple of strikes against him. First of all, he is genetically predisposed to rapid aging. Secondly, he took a whopping dose of radiation when

Shiva self-destructed during his escape." He pointed at the report. "You can read the consequences for yourself."

Jessica scanned the list of medical jargon. It set forth a veritable feast of physically fatal indicators. Three different forms of cancer had metastasized in MacBride's body before being pummeled into remission. A brain tumor the size of a pea underwent regular inspection for signs of growth. His left kidney operated at fifty-three percent efficiency, and his right kidney was on its fourth replacement—Morgan's immune system had rejected each of the first three within weeks, despite advanced cloning techniques. The problems with his heart had names she had never heard of before, but they looked bad. Half a dozen doctors swore that a heart transplant for a person with such a history of systemic rejection was going to be fatal.

The feeling of panic from last night, as she watched the disastrous assault on *Shiva V*, came back to her. "Oh, God! He's been the Controller against every last one of them!"

The General's voice became a whisper. "That's right, Jessica. For every *Shiva* since that first one, we've sent out at least two Angel teams. Angel One has always been run by the brightest, fastest combat controller we could train. No Angel One team has ever succeeded. Starting with *Shiva III*, we've always had Morgan run Angel Two. As you just said, no *Shiva* has ever gotten past him."

Jessica felt lightheaded. "He's the only one who can stop them. What are we going to do?"

The General's eyes commanded hers. "You're leaving with me, Jessica Travis." He looked around the room, at the clutter and the comfortable chaos. She could see that he knew this was not merely her house, but her anchor. "I don't think you'll be coming back." Jessica knew what he meant. The house might remain her possession, but it would never again be her home. She rose in response to the General's order.

And still the question reverberated in her mind. What were they going to do?

Reggie's trip from Laker's Inn to the Ng'eno residence was uneventful. Skycars crowded the air; periodically you could see one or another of them turn sharply as their proximity radars warned of a close approach. Cars were the first thing people bought with their newfound wealth, so Kisumu's skies were almost as busy as Colorado Springs, where the EDA had its headquarters.

From the air Reggie could also see trains coming in from both directions on the Ugandan Railway. A fleet of ships steamed across the lake. Reggie wondered if Kisumu would still be here in a month. Could the enemy ship recognize this place as a potent military staging area? Would it blast Kisumu as one of its first actions?

Of course, Reggie knew something *Shiva* did not know: that one single individual here in Kisumu personally threatened the giant warship more than all the equipment lifted from the drop port. And that person lived in a modest, red-brick, two-story house outside the bustle of the city. Reggie could see it as his skycar slowed to a hover near its roof.

A plain-looking family car sat next to the landing pad. Everything about this dwelling seemed completely unremarkable, considering the abilities of the forecast trader who lived therein.

Touchdown complete, Reggie headed for the front porch. The tall, ebony woman with short, kinky hair who opened the door looked substantially older than himself. This surprised him. He had dug out a little information on her on the Web, and Selpha's bio showed she had no more than two years on him. He recognized the suspicion in her eyes, though she gave him a tired smile. "Ms. Selpha Ng'eno?" he inquired.

"Yes, Mr. Oxenford," she replied, clasping his hand in a firm grip. Her speech surprised him. Not only did her voice have a strong, even commanding tone, but it rose clear and beautiful . . . rather like his own, in fact. It was free of the twangy American accent so common in the world these days. He should have expected that . . . after all, she had learned English here in her native Kenya.

Reggie smiled broadly. "I'm Reggie Oxenford. And I must say, it is delightful to find someone who speaks proper English, not that intolerable American slang."

That drew a cough from Selpha he interpreted as a suppressed laugh. "English is the official language of Kenya," she said, "though it is a bit hard to keep up the tradition, with American so popular on the Web." She led him into the living room, where a younger woman stood smiling brightly. "Mr. Oxenford, this is my sister Dorothie."

Reggie nodded to the girl. She was a beauty, with shoulder-length hair that curled rather than kinked, and smooth clear skin the same rich color as Selpha's. Only three years separated the sisters, yet they appeared to be from different generations.

Dorothie cocked her head and inquired, "Would you like something to drink, Mr. Oxenford? It's a long trip from England." Dorothie spoke perfect American. Clearly a child of the new order.

"That would be delightful. Some tea, perhaps?"

A coldness permeated the room as Selpha and Dorothie exchanged glances. Reggie knew that somehow he had lost what little goodwill he had earned in the earlier exchange. Dorothie said apologetically, "We don't have tea here, Mr. Oxenford. Coffee, perhaps? Or a Coke?"

"Coffee would be good. Thank you."

Dorothie departed and Selpha stepped back into the role of hostess. "Please sit down," she said, pointing at a high-backed cream-colored chair.

For the first time Reggie took a measure of the room. The chair appeared quite new, with hardly a hint of wear on the soft cloth. Indeed, everything in the room was new-ish. Suddenly Reggie understood the significance. "Did you buy this place about four years ago? After *Shiva IV*?"

Selpha nodded. "Most astute, Mr. Oxenford. I bought it with our earnings, helping the Angels in the last go."

"How did you do in the Angel One assault yesterday?" *Blast*, Reggie thought even as he said it. He was coming a bit too fast.

Selpha looked away. "We certainly did better than the Angels themselves."

Reggie took a deep breath. Somehow, he needed to get Selpha's trust if he was to achieve his goal. "It was quite terrible," he said softly, "I'm sorry I brought it up."

Dorothie returned with coffee, some cookies, and a Coke for Selpha. She hurried from the room.

Selpha spoke next. "I, uh, suppose I should apologize to you as well, Mr. Oxenford. About the tea."

Reggie looked at her in surprise. "Not a spot of bother, Ms. Ng'eno. The coffee is delicious."

"Yes, well . . ." Selpha sat up straight, as if making a confession. "I should explain. You know we're from Kericho."

Reggie nodded. "That was why I thought tea would be an easy choice, actually." Kericho's main claim to fame was still its tea, despite all the changes in Kisumu just a few miles away.

"Well, I worked on the tea plantations for six years. It is not a pleasant memory. Tea is simply not allowed in my house."

Reggie realized then that Selpha had probably grown up in a thatched hut, quite possibly married off at the age of twelve for a few cows. No wonder she looked older than her age. "Congratulations on your escape."

"Thank the Earth Defense Agency."

Reggie waited for her to elaborate. As the silence became awkward and Reggie decided to fill the void, Selpha continued. "After the Top Drop, Dorothie tricked me into learning how to use her palmtop, and I became the satlink admin for our village."

Reggie nodded. "I see." That explained many things. Top Drop had been a part of the WebEveryWhere initiative. In parts of the world where the governments stole more than the bandits, and used even food as a tool of control, Earth Defense had bypassed them and dropped millions of palmtops from the air. Solar powered and capable of vocal as well as written communication, the palmtops did best with children, playing games with them till they learned to read, write . . . and eventually to do calculus. If Dorothie had had to trick Selpha into learning about computation and communication, Selpha had been right at the cusp of the change. The three years that separated the sisters was indeed the transition across generations. Reggie realized there was an award-winning story here, two women so close in age yet so far apart in the civilizations that controlled their formative years. By accepting the precious but difficult satlink admin job, Selpha had been able to shield Dorothie from the harshest truths of poverty as they climbed, together, into a brighter future. Dorothie's youthful nature stood as another testament to Selpha's formidable strength.

Now he needed to somehow make Selpha understand him as he understood her. Perhaps telling her his goals would make the difference. "Please let me explain why this interview is so important to me."

Selpha snorted. "You explained yourself in email reasonably well." She pointed a finger at him. "You're doing a series of Web pages on, what do you call them? Ah, yes– 'Unsung Heroes—Behind the Scenes in Earth Defense.'"

Reggie winced at the sarcastic tone in her voice.

"Maybe, Mr. Oxenford, the 'Unsung Heroes' are unsung because they want to be left alone."

Reggie closed his eyes and prepared to try again. "It's true that I make my living as a journalist. But my series on 'Unsung Heroes' is more than just a commercial piece, Ms. Ng'eno. In my own way, I am trying to help defeat these bloody machines." He looked into her eyes. "The world needs more people like you. Out of the billions of people who have never submitted a solution to the prizeboards or offered a new prediction on the 'castpoints, there might be another person somewhere who can do what you do."

Selpha smiled bitterly. "But if someone else could make the forecasts I make, I would be out of business, would I not?"

"You wouldn't make as much money," he admitted. "But answer me this. Ms. Ng'eno, if you died, what would happen to Dorothie when *Shiva VI* came? If you hadn't warned Whitaker about the three minitanks of a new enhanced model, lurking in the materials storage room on *Shiva IV*, the whole team would have died right there."

He paused; Selpha looked stricken. He continued, "Ms. Ng'eno, if you insist, I will write a contract with you, right now, stating that I will not reveal your technique of forecasting until and unless you die or are mentally incapacitated. But please . . . tell me about your methods, or at least make sure someone else reliable knows it so that all of Earth will not lose it even if we lose you."

Selpha slumped as she thought about the larger issues.

Reggie pressed the attack. "You will not find a more reputable person in whom to trust your story. Let me show you." He pulled out his palmtop, and popped up a list of his recent publications. He moved, low and quick, to kneel beside her so she could see the display. "Please pick any of these articles at random, and examine the comment links. Most of these articles have actually been endorsed by the people described in them." He picked one from the middle of the screen, and showed her the endorsement and comment made by the interviewee.

Selpha raised an eyebrow. "Does *everyone* endorse your pages, Mr. Oxenford?"

He laughed. "Not everyone." He opened another page, and showed the ragingly hostile attack on him the subject of another article had made.

Selpha stared at the comment. "Goodness," she muttered, "that is rather vehement."

"Yes, but look at the comments the fellow has made about other biographers, and about other people in general." Reggie ran a search of the Web for other critiques with the same brand to show her a sampling. A blistering attack on a corner florist for a box of a dozen roses that had contained only eleven flowers nicely captured the fellow's temperament.

"He rather seems permanently angry," she confessed.

Reggie held up a hand. "Let me be very honest. I didn't go out of my way to mollify this poor chap, either. I try to write the truth, and that includes not sugar-coating the troubles a fellow has."

Selpha smiled. "Do you ever make mistakes?"

He snorted. "Of course. But," he played with the palmtop, "I correct them." On the screen she could see a correction link attached to one of the biographies, in which Reggie apologized for an error.

"I know it's hard to trust reporters, but believe me, I'm the one for you." Reggie flashed a big smile up at her from his kneeling position. "Really. I'm the best!"

At last Selpha laughed. "And modest, into the bargain. Very well. But I'm afraid my technique won't do you much good. Or anyone else, for that matter."

Reggie's knees were starting to ache and so, having won the critical battle, he retreated to his chair. "Really? Your forecasting has something to do with sound analysis, right?"

Selpha nodded. "Very astute again, Mr. Oxenford. We . . . *analyze* . . . sounds, and extract the nature of the objects involved from them."

"I thought so. There were several interesting forecasts, like the one about the minitanks, and another about going clockwise to the nearest slidechute, that appeared on the 'castpoint shortly after sharp sounds echoed down the halls. And of course there were postings on the prizeboards requesting occasional sharp raps on the wall, which were new and rather unusual requests during the assaults on *Shiva IV*."

"Those requests were ours," she admitted. "You missed a career as a forecast trader yourself, Mr. Oxenford."

"Call me Reggie." He chuckled. "I had hoped that you had developed some new type of digital signal processor that did this analysis for you. But if no one else can duplicate your success, what is your secret? Do you just listen carefully?"

"Not exactly. It's . . ." Selpha's shoulders slumped again. Somehow the answer caused her pain.

"Do you want that contract from me now?" he offered.

"No, it's just that . . ." She stopped again.

The sound of a loud crash came from a back room. Selpha leaped to her feet, and Reggie followed her without invitation, hoping he wasn't intruding but determined not to let her escape now that he had her convinced.

A left turn into the hallway and a right through double-wide arches led into a glassed-in rec room. The scene before him elicited puzzled anguish. A teenage boy lay huddled on the floor, shivering as if from an unknown ailment. Dorothie knelt beside him, her arms extended, her hands not quite touching the boy. A plastic globe of the Earth still rolled in a slow drunkard's walk across the hard floor. Selpha spoke to Dorothie rapidly in a language incomprehensible to Reggie.

The boy spoke. "Plastic sphere. Hollow. Shell four millimeters thick. Bumps on the surface. Hit vinyl tile, two millimeters thick, on five-millimeter mahogany plywood backing, three centimeters from a steel cross-strut."

It took Reggie a moment to realize that the boy had just told him Selpha's great secret.

Selpha knelt by the boy and looked up at Reggie, once again filled with bitterness. "Reggie, meet my son, Peter."

Not quite knowing what to do, Reggie knelt down as well and held out his hand. "Nice to meet you, Peter."

Peter did not respond.

Selpha explained. "Peter is blind." Her hands clenched and unclenched. "He is also autistic." She looked at Reggie as if she had explained everything. Reggie's blank expression clearly told her she had not. "You may know that some autistic children can solve remarkable mathematical problems in their heads. They are known as 'idiot savants.'" Tears welled in her eyes. "My child is also an idiot savant, Mr. Oxenford. But he doesn't do math. He just listens."

At last, Reggie understood.

Fort Powell, southwest of Las Vegas, could be described as beautiful only by someone with the esthetics of a Franciscan monk. But for such a person the windswept, scrub-blanketed lands presented a study in sublime beauty.

The austere simplicity of the land reached into the buildings of the base as well. Now barely at midmorning, the fierce desert sun already beat through the tinted windows, reflecting off the polished floor tiles, flooding the classroom with harsh light. The room's fluorescent ceiling tiles might as well have been blackened, for all the value they added.

Morgan MacBride knew what his new people were seeing in that stark light: a bald and decrepit wreck of a man with a parrot perched on his left shoulder. And he knew what they were thinking: *Is that really him? Jeez, I had no idea he was so . . . old!* It made no difference.

Whatever their thoughts, they looked at him with that absolutely sober earnestness shared by young people who believed in themselves and in their mission. He would hate himself for it, but he would use that dedication, exploit it for his own mission. Of course, his mission was only a little different from theirs.

He began. "Welcome, Angels."

That created a stir; now they knew that they had been selected.

"Yes, that's right. You're the Team now. Earth's last hope. If you succeed, your names will be remembered for as long as humankind lives. If you fail, you will still be remembered for as long as humankind lives. But it will be a much shorter memory." He smiled grimly and shifted in his chair. "However, you don't know who I am. You may think you do, but you don't. Let us be very clear about this. I am the man who will cause your deaths. Each and every last one of you will die at my command."

He let the silence hang in the air for a long minute. When he thought they had recovered, he flexed his huge shoulder muscles, lifted himself out of the chair, and swung onto the desk. The parrot had known what was coming, and took the sudden shift smoothly. "I have led twenty people into *Shiva* ships. Only one man has ever gotten out of a *Shiva* alive, and as you can see, he didn't do so well."

The five people in the room stared at the stumps where Morgan MacBride's legs had been; he let them protrude from his shorts in defiance of the unspoken convention that such disfiguration should be hidden. Everyone knew, of course, that the final explosion of *Shiva I* had cost Morgan MacBride his legs, but they'd never seen it—no pictures had ever been posted on the Web that showed the price of his victory. Morgan actually had a pair of prosthetic legs, but they were uncomfortable, and besides, he needed his legs like they were for this one day that came every five years.

"I know that you have gone through the most intensive training process in the history of Earth. Some of you have been training for this mission all your lives. I have news for you: your training has just begun. The next twenty-four days will be the real training. It will also be your last."

He looked down at his palmtop. "Locks and Blocks Specialist . . . Axel Sturmlicht," he called out. A sturdy young man leaped to his feet. "Heavy Weapons and Logistics . . . Lars Moreau," and a hulking Swede stood at attention. "Recon . . . Roni Shatzski." A tall, gangly fellow with a jagged smile stood up. "Medic and Alternate Lead . . . Akira Tanaka," and a small Japanese man joined the others.

"And the Angel Leader . . . C. J. Kinsman," he bellowed. The thin one that looked too young stood up and saluted. "Yes, sir!" he shouted in a voice that struck MacBride strangely. The voice was too high-pitched, too melodious, too . . .

Morgan stared at the Angel Leader. "You're a woman!" he accused her.

"Yes, sir!" she repeated, with the barest hint of challenge in her voice.

Morgan continued to stare for a long moment. "Dismissed. See you at Mission Training Alpha at oh-nine-thirty." He lifted himself up, swung into his wheelchair, and barreled out of the room so swiftly that the members of his new team were still staring as he disappeared into the hall.

Morgan knew exactly who to strangle for this, and he wasted no time. His target was only a short distance away. He rolled through the outer office, where the military aide barely had time to look up before Morgan crashed into the inner door, slamming it open in his rage. He rolled forward and crashed into the desk. General Samuels sat quietly with a raised eyebrow, watching his visitor, his fingers steepled in front of him. He had clearly expected Morgan's arrival.

"What can I do for you, MacBride?" he asked, too casually.

"She's a woman!" Morgan sputtered.

"That's a tautology," the General replied.

"We can*not* send a woman on a suicide mission!" Morgan practically screamed.

"You are indeed a Neanderthal, Morgan. You knew that, didn't you?" The General clicked his tongue. "Well, I won't tell anyone if you won't."

Morgan slammed the desk with his fist. This time the parrot was taken by surprise, and had to flap for balance. "You can't do this!"

"Ah. I can't. Indeed." He cleared his throat. "Perhaps, before you go on, you should read C. J. Kinsman's bio. If you had done so before bursting in here, you would have found that, despite your old-fashioned though honorable opinion, I *must* send her." Samuels rose from the desk, towering above the still raging Angel Controller. "But don't bother, Morgan. I know you don't like to read, so let me just tell you about her. She's the best person we've ever fielded against a *Shiva*." He held up his fingers and started ticking them off. "First of all, you should have heard of her before. She won the gold medal in the triathlon two years ago." He ticked another finger. "She has five percent more endurance than Whitaker did." Whitaker had been the Angel Two Leader against *Shiva IV* and they'd thought they'd never get anyone that remarkable again.

Morgan interrupted. "What about her strength, Samuels? How big a load can she carry?"

The General continued unperturbed. "Whitaker was twenty percent stronger than CJ," he admitted, "but she's got an IQ of one-eighty. She's smarter than you are, Morgan, and some of her highest marks are in spatial and mechanical analysis." He ticked one last time, closing his hand into a fist. "And here's the kicker . . . she has the fastest reflexes in history. Period. She can devise and execute a new combat strike faster than a mongoose can snatch a cobra." The General smiled wryly. "We have a separate research effort going on just to try to figure out what's different in her neural transmitters. She is so good, in fact, that she'd be a freak in any age except our own."

Morgan was listening now, past the rage, and into a pensive contemplation of the possibilities. The General knew it was time to deliver the *coup de grace*. "In short, Morgan, there's never been anybody with a chance like this. Together, the two of you can do it. Morgan, this time you can bring somebody home."

Morgan sat motionless in the wheelchair. A part of him felt the rage bubble back up, knowing that Samuels was manipulating him, using his weakness against him. But he knew the General was right.

Morgan's mission differed from the Angel mission in one small detail. He'd never revealed the difference to any Angel. He never would.

The earnest young people of the Angel team went forth merely to destroy *Shiva*. In that goal, Morgan's mission mirrored theirs. But beyond that, Morgan needed to bring those earnest young people home again. He had never yet succeeded. CJ might be his only hope. "You win, Samuels," he growled.

"Thank you," the General replied, as the sorrow slid across his eyes like a nictitating membrane. Morgan recognized the look, and immediately understood.

In all probability, they had just imposed a death sentence on a remarkable young woman.

Jessica watched impatiently as Morgan and the General went at it. Her monitor displayed the confrontation in living color, courtesy of a vidcam set up in General Samuel's office. Eavesdropping, even at the General's order, made her twitchy, especially when she was listening to arguably the two most important men

on Earth in the middle of a private row. But the
General had insisted that she study every aspect of
Morgan MacBride's life, and the General himself had
granted her the viewing rights in his private office. Of
course, her viewing rights ended automatically when
MacBride left the room.

But for now she'd forgotten her discomfort with the
vidcam arrangement. She was steaming with disbelief.

How could Morgan MacBride question a person's
qualifications just because she was a woman? What was
MacBride's problem, anyway? Hadn't he ever met a
woman soldier before?

It didn't make any difference. She'd been watching
the world's most revered hero for less than an hour, and
she already disliked him. She couldn't do the job.

She watched as Morgan spun his wheelchair out of
the room. Her view cut to the hallway, following him.
The next important episode in Morgan's life would start
in about half an hour. This would give her the time she
needed.

She walked briskly down the hall, passing Morgan
with a curt glance. The parrot gave her a wolf whistle,
but Morgan was distracted and hardly noticed that there
was another human being in the hall. She reached the
General's office and entered almost as forcefully as
Morgan had. She could see that the General's aide had
a very difficult job.

With a disarming smile, Jessica slid passed the aide,
a young man in uniform. The aide tried to intercept
her, but her smile penetrated his defenses easily, throwing his attack into disarray. In the end he threw up
his hands and let her go past. She wondered if she
had just gotten the kid into trouble, though he did
smile back at Jessica, briefly, as Jessica forced the door
to the inner office.

The General had not yet returned to his seat. He
looked at her in mock dismay. "*Et tu, Brute?*" he said,
with a hint of humor.

"I can't do it, General," she said in flat tones. "I cannot think like him."

The General pursed his lips. "Sit down, Jessica." He pointed to a chair.

She didn't like being ordered around, but he was so charming she found she couldn't refuse, any more than she could have said no when he demanded that she fly out here this morning. She wondered if this would be a recurring theme in their relationship. She was not going to stand for that kind of treatment. Who did he think he was anyway?

She sat in the chair as she was told.

The General owned a quiet office, with plush beige carpet and walls lined with old bound-paper books. She'd read paper books before, but not often, and not recently. It was quaint, really. But as the decor of office of the most powerful man in history, the room's elements suggested strength and ancient wisdom. She felt safe in this room.

The General returned to his chair as well. He picked up his coffee cup, wrapping his hands around it like it was his last hope of salvation, then made himself set it down again. She saw a curious design embossed on one side of the cup: a red dartboard with a small but glaringly bright bull's eye. Five blue dots of varying sized marked hits, scattered randomly across the target. None of the hits had struck near the center. Despite the shortcomings of the markers, however, the caption read, "High Accuracy." Strange—how could you have high accuracy without hitting the center of the target?

Jessica brought her attention back to the General, who was now speaking in abrupt, military tones. "Ever had a real enemy? Someone determined to block your every move, thwart every plan and goal?"

"No, not . . . uh, Charley?" Jessica thought back. Charley Wenig. Charley had been a division chief for FabChip Consulting. Polished, not unlike the General.

Very, *very* smart, again like the General. But with the delicate moral rectitude of a copperhead.

Jessica had been brought in to FabChip to stop the interdivisional slugfests, the internecine cross-group stealing of hot employees by promising salary increases just for switching teams, and worse, the stealing of customers by spreading rumors about the other divisions. FabChip was its own worst enemy, and its competitors were starting to figure that out.

Charley had loved it at FabChip. The company had a great customer list, and Charley had figured, why go through the agonizing, usually unsuccessful effort of attracting new customers when plenty of in-house customers made easy pickings? Charley had loved the internal corporate disputes—he thrived on them. From the first day he had known that his vision of FabChip and hers could not coexist.

For her part, it had taken Jessica a while to glean the same understanding. She learned about a series of not-quite-lies Charley was telling people about her, just about the same time she deduced when and how the corporate fighting had begun. Trouble had started brewing shortly after Charley had joined the company. Charley had created the environment he so enjoyed working in.

Never in her life had Jessica spent so much mental energy gaming out a single person. By the time she forced his departure from FabChip, she could quote the words he would say in meetings she did not attend, much to the amazement of the people who actually heard them. One devout follower of Charley's who later switched sides had told her that, toward the end, Charley had hired a team of sweepers to check for bugs.

The General watched as she reminisced. "You never played pinball better, did you, than with a person you detested utterly."

Jessica sat forward in her chair. "It was different."

"It is always different. But don't tell me you can't

game out Morgan just because you don't like him. Study
him till he can't twitch an eye without your knowing
it before it happens. Figure out how to beat him at his
own game. How would you defeat Morgan MacBride
if you were *Shiva V*, Jessica? And how would you defeat
a *Shiva* that could defeat MacBride? Tell me that,
Jessica, and our children's children will sing songs about
you for a thousand years."

She sat quietly in her chair, trying to look unconvinced. She just wanted to live through the next month.

The General stood up, and the full power of his
personality pressed upon her. "Jessica, when we picked
you out of millions of candidates because of your success
at *Angels' Gambit*, I had my doubts that you were the
right one for this job. But when you told me about
human pinball . . . You have all the right characteristics—the speed of thought, the innate tactical and
strategic ability, and most of all, the empathic people-
reading skills. This is your destiny, Jessica Travis. Accept
it. Grasp it with both hands. Make history." He picked
up his coffee cup and took a sip. "And go do it in your
own office, so I can get some work done."

Her mind turned back to the night before, the
moment when *Shiva* blew up and she knew she had
won. She remembered her feeling that, if she had the
chance, she could destroy that bastard machine. She felt
calm. She rose, and stood with the straight-backed
precision of Samuels himself. "Very well, General." Her
skirt swished gently as she departed.

Missile Commander Anatoly Vinogrado concluded
that being in the lifepod was scarier than dying. He
huddled there in the recommended fetal position. He
cursed the people who wrote the instruction manual and
the people who designed the pod, even though they
might have saved his life.

He did not yet know whether they'd saved his life,
because he had no way of knowing whether anyone was

in a position to rescue him. The pod was pitch-black, blacker than space itself. It had no windows. It was a simple shell of styroflow that now totally encased him and, incidentally, locked him in the fetal position that he had taken as he popped the thing around his skinsuit. The styroflow—liquid at that point—billowed around him, forming an egg-shaped container that protected him from the cold of space.

He had no idea how long he'd been here. He couldn't even tell how much oxygen he had left in his skinsuit's minuscule tank, much less how far away a rescue vehicle was—if indeed any rescue vehicles had themselves survived. At least they had a better chance of surviving than Vinogrado's cruiser had had. The Earth Defense Ship *Canberra* had been part of Task Force Eight, with the mission to attack *Shiva V* with a huge volley of missiles. The mission had not, however, included a requirement to destroy *Shiva V*. They knew they couldn't do that, not after the pounding Second Fleet had taken trying to ambush the damn thing as it passed the asteroid belt. No, Task Force Eight's goal was merely to distract it from the real attack—an attack that took the shape of a small dead-black cylinder with five men on board, the *Argo*, sneaking up on *Shiva's* docking bay.

Despite his discomfort, despite the screaming of his muscles to find any slight movement he could make to ease the cramps, Vinogrado smiled wolfishly at the darkness. He personally had done better than all of Second Fleet—one of his missiles had penetrated all of *Shiva's* defenses. He had hooked in with a two-megaton warhead and gotten a direct hit on one of the plasma-beam tubes. The tubes were necessarily weak points in the hull, openings that ran hundreds of kilometers deep into the guts of the ship. A two-megaton burst on *Shiva's* bare armor, ten klicks thick, would have merely scratched the surface. But hitting the tube as he had just had to cause some real internal damage. Really. He clung to the belief that he had hurt *Shiva V* as the long wait in the black silence of the lifepod robbed him of hope. That one hit was his only real testament to having fought with all his might.

So many of his friends had no testament at all. Every assault on a *Shiva* was a suicide mission. Less than a quarter of the ships in Second Fleet had survived their all-out attempt to destroy *Shiva* V. He didn't know the casualty rate for Task Force Eight, but judging from the explosions that dotted his combat screen while he was coaxing his missiles into detonation range, he had the cold, sick feeling that their losses had been even higher. Only the Angels themselves had a lower survival rate than the men who covered the Angel approach. A typical feint at a *Shiva* to camouflage the *Argo's* arrival cost as many lives as the Battle of Stalingrad.

Gloom descended further on him as he reflected upon friends he had lost.

Suddenly the lifepod jerked, half-spun, stopped, and bounced. It could only mean one thing—they'd found him!

He could hear the high-pitched squeal of ripping styro as they tore the lifepod apart. The instruction manual said that he should close his eyes; the brightness of the light would be painful after his prolonged sojourn in perfect blackness. He disregarded the manual and watched for the light.

The manual writers had been right. The light was excruciatingly painful. It was the most wonderful experience of his life.

Chapter 3

T minus Twenty-one

CJ trotted easily down the middle-ring corridor of the center-level. The three surviving members of her team followed closely behind. As she passed a missile storage bay and a power substation she had a nagging feeling that she had seen this layout before.

Finally, in the distance, she could make out a half-cylindrical mound running across the corridor. She knew it was not merely a random obstacle. Rather, she was looking at part of a plasma beam tube—a cylinder that flared slowly as it extended from the core to the hull of the ship. The full tube diameter was probably about eight feet, but only a four-foot wide section protruded through the floor.

When CJ saw the plasma tube, in that location, she knew where she was. She was in a *Shiva II* mockup. Like most of the training facilities, it was scaled down by a factor of ten; it had just as many combat robots as a real *Shiva*, but it didn't have the vast miles of distance to run—so you could pack a full day's campaign into a couple of hours. CJ and her teammates would get plenty of practice running in their exoskeletal armored frames on the racetracks before the fighting.

They hugged the inner wall as they ran. Then Morgan's voice came through her earpiece: "CJ, hall middle."

CJ hopped to the center of the corridor even as she considered the consequences of running a *Shiva II* mockup. The good news was that there shouldn't be any advanced robots in the simulation. She *had* wondered why they hadn't encountered anything more challenging than a roboguard; now she knew.

She had sprinted barely three steps before she saw an intersection coming up. At the same time she saw why Morgan had moved her to the center. She could just make out the shoulder of a roboguard lurking around the corner.

She did not hesitate; she raced down the hall and swept around the corner, hitting the roboguard with the blunt end of her spike even as Morgan commanded, "CJ, freeze!"

The spike, a pole almost as long as CJ was tall, with a sharp tip and a hook at one end, struck the robot in the center of its breastplate. The machine took no damage. No surprise there—the breastplate was the machine's thickest armor. But the force of her charge had knocked the machine back. It swayed on both legs and whirled all four arms in a desperate effort to regain its balance. CJ quickly flipped her staff and jammed the sharp tip beneath the plate. She thrust and levered, and the roboguard split apart with a shattering crack.

Unfortunately, the roboguard had not been alone. CJ already knew what Morgan was now telling her team: "Two minitanks, Mark II. Akira, sweep. Lars, decoy. Axel, ambush." Morgan said nothing to CJ. She guessed that Morgan had assumed she would be killed by the minitanks before he could even give her instructions.

But CJ was leaping in the air even as the closer minitank swung its blade. The minitank was fast, but

CJ was faster. The blade missed her leg by a fraction of an inch as she tucked, spun, and landed behind the robots. She snapped the spike into its sheath on her armor frame while she unholstered her pellet pistol.

The robot that had swung at her was out of position and vulnerable, its back to her. CJ pointed the pistol at the floor behind the tank and pulled the trigger for a short burst. Three pellets hit the floor, ricocheted underneath the tank, and struck the robot in its unarmored belly. The minitank's four legs collapsed suddenly, its pair of arms waving in the air.

The other minitank had already turned on her, and its blade-arm hissed through the air as it rushed her. CJ jumped back, but this time she was not quite fast enough. The blade struck her frame. A real *Shiva* blade would have shattered the frame and removed her leg, but this was a trainer, not an enemy, and the frame responded to the strike by bending CJ's leg at the knee. The frame locked her leg in this awkward position, simulating the loss.

The minitank swung for another strike, but Akira was already firing his pellet gun, and this minitank stopped as suddenly as its brother had moments earlier.

Morgan spoke, "Akira, lead. Double-time. Left wall."

CJ once more swapped her gun for her staff, but this time she used the staff as a crutch. She trailed behind. Her exertion started to take a toll; soon her lungs felt like bursting. She hobbled along faster.

Even with a one-tenth scale mockup the distance from the middle-ring to the ship core was four miles. Everyone had their suits set to carry only the weight of the frame to save power—everyone except CJ, who had to pump up the suit amplification, just to keep up. She watched the pressure gauges on her compressed air cylinders fall with alarming speed. A sinking suspicion took root that she would not make it. She, like all Angels before her, found herself wishing desperately that she could carry a real power pack and a full-sized fuel cell or two to drive electrical motors for the suit. But all the stealth technology in the world couldn't protect *Argo* from detection if the ship had even small chunks of ferrous metal on board. Electric motors were simply out of the question.

Finally the arch of the Gate came into view. Three minitanks and four roboguards patiently awaited their arrival.

"Lars, pellets, roboguards," Morgan said. Lars stepped to the center of the hall, lifted his pellet rifle, and started firing as CJ hopped passed him. Using the rifle against mere roboguards seemed profligate to CJ, but they only had to get past this one squad to win. MacBride undoubtedly knew what he was doing.

"Lars, cease fire. Catch up. Akira, sweep right. Axel, left. CJ, pellets as the tanks turn."

As MacBride predicted, one tank turned toward Akira and another toward Axel. The angle wasn't great, but CJ got a pellet into the belly of the one attacking Akira. Axel's left arm snapped up in a locked position as the minitank got in a blow. Akira popped Axel's assailant with pellet fire. And the third minitank swept its blade in a killing blow that CJ could not dodge.

But instead of catching CJ in the abdomen, the blade ran into Lars' spike. The spike shattered, but Lars grabbed the robot's arm and with brute strength lifted the thing bodily into the air. Its legs flicked out to kick Lars a crushing blow to the ribcage, but missed as Lars slammed it onto its back. CJ brought her spike down into the thing's guts. It lay silent.

"Axel, the acid."

Axel dug out his gear with his remaining hand and sprayed the edges of the door with the blue canister. Lars trotted up with the extra explosives, which Axel applied with precise care. For a minute they stood watching for more enemies. The acid did its job, and then the explosives did theirs. Lars put his shoulder to the door and it went down with hardly an argument.

CJ hobbled through the Gate into the control room, pulled out the air-fuel bomb designed just for *Shiva* control rooms, and pulled the pin. "Ta daaa!" she warbled.

"Congratulations." Morgan rarely let his voice sound anything but level, but CJ thought she could hear a bit of satisfaction even from him.

Paolo sat down in the breakfast nook protruding from the kitchen. Actually, he considered the terms "breakfast" and "nook" a bit over the top. Was it really still breakfast if you sat down at the table at eleven A.M.? And could you really consider it a "nook" when it was a six-meter-wide room with a curve of glass constituting two of the walls? Well, his wife Sofia certainly considered it to be so.

The nook was on the second floor and the windows overlooked the Yucatan jungle. Sipping his hot chocolate, he reached for one of the *pan dulces naranjas* thoughtfully put out by Rosa as a breakfast appetizer and scanned the surroundings. It was a beautiful day, and in the distance, it was a beautiful view. As his gaze traveled back to the landscape just beneath him, however, a frown formed on his lean, sharp features.

A flurry of motion came up behind him. It could only mean one thing. Paolo held steady as the flurry kissed him on the cheek and said, "Hi, Daddy!"

Paolo looked up at his daughter, trying to keep his adoration from showing. "Princessa, you still say 'Daddy' the same way you did when you were six years old."

The Princessa, known to people other than her father as Mercedes Ossa y Pirelli, slid into the seat to his left. "Of course I do. It makes you so . . . malleable." She gazed at him with limpid innocence.

Paolo laughed. The term "innocence" had very little in common with his twenty-one-year-old daughter, recently graduated from Stanford with a degree in arbitrage and a specialty in forecast specification.

"What were you frowning at when I came in?" she asked after she took a sip of her coffee.

He pointed down at the old driveway leading up to the house.

"Ah," she said, immediately understanding.

Their house had originally been built back at the turn of the millennium, when people traveled by road. The couple from whom they had bought the house had not kept the driveway up. Now the concrete was breaking apart as the philodendrons, driven by forces far beyond the powers of mere humans, slowly coerced their way back into their rightful habitat. In a couple of places Paolo could even see saplings taking root.

Mercedes continued, "Still, I'm a bit surprised that it bothers you. Since when did you start caring about the landscaping?"

"Oh, don't get me wrong. It doesn't bother me in the slightest. But your mother . . ."

"Ohhh . . ." Mercedes' understanding took on new depth.

"Indeed. Your mother is bound and determined to rip the whole thing out and replant it."

Mercedes nodded. "It will cost a fortune, won't it?"

Paolo threw up his hands. "You know how your mother does these things." He took a deep breath. "She's already coming up with some truly remarkable and creative landscaping ideas. It will be," he choked for a moment, "a work of art far beyond anything heretofore wrought by Man. Or Woman."

Mercedes stared thoughtfully out the window, and bit into a sweet roll of her own as she pondered the implications. "You know, I think the driveway has a certain panache just the way it is. Don't you think it looks a lot like the ruins of the Castle of Kulkulan?" She turned her wide-eyed gaze upon her father once more. "Really, doesn't it have that same elegant, ancient look about it? Daddy, I think we need to preserve this monument for future generations."

Paolo looked out upon the crumbling concrete with new eyes. "I think you're absolutely right, Princessa. I think it would be a shocking blow to our national heritage to remove this historic monument." The left side of his mouth screwed up in a cockeyed smile. "Umm . . . you think your mother will buy it?"

"Not a chance."

They laughed together.

A high-intensity energy source flounced into the room. "Paolo!" his wife exclaimed, wrapping him in her arms and giving him a big kiss. She turned. "Mercedes!" she said, and repeated the performance with her daughter.

Paolo watched his wife with bemused affection. Even though they were now pretty deeply into their forties, Sofia was an attractive eyeful. Other men might consider her platinum-blond hair a bit too much, but for Paolo it simply made a striking and beautiful contrast to her smooth copper skin. Other people might consider her too thin, but her oft-frenetic pace kept her physically fit and her shape remained well-sculpted.

Sofia broke his reverie. "What were you two talking about when I came in?"

Mercedes looked over at Paolo with a raised eyebrow. Paolo answered reluctantly, "We were, ah, *conferring* about the driveway."

A clatter of plates announced the arrival of breakfast, carried in Rosa's devoted arms.

"Excellent timing," Paolo told her. "Thank you."

"*Sí*, Señor Ossa," Rosa replied brightly as she distributed the plates. Paolo received his traditional poached egg, Mercedes received her traditional two, and Sofia had one egg over-easy, with just a pinch of cumin and a sprig of parsley.

Rosa departed, and Sofia muttered, "I'll have to tell that girl these eggs are somewhat overdone." She paused in her culinary examination and picked up the earlier conversation. "Anyway, the driveway just *has* to be cleaned up. I can't live with it any more the way it is."

She looked her husband in the eye. "And it won't be very expensive, either. Besides, with *Shiva* coming, even if it does cost a little more than I expect, we're covered."

Paolo felt a chill run the course of his spine. It made him a little queasy to make so much money from the *Shivas*. He didn't like having a reason to be happy about the arrival of a machine of pure, malevolent destruction. Was he just the twenty-first-century equivalent of the arms dealers of the twentieth century? Or did he have more in common with a pragmatic businessman who, having been given lemons, made lemonade? Surely he was the lemonade guy—but at moments like this he had to wonder.

Paolo had grown up rich, and had been taught by his father to view his wealth as an obligation as much as a privilege. He'd studied economics, started a pair of very successful microlending operations—one in the depths of the Yucatan, one in the cities of Haiti. Then he'd won the contract to distribute the EDA palmtops south of Mexico City, part of the Earth Defense Web-EveryWhere effort to upgrade the quality of its work force—namely, the whole human race.

None of this had been wildly profitable, though, and Sofia's appetite for remarkable *objects d'art* like this house had imbued him with a slowly rising panic about their finances. No one in his family had had so much wealth locked up in real estate since his great-grandfather.

The development of the forecasting markets—the "'castpoints" as people now called them—in response to the *Shivas*, had changed this. He'd quickly found that forecasting was his destiny. Remarkably, it fulfilled both his desire to make a contribution to the world and his need to keep the bills paid. When *Shiva* came to town, the amount of money in the prizeboards and 'castpoints surged to astonishing levels, and no one made forecasts as wisely as he. So during the "Month of *Shiva*," as they called the twenty-odd-day period from the first Angel assault on *Shiva* to the second, their income always bulked up. The bad news, as his wife's comment just indicated, was that now Sofia assumed a big increase in their income, and compensated by expanding her spending plans.

Ah, well. The truth was that even Sofia could no longer really dent the family's financial position. She ruthlessly drained the household account down to empty, but that was mostly just interest on the business account. Paolo needed a lot of capital to work the 'castpoints, and he had it. Indeed, he had a rather staggering amount of capital, more than anyone, even himself, truly appreciated. So the work on the driveway was really of no consequence. *Really.* He shook himself, forcing himself to remember just how much difficulty even Sofia would face to really spend the family into debt, even with great creativity and insight.

Mercedes cleared her throat. "Who's that, Daddy?" She pointed out the window.

Paolo followed her hand. "Sofia, were you expecting anyone?"

Sofia did not look up from buttering a biscuit. "No, dearest. Why?"

"Because someone is landing." Paolo frowned out of the window as the dark blue car descended onto their landing pad.

Morgan watched the Angels as they watched the instant replays. Everyone sat quiet and still, totally focused on the screen—except for CJ. Her hands danced to a tune of their own, and her whole body periodically writhed. Morgan finally realized that this motion was part of her concentration; she was playing out the actions of the people on the screen. CJ was so supercharged that the energy poured out—like a nuclear reactor driving its generators even when unneeded, just to avoid meltdown.

On the screen, CJ once again cut around the corner, clobbered the roboguard, and turned to the minitanks.

Morgan paused the recording. "This was the first and only real surprise in the setup."

CJ muttered, "You mean the multiple robots, or do you mean minitanks on a *Shiva II* mockup? I did expect more 'bots 'round that corner. But," she confessed reluctantly, "I didn't expect minitanks."

Morgan bit back the cutting reply. Too obvious. Go straight to the point. "Never go around a corner without my directive. Unless of course it's unavoidable."

CJ smiled wryly. "I guess I can't really plead it was unavoidable, can I?"

Morgan grunted. "We have to accomplish several goals in these easy training runs. We must work out our mutual understanding. You need to know what it means if nothing is being said, whether you should move with speed or caution. But I also have to learn your capabilities. Each of you has remarkable talents." He watched them as they sat just a bit more proudly. "Which just makes you typical."

He pointed a finger at CJ. "Truth be told, CJ Kinsman, you are incredibly fast." He frowned. "Impossibly fast. Since our recon triangles were all gone, that corner was a danger no matter what we did. Had I known your speed, I would have ordered you to take that corner."

"I'm that good, huh?" CJ leered at him.

He glared back. "I'd still expect you to get killed. But you'd make hash out of the enemy position. And that close to the control center, I'd accept the loss."

Solomon gave her gravelly African Gray parrot-chuckle and said, "No lose CJ." She whistled a few chords from the *Godspell* number, "Could We Start Again Please?"

Morgan gave the bird the same glare he had just turned on the Angel Leader. He turned back to the team. "I've got to learn to use each of you to the fullest advantage, just as you must learn to react instantly to my commands." Since coming into the room, he'd been holding a wired chunk of duodec explosive quietly in his lap. Now he tossed it to CJ. "Press the button," he ordered.

CJ stared at the duodec, looked back at Morgan, and asked, "Really?" Her thumb rose over the button.

Morgan frowned in dismay. "I can see we have a long way to go." He forced the frown from his face; he knew he frowned too much. He held out his hand, and CJ gingerly gave the bomb back to him.

They played out the rest of the tape. Only Roni escaped a battering discussion of his mistakes; as recon, Roni had performed a miracle by surviving for three-quarters of the distance.

"Not bad," Morgan summed up at the end, "but not great. You took the most effective weapons Earth Defense has devised. You faced a very old *Shiva*. We saw one little surprise: the minitanks near the end. Most of you handled that surprise well enough for a first try."

Morgan noticed that he was subconsciously avoiding CJ's eyes, and he forced himself to look at her. She smiled back with that bright winning radiance that filled her, and he swore silently to himself.

Christ, it was hard enough sending guys like himself off on this mission. Why in hell did the next assault leader have to be a woman? And a remarkable one at that.

Thinking about her fate, seeing her die in his mind's eye, he once again felt the manic impulse to get out of the room and never come back. He squeezed the arms of his wheelchair with all his might and did not move at all—an act that took all of his formidable will to achieve.

She still smiled at him; he continued to consider her. Truly, she had no discipline. She did not respond to commands like Bill Whitaker. But when he got down to it, she was better than Pavel Solovyev had been when he arrived. And Solovyev had turned out pretty well. In fact, Solovyev had turned out to be great . . . but not great enough. Of course, that hadn't been Pavel's fault. It had been Morgan's.

Morgan could feel the tension gripping his back again as he walked amongst the tombstones in his mind. The parrot on his shoulder could feel it too; Solomon started grooming him, a futile attempt to calm him down. Morgan spoke. "Live weapons practice commences at oh-two-hundred."

Morgan rolled his chair into the corridor, wanting only to escape the pressure of his own emotions. Suddenly a shadow passed directly over his head. A gust of air announced the passing of a hurtling body, and CJ appeared before him, using the same trick she had used on the minitanks.

Morgan laughed. "Please remind me never to play poker with you."

CJ didn't understand. "Why not? Think I'm good at hiding my thoughts?"

Morgan snorted. "Of course not. You're an open book. The problem is, you'd always pick up a straight flush." He waved his hand. "Oh, I'd always know you had a straight flush just by looking at that smug expression on your face. But you'd still win."

CJ looked away thoughtfully. "I guess that's okay when fighting *Shiva*. I mean, you can't really bluff it anyway, can you?"

"No," he said. "You can only beat them with a straight flush." Morgan skillfully snapped his wheelchair in a half circle to get around her.

Solomon chirped. "Pretty CJ," she said, and the first few notes of "The Girl from Ipanema" echoed down the hallway in their wake.

Morgan muttered, "You're a damned impertinent bird."

He thought he'd spoken to himself, but CJ heard it. She caught up easily. Laughing, she asked Solomon, "How long have you had this curmudgeon with you?"

Solomon waggled her head with pleasure. "Always. Mate of teacher."

Morgan explained. "My wife was an ornithologist. She followed up the work done by Dr. Irene Pepperberg."

He added, "She also loved twentieth-century music, particularly the later half, if you're curious about Sol's repertoire."

CJ continued to look puzzled as she asked him to tell her more about Irene Pepperberg.

"Pepperberg was the woman who first taught parrots to talk, really talk with semantic meaning. She lived somewhere in Nevada . . . no, Arizona, I think." He waved his hand. "It all took place before the Crash. Anyway, Elisabeth built on Pepperberg's ideas. She did some fairly amazing things with parrots." He glared at the preening gray form on his shoulder. "Not all of her experiments were successes."

CJ mouthed the name. "Elisabeth MacBride." Her mouth formed a large "O" of realization. "Dr. Elisabeth MacBride was your wife? I hadn't made the connection."

Morgan smiled. "In some circles she was more famous than I am."

CJ turned back to Solomon. "So what do you think of Carnack?" Carnack was the bird that had led a flight of parrots into *Shiva IV* to do recon, using an *Argo* dropped into *Shiva*'s dock during the primary battle in the asteroid belt. Carnack and his flock had mapped out the passages before Angel One's assault. Carnack been very successful, too. Unfortunately, when Earth Defense had tried the same trick against *Shiva V*, a team of repair mechs had been waiting for them. The parrots hadn't even gotten out of the Alabaster Hall.

CJ gave a wolf whistle. "Carnack brave. Carnack crazy. Carnack hero." She flapped her wings enthusiastically. "Cute tailfeathers."

Morgan ground his teeth. The last thing he needed was his Angel Leader getting chummy with his dead wife's blasted bird. "Yes, Carnack was every bit as good as some of my Angel Leaders. And he's just as . . ." He trailed off, not really wanting to finish the sentence.

"He's just as dead," CJ whispered.

Solomon replied. "All go sometime."

CJ answered, "Yeah, so we do."

Solomon rolled her head at the impossible upside down/sideways angle used to persuade a human to pet her. CJ instinctively understood, and started running a finger up and down Solomon's neck. As CJ stroked the bird, she said, "Solomon, I was thinking of flying to Vegas to Ruth's Chris for lunch. Steak and a chocolate malt. Would you like to come along and check it out?"

Morgan cleared his throat. "We have other business. Sol can't have chocolate anyway—it's poison for parrots. Although, I have considered giving her Oreos from time to time."

Sol bit him. "Business wait. Steak great!" She whistled "Walk Like an Egyptian."

CJ looked at Morgan triumphantly. "Well, Angel Controller, whaddya think?"

Morgan would have said no again, except that, for the first time, CJ had used his proper title. Perhaps it would be a good start.

Convinced that the unknown visitor had to be a friend making an unscheduled stop, Sofia swept down the stairway as a full-powered reception committee of one. Paolo, being slightly more paranoid, opened the wallscreen in the breakfast nook and alerted security to the surprise intrusion.

It was quite unusual for somebody to just cruise up to the house uninvited. They didn't advertise the location of their house, like some people on the Web, and Paolo strongly preferred a life of quiet anonymity. He'd made over a billion dollars off the 'castpoints. He didn't relish publicity as some people might. Ask anyone who'd won a lottery how much they liked having ten new best friends pop out of the woodwork every day, all with great ideas on how to spend the winner's money.

Paolo and Mercedes watched as Sofia strode across the courtyard to the landing pad. Mercedes poked her father in the ribs. "I'll bet he's from out of country,

Daddy. That's a rental car, or I'm a blonde." She crossed her eyes, giving him her best goofy dingbat expression.

Paolo laughed. "No forecasts today, Princessa. Besides, I think you're right about the rental." The skycar was a plain vanilla model; he couldn't even tell who manufactured it. Toyota? Boeing? Ford? The answer lay outside his areas of expertise.

A pale but distinguished young man in a camel's hair jacket, button-down Oxford-cloth shirt open at the neck, pressed khaki pants, and Docksiders stepped lightly from the car. He was only a little taller than Sofia, they could see as she greeted him.

Paolo clapped his hands. "What a delightfully elegant gentleman! Your new boyfriend?"

Mercedes hit his shoulder. "Don't be silly. He's way too clean-cut for my taste."

"Too clean-cut! Would he be better if he rolled in the mud? Should I tell him this secret to winning your heart?"

Mercedes hit Paolo again, harder this time. "You know what I mean. Look how short his hair is. He's a mama's boy."

"Princessa, you may say that to him, but I could not. Observe the muscles across his shoulders and back." As Sofia danced about him in her normal animated conversational style, they could see the fellow from every angle as he politely twisted and turned in a vain attempt to maintain eye contact with her.

Mercedes saw and understood. "Competition swimmer."

"Or gymnast."

"Swimmer," Mercedes replied authoritatively. She should know; she'd been a competition swimmer herself in high school.

Sofia led the visitor in another do-si-do beneath their watchful eyes.

"Cute butt," Mercedes conceded in a slight change of the conversation.

"What!? I am shocked, Princessa!"

Mercedes laughed. "Don't worry, Daddy, he's still not my type."

"Shame. He looks like a nice guy. Or perhaps I should say he looks like a decent chap, as they'd say in England, since I'd guess that's his home." Paolo smiled slyly and looked at Mercedes out of the corner of his eye. "You haven't started dating yet, have you?"

Mercedes held up both fists and uttered a guttural scream. "Father!" Her eyes filled with fire.

Paolo laughed. They'd had a running joke that she wasn't allowed to date till she was twenty-five. His heart skipped a beat as he realized that even according to that outrageous timetable, she would soon be finding other men to replace him. He knew it was foolish, but the thought upset him nonetheless.

Paolo turned back to watch as Sofia gesticulated, communicating with her graceful hands as only Sofia could.

Mercedes spoke again. "Okay, if you won't take the first bet, let me try another one. I don't think the gentleman is going to get past Mom."

"Um. You're wrong, but I don't want to take your money on that one, Princessa." Sofia's movements from the beginning had had a defensive air to them. The stranger spoke again—the second time he'd been able to get a word in edgewise—and Sofia's arms stopped in mid-gesture. She burst into laughter.

Paolo raised his eye at his daughter. "Battle over. Stranger, One, and—"

Mercedes interrupted sadly, "—Mother, Zero."

Sofia and the visitor headed for the door. Paolo looked hard at the man. "He looks awfully familiar."

Mercedes nodded her head. "Yeah, he does. I'll remember who he is in moment." She paused. "Daddy?"

"Yes?"

"How did you know he'd get past Mom?"

Paolo raised his chin and sniffed the air. "Well, you know, that's why they call me the 'Predictor.'"

His daughter hit him in the arm again; he had to admit, he seemed to be earning his beating today. "Daddy!" she said with conviction. "The Predictor is just a Web myth, like alligators in the sewers in New York City. You know that. Stop joking with me."

Paolo squeezed his daughter's shoulders. "I'll never stop joking with you, Princessa."

Sofia entered the room and beckoned the visitor to follow her. "Paolo, I'd like to present Reggie Oxenford."

Oxenford reached out his hand.

Paolo's expression blanked even as he automatically accepted the handshake. "Oxenford," he muttered.

"The reporter," Mercedes said in the flat tone that told Paolo she, too, had immediately recognized the name. He didn't have to look to know that her face was now as deadpan as his own.

Oxenford looked back and forth at the two of them, eyes alert, knowing that he had at least two strikes against him already for some unfathomable reason. "Call me Reggie," he said as a start.

A cold pause followed his overture.

Paolo felt a measure of dismay, knowing that his daughter hated reporters solely because he himself had hated them. News people—the media elite—had been a terrible scourge during his childhood. But they had gradually lost power with the advent of bidirectional, reputation-endorsed public commentary via Web links shortly after the turn of the millennium. People who published on the Web—especially people who wanted the title of "reporter"—had to tell the truth, the whole truth, and nothing but the truth. Failure was brutally and swiftly punished with electronic tar and digital feathers. Despite a rocky start, honesty had taken over as the currency of the Web—a devastating if subtle blow to manipulators of public opinion. Weakened by the Web, the media elite had died alongside their political bedfellows in the Crash.

So reporters really weren't a bad thing anymore, and hadn't really been much of a scourge even when his daughter was born. But Paolo had instilled his prejudices into her and now, even though he himself had finally grown out of his distrust, his daughter had not.

Sofia was too astute not to notice the icicles hanging from the words of greeting, but she was in hostess-mode now and performed the rituals with the easy grace that rose above such problems. "Reggie—as you can see, we were just eating. Would you care for something? A *pan dulce*, or scrambled eggs perhaps?"

Reggie shook his head. "Thank you, but I just ate." He held his head in mock dizziness. "Jet lag, you know. I've been to three continents in three days. I fear my body clocks are a bit confused."

Sofia pursued him with typical tenacity. "Coffee, then?"

Reggie nodded. "Perhaps that would help."

Sofia departed, calling for Rosa.

Reggie stood very quietly, looking out the window. "You have a truly marvelous home here, if you'll permit me to say so."

Paolo nodded. "I have to agree. Sofia is nothing if not gifted as a house buyer, renovator, and all-round decorator. The results of her efforts are invariably spectacular."

Mercedes chimed in. "You should have seen our *last* house. Smaller, but even more amazing."

Reggie smiled at her. "You must be Mercedes."

Mercedes gave him her most dazzling social smile, which looked to Paolo like the smile of a shark about to strike. "That's me."

Sofia returned with coffee for Reggie. Paolo turned to the table and picked up his own hot chocolate. The liquid in the cup had turned cold, but it gave him something to do with his hands.

Everyone stood in silence for a moment, drinking, and watching and listening to the black-headed gros-beaks flitter outside. They were red birds with black heads and black on their wings who wintered in Mexico and sang beautifully. Sofia always had their favorite safflower seeds in an aboveground feeder, just to attract all that she could.

Reggie spoke in surprise. "What a remarkable song those birds are singing. I wouldn't have expected to hear them from inside. Are the birds really that loud? Or have you done something to this window? I can even hear the wind rustling the trees."

Sofia smiled proudly. "We have microphones scattered about outside, and the sounds of nature can be piped into any room."

Paolo nodded. "Yes, Mercedes and I were serious when we told you how creatively Sofia builds a home. This is just one of her brilliant touches."

Reggie sighed in admiration. "Magnificent. You are a very lucky man, Mr. Ossa y Santiago."

Paolo winced at the full use of his name. "Please call me Paolo. But let me say that you performed magnificently, pronouncing my name correctly. I've never even heard an American say it right, and I'd never have expected it from a Brit."

"Thank you," Reggie said humbly. "I try very hard not to botch people's names. It quite ruins the interviews before they begin."

Mercedes stepped forward. "So you're here to interview Father?" she demanded.

Reggie slouched over slightly and opened his palms as if to beg forgiveness, or at least to show that he wasn't armed. "If he will permit it. And you too, of course." He gave her his most winning smile. His hazel eyes carried a challenge in them, but even so his smile did not look as predatory as Mercedes' had.

The smile triggered a surprising reaction in Mercedes. Her mouth opened wide. "Olympics. Ten years ago. Gold medal breast stroke."

Surprise made Reggie's smile sparkle. He clapped. "See? I'm not just a reporter. I'm a person, too." He folded his hands humbly. "But my story is not half as interesting as your father's." He turned back to Paolo. "Sir, if you are the chap I think you are, I believe you have something of a story to tell. Am I correct?"

Paolo's heart leaped in his throat. He was tempted to deny Reggie's assertion, but his expression betrayed him. He'd often wondered if this day would come, if someone would finally figure out that the legend invented in foolish Web gossip actually fingered a real human being. He started to speak, but Mercedes, after a quick look at her father, mentioned in a voice full of sweetness edged with steel, "Before you start the interview, I think we should set up a contractual understanding of what you can say about what we tell you, don't you think?" Her smile grew even more charming now, but the sharklike quality had turned into a rapier-edged gleam in her dark brown eyes.

Reggie laughed in relief. He hadn't known quite what she had been going to say. "Of course. Actually, I insist." He pulled out his palmtop and held up the display. "I have a standard contract here. Of course, I expect that you will want to change it." He smiled at Mercedes. "And of course, there is no one better qualified to make modifications than you. Indeed, I'd appreciate your help improving my standard contract."

Mercedes' anger dissolved in astonishment, which she quickly covered with a frown of suspicion. Paolo fought to hide his surprise, but could not help a short laugh.

Sofia was the swiftest to recover. She beamed proudly. "So you've heard of my daughter," she said.

Reggie replied, keeping his grin and his gaze focused on Mercedes. "Of course I have. Unless there's more than one Mercedes Ossa y Pirelli, Salutatorian of her class at Stanford University, protégé of Mike Lacobie. I hear you've been tapped to write detailed specs for the forecasts on the Angel Two assault 'castpoint."

Paolo now turned his surprised eyes on his daughter. "Really?"

Mercedes blushed. "Well, yeah, actually, he's right."

Paolo huffed, "Were you going to keep this a secret from us?"

Mercedes winced. "It was going to be a surprise. I was going to tell you at dinner. *Really!*"

Paolo harumphed. Sofia shrieked, "That's just wonderful!" She swept Mercedes into her arms and gave her a kiss on the cheek.

Mercedes glared at the reporter from her current location, trapped in the spine-tingling embrace of her energetic mother. "Thanks, Mom. Uh, could you let me breathe a little bit, please?"

Sofia released her daughter. "To think we needed to have Reggie Oxenford come here for us to find out. Goodness!"

Now it was Reggie's turn to wince. He even blushed—easy to see in such a pale face. "I'm really sorry. I had no idea . . ."

Mercedes sighed. "You had no way of knowing I hadn't told them yet." Her brow folded down like thunderclouds gathering round a tornado, despite the soothing words.

Paolo just shook his head. "Well, Reggie, you just broke a first-rate story. I guess that pretty well establishes your credentials. But I'd still like to verify your identity the old-fashioned way." He raised an eyebrow at his daughter. "Even before we enter into a contract."

Reggie agreed immediately. "Of course. Truth be told, I don't even look enough like my Web photo to convince *me* that I'm myself." He laughed. "I spent an entire day with a photographer getting a shot that made me look older, more mature. People don't think young newscasters are reliable, you know."

That was why, Paolo suddenly understood, he hadn't recognized Reggie right off. He'd seen Oxenford's picture on the Web, but the picture was intentionally unlike the man! How ironic. Both modern photography and modern plastic surgery made it easy and inexpensive to fool the eye. But modern encryption systems made electronic forgery virtually impossible. So it was easier to trick people with someone else's physical appearance than with their Web brand. Such a strange world. Of course, Paolo's grandfather had said much the same thing in his time.

Paolo turned to the wallscreen. "Luis, please show us our email accounts."

Luis, the central computer server for the house, replied, "Okay." The images of four inboxes appeared on the wall, one for each member of the family.

Paolo continued, "Close Fernando's box." His son's email closed down.

All three boxes were currently empty. Reggie tapped on his palmtop, and seconds later, Luis spoke again. "Mercedes, you have new mail."

"Show me," Mercedes said.

A new piece of mail appeared; the subject line of the mail just read, "Proof." Paolo spoke. "Luis, could you show us the latest article by Reggie Oxenford?"

Reggie looked at him in mild surprise, and Paolo admitted grudgingly, "I have a subscription to your site."

An article about an "Unsung Hero," a woman in Kenya, appeared on the screen. Mercedes compared the author of the email to the author of the article. She nodded. "It's the same brand, all right."

Reggie raised an eyebrow. "Aren't you going to read the mail I sent you? There's more there than just my brand."

Mercedes eyed him suspiciously. "I suppose so. Luis, please show the whole message."

The message read, *Mercedes, I am really sorry I spoiled your surprise. Please let me make it up to you. After you modify and approve the contract, of course.* Attached was a separate document, endorsed by the reporter. The contract, no doubt.

Mercedes harumphed; Paolo chuckled.

"Okay, let's see it," Mercedes said.

Reggie and Paolo walked over to the window while Mercedes approached the wall to peer at the clauses of the document Reggie had sent her.

Sofia turned to the doorway. "Well, people, if you are settled, I have things to do." Paolo smiled and waved, and she was gone.

Reggie muttered to Paolo, "Your daughter's pretty feisty, isn't she?"

Paolo's smile broadened. "Yes, she'd give Boadicea a run for her money." Reggie looked sharply at him, visibly surprised and pleased by his knowledge of the greatest virago in history.

The men waited patiently as Mercedes scrutinized the contract with meticulous care. At last she said, "Okay, Dad, it looks decent. He promises to publish the interview only under his Oxenford brand." Paolo nodded; the promise ensured that Reggie wouldn't sell or publish the interview on any of the lurid scam sheets on the Web.

Mercedes smiled wickedly, "Of course, he does have a little wiggle room here." She pulled a touchpen from her pocket and marked briefly on the wallscreen; the digital ink turned quickly into edited text.

Reggie joined her at the wall and examined her revision. "My, you are paranoid, aren't you?" He tapped on his palmtop, endorsing the revised contract.

It was time to get to business. Paolo offered Reggie a chair. "Okay, now please tell me why you came here."

Reggie spread his arms wide. "Surely you know. I came here to find out the Secrets of the Predictor."

Mercedes stared at Reggie. "The Predictor? But that's a myth! A harebrained invention of the gossip mongers on the Web!"

Reggie raised an eyebrow at Paolo. "When were you going to tell her *your* little secret?"

Paolo held up his hands to block the puzzled look from his daughter as it turned into a lioness' glare. "Um, Mercedes, did you make sure the contract guarantees he'll keep my name and my brand out of this?"

Mercedes waved her hand to indicate it was not a problem, but continued to hold him with the full force of her gaze. "Father! Are you really the Predictor?"

Paolo writhed for her. "Not exactly. The Predictor really *was* invented by the nutcakes on the Web. But, ah, the hypothetical character they dreamed up does, uh, sort of have a lot of features in common with, uh, me."

"Why didn't you ever tell me?" she demanded.

Paolo said weakly, "Well, I was going to tell you at dinner. *Really!*"

This time it was Reggie's turn to laugh.

Chapter Four

T minus Nineteen

Her back was turned to her father as she neatly folded and tucked a soft green sweatshirt into her suitcase. "Is my room properly cleaned up?" Mercedes shot the question archly at him over her shoulder.

She could feel her father's eyes sweeping the room automatically. "It is beautiful, Princessa. You are far better at cleaning up than I. Rather remarkable, really, considering how you kept your room at the age of seven."

Mercedes was irritated to feel her muscles relax. After all these years, she still dreaded her father's disapproval. Dad said you never get over that—that his father could still do the same thing to him even today—but it was still irritating.

"I don't suppose you could stay just one more day," Paolo wheedled. "We could go climb Chichen Itza and get a better feel for how to preserve our ancient and revered driveway."

Mercedes bit back a laugh. She straightened, snapped the suitcase closed, and turn to her father. "I'm sorry,

Daddy, but I really do have to get back to work. Body contact and all that."

Paolo glowered. "Not too much body contact," he warned.

Mercedes glared back. "You know what I mean."

Paolo laughed. "Of course I do. I'm the one who taught you the phrase, if I recall correctly."

"Probably." Mercedes jerked the tan leather suitcase from the bed, but Paolo was right there and he plucked it smoothly from her hand. "Let me get that."

Mercedes let go, and Paolo let the bag fall a short distance with a strangled gasp. "Princessa, you inherited your packing skills from your mother, not me! Do you have a *Montana*-class battlecruiser in here as well as your clothes?"

Mercedes found herself choking on her laughter, unable to retort, as her father grappled with the suitcase. He mimicked a wrestler struggling against a heavier opponent. "Daddy!"

Paolo chuckled and stopped swinging the case. They walked down the hall toward the stairs together, but as Mercedes turned to the first step Paolo took her arm. "Before you go, I have something for you." He led her farther down the hall, to his office.

Mercedes felt a soothing warmth as she entered her father's inner sanctum. Daddy's office was a very private place—anyone except Daddy himself entered on an invitation-only basis. But when Mercedes had been a small child and her mother was away, Daddy would often let her come in even when he had work to do. She would sit at the worktable and play with her Barbies while he concentrated at his desk, telling her periodically to keep quiet. For an energetic, talkative child it had been too restrained an atmosphere, but she knew how special it was even then. There was no place on Earth as secure and comforting as Daddy's office.

They had lived farther north in those days. This was a different office from the one she remembered so fondly, but it had the same feeling. The carpet was thick and soft, beige with ropes of woven gold forming a gentle paisley pattern. The two walls with neither screens nor windows held a careful selection of pre-Crash artwork. As a child, her favorite painting had been a picture of a flying battleship, dashing fiercely across a field of fire where every color of the rainbow danced in a frenzy of light. The painting was the original cover art for an early SF book about the coming age of global networking. She had read the book once, as a child, and had received a small shock that prepared her well for a future of Web literature. The book had not contained a single word about flying battleships. She liked the painting nonetheless.

She ran her fingers idly across the worn surface of the old worktable where she had once played. The table would have looked out of place to a stranger, but for Mercedes it was just one more element in the composition that spelled cozy familiarity.

Her father broke the spell. "I just thought you might like to see the video I've emailed to you at home," he said, and waved at the wallscreen by the door. "Luis, start the video please. Mute the sound."

The screen came to life. Mercedes watched herself on the screen, standing in the breakfast nook the day before. Onscreen, Reggie entered the room.

Mercedes clapped. "Daddy, you recorded the entire thing."

"Luis automatically records most of this house. Except your bedroom, of course. Though I might change that if you try to bring a boyfriend down here."

Mercedes growled.

Paolo chuckled. "Anyway, I thought this might be useful to you. The contract you made with Reggie specifies the Stossel Rule Book, right?" As Mercedes nodded, Paolo continued, "I thought so. And under Stossel rules, everyone assumes that everyone else is recording, so these tapes are valid evidence in an arbitration."

Mercedes smiled so widely it hurt. "I didn't know you knew so much about arbitrage, Daddy."

Paolo folded his hands modestly. "Hey, I get around."

"Hey, yourself! Don't be so . . ." Mercedes watched the tape of Reggie and thought back on his visit. "You know, I think you really vortexed his mindspace yesterday."

Paolo raised an eyebrow. "Actually, I think *you* vortexed his, uh, mindspace more than I did. Few arbiters are as lovely as you, Princessa."

Mercedes blushed. "Well, I have to confess you vortexed *my* mindspace. He at least knew who you were."

A hurt look spread over her father's face. "You can't mean it. Is my true identity really the 'Predictor'? Can't I keep on as Paolo Ossa y Santiago, father of the world-famous Mercedes?"

Mercedes pouted. "Well, now that I know your secret, will you let me be on your team?"

Paolo took a deep breath. "Ah, Princessa, I wish you could join me. But I think it is not such a good idea." He shook his finger at her. "*You* tell *me* why you can't be on my team."

Mercedes wrinkled her nose, and after a moment uttered a small, "Oh."

"Oh, indeed, darling daughter. Or should I say, 'Your Majesty, Queen of Contract Specification for Earth Defense'?" Her father swept into a deep and noble bow.

"Rise, gracious lord," Mercedes offered with a wave of her hand. "I guess it *would* be a bit of a conflict of interest, at that."

"Mercedes," her father began, and she knew he was serious now, "just being the Predictor's daughter would force Earth Defense and your insurers both to review your qualifications." Her father looked grim, knowing that his own career might one day end hers.

She huffed, "Hey, don't go serious on me, Daddy. I'm not the queen, you know. There are five of us—Blake Gosling is really the king."

"Okay," Paolo continued softly, "You're just a princess, then. A remarkable fairy princess. Have I mentioned lately that I'm very proud of you?"

Mercedes turned to the door, embarrassed, and prepared to get on with her departure. "Cut the mush, Daddy. I'll be back after we nail this *Shiva*, maybe even before." She looked back at him. "And we both have a lot of work to do in the meantime."

Her father made no response to the truth she spoke.

She frowned. "You surprised me another way with Reggie Oxenford. Why did you tell him so much about your team? And your techniques? I'd have thought that stuff would be an important trade secret for your business."

"Hey, if I hadn't talked to him we wouldn't have gotten him to sign a contract, right? So he would have been free to write anything he damned well pleased about us, spreading a rumor that I was the 'Predictor.' With his reputation half the world would have believed him, and we'd have people flying in here just to look at our house. We'd have to sell tickets—if we didn't someone else would." He looked grim again and walked to the window. He tapped on it. "Remember when we retrofitted these windows?"

Mercedes chuckled. "That poor bulletproof glass salesman! I thought he was going to throw himself in front of the window!" Paolo had insisted on a full-power test of the first window they'd replaced, using his father's antique ArmaLite AR-10 assault rifle. He'd splashed a full twenty-round clip against the pristine clarity of the glass before stopping. The glass hadn't been pristine afterwards, but it had held. Paolo had happily paid for a replacement pane for the window, but not before the company rep had come close to a heart attack.

Her father pointed out the window into the majestic distance. "There are still angry people beyond those trees—the children of the Zapatist rebels, nursing grievances once not unfounded. How do you think they'd feel knowing there's a billionaire living here?"

Mercedes pursed her lips. She came to her father and took his hand. "You know, Daddy, somebody else is going to find out. Now that everyone knows there really *is* a Predictor, people are going to look harder."

"I know." Paolo shrugged. "Well, it was bound to come out sooner or later." A twinkle came into his eye. "Eventually, your mother would have figured it out and told just a couple of her best friends."

Mercedes giggled. "At that point, it would have been better to publish directly to the Web—it would take people longer to find out."

Laughing, Paolo picked the suitcase back up and led Mercedes out the door.

The preliminaries were all behind them—simulations of the older *Shiva* battleships made good targets and gave Morgan the opportunity to work the new Angels into a team. But, much as they may have sweated, uncomfortable as they may have found it trying to run with an arm or a leg locked by the suit, all those sims had been simple preliminaries. Now they moved on to SimHell. It wasn't a pretty sight.

This time the pain was considerably more real. An agonizing electric shock accompanied the simulated loss of a limb. And the sweat was more real too—even CJ was dripping this time, without having lost a leg. In SimHell the corridors hooked together in an almost random fashion. Without the accelerometers on their suits they couldn't even tell where they were, and there was no way of telling where they should be going. Mark II minitanks lurked around every corner, and as often as not they were accompanied by hastily snapped-together replicas of the new Destroyers—the two-legged robots that Angel One had encountered on *Shiva* V. The Destroyers were quite unlike any other robot they'd ever seen—as much of a surprise as the minitank Mark I had been on *Shiva III*. Whereas the repair mechs and roboguards had two legs and four arms, the Destroyers had only one pair of arms—where the lower arms could have been attached, the Destroyer carried a dart launcher more powerful than the Angels' pellet rifle, and a broadsword every bit as tough and sharp as the Angels' spike. Angel One had encountered six of the things, and hadn't killed any of them. Instead, the Destroyers had accounted for three Angel deaths, including the death of Angel Leader Buzz Hikmet, last surviving member of the team, in the intersection where the Gate should have been.

Roni, the first member of Morgan's new team to encounter a simulated Destroyer and the first one to be killed by it, waved his hand at the replay. "What are we supposed to do with those things?"

Morgan shook his head. "There's a strongly favored forecast on the Web now, that if you can jam a cubic centimeter of duodec underneath each shoulder and light them off simultaneously, you can cook one."

Axel rubbed the spot on his chest where he'd taken a punji stick during an EarthDay festival three years earlier. He smiled in a vain attempt to hide his disbelief. "Are we just supposed to ask nicely before we tickle his armpits? Any proposals for that little problem?"

Morgan shrugged. "There's a ten-million-dollar prize on the board for a reliable Destroyer-killing strategy. As you may remember, a similar prize led to development of the strategy for killing Mark II minitanks. Hopefully someone will come up with a solution in the next two weeks."

Akira waved the matter aside. "We shall approach with stealth and deception. The Destroyers will not be a problem."

CJ smiled. "Check, Akira. You take the left side, I'll take the right."

Lars spoke lightly, "And I'll hold its arms up to give you easy access."

Axel grunted. "I guess that leaves me with the job of disarming the thing. Think I can shoot its gun and broadsword off their bases?"

Morgan interrupted. "More likely, Axel, after these three get killed playing with the Destroyer, you'll be the one to deliver the football."

Axel smiled. "I'll take that assignment."

"We all will," CJ said. "We'll all deliver that football."

Morgan choked back a sharp retort. "Okay, break time, folks. You've been real good, so maybe we'll practice Destroyer eradication when we get back." He rolled out of the room.

CJ loped up to Morgan in the corridor, but turned her attention directly on his gray-feathered companion. "So, Sol, ready for a snack?"

Solomon fluffed her wings and agreed. "Lunch time."

Morgan looked at each of them in turn. "Don't I get a vote?"

CJ and Sol answered in unison, "No." Sol simultaneously sang the words and whistled the first verse of the Fred Astaire classic, "Let's Call the Whole Thing Off." What really scared Morgan was that CJ joined in, right on cue. Sol was actually pretty good with a tune, though he'd never tell her so. Might give her a swelled beak.

They went toward the buffet room. Most of the people on the base ate there. With silent assent, they passed it by; too much noise emanated from the double doors. They continued on to the dining room and its relative quiet. The dining room was considerably more expensive, but that didn't matter at all for the next two weeks.

CJ made that peculiar shake-roll motion universal to women with long hair as they sat down.

Morgan chuckled. "Your hair used to be longer."

CJ smiled in surprise. "How'd you know?"

"My wife used to flip her head just like that in the winter when she wore her hair long. Then when spring would come she'd cut it off, but it still took her a few weeks to break the habit." He flipped his head in a gentle caricature of his wife, or C, or both; even he wasn't sure which.

CJ's eyes laughed as she said, "Very observant. A rare quality in the male of the species."

Morgan just looked at her for a long moment. Finally, for no reason he understood, his mouth spoke the word at the front of his mind. "Refulgent."

CJ blinked at him. "Excuse me?"

Sol answered for him. "Beautiful bright."

CJ turned to Sol. "Could you tell me exactly what you mean by that?"

Sol whistled mournfully.

Morgan explained. "CJ, just an hour ago you were trapped in an armored frame with one arm and one leg locked out, with periodic shocks hitting you. I know what those shocks feel like, too."

The waitress arrived with their orange juice. CJ sipped as Morgan continued, "You'd just run six kilometers, killed fourteen murderous robots, and dragged yourself the last hundred meters to the control room." He held up his hands in wonder. "Now you're as bright and cheerful as if you'd spent the whole time napping. You're refulgent."

CJ tapped her chin with her forefinger. "Hmm . . . you make me sound sort of like one of those old watches. CJ takes a licking and keeps on ticking."

Morgan spluttered in his orange juice. "Exactly what I meant," he said in mock reproach. They started to laugh. Morgan stopped abruptly, as an alarm bell went off in his head—*nineteen days*.

CJ picked out the thought as if she had originated it. She reached across the table and put her hand on his. "You can't think about it like that, Morgan. You've got to learn, somehow, to live today even though tomorrow you may die."

Sol chirruped, "CJ smart, boss."

The waitress arrived again, with CJ's shrimp salad and Morgan's onion soup. Morgan idly poked at the cheese on top of the soup, wishing he had something to say in reply.

CJ broke the silence. "Well, *I* think it's time for you to live a little."

Morgan looked at her with the beginnings of alarm.

She continued. "Go ahead and be a sourpuss for the rest of today. But tomorrow, at sixteen-hundred, be ready for a change."

Morgan asked, "What exactly is going to happen at sixteen-hundred?"

"Well, for one thing, that's when our last sim ends, right?"

Morgan nodded. "It may take longer if you're still alive, of course."

CJ laughed. "Yeah, but it'll take less if we beat tomorrow's SimHell the same way we beat this one."

Morgan grumbled. "True enough."

CJ recognized the irritation in his voice, and somehow brightened even more. "So, I'm still surprising you, aren't I? Go ahead, confess." She leaned forward and spoke in low tones. "Nobody else has to hear it. Go ahead, just whisper it in my ear."

Morgan closed his eyes for a moment, and then leaned forward. "You are a wicked, wicked woman. And if you aren't careful, tomorrow I'll help the robots."

CJ sat back up. "I knew I was still surprising you," she said cheerfully. "I'm going to surprise you at sixteen-hundred tomorrow, too." She looked at his bird. "I'm sorry, Sol, but this is a trip just for two. You'll have to stay here."

Sol grackled, "No problem. Boss go." She whistled a few bars of "Moon River."

Morgan retorted, "There is no way I am going anywhere with you alone."

Sol answered, "Gotta go, gotta go." She nipped Morgan on the ear, then said, "Ouch!"

Morgan snapped his head over. "Ouch!" he grunted, just a second late. Sol always beat him to that punchline.

Morgan glared at the bird. "Bite me again and you're cat food," he promised.

Sol whistled a few notes of "Don't Worry, Be Happy." She then defended herself. "Sol good girl. Boss go."

CJ held her hand over her mouth to muffle a belly laugh. "Listen to your bird, Morgan MacBride."

"CJ good girl too," Sol said. "Boss go."

Morgan growled. Sol was so insistent that he undertake this venture with CJ, he wondered if Sol already knew what CJ had planned. But how could Sol know if Morgan didn't? He opened his mouth to ask, but then thought better of it. If Sol had learned how to read minds, or CJ had mastered telepathy, he didn't want to know. He felt outnumbered badly enough as it was.

Paolo shook his head as he jammed the suitcase into the front trunk of his daughter's vehicle. "Honestly, Princessa, I think they're paying you too much money."

Mercedes looked at him with suspicion, knowing she was being set up. "What do you mean by that, exactly?"

He pointed at the sleek white racing stripes streaming down the sides of her cherry-red sports car. "For one thing, this vehicle is far too fancy for a kid of your immature and inexperienced years." He swept his accusing finger back to the rear engine cluster. "Second, this box is just too hot for a speed glutton like you."

Paolo could see his daughter's grin appear as she walked to the rear of the car and caressed the top engine nacelle that distinguished the speedster from a run-of-the-mill family car. Paolo cleared his throat. "I think you should leave this machine with me and take the family boat instead. I'll take the risks and work out the bugs. What do you say?" He continued to point at the offending car with his finger.

"You know what I say to that, Daddy." She swaggered over to him, grabbed the offending finger, and twisted it till it pointed back at him. "I have to have this car for your own sake," she said with wide-eyed innocence.

Now Paolo knew he was being set up. "Oh, this should be good. Go ahead, strike me down with the brilliance of your rationalization."

"I bought this sports car because it's faster, so that I can get here more quickly and easily, so that I can come down and visit more often, and stay longer when I arrive." Her eyes twinkled with effervescent fire. "You know how I love to come down and visit."

Paolo laughed. "Well done, Princessa. A brilliant defense."

Paolo heard quick footsteps coming down the steps. He turned to watch Sofia hurry over.

Sofia waved. "You can't leave without a hug, darling." She came up and caught Mercedes in her traditional bear hug. Paolo watched Mercedes gasp for air with his usual amazement; Sofia looked too thin and small for the wiry strength she put into her *abrazos*.

Tears filled Sofia's eyes. "We'll miss you so much."

Mercedes looked away. "Don't cry, Mom." Now there were tears in Mercedes' eyes as well. "If you cry every time I come down here, I might not come back."

Sofia laughed and wiped her face. "I know. Maybe you'd better get out of here quick, so you don't see it."

Mercedes smiled as she hugged her mother again. "Okay, Mom." Mercedes turned to hug Paolo one last time.

Paolo murmured. "Go get 'em, kiddo."

Mercedes frowned. "I'm not a 'kiddo.'"

Paolo smiled as he completed the ritual. "You're absolutely right, kiddo."

Mercedes sighed and climbed into her skycar. Paolo took his wife's hand and they stepped off the landing pad. The air filled with the soft whine of the turbofans as Mercedes lifted off and accelerated north.

As the car disappeared, Sofia wrapped her arms around him and nuzzled his neck. "Darling, there's something I have to ask you."

Paolo recognized the tone of her voice, and tried not to let her feel his muscles tense up as he prepared to encounter whatever terrible, sneaky question she had. "Uh, oh, what is it?"

Sofia laughed gently, and her soft warm breath tickled Paolo's ear. "Are you really the 'Predictor'?" she asked.

Paolo squirmed in her arms and held her more tightly. "Well, not exactly. After all, sweet Sofia, the 'Predictor' is a mythological creature of superhuman powers."

She lifted her head and looked into his eyes with her most dangerous form of sincerity. "But, *corazon*, you *are* a mythological creature of superhuman powers." She put her head back on his shoulder, snuggling even closer somehow. Paolo started to rock sideways, holding her in his arms. Sofia continued dreamily, "I suspected you were the Predictor." She sighed. "I guess I can't tell anybody, can I?"

Paolo suppressed a shudder of terror. "I think that would be unfortunate for all of us, *mi alma*."

A soft mewling of passing sorrow escaped her lips. "I didn't think I could. Oh, well."

They walked back to the house awkwardly, wrapped around each other in a hold they had perfected long ago.

Selpha ate breakfast while carefully keeping her eyes off her touchscreen. She had mustered the courage to go to Reggie Oxenford's site and buy the article about herself, but now that his text filled her screen she found it quite impossible to bring herself to read it. For the first time in over a decade she was afraid.

The *Shivas* had never frightened her, really. They had never struck anyone or anything close to her, and although she would soon be able to see it as a bright

spot among the stars, even then it would just be a dot,
it would not look dangerous. And the scenes she
watched of the Angels, fighting and dying in the sandstone corridors of the beast, seemed no more real to
her than some of the serialized movies on the Web.

But she could still remember her sense of fearful
uncertainty when the airplanes flew over her village and
scattered huge loads of palmtops across the landscape.
Thousands of bright red little parachutes filled the sky,
dangling little gray boxes beneath them. She had known
that something momentous was happening, something
that would change her life, something that she did not
yet not understand.

Selpha almost laughed, looking back on her fear then.
Working at the tea plantation, taking care of her sister
Dorothie and her autistic son Peter, how could her life
had gotten worse? Well, she considered, it could have
gotten worse if her husband had come back from
Uganda, or if her father had returned from the dead,
but the Top Drop had hardly seemed likely to produce
such ill consequences.

And Reggie's article was even less likely to hurt her.
Indeed, what possible damage could it do? She turned
to the touchscreen and began to read. A tentative smile
slowly grew across her features, unfolding into a grin.
Goodness, Reggie wasn't joking when he called this a
series about unsung heroes. Had she not intimately
known the person he described, she would have thought
that this woman in Kenya was a hero too. Of course,
she had not told Reggie her real motivation for her
assiduous work on the 'castpoints for *Shiva* assaults. She
didn't know whether Reggie would really understand.
As she read further, though, she concluded that he
probably would have understood, and would not have
changed the article. He would have made her sound
heroic anyway.

Selpha heard Dorothie's bare feet half-skip into the
room. Dorothie's eyes went wide as she saw Selpha in

a rare moment of good cheer. "Goodness," Dorothie exclaimed, "Did someone pump laughing gas into this room?" She sniffed the air cautiously.

Selpha looked away in confusion. "I was just reading Mr. Oxenford's article," she said.

"Ah, did he make you out as a true and wonderful Hero?" Dorothie asked, scurrying around the table to peer over Selpha's shoulder at the touchscreen.

Selpha flicked the screen off.

Dorothie exclaimed, "Hey!"

"If you want to read it, buy your own copy." Selpha said. "It isn't very interesting. I was just being impressed because Reggie knew things about our lives that we didn't even know."

Dorothie put her hands on her hips. "Indeed? Like what?"

"Well, did you know that here in the Nyanza region was the first place they ever dropped palmtops?"

Dorothie nodded. "Of course."

Selpha clapped her hands together. "Ah, but did you know why?"

Dorothie watched her through narrowed eyes. "Nooo . . ."

"As you'll recall, General Samuels had just taken over Earth Defense. He made the first palmtop drop here because, even then, he was thinking that they'd eventually want to put a heavy lift drop port here, and they'd need a skilled labor force to make it work."

Dorothie looked out the window as she pondered that, and nodded. "Makes sense, in a way, but . . ."

Selpha completed the unfinished thought. "But it would require a lot of planning ahead. He had to know that he couldn't build a useful drop port here until after the next *Shiva* had come and gone. On the first day he took over, he must have already been planning multiple *Shiva*-attacks ahead."

"Smart guy," Dorothie agreed. She pointed out the window. "What's going on out there?"

Selpha got up to look where Dorothie was pointing. She saw a huge stream of trucks fly by.

Dorothie asked, "You think they're going to the port?"

Selpha shook her head. "No. The heavy lift cargoes can't be trucked in. They come by boat, or they come on the railroad." She clucked her tongue. "They must be on the way to the General Dynamics missile plant." Selpha couldn't see the plant from here, but there wasn't another place such a continuous stream of trucks might be going.

Selpha herself had worked at the General Dynamics plant for a while after moving to Kisumu. They had needed network-admin-level software expertise, and she had been a natural fit. So she'd let them employ her while she was getting the people and material organized to start her MindTools Elementary school franchise. Her stint with General Dynamics had been short but informative. They had taught her a great deal about the HellBender series of missiles. Even then, those missiles had seemed too fast and powerful to be stopped by anything, but *Shiva III* had stopped them cold. She knew from her friends at the plant that the newer HellBenders were even more remarkable, but *Shivas IV* and *V* had stopped them just as easily. Well, almost as easily—she'd read that one HellBender had gotten a good hit during the Angel One assault.

Selpha continued, half to herself. "I can't imagine what they're doing. You only send truck fleets like that to ship new kinds of hard-to-manufacture parts."

"Like specialized electronics?" Dorothie asked.

Selpha nodded. "Right. But you'd only go to new parts like that if you were making a serious model upgrade."

"So? What's wrong with a model upgrade?"

Selpha shrugged. "It just seems incredible to me that they'd change models right now, in the middle of the Month of *Shiva*. Right now they have to be cranking out missiles as fast as they can—as you should know, because your no-good boyfriend Joseph is working the midnight-to-eight shift, right?"

"Joseph's a very good boyfriend, Sis. Stop digging at him."

Selpha continued, ignoring Dorothie's reply. "That plant is running twenty-four hours a day." Selpha shook her head again. "They wouldn't risk such a disruption unless they thought the new improvements could make a big difference. A really *big* difference."

Dorothie approved. "Good. I hope they've found something that can knock that cursed *Shiva* back where it came from."

"I suppose." Selpha turned. "It's time for you to go to work, young lady," she said. "And time for me to work with Peter."

Dorothie gave Selpha a quick peck on the cheek and headed for the door. Selpha went into Peter's room.

Peter sat in his chair, shaking his head, tapping his feet together. She walked to the computer and turned on the recording of an Angel's armor frame tapping on the wall of the Alabaster Hall of *Shiva V*.

Peter stopped wiggling in his chair, then said, "I don't know what it is."

"Please try, Peter." Selpha played the sound again.

Peter curled up into a fetal position and fell sideways in his chair. Selpha turned from the computer and knelt beside him. Her every instinct screamed for her to wrap him in her arms, to hold him till he felt better. But she knew that he didn't like to be touched, particularly when he was in this state.

Taking a deep breath, Selpha rose and walked quietly back to the computer. This time she turned on the music. The sound of "Tugatigithanio" by Joseph Kamaru, the King of Kikuyu music, filled the room.

Peter started to relax, and Selpha relaxed as well. For whatever reason, classic Bengan music from before the Crash soothed Peter better than anything else she had ever found.

Someday, she would be able to hold her son to comfort him, she swore. And they would laugh together, and talk like other families.

The thing Selpha hadn't told Reggie was her real dream of the future. If she and Peter did well enough helping the Angels with this assault, she would have enough money to explore the hints she'd found on the Web—hints of cures for Peter's autism.

She could already have cured his blindness, she knew. It would have been expensive, but the technique was straightforward.

But what was the point of repairing his eyesight if the mind behind the eyes could not see? And if she gave him sight, would he still be able to interpret the things he heard when an Angel tapped on the wall of a *Shiva*?

She sometimes felt sharp stabs of guilt, denying him the ability to see, but his blindness was, ironically, the only thing that gave her a chance of helping him. He had to help her earn enough money to bring him all the way home.

Peter was calm now. She allowed the music to fade away, and began again.

It had been a good interview after all—even a remarkable interview.

Reggie stood by the window looking out into the dark gray drizzle. Past experience told him that if he were foolish enough to go outside he would have trouble discerning which was thicker, the fog-drowned air or the rain-drenched mud.

The Predictor was a remarkable fellow. Indeed, his whole family was quite astonishing. Reggie laughed again, remembering Mercedes' reaction upon learning that her father was the Predictor. Her surprise would not wear off any time soon. And that was just fine. She deserved a spot of surprise in her life, as nearly as Reggie could tell. Quite a fireball! If he put her outside in the wet of Dover, he was not sure who would win—

whether her fire would be quenched by the penetrating cold, or whether her personality alone could burn off the fog and bring forth sunshine.

Reggie was quite sure that she could at least saturate his penthouse with incomparable warmth. Too bad she wasn't here right now—he could feel a cold draft off the window glass, and though he kept his apartment rather warmer than most people, he felt a chill.

The reason he felt so cold, he rationalized, was that he'd just spent the last week haring off to some of the hottest places on Earth, from Kenya to Mexico. His blood was thinned out by the travel, and the jet lag was catching up with him. This diagnosis led him irrefutably to a sovereign prescription. Turning from the window, he went to the bar and poured himself an armangnac.

He thought back on the interview with the Predictor again. Paolo Ossa's forecasts were directly responsible for over a dozen planet-saving decisions. He deserved every accolade the people of Earth could provide. For a moment Reggie regretted that he couldn't reveal the Predictor's identity, so that people could thank him directly. But the contract had bound him, and any arbiter in the world would screw him to the wall if he reneged and published that very important detail. Besides, Paolo was probably right that, however justified the accolades, the difficulties of being a public figure would hinder him intolerably.

At least Reggie could now tell the world that the Predictor really did exist. And more, he could tell the world that the Predictor was for the most part a normal human being—someone just like everyone else, at least in a lot of ways.

Of course, the Predictor was also a genius. But though Reggie wrote about that genius in his article, the real thrust of his report was to describe the Predictor's ordinariness. That fit in with Reggie's personal contribution to the defense of Earth, and his own private crusade. He smiled, and wandered over to the table where his touchscreen lay. He read once more the summation of his article:

The Predictor's ascent to greatness highlights this important truth: since Earth Defense started the military 'castpoints, you can help stop Shiva if you can read this article. The method is simple: watch the prizeboards and the 'castpoints for questions and forecasts about matters on which you are an expert. You don't have to be a computer programmer or an explosives engineer to answer these questions. Frequently, a mechanic or a plumber can be the fellow with the right knowledge to find the right solution or make the right forecast. If you buy positions on forecasts based on your expertise, you can do two things at once: you can improve the quality of the military decisions vital to our survival, and you can earn a profit. What could be more noble, more honorable, more just, than doing well by doing good?

Reggie read the words again, editing out a few commas, crisping up sentences, adding another increment of punch. He wanted this message to be so perfectly stated, so clear and correct, that no one could miss the dazzling truth. After a few more changes, some of which probably hurt rather than helped, he shrugged and stopped. Persuading all of humanity to participate in the defense of Earth was not something to achieve in a single article, or even a series of articles. And actually, humanity had pretty much gotten the point—over two-thirds of Earth's population actively watched the real-time 'castpoints during *Shiva* assaults, and about twenty percent of those actually put their money where their mouths were, making it the largest single commercial transaction system in history with over a billion financially-active participants.

And based on what the Predictor said about his system for making forecasts, the number of real participants in Earth's defense could be higher than the estimates. The Predictor wasn't a one-man band—he had a fifty-person team. His team included an architect from

Lithuania, a software engineer from India, and an expert systems guru from Seattle.

Anyway, they all worked together on a set of wildly tortured genetic algorithms that studied the patterns of layouts from all the *Shiva*s. They compared and contrasted this as they watched the assault in realtime, as information about the layout of the current *Shiva* came in. Then every individual in the team—including the genetic algorithm programs as individuals—participated in an ingeniously customized private 'castpoint using a token economy. The predictions that came from the combined analysis of the Predictor's team were surreal in their reliability—often obvious after the fact, but generally a surprise before.

Reggie noted in his Predictor article that other people could form teams like this too. Perhaps, Reggie thought, one such team, inspired by his article, might make the difference in saving humanity's skin this time . . . or the next time . . . or the next.

Keeping that hope in mind, he tapped a button on the touchscreen and published his newest article to the Web.

When Morgan and CJ broke for lunch, Jessica instantly stabbed the button that opened the door of her cocoon. Fresh air and light seeped through. She appreciated the air, but the light was unwelcome. Jessica closed her eyes and took a deep breath.

Her head throbbed, and if she could have popped her eyes out of their sockets, she would have done so— she was sure it would have felt better. It would have relieved the cranial pressure . . . or would her brain have oozed out? Well, that might feel better anyway. Cripes, she had a lot to learn.

Even when she'd been in school she'd never had to learn so much so fast, and she'd quit school when she was sixteen and a half. Of course, she'd quit school as much because it was boring as for any other reason.

Jessica's grandmother still fumed that her parents were at fault. They'd sent Jessica to one of the last government-style schools in America. Unbelievable. The school didn't even teach its high school kids basic communication skills, like dissective analysis of advertising hype.

Still, Jessica doubted that the school's incompetence fully explained her failure. Jessica's grandmother wore her certainties like a coat of armor, and some of her certainties were clearly just the habitual opinions of someone scarred by the Crash.

Of course, the truth about the school and her parents didn't make any difference any more, anyway—both school and parents had been wiped out by *Shiva II*.

Jessica rubbed her temples, then dimly sensed a presence stopping just outside her cocoon. She didn't have to see, however, to know who it was. "Hi, General," she said with more cheer than she felt.

The General stepped across the threshold of the cocoon and smiled at her. "I've always hated trying to do more than one thing at a time. Your job would drive me nuts."

Jessica followed his eyes as he glanced around at the battery of viewscreens and speakers through which she reviewed Morgan's every action. Studying Morgan required that she watch not only Morgan himself, but also the seven viewscreens that he maintained to track the Angels, the prizeboards, and the 'castpoints. Morgan had also mastered the incredible technique of listening to two conversations at the same time, one in each ear. That was the proximate cause of Jessica's headache. "I've done easier things," Jessica confessed. Her voice fell off, "And I've done less futile things as well."

"Futile?" The General's eyebrows crunched up.

"Futile." Jessica pulled the 'plugs from her ears and motioned to the General to get out of her way. The General retreated from the cocoon. Jessica stepped out into her office. "I have no real way of knowing if I'm succeeding. How can I tell how well I understand the man?" She shook her head. "Worse, how can I tell if I understand him well enough to duplicate his thoughts years from now? What if my interpretations of him drift?" She squeezed her eyes. "Worse. What if I can't do it after he's gone? What if I panic under the pressure?" Head still hurting, Jessica went around to the front of her desk and opened the bottom drawer, where she kept the orange juice.

"At least dealing with the pressure will be easy."

Jessica blinked in surprise.

"If you break under the pressure, we'll just give you hypnotherapy and drugs till you're calm. Understand, Jessica, that there is nothing I would not do, no extreme I would not go to, no amount of money I would not spend, no law I would not break, no moral or ethical principle I would not corrupt, to ensure that we have a successful replacement for Morgan MacBride."

Jessica took a gulp of orange juice to clear her head. As the throbbing eased off, she replayed General Samuels' last words with a growing sense of fear. His intensity, his emphasis—both were clues. In that moment, Jessica knew the General was telling her something she needed to understand but couldn't decipher. And she knew that if she asked straight out, he wouldn't tell her. She took another gulp of juice and followed the General out the door.

"Lunch?" he asked her. She shrugged; she didn't feel hungry, but knew she wouldn't have many chances to pump the General. They strolled toward the cafeteria.

The General continued where he'd left off. "I can't tell you how to avoid 'drift' in your extrapolations of Morgan's decisions, but you'll get plenty of chances to test your skills. After we've nailed *Shiva V*, your next training phase begins. You'll learn by doing."

"Learn by doing?"

The General smiled. "Jessica, two months from now, unless disaster strikes, you'll be running Angel teams.

Or rather, you'll be running candidate Angel teams that are in training the same way you are."

Jessica looked doubtful. "Maybe, but training's not the same as live action."

"Oh, but there will be live action. Too much live action."

Now Jessica was really puzzled. "But, without a *Shiva* . . . ?"

The General waved his hand. "Combat teams are not without duties here on Earth, Jessica. Consider the annual EarthDay Festival. Who do you think we send in to the winning country for the cleanup?"

"Are you telling me the Festival cleanup teams are really Angel teams in training?" Jessica suppressed a laugh; there was nothing funny about the EarthDay Festival. The meaning of EarthDay had evolved quite a bit since its first questionable incarnation as a day to educate children about the environment. It had become a matter of serious action. In theory it was straightforward—send a small team into the country with the most corrupt, vicious government, grab the fifty most powerful people in that government, and cart them away to the World Court at Den Hague. On principle, it was a chilling aspect of the global effort of self-defense— it was hard to put aside the sense of big countries ganging up on little ones, despite the safeguards. In practice, of course, the governments who received the Festival were composed of torturers, murderers, and madmen, and no one regretted their loss. But also in practice, the Festival was always brutal: the worst government bosses knew they were targets, and built up their armies just to protect themselves. "I should have realized that Angels worked the Festivals. After reading Axel's background, it should have been obvious."

General Samuels shrugged. "Anyway, my people tell me they've heard you muttering, trying to forecast Morgan's next orders. They tell me you're making a lot of good predictions."

Jessica shrugged. "I guess I'm getting it about half right."

Samuels stopped and studied her in amazement. "That's fantastic, Jessica! You've only had five days on the job, and you're halfway there!"

Jessica laughed. "Well, the first half is pretty easy. It's the clever little surprises that are hard to predict. And it's the clever little surprises that make the difference. It's kind of like character recognition on the old paper scanners, when they were switching over to digital—ninety-nine percent accuracy sounded good in the advertising, but the result still wasn't very useful."

"I see your point. Still, whether you admit it or not, you're doing extremely well for such a short period of study."

Jessica wrinkled her nose and looked up into the General's eyes mischievously. It was one of her best looks. She enjoyed having the opportunity to use it. "I'll make one shocking forecast right now, General. I know you won't like it, but it's going to happen. *This* one I'm sure about."

Samuels raised an eyebrow. "Aha. Well, don't keep me in suspense."

Jessica shook her head wisely. "CJ is going to get Morgan into bed. He can't hold out much longer."

The General burst out with a laugh of disbelief. "It can't be. Morgan is too . . . too . . ."

Jessica watched his struggle for words with amusement. ". . . too disciplined to be seduced, Jessica."

"You wait and see. I'll bet you dinner at Spago's in L.A."

The General clasped his head in horror. "You're playing for high stakes on that 'cast, lady. Very well. Done." They shook on it.

"You're going to be sorry, General."

Samuels shook his head. "I hope not. Morgan is the lynchpin. If he somehow loses his focus . . ." He didn't have to finish the thought.

Though Samuels had to care first about the impact of a crazy romance on the defense of Earth, Jessica found herself visualizing the impact of such madness on Morgan the human being. If CJ got killed on *Shiva V* . . . her head ached as she played pinball with the results. The vision left her cold and sick. Her forecast of MacBride and CJ's entanglement didn't seem funny at all any more.

The two of them turned into the dining room and took a table. Samuels continued to speak. "Still, in a professional sense I hope you're right. If you predict this correctly, you'll show remarkable mastery of your subject."

A loud laugh broke the hush of the room for just a moment. A brief parrot chuckle followed the laughter. Jessica didn't have to look to know the laughter came from CJ and MacBride's table at the far end of the room. Jessica looked into the General's eyes with a triumphant stare—*I told you so*, she said with her eyes.

As she expected, the General looked back into her eyes and sadly nodded his head. "Perhaps I should make the reservations at Spago's now," he muttered.

They ordered lunch, and the General put his hands on the table. "Meanwhile, there are other things you must learn to become a Controller, Ms. Travis."

"Really. Such as?"

"Such as how to read the 'castpoints properly. How much do you know about Web forecasting—or 'idea futures,' as they are called by economists?"

Jessica shrugged. "I know the story of how they started. Earth Defense invented the 'castpoints after *Shiva II*." She closed her eyes tight in thought. "Didn't somebody make a ten-thousand-dollar bet on something?"

"The dogs," Samuels prompted.

"Right. Somebody posted a wager for ten thousand dollars that you could get better recon data on the next *Shiva* if the first *Argo* didn't carry any people at all, but instead carried a team of trained dogs with vidcams on their harnesses." She paused. "Then there was a millionaire, right?"

The General nodded reluctantly. "You're remembering the popularization of what happened, which has the right facts but not the right causality. Go on."

"Anyway, the bet would have been just one more random chunk of Web junk, but a millionaire saw the bet and plunked a million dollars on the proposal. Then one of his friends dropped two million on the prediction that the Earth Defense Agency was already too bureaucratic to use such a novel idea. Earth Defense was brand-new, and was kind of getting kicked around by the UN and NATO and everybody, so I guess it was acting like a pre-Crash government."

Their hamburgers arrived, and Jessica added ketchup as she continued. "Well, that prediction made a pretty big ruckus, and somebody else saw an opportunity. They created a website to manage the bets heaping up—the bets couldn't be paid off for five years, and if nobody managed 'em, the contracts would get lost, the money wouldn't be escrowed, etc."

"You really do know something about this," the General said with pleasure. "That bet-management website was, in effect, the first full-service financial 'castpoint."

"Yeah, I guess you're right. Didn't they make it possible to add new forecasts? And buy and sell positions on all of them?"

"They certainly did, Jessica."

Jessica looked hard at the General; there was something funny in his voice again, but she couldn't tell what it was. "Anyway, in the end Earth Defense surprised everybody. Not only did they embrace the idea of using dogs for recon, they encouraged people to use 'castpoints to stimulate the general development of new ideas. EDA even funded a couple of the first 'castpoint startups, right?"

The General grunted. "Like I said, you're telling the pop version of the story, though you've got it down pat. Actually, idea futures are much older than Earth Defense. There are some fragments in the pre-Crash Web archives pointing to an idea futures market formed before the millennium, back in 1989."

Jessica laughed in disbelief. "But there wasn't even a Web then."

Samuels shrugged. "It was a local market. The buyers and sellers and the 'castpoint manager all lived around Palo Alto." The General smiled. "They weren't dummies back then, you know. After all, they had to invent the Web for us."

Jessica bit into her hamburger. They continued to talk about various things, but she was distracted. Twice in this conversation General Samuels had said things that rang warning bells in her head. There were things he wasn't telling her, things she should know. She knew what she was going to do about it, too. Right now, she had no mental energy to spare. But after they killed this *Shiva*, she was going to turn her attention to the General. She would empathically learn his behavior as she had once learned Christina's, as she was now learning MacBride's. Once she had his mind inside hers, she would study him. And there in his mind she would discover the truth.

Chan Kam Yin shut off his welding torch, looking up at the undercarriage of the antique '67 Mustang with satisfaction. He loved the old groundhuggers. They were so mechanical, so visually understandable. It made them entirely different from computers and integrated circuits—you could look at an integrated circuit through a blasted microscope and still not see anything you could understand. Even with a modern skycar the real action was in the methane fuel cell, where molecules quietly changed their arrangements and brought forth electricity with stealthy efficiency. A piston engine like the one in this baby was, however, a beast of another kind. What could be easier to understand than driving a piston with periodic detonations? He could wrap his head around it.

He ducked out from under the car and released the hydraulic lift. The Mustang settled gracefully to the ground. He looked at the polished chrome and sighed. Someday he'd have a car like this, just for show, the way the owner of this one did. And he'd have a ten-fan skycar for serious travel, the way the owner of this one did.

The Dealer washed up and flipped on his palmtop. "Honorable Lao, your Mustang is all fixed up. Wanna come down and check it out?"

Kee Sun Lao replied, "Thanks, but I've gotta jump out of here in about five. Can you come back next month for the maintenance check?"

The Dealer tapped his palmtop. "Already scheduled. Catch you later." The Dealer strolled out of the garage, looked up at the mansion towering over it. Well, even if he didn't own the old car, he had to confess he enjoyed working on it. Indeed, in some ways it was better; after all, with the current arrangement *he* was the one who got paid, while the owner wound up doing the paying. It was almost as good as a scam. He turned and fired up his own groundcar, a clunky old (as opposed to antique) hunk of lime-green junk (could you believe that color was ever popular?). It took him only twenty minutes to get back to his apartment. Traffic, he noticed, was lighter than it had been a year ago, just as it had been lighter a year ago than the year before. Skycars and telecommuting were at last taking over in Guangdong Province. It was about time.

He grabbed some left over *chow fun* from the fridge and heated it in the microwave, then threaded his way around the table and the bed back to his desk. He tapped on the touchscreen, being careful not to spill lunch on it. His Webcrawler brought forth his daily dose of news and information, his logon Factoid followed by serious subject lines only. He stuffed a chopstick's worth of chow fun into his mouth and began reading.

His Factoid of the Moment told him:

When a frog vomits, it first expels its stomach and then scrapes the contents out with its hands. It then swallows its stomach again.

The image quite overpowered him. He swallowed quickly, then carefully put the rest of the *chow fun* at the far corner of his desk.

He scanned the subject lines. One article's topic made him blink in amazement, and he popped over Reggie Oxenford's website. He had a subscription to Oxenford's news stories, so there wasn't any payment hassle.

The report "Interview with the Predictor" knocked him flat. He'd known there was good money in the Earth Defense 'castpoints, but this guy was a billionaire! Dragon's teeth!

There just had to be a way to get in on the gravy. His work as a fence paid the bills well enough. He was even putting the occasional chunk of change into the mutuals. But he'd still never own Kee Sun Lao's Mustang the way he was going.

Then he remembered the one time his father had bet on a cockfight when the experts were playing. His father had found out where they were putting their money and had very quietly bet the same way. Needless to say, the loser of the fight had been the "favorite," the one the amateurs had backed, and the experts—and the Dealer's father—had made a handsome killing.

Now it was obvious to the Dealer how to scam the 'castpoints. All he had to do was figure out who the Predictor was, and then he could ride the expert forecast the same way his dear old dad had done.

Of course, figuring out how the Predictor took positions in the 'casts wouldn't be easy. Reggie Oxenford had actually taken the simpler path when he merely found the Predictor's true name and home. The Dealer didn't care what the Predictor's name was, or where he lived. He just cared about the Predictor's anonymous identities, the ones he used to buy and sell positions on forecasts. If the Dealer could map the Predictor's brand, or even just his behavior, to a set of identities on the 'castpoint, he could ride the forecast.

The Dealer looked out his window toward the glow of light above Hong Kong. He wasn't exactly sure how he'd do it—after all, anonymous identities *were* anonymous because they had no traceable link to a brand— but he'd pull it off.

"Thanks, Dad," he murmured. This time he was partly sincere.

Chapter Five

T minus Eighteen

The moment of decision came. The sudden transformation of Jessica's palmtop from a quiet companion into a Demon from the Depths heralded the event. The offending palmtop vibrated the room with the thunderous clap of electric guitars. The country metal group Avatars had a new hit single, and Jessica's computer had shown great inspiration by choosing the melody to sing her to consciousness.

Jessica made an executive decision. She slapped the palmtop more forcefully than it deserved. The Avatars' music disappeared from the room as quickly as it had arrived. Jessica muttered to no one in particular, "Ten more minutes."

Jessica drifted in and out of sleep. She scrumaged through the sheets, searching for the warmest spot remaining in the bed. She wished the bed were her own. If she were in her own bed, she could merely worry about Andrew Clay's problem with building a management team around his socially-retarded-but-brilliant VP of engineering. If she were in her own bed, she wouldn't worry about the survival of Earth. She wouldn't dream about pain, blood, and lost lives.

Jessica had never liked working in her sleep, though she did it often. Normally working dreams kept her in limbo, left her unrested. Now her dreams kept her in hell and left her exhausted.

She tossed to the other side of the bed, tumbling like a soccer ball in a brutal game. Her training cycle was only going to get worse. Soon she would start work as a Combat Controller. Real people would die; those deaths would be her responsibility. Those deaths, those people, would haunt her dreams forever. And she hadn't even met them yet.

The alarm came to life playing yet another tune. She did not recognize this one, but it ground her nerves even more than the Avatars. Only surrender could save her. She struggled to her feet to greet the day.

Jessica bent over and plunged her hands deep into her thick mane, massaging some life back into her scalp. Her brain felt as thick and tangled as her hair. At least she knew how to comb out the wild disarray in her hair.

She was fastening the silver belt of her green jumpsuit when a polite knock wrapped at her door.

"Coming," she yelled. "Just a minute." She dropped her brush and grabbed the deodorant. After two quick blasts, she realized it didn't smell quite right. When she looked at the can, she realized she'd just used her hairspray under her arms. She closed her eyes and groaned softly. It was going to be one of those days. At least she was dressed.

She opened the door to find General Samuels towering over her. "Breakfast?" he asked.

Jessica raised an eyebrow. "What about the morning sim?"

The General shrugged. "We're videotaping it; you can study it later. I want to hear how you're doing with 'castpoints, which are now as important to our victories as MacBride himself."

The General walked down the sandstone hallways with an easy stride; Jessica found herself skipping from time to time to keep up. They reached his office, where Jessica found the aide laying out coffee for her, tea for the General, and danish pastries for all parties. She couldn't resist harassing the aide. "Coffee and danish, my favorite breakfast. Tell the truth now. Have you been videotaping me, learning about me the way I'm learning about Morgan?"

The aide laughed graciously. "General Samuels told me what to procure for you, Ms. Travis."

She raised her eyebrow at the General. He shrugged. "I knew you drink coffee because when we first met, I caught you staring longingly at your autoperk, wishing the coffee would hurry up. The danish is a lucky guess. But don't get confused, Jessica. Although we haven't been videotaping you outside the cocoon, remember, our contract authorizes it. So don't be surprised if we do it sometime." He sipped tea from his High Accuracy mug. "Actually, I can't imagine why we'd want to any time soon."

Jessica's eyes flickered around the room as she tried to think of a circumstance under which someone like the General might want to scrutinize her life. She found it. "But later, if I lead an Angel team and destroy a *Shiva*, you'll want to do to me what I'm doing to Morgan. That's why you've got that clause in the contract, isn't it?"

The General smiled. "Excellent analysis. Even if you don't take over Morgan's job, perhaps you can take over mine."

Jessica snagged a cherry danish from the table and sat down. The danish was fresh and warm. She rolled her eyes. "Heavenly."

The aide nodded his head to her and departed. General Samuels turned to her. Suddenly, he was every

bit the professor. "What new have you learned about
'castpoints since our last discussion, Ms. Travis?"

Jessica took her time and swallowed before answering.
While working through college she'd done a stint as a
researcher for Pacific Arbiters Inc., and in applying those
research skills she had uncovered some very interesting
tidbits. Her immediate problem was how to sneak up
on Samuels with her surprise. "You know, before coming
here, I'd always sort of looked on the 'castpoints as a
big gambling game, like Vegas and Anguilla." She shook
her head. "I must confess, there's more to them than
meets the eye."

"That's a beginning. Can you tell me why Earth
Defense spurred the development of 'castpoints in the
first place?"

Jessica smiled; this was a question to which she knew
the answer. "You were swamped with ideas coming off
the Web. Worse, you were swamped with good ideas."

The General just shook his head in delight. "Won-
derfully put. Go on."

Jessica shrugged. "During the final *Shiva II* assault,
over half a billion people were watching the battle
through the live webfeed." She took a sip of her coffee,
which was, she found, fresh roasted and almost as sweet
as the danish. "Lots of the people who were watching
were talking at the same time. I've looked at some of
the Web archives, and the whole world was alive with
newsgroups and chatrooms full of proposals for how to
deal with the new roboguards, guessing how *Shiva* was
laid out, arguing about what kinds of opposition you'd
get going different directions. A lot of it was garbage,
of course, but here and there it was brilliant."

The General's eyes reflected agony as he stared past
her, past the wall, and into history. "You were what,
fourteen at the time? You can't imagine how frustrating
it was to know that, somewhere in those twenty-five
million conversations, someone was predicting exactly
what would happen, for exactly the right reasons. But

we had no way of finding that one thread of genius."
His eyes focused on her again, waiting for more.

Jessica felt her face warm, blushing for no reason
she could find. She felt like a wayward student speaking to a kind but determined professor. "Anyway, I
found three different people in the archives who
independently suggested the eventual strategy for killing
roboguards. One of them came up with the idea seven
hours before Morgan and Cochran figured it out. If
Morgan had been able to find that idea on the Web,
two of the Angels would not have gotten killed early
in the engagement. We might have even gotten somebody out." For Jessica personally, the consequences of
the lost opportunity had actually been much greater.
Because it took the Angels so long to reach the Gate,
Shiva II had survived long enough to light off a missile
at Silicon Valley. A lucky countermissile had gotten a
piece of it, enough to deflect it from its target, but
not enough to avoid tragedy: the multimegaton warhead
had detonated near Sausalito, where Jessica's parents'
home had been located.

The General looked into her eyes like he was reading
her thoughts. "A terrible tragedy, the loss of northern
San Francisco." He sipped his tea. "At least *Shiva*
warheads don't produce a lot of radiation. If they did,
we'd have lost far more, and wouldn't be rebuilding for
a hundred more years."

Jessica had a tangential thought. "You know, if we
didn't have 'castpoints today, not even Morgan could get
an Angel into *Shiva*'s control room. But if we'd had the
'castpoints then, I think we could have beaten the early
Shivas without him."

The General nodded. "Undoubtedly." He returned
quickly to professorial mode. "But now, please explain
how the 'castpoints solved the problem of finding the
widely spaced threads of genius in the Web."

Jessica squished up her eyebrows. "Well, it's sort of
obvious."

"I wish everyone thought that. There are still plenty of people in the military who don't get the point."

"Well, how do you spot a good idea or a good forecast? Obviously, you make people put their money where their mouths are. Let them back a forecast with real bucks, and the serious ones will go for it, while the rest just hang out in the chat rooms. No muss, no fuss. No debating. No mediocre compromises. Just say it with money."

The General swallowed the last of a danish and sat back, finished. "Any other critical new insights, Jessica?"

Jessica started circling her biggest revelation. "Another thing I found in the archives was the startup of the first 'castpoint. It would seem, General, that that first one didn't get started the day after the million-dollar bets were made."

"It didn't? Really!" the General asked with mock surprise. Jessica could see he was laughing again—with her or at her, she wasn't so sure.

"Not at all. Those bets were actually placed a while before the US, NATO, and the UN worked out the Earth Defense concept."

"So the idea was already in place, ready for Earth Defense to pick it up."

"Well, Earth Defense didn't pick it up right away, either."

The General sipped his tea. His expression said he knew where Jessica was going, but that he would let her get there in her own time. And he would enjoy the journey. "Shocking! Perhaps they were bureaucrats after all."

"Perhaps. General Celenza, who'd commanded the US attack on *Shiva II*, was in charge for a little while, as caretaker while they picked the new Chief of Staff." She paused. "It would seem, General, that idea futures really took off just moments after you took over."

The General nodded sagely. "Interesting. Coincidence?"

Jessica stood up. "Coincidence my ass." She pointed a finger at him. "It was you, General Samuels. You started the 'castpoints."

The General clapped. "Congratulations. You have gotten much closer to the truth than most people." He sipped his tea. "You said earlier, you had originally thought the 'castpoints were big gambling games. Aren't they, really, just a form of gambling, like the office football betting pool?"

Jessica gave him a sidelong glance. "You're trying to trick me, I can tell. When the 'castpoints first went into operation, a kind of gambling fever did sweep the markets. You might say that the 'castpoints first got their energy from their similarity to a football pool. But it didn't last."

"Why not?"

Jessica took a deep breath. "An office betting pool has a very limited selection of participants, and in general the participants are not experts who can discriminate small differences in probabilities and risks. But the 'castpoints are inherently global. Statistics guarantee that over the long run the money will flow to the people who make the best predictions. It doesn't work out for the amateur the way a small, closed football pool does." She shook her head from side to side the way she did when she was pretending to be a blonde. "Of course, the first wave of gambling fever on the 'castpoints ended sort of suddenly. One of the billionaires at the time—a guy who had made a fortune in computer software before the Crash—made a claim in public about the demise of the most popular operating system of the day. There were gales of laughter at the time, and a lot of people said, 'Hey, if you really believe that, back a 'cast on it.'" Jessica laughed. "The old geezer must have been in his eighties at the time, but he was still pretty savvy. He went ahead and backed the 'cast. A lot of people lost their shirts on that one."

The General steepled his fingers. "So that was the end of the gamblers?"

"Well, the end of the fever, anyway; I'm sure there are still gamblers out there playing the 'castpoints for kicks. But now the commercial 'castpoints work a lot like the commodities futures markets—engineering companies and insurance companies that need to hedge their bets in the face of technological change use them, the same way they use commodities futures to protect themselves from sudden changes in materials availability." She shrugged. "'Course, at this point, there are billions of people who are experts in some aspect of some technology, so the world-wide pool of participants for the 'castpoints is much larger than the pool of commodities experts, even without the Earth Defense interest. So there are more people involved, and more money at stake."

The General sat back in his chair. "Whew! You really did learn a lot about this, didn't you? I'll have to be more careful in the future, if I'm going to keep any secrets at all."

Jessica frowned. The General's eyes twinkled as he said it, but in back of the twinkle there was something . . .

The General's aide knocked on the open door and looked in. "Sir, General Dehnad is on the line."

The General looked back at Jessica. She took a last drink of her coffee, snatched a last danish, and departed as the General picked up the line.

With slow, careful motions, the Dealer held up his palmtop to unlock his apartment door. He could feel his hand trying to shake. He refused to let it.

He could not, however, stop the chill that went down his spine. He knew, just *knew*, that they were still watching him.

Cops. He hated the damn creatures. Well, that wasn't quite true. The cops were just trying to make a living too, after all. And when you got right down to it, even he liked having the cops around—without the cops who watched over his apartment complex, all kinds of lowlifes might threaten him.

But the apartment cops worked for him, and they knew it. They were always polite—polite in that warm, helpful way. The cops working for the Shao Lin Computer Parts Company did not work for him, however, and they also knew it. So though they'd been polite when they accosted him on the street in front of the apartments, it'd been tainted with the coldness that they'd always shown when talking to his father.

The cops couldn't rough him up—indeed, the Dealer was sure they'd stopped him in front of the complex just so the Dealer's own security people could watch and see how nice they were. But it had been unpleasant nonetheless.

Somehow, those bastards had fingered him as the fence for that truckload of motherboards. They couldn't prove it—if they could, they'd have had a chat with the Dealer's residential cops and dragged him to an arbiter in a flash—but they knew.

The Dealer closed the door behind him and took a slow deep breath. The room seemed cold. He turned down the air conditioning a couple of notches. He sat down at his desk and stared at his blank touchscreen, deep in thought.

Considering the risks involved, fencing stolen goods had a pathetic profit margin. He'd always figured it was a stepping stone on the way to something bigger. But he'd never figured out exactly what that bigger thing might be. Now he had to seriously consider the possibility that, unless he figured it out really quickly, the fencing operation would be a stepping stone to something smaller. Something a lot smaller, like a plasfoam box in a cold doorway.

Unconsciously, the Dealer opened the middle right drawer of his desk. He kept his old palmtop there, his first one, the one he'd gotten from the government when he was eight years old. It had been the one thing he had taken with him when he left his father at the age of twelve, his one contact with people whom he could consider friends because they couldn't hurt him through the simple electronic interface. He picked it up. The dull gray surface of the plastic box, once textured, was now worn smooth. The screen surface, once smooth, was now scratched from too much writing, too many commands entered in rough haste. He flipped it over and saw the seal of the Republic of Guangdong, big and bold. Beneath that, in very tiny English characters, lay the real truth behind the box: *Earth Defense Agency*. Earth Defense had supplied the Republic's government with enough of these to make sure everyone had a chance to hook into the Web and educate themselves. The Dealer discounted the wild claims for the difference the palmtops had made. Nevertheless, for the Dealer himself the program had worked, though the successes he'd had with his palmtop could not have been part of the EDA plan. He smiled despite his predicament. His successes would have turned the EDA bureaucrats inside out with horror.

Chan Kam Yin returned to his current problem. If the cops nailed him to the crime, victim reimbursement plus investigation costs plus damages would strip him clean. He'd be back on the street again with nothing but his once-loved, now-antiquated palmtop. He couldn't risk that. He'd have to find another scam, at least till the heat died down. Fortunately, he had a plan.

He just had to figure out how to find the Predictor. It wouldn't be easy. Anybody like the Predictor, who did that kind of successful, insightful, but expensive analysis, would want to maximize his profit from it. That meant using a series of anonymous identities to buy and sell your forecasts. After all, if you used a consistent brand, people would watch your reputation grow and start tailriding once it became obvious you were a winner. Once that happened, you'd never get good odds.

Furthermore, to keep your tracks hidden, you'd use multiple anonymous identities for each forecast, spanking-new each time, each betting only a little money rather than making a big purchase. After all, even an anonymous identity that bought a big position on a 'cast would draw attention. Who but an expert with deep analytical knowledge would take a chance like that, particularly with long odds? Even such a hint as this would pick up riders that would send your odds into the toilet.

So the Predictor would surely be subtle about his purchasing. Consequently the Dealer would have to be subtle. too. He'd been watching for patterns in the anonymous bets but hadn't found any yet. He had to take this seriously, now, and nail it down.

With fresh, fear-driven enthusiasm, he flipped his touchscreen to life and poured over the results of the recent forecasts.

The car wove back and forth across the road, dodging the potholes and the people on bicycles as they hurtled along Interstate 93, down the long sloping hill from Boulder City to Lake Mead. The taxi driver, complacent about the whole matter, ventured another look at his fare; Reggie saw the man's eyes staring at him in the mirror. "You aren't one of the Faithful," he asserted confidently.

Reggie smiled weakly; he was getting carsick. Funny, he never got airsick in a skycar, but the stop/start weaving of the groundhuggers invariably left him quite undone. He answered, "You hit the jackpot on that 'cast. 'Course, the odds left you the heavy favorite, wouldn't you say?"

The driver chuckled. "Yeah. You're too normal for the Faithful."

Being normal certainly did make Reggie stand out here. Even the taxi, a nondescript Ford, stood out, though not for its archaic use of wheels instead of turbofans. Most of the crowd was coming by ground transport. Though not all, as he could see by pressing his face to the window and looking up. Numerous skycars homed in on his destination as well, and he watched them enviously. Though, he reluctantly confessed, even if he *had* been able to get one of the handful of landing permits authorized by the Church of the Stellar Light, he would have had to come by groundhugger anyway. Most of the participants were taking the road from McCarran InterPlanetary in Las Vegas. For his story he needed the full experience.

Reggie turned green as the cab swerved again. At last he saw the break in the old fencing along the interstate and the crude dirt path snaking off to the left, down to the revival's extensive site on the lake front. He could hear the music from here, even with the windows closed. He groaned quietly; he hadn't brought any earplugs.

He was still not quite sure why he was here. Rather, he knew, but didn't like admitting it. The editor of the *Newsweek* website had begged him to do a story about lost souls and the Month of *Shiva*, challenging Reggie's assertion that their numbers were declining. Reggie had apologetically said no, and had held to it . . . until all nine full-time members of the *Newsweek* staff had sent him a singing email, reiterating the request. They were all friends from earlier in his career. How could he refuse? Besides, the singing was awful. He'd do anything to avoid another email like that.

The coming of *Shiva* set off a host of contradictory trends. The high end of the economy and the low end gained strength as the middle dwindled. Top-flight sports cars—particularly the new supersonic twelve-fan models—sold so fast it was hard to get a test drive. But you couldn't sell a used family skycar no matter how fine its maintenance record. People were buying fantasies—why not, if you've got only a month to live?

At the other end of the spectrum, sales of microwave

dinners suffered as people ate more meals at restaurants, sharing some kind of herd instinct . . . but brown rice and dried beans sold well as born-again survivalists stocked up for the post-apocalyptic siege.

Each of these trends suggested distinctive individual coping strategies. Another trend had emerged as well, however. The Church of the Stellar Light faced dramatic growth in devotees.

The Church knew the truth, and broadcast throughout the world for anyone who would listen: *Shiva* would one day destroy all the weapons of Earth. It would then proceed to wipe every trace of evil human habitation from the planet. Finally *Shiva* would collect the Faithful from the six safepoints scattered around the globe. Lake Mead, just south of one of the most sinful cities of the planet, was such a safepoint.

To Reggie, though, this safepoint looked more like Hell.

The cabbie stopped; Reggie left a tip and stepped out. He stopped as if hit by gunfire—the burning sun slapped his face like a hot metal hand. The dust kicked up by the cab itself choked him.

Come on, people now/Smile on your brother/Everybody get together/Try to . . .

Reggie listened to the music. The beat had a classical cadence to it. Something from before the Crash. It was catchy in its mellow sort of way. He just wished they could turn it down a little; even mellow music drummed like a war cry at that many decibels.

A fellow in faded camos drifted past him. Stoned. A striking woman arrayed in silk scarves circled close to him, one breast ornamentally displayed. Biosculpted. She was chanting in a singsong voice.

He could see litters of discarded trash here and there amongst the Faithful. The wind picked up a plastic bottle and whirled it across the field, bouncing off the participants in a reticulated dance similar to the whirling motions of the younger, more enthusiastic members of

the crowd. The whole scene looked to be straight from
that old documentary he had seen about Wood-some-
thing. A pause came in the music. For a moment he
could think clearly. The dust and the people faded from
view as, with his mind's eye, he could see the one person he most wanted to talk to: Mercedes Ossa. Yes, he
needed her here, her eyes laughing as she turned her
clean incisive wit on the people inundating him. Standing
alone in the crowd, he felt neither the clever laughter
Mercedes might supply, nor the primitive joy of the
Faithful dancers.

A gap separated him from these people, a chasm he
doubted he could ever cross. Did they believe in some
deep, subliminal fashion that if they denied *Shiva's*
existence vehemently enough the ship would disappear?
Or did they feel themselves so helpless, only denial
remained for them?

The idea of denial was as hopelessly foreign to him
as the idea of fighting might seem to the people around
him. He'd spent his teenage years as a fierce competitor.
Just ask the guy who'd had to settle for the Olympic
silver medal.

Did the Faithful think the race with *Shiva* was
already over? Who had won?

The lake drew his eye. Like Mercedes, it too was
clean and incisive. A lone waverunner skimmed the
surface on the far side of the lake, as far from the
Faithful as it could get. Soon the music would begin
again, and Reggie yearned to join the runner.

A rumbling sound bellowed down the hillsides behind
him. It was a sound mostly heard in old movies—the
sound of a gasoline-powered motorcycle engine. Only
one group still wandered the desert lands with honest-
to-God motorcycles. Reggie didn't have to turn or look
to know who had just arrived, who now gazed over the
crowd like a hawk studying baby mice. The Brute Squad
motorcycle gang and their leader Chuck "Wire" Goldstar
had just arrived. A very different subculture had just

come to the party. Reggie's story was about to get more exciting. He hoped he'd live through it.

Reggie had met Chuck once before. Reggie had been doing a story about the Defenseless, people who didn't have arrangements with any conventional security agencies. Sort of like the pre-Crash homeless people. An impoverished Defenseless girl, terrified of her violent possessive boyfriend, had been going through Chuck's initiation ritual. It looked more like a gang rape. But the girl didn't object; she judged the boyfriend the greater of the dangers.

Reggie and the Wire had both walked away from that encounter with whole skins. Neither had been entirely happy about it.

Reggie reached for his palmtop, to call for help. He could feel the skin tighten on the back of his neck as multiple pairs of biker eyes turned on him, picking him out easily as one of the few people there who might defy them.

But the Church had apparently anticipated the Brute Squad's arrival. A dozen blue-and-gold skycars, all with the BKM logo embossed on the side, swept down out of the sun. They filled the sky with the low drone of a million hummingbirds. And though they might sound like hummingbirds, they had more in common with T. Rex. The cavalry had arrived.

Reggie pocketed his palmtop. His security agency in Britain, Velvet Glove, had cross-contracts with BKM. The Church had made his call for him. Reggie turned, and looked out at the bikers for the first time. Most of the bikers were now looking up at the BKM skycars. A few sat back on their bikes so he could see metal tubes aiming into the sky—enough missile launchers to start a war.

The thin chap in a leather vest and yellow bandana had his arm pointing to the sky, but he still watched Reggie. Muscles like thin steel ropes whipped beneath his skin. Reggie stared into the man's angry brown eyes, a contest of wills, eyeball to eyeball. "Well, Wire, we meet again," Reggie muttered.

For several moments the situation hung in a delicate tableau. It could not last.

Reggie found himself working through the logic the leader of the Brute Squad now faced. The Squad had no mutual arbitration contracts with the BKM. So if a fight broke out, it would go to a government court rather than an arbiter. The case would take a tremendous amount of time, cost a lot of money, and produce uncertain justice. All these problems weighed on BKM more than the Brute Squad—uncertain justice favored the aggressor, not the victim.

However, the BKM, understanding this scenario, would engage in massive intervention if the bikers started a fight—massive enough so that it would be the BKM, not the bikers, who owed damages at the end of a long court battle. The BKM would do just about anything to minimize unreclaimable damages to their clients.

The Wire would have to go for the total destruction of the BKM contingent to come out ahead. Very unlikely. And worse for the Wire would be to succeed—BKM would surely pay Pinkerton a big premium to finish the job if BKM got chewed up.

The Wire lowered his hand and spoke into the microphone in his helmet. The rocket launch tubes rotated on the bikes of the owners, to point down to the ground. There would not be a war today.

The Wire smiled at Reggie, displaying jagged teeth that had seen too many fists, not enough dentists. He reached into his saddle pack, pulled out two long-necked, dark beers, and walked on over to Reggie. "You get around," the Wire commented, offering him the beer.

Dry as the Nevada air might be, the beer was so cold that a fine mist already clung to the glass bottle. Reggie suddenly realized how thirsty the desert was. He shook his head, declining the offer nonetheless. "What brings you to the Church of the Stellar Light, Wire?"

The Wire shrugged. "My guys are tense. I brought them down here for a little fun in the sun."

Reggie looked into his eyes in disbelief. The Wire wasn't a dummy. "You knew the BKM would show up."

The gang leader looked up at the skycars from beneath bushy gray eyebrows. "Yeah. I figured a little polishing of the old shooters would be good for 'em, and once they saw the opposition, they'd cool down." He smiled again. "So now we aren't shooting each other."

It was a revelation. The Wire had counted on the BKM to calm down his own people!

"How many days left, Wire?"

The Wire answered instantly. "Eighteen."

There was a long pause. Reggie said softly. "It gets to your people too, huh?"

"Yeah." The Wire took a last deep swig from one of the beers, dropped the empty bottle on the ground. He waved the other one at Reggie. "See ya 'round." He turned and walked back to his followers.

Reggie now had a very different angle on his story than he'd had before.

Music blared forth. A fight would have been quieter.

Reggie turned from the noise and the two distinct crowds that now overfilled the desolate countryside. He trotted up the hill, cutting a little to the west. It took a long time, and he was sweating by the time he arrived, but eventually he made it to the far side of a large boulder. Out of the line of projection of the loudspeakers, he found an oasis of quiet. He opened his palmtop, linked to Mercedes. One of the side benefits of working with her on the contract at her father's house had been that he'd gotten her email address. He hoped she'd answer his request for a realtime chat.

"Mr. Oxenford," Mercedes voice sounded suspicious and irritated from his computer's tiny speaker. "What do you want now?"

"I want you to save me. Please," he begged, holding his palmtop close to his lips and shouting—though he was out of range of the bands, even the wind here whipped loudly.

"Save you?"

"I'm at the Stellar Light Revival on Lake Mead," he continued. "I am being destroyed by the Twin Mysteries of the Pyramids and the Crop Circles."

"What are you talking about?"

Reggie smiled. "Meet me and I'll tell you." When Mercedes did not respond, he continued on a pleading note. "If you don't rescue me, I shall go mad. And deaf as well," he said.

There was a long pause. At last, the tinkle of laughter came through his palmtop. "Well, it's too late to save you from going mad. But I guess it would be a shame if you went deaf. How do I save you?"

Having turned off the cooling in his apartment, the stifling air had now grown too warm. Chan Kam Yin wiped his forehead where a thin bead of perspiration had taken shape. He hardly noticed the heat, or the sweat, or his own action to brush it away. He had entered mental overdrive. The whole world narrowed down to a few lines of text on his screen.

It had taken him countless hours to find the pattern. But he had it now. Anonymous identities danced the markets, making purchases in a certain size range, clustered over an extended but nonetheless well-defined time interval. The anonymous clusters tended to buy positions where the odds were against them. Even more interesting, they tended to win. If they weren't controlled by the Predictor, they were controlled by someone just as good for the Dealer's purposes. He knocked out a simulation of what would have happened in the past couple of weeks if he'd ridden the predictions of these anonymous clusters. The ride generated pure wealth. Pushing himself for one last effort, he found an open 'cast with the same pattern in place. He moved into play. Success. He had just locked his own fate to that of the Predictor.

The Dealer sat back, relaxing in perfect satisfaction. He rubbed the crick in his neck; someday, he promised himself, he'd get ergonomic furniture, to go with the wallscreen of which he dreamed. The days of comfort, he promised himself, drew closer.

He felt tired but not sleepy. With his eyes glazed open he scanned the Web markets, just surfing the goods for sale, the prizes for winning, the jobs available. It seemed a good moment to look for additional opportunities. In due course, an intriguing Request For Proposals drew his eye.

He'd found the RFP posted in the Anguilla Seaside Web Market. The solicitor, Supercon Intercepts, had requested a custom-designed skytruck to cart a large, awkward device to the top of Mount Everest. Doing a global search on the Supercon Intercepts brand, the Dealer could see that they did a lot of contracting for Earth Defense. That made sense: who but Earth Defense would want to drag something that unwieldy to the remotest pinnacle of the planet? Particularly during the Month of *Shiva*, when just about everybody else on the planet put aside their long-term projects and concentrated on the next couple of weeks.

The Dealer spent but a moment puzzling over the purpose of the ungainly payload: the description of the object only gave aerodynamic information, and its purpose didn't really interest him that much. What fascinated him was the set of constraints on the skytruck. The requirements were fierce.

The truck would have to be a brute. A big brute, with huge lungs—the truck would gasp for breath, hovering in the thin air above Everest.

For a moment he thought about just shipping the thing with a roton . . . but the ungainly shape really ruled a roton out. No, the RFP writer had been correct specifying a skytruck.

The engines would constitute the biggest problem.

Conventional skytrucks used electrically powered turbo-fans, fuel-efficient but not as powerful as you'd like for this application. Worse, you'd need a custom-designed supercharger to supply oxygen to the fuel cells, adding yet more weight and considerably cutting down on the efficiency of the full engine assembly. You might be able to lift the cargo that way, but the Dealer sure wouldn't take a 'cast on it. At best it would cost a fortune.

Most people would have had to give up trying to solve the problem at that point. But the Dealer knew something most people didn't know: Saab had built a next-generation combustion engine, using the same principles as the original Moller engines that powered the first skycars, but updated to use ceramic materials and burn pure hydrogen. He'd run into the Saab spec sheets while perusing the websites for antique car buffs, antiques being about the only things around these days that still used combustion. Saab had been trying to build a business in engine retrofits.

Anyway, the Saab engines were just the monsters for this job.

The Dealer suddenly realized that his expertise on combustion engines gave him the inside track on this deal—could he really win the contract? Why not? He could surely undercut anyone foolish enough to bid using conventional technology!

He searched the Web for a suitable airframe; he needed something sturdy but open-framed, so the odd corners of the package could stick out. The frame was pretty easy to find, though it took a bit more surfing to find the bottom-end price he wanted. He needed to buy the frame cheap, because he couldn't go cheap on the flight control system: Because of the complicated effects of the payload's center of gravity, with all the appendages exposed to the fierce turbulence at twenty-nine thousand feet, he'd need top-of-the-line flight control. Only the shortest response times, the most precise corrections, would satisfy the demand. He hated going with expensive parts. It hurt deep inside. But it was necessary.

He wasn't sure how to carry the hydrogen for the engines, whether to use an adsorptive powder, a simple pressure cylinder, or whether to liquefy it; he didn't trust the pressure cylinders, but the adsorptive power was heavy, and refrigeration would surely be both heavy and technically tricky. After staring at the alternatives for a while, he realized that he wasn't the right guy to make this call. He posted a request for consulting services on the Web, to see if he could get a real expert to give him a quick answer.

Meanwhile, he turned on his CAD package and started integrating the pieces he'd already identified. His CAD system wasn't really up to this, it was almost a toy—you don't need fancy stuff for working on Mustangs—but despite its flaws it could still give him some sense of whether the pieces of his plan could sing in harmony.

Four in the morning came and went. He knew he ought to hit the sack, but his mind was flowing with the elements of the operation. He fiddled with the design till it looked as good as he could get it in his CAD system. Satisfied with that phase of the analysis, he rented a little time on a high-end system from the server complex in Novosibirsk. With that he could run a professional simulation of his new invention.

Meanwhile, a hydrogen power specialist in Germany answered his consulting request. The pressure cylinder was the way to go, though the German gave him a pointer to a particular Australian manufacturer who had a million-dollar bond backing the reliability of his products. If the cylinder failed, the Dealer could make a bigger profit than if it worked.

He still had twenty-four hours before he had to submit the proposal to Supercon Intercepts, and the CAD servers still needed a couple of hours before reporting on their simulations. It was time to get some sleep.

❖   ❖   ❖

Morgan tapped the control, and the hatch of his cocoon opened in smooth silence. He rolled out into the brighter light of the office. The clock read 1600.

The office door swung wide. Morgan looked up to see CJ, her hair still glistening wet from the shower, sweep into the room. He considered making a tart remark about knocking first. Futile, he knew.

His momentary pause gave CJ the chance to initiate combat. "I told you we'd finish early."

Morgan pursed his lips. "So you did. Congratulations."

CJ rubbed his shoulder, the shoulder that wasn't supporting Sol. "No, congratulations to *you*, oh Mighty Angel Controller. You're the one who supplied the inspiration." She watched for the puzzled expression on his face before explaining, "I was excited enough about our date that I couldn't help winning."

"So it's a date now, is it?" Morgan said with an edge of steel in his voice.

"Sure." CJ placed a finger in front of Sol, and commanded, "Up."

Sol obediently climbed up on her finger, and contorted her head to rub it against CJ's thumb. "Solomon, there's someone I want you to meet," CJ said. "Since you can't come with us, I thought I'd introduce you to a new friend."

Morgan watched CJ dash down the hall with his parrot, and for a just a moment, he felt a shock of isolation. He was alone with no one, not even his arrogant bird, as company.

Then CJ reappeared, moving with the speed of a tornado, and suddenly Morgan wished for his isolation to continue. He knew it was to no avail, however. "Okay, Angel Leader, where did you ditch my bird?"

"With someone who can use Sol's skills better than you can," CJ answered smugly. "Don't worry, she's in fine hands." CJ climbed onto one of the reinforcing steel bars across the back of his wheelchair, and stretched over Morgan's shoulder to reach the joystick under his right hand. She grabbed the control and pushed forward, causing the three of them—the captive Morgan, the maniacal CJ, and the submissive wheelchair—to charge down the hall at a speed Morgan hadn't attempted in years.

Morgan considered closing his eyes. No, if he was going to die, he wanted to see it coming. He stared straight ahead and said casually, "You're going to get us killed, you know. Wouldn't it be better to save your kamikaze instincts for the mission?" He raised an eyebrow and tried to smile into her eyes, but her breast was in the way, and her head was held rigidly up as she concentrated on the driving. Morgan noticed that his hands were clamped tight around the arms of the chair. He forced himself to relax.

The chair bounded toward the door, which opened automatically just fast enough for CJ to squeeze them through the center without a scratch. "How was that?" she asked her kidnapping victim.

"Typical," he snorted.

In moments they'd reached a drab green skycar, too ugly to be anything but military issue, even without the small label, *Property of Earth Defense Agency* on the side. It was specially designed to accommodate wheelchairs, and Morgan had to wonder who CJ had wheedled to get control of this vehicle for the afternoon. He wouldn't put it past Samuels to support this effort . . . though on reflection he didn't buy it. Samuels understood the dangerous consequences of this fraternization as well as he did.

Once again, Morgan wished he had the strength of personality to stop CJ's playfulness. But he could dimly remember what it was like to play. The part of him that had died with his wife Elisabeth stirred briefly to life once more, urging him on.

Their car leaped in the air, and CJ piled on the speed. She started to whistle; the notes melted on one another in a fashion that did not quite add up to a melody. Eventually it dawned on Morgan that CJ was whistling a parrot tune. Very scary.

Morgan cleared his throat. "Dare I ask where we're going?"

"Sure, ask all you like."

Silence fell. No further answer ensued.

Morgan watched the barren landscape of Nevada flow underneath them, then saw the line of hills that surrounded the Colorado River on the Arizona border. The skycar began to descend. As they closed in on an inlet to the river, he could see a row of boats, and eventually he made out the sign on the establishment: Golden Shores Marina. "We're going boating?" he asked.

"Almost," CJ said. She dug in the backseat of the car. "Here, put this on." She handed him a bulky but lightweight vest.

Morgan looked at the thing doubtfully. "A life preserver?"

"Safety first," CJ chirped. "Now put it on." The car landed itself, and CJ started stripping out of her clothes.

Morgan blushed and started to look away before he realized that she was wearing a bathing suit underneath.

CJ caught his eye and smiled. "Like the suit? Sorry it'll get covered in a minute." She grabbed another vest from the back and pulled it on. "Let's go," she said. She popped the doors. Morgan reached for his controls, but CJ was already reaching for him. "You really ought to wear your legs, old man," she complained. "Then you wouldn't have to put up with me so much." She lifted him out of the wheelchair and swung him onto her back. She set off at a fast march down the ramp to the slips.

"This is undignified," Morgan barked in her ear.

"Like I said, wear your legs next time."

Morgan tried to guess which boat they were going toward: was it the long, lean, jet boat, or the clever little catamaran? Suddenly CJ stopped, and he knew the dreadful certainty: they were not getting on any of the real boats. Rather, they were getting on the itty bitty, green-and-white waverunner bouncing in the gentle waves of the dock.

CJ did not hesitate for even a moment before grabbing the left handlebar and stepping across with her right leg. Balancing carefully, she lowered the two of them onto the runner. "Wrap your arms around my waist," she ordered him, and Morgan obeyed automatically; he now understood in the most primal sense why CJ was the Angel Lead.

CJ pressed the throttle with her thumb, and they pulled away from the dock. The departure was leisurely.

"What's this, speed demon, why are we traveling slower than my wheelchair?" he needled her.

She looked back at him with a sweet smile. "This is a no-wake zone," she said. She was still looking at him as they crossed the slightly narrowed mouth of the inlet, into the river. Her smile twitched just a bit wider, and that was all the warning Morgan had as her thumb squeezed down and the waverunner exploded forward. "This is not a no-wake zone," she yelled at the top of her powerful lungs, barely loud enough to be audible against the noise of the rising wind and the bubbling water spray. Moments later they were going fifty miles an hour, leaping out of the water in time to the waves that crashed against them. "Now we're traveling," she screamed in satisfaction.

Morgan held on for dear life.

Jessica looked intently at her new acquaintance. "Okay, Solomon, I hear you like chicken. Right?"

Solomon whistled a phrase from "Joy to the World." "Chicken good. Yummy!"

"The next question is, do you like white meat or dark?"

Solomon's head rocked back and forth eagerly. "White. White."

"Your wish is my command." Jessica reached across the table to the box of Kentucky Fried, pulling it close. She walked around the coat rack serving as a makeshift bird stand, and pulled a substantial knife from a drawer in the kitchenette. With swift strokes, she cut the chicken into Solly-bird bite-size pieces.

Solomon gave her a wolf whistle and dug in.

Jessica chewed on a chicken wing herself and watched Solly pick her piece apart. The thought struck her that the bird was more or less engaged in an act of cannibalism. But then, how closely related was a chicken to a parrot, after all? Would Solomon consider it cannibalism for her to eat beef, just because humans and cattle were both mammals?

Cannibalism or no, Solomon snacked her way through the chicken breast at an impressive clip. Upon finishing, she asked Jessica for the second time that evening, "Solomon stay all night?"

Jessica nodded. "That's what CJ said. I think your Boss is in trouble with her." When it had become obvious through her video spying that CJ would need to plant the bird with someone, Jessica had quietly let it be known around the base that she had dealt with birds before—which was the simple truth, her mother having kept an aviary, a veritable Noah's Ark for the bird kingdom, during Jessica's childhood. So Jessica had not been surprised the previous afternoon when, stepping out of her cocoon, she had found CJ standing in her office, looking for someone to take good care of Solomon this evening. Jessica had quickly agreed to the planned overnighter because, in her role of learning everything about Morgan, it seemed reasonable to become acquainted with Morgan's oldest surviving friend.

"CJ good girl. Solomon good girl. Boss needs us."

"Frankly, Solly-girl, I'm surprised you aren't jealous of CJ."

"Jealous of people-girl? No, no. She not parrot!"

"I guess that makes sense." Jessica put her chicken down. "You know, Sol, I'm supposed to learn everything I can about your guy."

"Okay. You next Boss?"

Jessica considered the question. "Well, that's the plan."

"Okay, okay. I help."

"Cool, Sol." Jessica slid closer. "I was hoping you could answer some questions I have." She watched Solomon's eyes wander over to the box of chicken. "And I have plenty of food."

"Ask, ask."

Jessica could see that it would be a pleasant evening, discussing her job with the most alien intelligence of her experience.

Free at last. Reggie took the rickety old taxi to Henderson, where he rented a skycar and took off for Lake Havasu.

He had offered to fly to Stanford to pick Mercedes up, but she had sensibly pointed out how it was ridiculous for him to fly for an hour to get her, then turn around to go most of the way back. She had assured him that she was a big girl, and her car worked perfectly well. He had bowed to her logic and her stubbornness.

He saw her at the Bridge, a light breeze ruffling the folds of her simple blue shirt; her cutoff jeans were too tight for the wind to catch them. "Mercedes!" he waved to her. She did not hear, and he tried again. The second time she waved back. He started trotting toward her. Realizing how undignified it was, he slowed to a quick walk. They met at the end of the bridge.

Mercedes brushed her hand across the old stones of the bridge. "Goodness, I had no idea what a sullen collection of gray rocks they'd used to make the London Bridge. Tell me, is this typical of your country's architecture? Is it all this dreary? Or did they run a big prizeboard to find the most sorrowful stones of the nation to build this bridge?"

Reggie looked at the stones beneath his feet. Someone with more money than sense had moved the Bridge to Havasu from London long before the Crash. "No, Britain is certainly not this dreary." He pointed to the cloudless sky. "Here, the sun shines brightly. Such sunshine gives everything a dash of luster. At home, in the gray fog, this bridge was surely much more dreary."

Mercedes laughed. He joined her. For just a moment, he was a little more serious. "Of course, if they'd left the bridge in London, the first *Shiva* would have vaporized it."

She shook her head. "I'm sorry. Did you lose anyone . . . important?"

Reggie shrugged. "It's hard to be British and not to have lost someone when London burned." He'd been eight years old at the time. He'd spent two days trying to dig his mother out of the rubble of their home before someone noticed and took him away. His father had been in the financial district. There hadn't even been any rubble there to dig through.

Reggie clapped his hands. "But enough of this. I thought I'd take you for a different kind of a ride."

Mercedes raised an eyebrow.

He held up a pair of keys. "Let me show you." He walked with her down to the wharf and pointed.

Mercedes laughed again. "Waverunners! You're right, it'll be a new experience. I've never been on one of these before." Her expression turned doubtful. She looked down at her clothes. "Umm, I'm not exactly dressed for this."

Reggie pointed at himself, with his creased pants and polished black leather shoes. He widened his eyes. "You think *you're* not dressed for it?" He pointed at the Catch'n Rayz sun boutique a short distance away. "I made arrangements. Pick a swimsuit; it's yours."

"Goodness!" Mercedes said. "You have all the bases covered, don't you?"

"Constant preparation and attention to detail is a British trademark." Reggie looked down his nose ever so smugly.

"Mmm . . . I thought it was a national form of obsessive-compulsiveness."

"No, you're thinking of the Germans," Reggie replied grandly. "Race you to the shop."

Mercedes won the race to the shop easily. However, Reggie was the first to pick a suit and get back to the waverunners. He watched the shop, and when Mercedes came out, his heart almost stopped.

She had chosen a metallic purple one-piece, about as conservative a suit as the shop had. But nothing in Catch'n Rayz could really be called conservative. Her copper-bronze skin glowed in the sunshine. She was so beautiful it hurt.

Reggie flexed his muscles. They were good muscles, he enjoyed stretching them. He hadn't raced in ten years. But he still swam laps whenever he was home in Dover . . . which wasn't really that often, if you got right down to it.

He threw Mercedes the bracelet that keyed one of the runners. He himself hopped on the other machine. She stepped onto her vehicle with less grace than normal as the runner rocked beneath her feet.

Mercedes moved the handlebars left and right. "Is this little thumb-lever the throttle?" she asked, pushing it down. Suddenly she was moving as the electric motor silently went into action. "Ooops," she said, releasing the control.

Reggie gunned his own steed and caught up with her. "Careful, it's a no-wake zone here," he chided her, and brought his own machine to a legal speed. Mercedes followed him out onto the main lake, hugging his port side.

Just as Reggie could still marvel at the roton, he was now amazed by his waverunner. He had seen old footage of the first waverunners. Nightmares on water. Those machines had screamed like banshees as you brought them up to speed, ruining the water's pleasure for everyone for miles around. Clearly detestable toys of the proletariat, at least from a proper British perspective.

These waverunners, though, were hardly louder than

canoes. At least, they were no louder than canoes at
canoe speeds.

The two of them reached deeper water. Reggie heard
the sound of rushing waves rise astern, off his port side.
Next a gale of laughter surged passed him, and Mercedes
picked up the pace, accelerating ever faster. He gunned
his own engine to catch up, but she had gotten the edge
and was not about to yield. The wind whipped her long
black hair in sinuous waves; the light of the sinking sun
caught the edges of the waves, splintering with flecks of
red and gold.

Mercedes veered to starboard to avoid a speedboat—
a boat that seemed big and clumsy to a rider of the
wave—and Reggie got caught in her wake, putting him
even farther behind. Finally, she noticed that he was not
by her side anymore and slowed down. He bounced out
of her wake and maneuvered to her starboard side once
more. "That way," he yelled, pointing north.

Mercedes nodded. She spun the waverunner on its
heel as if she'd been born to it. Once again her vehicle
rose out of the water as she glided to full speed. This
time Reggie expected it and clung doggedly to her side.
They sped along for a couple of minutes before they
reached the mouth of the Colorado River that fed the
lake. Reggie glanced at the GPS-location map, the only
instrument the vehicle had besides the fuel gauge. He
waved Mercedes slightly to port, and soon they were
running out of the lake, up the river.

Finally, Mercedes slowed down. The rush of wind
and water subsided, and they could talk. "Goodness, it's
beautiful out here," she exclaimed. Her eyes swept over
the hills and low-slung mountains that staggered away
from the river.

"Yes. Quite austere, but quite beautiful in its own,
different way." He pointed at the hills. "How can you
have such a barren desert, just a few meters away
from a veritable flood of water?" Despite the sometimes thick clusters of reeds and other greenery at

the water's edge, the hills stood starkly barren, high-lighting the naked beauty of the red and golden-yellow stone that embodied the region.

Mercedes saw, and understood. "You're right. It's odd," she replied. Her face lit up with a wonder that mirrored Reggie's own feelings, and Reggie could not help believing he had met a soulmate.

"This section of the river is called Topock Gorge, by the way, if you ever want to come back." Reggie spotted a tiny beach on the eastern shore of the river up ahead and waved to his companion. "Come with me," he said, and led her onto land. "Let's go on up the hill," he suggested.

"Not yet," Mercedes replied. Unbuckling her life jacket as she went, she ran back out into the water, her long legs splashing water in all directions.

"Hey!" Reggie called. "Come back here!"

Mercedes dived headfirst into the water.

Reggie had no choice but to follow.

He dove into the water, a shock as cold as the air was hot. But he'd expected that, and started cruising toward the escaping girl. He'd catch her in less than a minute.

But somehow he seemed to have trouble catching up. He lifted his head for a moment to get a good look and saw why. Mercedes was pulling away with a flat-out butterfly stroke. Only a pro could master the rhythm of the butterfly with Mercedes' sinuous grace. He was being hustled!

Reggie surged back into the water, pulling out all the stops. He followed his butterfly in a wide arc as she tried to outrun him and get back to the beach. Finally he came close enough grasp her foot on the upstroke of a dolphin kick.

"Hey!" Mercedes spluttered, laughing and catching her breath at the same time. "Thought I'd be easy just because you got a medal, right?" She tread water and splashed his face with one hand. "Wrong, buster!"

Reggie puckered his lips, blew her a kiss, and slapped

a huge wave back at her. They swam back to the beach side by side.

They reached the beach. Reggie once again pointed up the hill. With wordless agreement, they started to climb.

The sun descended. The air felt cool as the water trickling down their backs dried. Mercedes started a new conversation. "You promised you'd tell me about the Twin Mysteries, crop circles and pyramids."

Reggie chuckled. "So I did. And now I am honor-bound to explain." He clasped his hands together. "Consider the pyramids. Could you have built them with your bare hands?"

Mercedes laughed. "Of course not." She traced a finger lightly across Reggie's chest muscles; he tried not to flinch. "Perhaps you could, though."

Her touch had destroyed his train of thought, and it took him a moment to recover. Her eyes were still laughing when he went on. "For you, perhaps I could. But lifting the stones into place, difficult as it is, is not the hardest part of building a pyramid. Laying it out with the required precision is even more remarkable, particularly without modern tools."

"I suppose so." She looked away, pursing her lips. "You're right, it would be pretty hard to do."

Reggie clapped his hands. "There you have it. Clearly, the pyramids are too big and too well constructed to have been created by mere primitive humans. Clearly, they must have been built by aliens from another star." He swung his arms out in a great arc, ending in the sky.

Mercedes reached out with her hand in an arc that came within millimeters of his chest but did not touch. He snapped his hands down in a defensive reflex, fast enough to grab her hand in his. He did not let go. She did not try to escape.

"The crop circles, of course, are more mysterious than the pyramids. How could you see what you were building except by flying, and how could you cut such a swath without a machine that would leave a telltale trail from the road?" He held his head in mock pain. "Impossible for the mortal man. Crop circles too must have been created by aliens."

Mercedes guessed where he was going. "And the Church of the Stellar Light turns that attitude into religion. If we can't even build pyramids and crop circles, how can we hope to fight these really, truly alien spaceships?"

Reggie nodded. "That's how it looks to me." He sighed. "It's hard to dent the faith, too." He chuckled. "But once in a while you get a special circumstance . . ." He became lost in a personal reverie.

Mercedes poked him in the shoulder. "Yes? I take it you brought someone some Light of your own?"

Reggie shrugged. "More or less. My grandmother was certain that aliens must have created the crop circles." The lines of his face drew back in pleasure at the memory. "I never could have convinced her with logic and diagrams that people made them. But I convinced her nonetheless. I gave her a coffee-table book—a real book, mind you, something solid and expensive that suggested it wasn't forged and couldn't be dismissed like a Web page. The book was a photo layout of all the winners of the annual crop circle competition, in Kansas. The winner with the red baseball cap didn't look like an alien at all." His chuckle took on a wicked tinge. "Though some of the other winners, I confess, looked rather strange and alien. Forced me to question my own beliefs."

Mercedes laughed, and put her arm through his. The warmth of her body drew a line up the side of his hip and shoulder.

They reached the summit. With the sun to their back, they looked out on the desert landscape.

"Very different from home," Mercedes muttered.

"And very different from Britain, as well," Reggie

replied. "The Yucatan has very little in common with
England, but at least they both are places where things
grow all the time. This is about as different from that
as you can get, short of the Sahara."

The rich red hues of the sinking sun transformed the
hills moment by moment, from gold to bronze to copper.
Reggie sighed. "It's time for us to head back," he said.

"Yeah," Mercedes agreed reluctantly. "I still have work
in L.A."

They turned and started walking down the hill. A
bright stream of white foam turned the northern bend
in the river, heading south toward them at a tremendous
speed. Mercedes pointed. "It's another waverunner," she
said. "*Miercoles*, were we going that fast?"

Reggie laughed. "Oh, yes, I promise, that's just what
you looked like a few minutes ago."

The runner charged closer, then started doing doughnuts in the water. Two people sat astride the vehicle,
a young woman and an older man. Mercedes stopped,
and Reggie saw her peering intently at the couple. "They
look familiar," she muttered. "Do you recognize them?"

Reggie looked more closely. The man, he could see,
seemed to have unnaturally short legs . . . and Reggie's
eyes widened with recognition. The waverunner spun.
Reggie watched the woman smile and recognized her
as well. "She won an Olympic medal a couple of years
ago," he replied limply; a discussion of the Angels
would have broken the mood. "I was watching as she
took the gold away from the leader in the triathlon."
He remembered her look of exhaustion as they came
into the last lap, how beaten she had seemed . . . and
how in those last moments she had called upon an
inner strength, perhaps the kind of strength that built
the pyramids. He remembered watching her power
grow till she reached the finish line. How remarkable
her victory had been.

The runner spun again, so Reggie could see the man's
face. Reggie's eyes widened even further in astonish-

ment. "He's smiling," Reggie observed, and the sense of wonder filled him.

"Who's smiling?" Mercedes asked.

Reggie nodded toward the couple. "The old goat over there. That smile, my dear, is more remarkable than anything else we've seen today."

Mercedes looked at the people, then back at Reggie. "It's unusual for him to smile? What kind of person is he?"

Reggie frowned, then relaxed. "He's a person who deserves a chance to smile. I just hope this is the right chance."

Mercedes ran a finger down Reggie's cheek. "Everybody deserves a chance to smile." Her eyes looked into his, and he looked back. He stepped closer, and then they melted together in an embrace where the waverunners, and the hills, and the water receded, shimmering into the distance.

They skimmed beneath an old bridge of some sort and plunged forward. CJ turned her head. "We're going into Topock Gorge," she yelled. "Quite beautiful, don't you think?"

Bouncing across the waves at fifty mph, with the water spray pecking at his eyes, and CJ's hair swirling across his mouth, Morgan attempted to look around and appreciate the beauty of nature. The effort was too absurd for even the most intent student, and in the end Morgan broke into a strained laughter. "You are a madwoman," he yelled into her ear. Every muscle in his body tensed up, both from the desperate desire to hang on, and from the desperate attempt to keep warm, as the frigid Colorado River water soaked his clothes with a cold that penetrated deep into his body. Yelling into CJ's ear, he found that the crook in her neck was the only warm place for miles around. He buried his nose there.

"Oooh!" CJ exclaimed, and heeled the runner over almost onto its side, into a series of tight doughnuts.

Morgan had finally begun to adapt to the rhythm of the full-throttle straight-on race down the river when CJ set them into the spin, and he jerked as the water rushed up to meet his face. It didn't quite reach him, but he tightened his body lock on her till he had surely given her bruises. It served her right.

They straightened up and took off down the river again. CJ glanced over her shoulder at him. "Your face is cracking," she yelled, and a smug expression passed over her face.

Morgan realized CJ's joke was approximately true; his lips were pulled back in a wild caricature of a smile, caused by a combination of the wind beating upon him and the cold that held his teeth clenched in a grimace. And there was one other thing that went into that smile, he reluctantly acknowledged. "This is a blast," he admitted to CJ.

The grin on CJ's face was as wide as his. "Then I have succeeded." She dropped the throttle, and the sudden deceleration pressed him against her even as he loosened his grip. "Now we can just cruise and enjoy the scenery."

They turned back up the river and puttered along toward Golden Shores. They traveled in eloquent solitude for a time. Finally, Morgan asked a question he had been holding back ever since the first day he met CJ. "How did you wind up training to be an Angel?" he asked softly. "Who did you lose?"

She turned to him, and though her smile still contained a hint of wickedness, her eyes were soft. "Not everybody who goes after *Shiva* has lost someone," she whispered. "My family lived in Rabbit Hash, Kentucky. Population three hundred seventy-nine. It's just about the last place on Earth *Shiva* will strike."

"That makes it all the more puzzling, then."

CJ wriggled in his arms. "When I was nine years old, my dad told me I should be an Angel. I've been training for it ever since."

Morgan hid his shock. "What kind of man would tell his daughter to go on a suicide mission?"

CJ pursed her lips. "It's not like that at all. Really." She gave him a short, harsh laugh. "For one thing, Dad doesn't really expect me to die on this trip. He thinks I, of all people, will make it back." She shrugged. "He thinks I can get back because I inherited his genes. You've heard of Hookshot Kinsman, right?"

Morgan blinked. "The basketball player? He's your father?" When CJ nodded, Morgan raised an eyebrow. "You're at least two feet shorter than he is. You sure your mother didn't have an affair?"

That made CJ laugh gaily. "She certainly could have, but I'm quite sure she didn't. For one thing, it wouldn't fit with her morality, being a policewoman and all. But we know I'm his daughter because I'm a natural athlete, just like he is. You should have seen his expression when he handed me a basketball at the age of six, and I dribbled it downcourt and swished it."

Morgan could see that expression, all right. It was the same expression Morgan wore half the time, watching CJ outmaneuver the robots in SimHell.

"Anyway, there's a second reason Dad would tell me to be an Angel. You're familiar with BKM Security, right?"

Morgan snorted. "Let me guess, the K stands for Kinsman, and your father was one of the founders of one of the Big Four security companies?"

CJ twisted and brought her nose up till it almost touched Morgan's. Her eyes were filled with mischief. "Right again, big guy. He sold out early, so he's not a billionaire, but when the Crash came and wiped out the government law-enforcement subsidies, he helped fund BKM. That's actually where he met Mom; he hired her after she got laid off from the Cincinnati police force."

"And what does that have to do with your being here?"

"Even though he started out as a basketball player,

Dad was always a person who cared about people. You don't go into security and rulebook enforcement unless you care." She turned away, though she squirmed to get deeper in his arms. "Anyway, he always believed in sending the right person to do the job. He never shirked a task in his life. And when I was nine and I won the gold medal in the American Junior Gymnastics competition, he looked at me and said, 'Girl, you're an Angel. They need you.'" Water trickled down from her eyes, and it was not just river spray. "He wasn't happy when he said it, but we both knew, when he said it, that he was right."

CJ was no longer the arrogant leader of the Angels; suddenly she was a young girl, and Morgan no longer held her tight to stay alive; he held on to soothe her. She continued. "So he moved me over from gymnastics to the triathlon. 'CJ,' he said, 'you're acrobat enough now. What you need most is endurance. Your heart and your endurance will get you through.'"

"And me," Morgan said. He brushed her hair out of her eyes. "I'll get you through, too." He took a deep breath, knowing he was about to make a terrible mistake. He leaned forward, and gently kissed her.

Chapter Six
T minus Fourteen

Paolo's hands didn't shake, although his breathing was a bit staccato. Jesus, it hurt him to damage people like that! Even when they were faceless strangers. Even when they deserved it.

Paolo stepped away from his desk. He ran his fingers over the luxurious leather of his executive chair, and left the room. How many people had he just sabotaged? How many had he driven into bankruptcy and abject poverty? He would never know.

He needed some air. A chance to walk around, collect his thoughts. He would risk a trip into Sofia's garden, a lush land of fragrant delight and hidden danger.

He could see a swatch of the garden from the two-story-high window through which sunshine coursed into the stairwell. As with all things within Sofia's purview, the original garden plot adjoining the house had been transformed. Repeatedly.

When they arrived, the garden had held some simple

flower beds. The parcel had been reclaimed from the jungle, tamed and domesticated.

Sofia had transformed the area back into a jungle, a place where dense green vines wrapped and twisted around the seemingly random clusters of bushes and aromatic flowers. A Spaniard arriving centuries before would have felt right at home on first glance—just another chunk of the Yucatan to hack through.

But upon closer inspection, he would have been puzzled. Perhaps he would have dropped to his knees to ask God about Satan's dark purpose. For the plants now bursting from the garden did not normally grow in the Yucatan. Here, these nonnative plants demanded unrelenting, intensive care to thrive in their carefully crafted, chaotically overgrown state.

Paolo stepped down from the staircase, around the corner through the kitchen, and out onto the short path that led into the garden. A tall bower laced with antique roses invited him to enter, at his own risk. He hesitated but a moment before plunging ahead.

The sound of burbling water drew him deeper into the hidden mysteries of Sofia's special place. Scores of vines and branches reached with delicate fingers into the path. Paolo winced as an errant rose branch reached out to strike, its thorns raking his arm just above the elbow. Tiny beads of crimson welled up along the scratch, a bright string of rubies glittering in the sunshine. Paolo cursed softly.

A sweet and innocent voice, surely the voice of Eve or one of her descendants (although it could have easily been the snake), floated to him from a distance. "Is that you, darling?" Sofia asked with dulcet charm.

"Sweetest Sofia," he responded with a voice of delicate happiness, while considering how best to saturation-bomb this place with napalm, "you have made this land of quiet splendor not only as beautiful as a jungle, but as dangerous as one, too."

Through the ivy vines of the central walkway, Paolo

caught a peek of beautiful female curves gliding around a Banyan tree. A few seconds later, behind him he heard a voice gasp. "You're hurt," Sofia said. She leapt catlike across the treacherous flowering almond bushes separating them. "Let me fix that for you." She cocked her head, studied the scratch, and delicately kissed it.

Paolo grunted his thanks.

Sofia looked up into his eyes, and as her gentle smile curved into a wicked grin, she bent her head and licked the blood from his arm with long, graceful movements of her tongue.

Paolo shuddered at the touch. "Ooof," he said, with the characteristic power of the male wit. He took a step back, thus nearly impaling himself on the rose bush once again. He was trapped like Adam, he realized, in a garden, between an alluring woman and a deadly danger. He also understood full well that the alluring woman was actually the more dangerous one. Nonetheless, like Adam, he stepped back toward the woman, on the verge of accepting the greater dangers presented by the female of the species. Then he remembered why he had come into the garden in the first place.

Sofia recognized the change in his expression with practiced ease. "Uh oh," she said teasingly, "I can see you're in no mood for teasing." She put her hands on her hips. "What terrible thing has happened?" She raised an eyebrow as her analysis of his somber mood yielded subtler nuances, leading her to correct herself, "Or rather, what terrible thing did you have to do?"

Paolo laughed with a touch of bitterness. "Ah, Sofia, I could never hide my thoughts from you." Well, sometimes he could hide them, mostly by accident. Periodically Sofia was so alert for his feelings and thoughts that she jumped at shadows, certain he was melancholy or irritated when he was perfectly fine. But today she was right on target. He took a deep breath; the perfume of Sofia's jungle garden undercut his depression. "I just shook down the tailriders," he explained.

Sofia looked at him in puzzlement.

"I created a set of trackable identities, to lure the scam artists to follow me, so I could sucker them on a bad forecast. The bad forecast—and it was a beauty, I must say—hung a hundred or so people out to dry."

Sofia closed one eye and wrinkled her nose. "You did this once before, didn't you, darling?"

Paolo nodded. "About six years ago. I never expected to do it again, but after Reggie left, I realized his article would spawn a whole new generation of gamers trying to get a free ride." He threw his hands in the air, slapped them down on his thighs. "I hate knocking people down like that, even if they ask for it."

She stepped up and wrapped her arms around him, laying her head on his chest. She had been covered with dirt from the plants; now he was too. "If it bothers you that much, why not just let them go ahead? We have enough money, let them be."

Paolo ran his hand through her hair. "If it was just the money, you'd be right, I'd just let them be. But tailriders have a more terrible effect than that. They distort the odds on the 'castpoint. Remember the mess I told you about for the Gate location?" He rocked Sofia gently in his arms. "If any tailriders were able to get a handle on my brand during the assault, they'd back my forecasts with more money, more strength, than the forecasts warranted." He shook his head. "In the normal course of events, those people would eventually lose their shirts. But there are too many life or death decisions in the next two weeks to let time and statistics teach the tailriders a lesson. Right now, the 'castpoints have to reflect mankind's best judgment."

Sofia squirmed restlessly in his arms. "Ah, yes, darling, I seem to recall this part of the conversation from the last time." She stood on tiptoes and breathed in his ear. "Let me see if I can get this straight. These tailriders, the scam artists that you just scammed, could lead Earth Defense to make the wrong decisions, so the

Angels would get killed, *Shiva* would get to Earth, and cities would get vaporized. Is that correct?"

"Pretty much." It always surprised Paolo when Sofia revealed how well she understood the Web and its machinery. Her grasp of the features of electronic commerce seemed incongruous and inappropriate.

"Well, then, congratulations, darling, on having saved ten billion or so lives this morning. What are you going to do this afternoon?"

"Hmph." He knew she was right, but he still wasn't happy with it.

Sofia's eyes gleamed; once again, Paolo knew he was in trouble. "Come here," she commanded, taking his hand and leading him around a corner. They crossed an intersection, bore left at a fork, and found a bench under the shade of a pair of Golden Chain trees. Paolo looked around wonderingly; he was completely lost. "This garden is only fifteen meters square, isn't it?" If necessary, he could just pick a direction, force his way through the plush growth, and come out into the open. He looked at the rose bushes and the bougainvillea, and realized that the plan was untenable. Only Sofia could lead him out of here. He was completely at her mercy. No doubt she had designed it that way.

"Paolo, you see the garden from the air every day. Does it look any larger than fifteen meters? Of course not."

Paolo shook his head. "This maze is more complicated than the corridors in *Shiva*," he muttered.

"See how fortunate you are that I'm on your side?" she answered his unspoken thoughts. On tiptoe again, she rubbed her nose along the line of his chin. "There's a price to be paid, though, for safe passage. *Quid pro quo*." She purred.

Paolo laughed, lifted Sofia from her feet, and flung her gently but masterfully upon the bench.

Sofia yelled, "Wooohooo!" as she put her arms around him in response.

✧   ✧   ✧

The aroma of lasagna wafted from the kitchen. It filled the house, reaching even Lou's little office hanging off the side of the rec room, an outcast from the family dwelling. Lou Scharanski inhaled the rich Italian aromas deeply. It was good to be alive. He could still enjoy many things, even if those pleasures were fewer now than they had once been, when he had been a spry eighty-year-old.

"Pops, get out here," his granddaughter yelled from somewhere deep in the house.

Lou heard his son's reproving voice from the rec room. "Quiet," he said in a loud whisper. "Let him sleep."

Lou flipped off his touchscreen and shouted back, "I'll be right there." He stepped out of his office into the rec room and swept his great-great-granddaughter into his arms. "Ugh," he said, "you know I won't be able to pick you up like this much longer."

Lanie hugged him. "Will you still be able to pick me up when I'm twelve?" she asked. Her twelfth birthday was just a few weeks away.

"I don't know," he said doubtfully. "Do you want me to?"

She squeezed him. "You bet, Pops."

He put her down, and they held hands as they entered the kitchen.

A ragged chorus of people shouted as he arrived, "Surprise!"

Lou winced, held up his arm to protect his eyes from the flash, then laughed, all in quick sequence. "You people really got me this time," he said. "I never would have guessed." They had done this for his birthday for over forty years—a hamster could have forecast this event. But he had to keep up the pretense for Lanie's sake.

His great-grandson lifted his finger in an orchestral motion, and an awful round of "Happy Birthday" filled the air. Lou's children had many gifts, but they did not have the gift of singing. Unfortunately, they did have the gift of strong lungs.

Lou sank into a chair. Lanie brought out the cake. Lou looked at it in surprise. "Only one candle?"

"Sure," she said. "Mom said you get to start over after a hundred."

Lou pondered that for a moment, nodded to his great-granddaughter-in-law, and said, "Makes perfect sense." He inhaled mightily, till his eyes bulged out for the youngest members of the audience. Finally he blew out the candle. Lanie enjoyed the show tremendously.

His son hobbled over on his cane with a present in his hand. "Happy birthday," he said.

One by one, each generation of Scharanskis gave him a present. Then Lanie brought in another present. "It's from Viktor," she said breathlessly. "It came all the way around the world." She shook it, and Lou almost leaped from his chair in horror. She continued. "It makes a funny sound."

Carefully, very carefully to conceal his terror, he held out his hands. "Here, child," he said with a big smile.

The package was rather smaller than the typical Viktor gift, which only meant he'd used the newest technology. Viktor had wrapped this one lovingly in maroon velvet, with a bright silver bow. Lou himself would have had trouble not running his hands caressingly over the warm surface.

With a silly grin on his face, he held the package gently to his ear. Yes, it was ticking, all right. Good old Viktor.

Lou turned his smile on his granddaughter, who was old enough to understand what he was about to say but young enough to act swiftly. "Sara, while I go into my office to thank Viktor, why don't you fly everyone up to the park? I think the flag iris may be just starting to bloom."

Sara looked at him, and he looked back at her, hard. Light dawned in her eyes, and as he had hoped, she started moving with swift efficiency. "Okay, everybody, let's go. I think everyone can fit in Ben's van, can't they?"

The roomful of people looked disoriented, but the outcome had become inevitable. Lou retired to his office and sat staring at the ticking package until he heard the door slam closed. Car fans whined to life, then changed pitch as the vehicle rose in the air. Lou waited till the sound faded before taking action. Viktor had surely not designed the package to blast a hole bigger than the house itself, but there was no sense taking chances.

Lou's old skills came back as sharp as ever. His hands were not so steady as they had once been, though. He hoped that, just this once, Viktor had sent him a dummy, not a live one. Fat chance.

The wrapping was not wired. He removed it easily. Penetrating the cardboard box was a bit trickier, but this too yielded to his careful vivisection. Eventually, he had the entire structure laid out, exposed. Sure enough, Viktor had sent a live bomb, and had used the newest technology. The charge was a small chunk of duodec, in the shape of a Hershey's kiss. Viktor's sense of humor remained as sharp as ever. And Lou appreciated the thoughtfulness shown in the size of the charge; even with duodec, the charge was only enough to blow up his office. His family would have been perfectly safe in the kitchen. It told him that Viktor cared about his family. It also told him that even Viktor was just a little concerned that this time, just maybe, Lou wouldn't be quite up to the challenge.

Lou spent half an hour working his way around the traps and dummies. Finally he made the ticking stop. No explosion accompanied the sudden silence. Lou sighed.

The bomb had been attached to a small touch-screen, which now lit up of its own accord. "Lou!" the broad Russian face smiled at him from the screen, "*Pozdravlyayu s dnyem rozhdyeniya*! And many more. Though you'd better practice more for my presents, *comrade*. Otherwise, next year will be your last!"

❖   ❖   ❖

Jessica's confidence that she had done a good deed by inviting her grandmother to come down from Montana for a couple of days was ebbing fast. "Granma, I just can't believe it! You can't even walk through a simple supermarket without ranting about the government." Jessica reached into the freezer and brought out a package. "I for one want a T-bone steak tonight."

Granma rapped her cane against the tiled floor several times, then swept the steaks out of her granddaughter's cart, and threw them back into the meat case. She stooped over it, tossing packages this way and that with a speed and forcefulness that belied her rumpled appearance. Her search proceeded relentlessly, as she dug down deeper into the stacks of meat, until a crowd started to gather.

Jessica whispered, "Granma, you're making a scene!"

A whoop of triumph echoed from the depths of the freezer. A wrinkled hand triumphantly held up a package of T-bone steak very much like the one Granma had originally thrown back in disgust. Granma stood up saying forcefully, "Now this is a label you can trust."

Jessica sighed as Granma tossed the steaks into the cart. Only the most miniscule difference separated Jessica's original steaks from her grandmother's: Jessica's steaks had been certified by the FDA, whereas Granma's had been certified by Underwriters Laboratory.

Jessica pushed her cart through the gathering of people, trying to escape the scene of the crime, but Granma wasn't quite done yet. Granma looked each of the half-dozen people in the eye and said, "Never trust the FDA! They'll kill ya." With that, Granma strode with dignified haste down the aisle to catch up with her granddaughter, who was thoughtfully eyeing the different brands of dishwashing detergent, trying to become invisible.

As usual, Granma had an opinion. "Get the detergent

from P&E, girl. *Consumer Reports* says it really does cut the grease better, and leaves fewer stains."

"Really?" Jessica asked with some amusement.

"Really." Granma whipped her palmtop out of her purse and performed a quick Web search. She held the computer out so Jessica could view the screen. "See?"

Jessica looked at the *Consumer Reports* analysis, just three months old. Sure enough, it said that the P&E brand of detergent was worth the extra cost. "Well, you sure saved me that time," Jessica said as she picked up a box of the expensive detergent.

"No, I saved you when I got you the good T-bones," Granma sniffed. "You know the FDA killed your great-grandfather."

Jessica checked off the dishwasher detergent from her shopping list, and saw she was done. She pointed her cart toward the exit. "I know, Granma, I know." Granma's father had died of sudden heart failure during the time when the Food and Drug Administration was still refusing to allow beta-blockers on the market. Tens of thousands of people had died. "But Granma, that was back in the 1970s, for God's sake. The FDA isn't even a part of the government any more. They're a respectable company, just like Consumer Reports or Underwriter's."

"Ha! I suppose you'd say that about the Post Office, too." Granma was still unconvinced.

As they reached the exit, all the packages in the cart talked to the store computer, which then beeped Jessica's palmtop. Hardly slowing down, she glanced at the tallied-up cost of her purchases and authorized payment.

Granma was peering over her shoulder. "Federal dollars?!" she wailed. "You're keeping your money in Federal dollars?"

Jessica groaned. Now she would get a lecture about government-backed financial instruments, and the merits of using Masterbucks instead. "I keep some of my money in Swiss francs, too," she said helpfully, just for the perverse joy of watching her Granma splutter in rage.

✦   ✦   ✦

The Dealer stared once again at the disaster upon his screen. An American, he believed, would have screamed in pain looking at the shattered results of his careful planning. But he was tougher than Americans. He really couldn't understand how those whiners succeeded so often, with all the crying and moaning they did.

Still, his loss hurt. The plan had seemed surefire. Somehow, though, he'd gotten himself taken to the cleaners on the 'castpoint, again. He forced himself to sit back in his chair and close his eyes, to review what he'd done, find the mistake.

That pattern of anonymous identities he had followed, he was sure it was the Predictor. He'd followed them on half a dozen forecasts, all winners. The Dealer's confidence in his scam had grown as he proceeded, encouraging him to plunk down bigger chunks of cash— he was reinvesting all his profits from the forecasts and then some. But then the Predictor's anonymous little cluster of buyers had forecast that the new generation of solar mirrors would be able to do some damage to *Shiva*, vaporizing at least one hundred tons of *Shiva* armor, before *Shiva* destroyed them. The odds, at five to one against, were terrific. With this 'cast, the Dealer would make a profit to party on!

But the mirror arrays had barely gotten focused on *Shiva* before the blasted planet-wrecker had started spinning, and whatever that alabaster white armor was, it could throw off a lot of energy before yielding. The Dealer had glanced at the post-attack analysis, and now they thought the damn stuff might be laced with capillary tubes pumped with liquid sodium, a huge cooling system. True or not, *Shiva* counterfired on the mirror control stations with a series of particle beam strikes. A salvo of those incredible high-speed Selk missiles followed the particle beams, and that was that.

And once again the Dealer was left holding the wrong 'cast.

Well, if things went well on the skytruck proposal, he'd recoup his losses. The sims had shown, pretty clearly, that his design would work. He'd have to tinker with the end result a bit, he was sure—the sims weren't perfect—but his underlying concepts were sound. He went out to the Supercon Intercepts RFP and clicked across the links till he found the webform to submit his proposal. He was immediately faced with the most difficult decision he had to make on this effort: which brand should he use?

The Dealer held two longstanding brands on the Web. One was his "reputable criminal" brand, the one he'd used when negotiating with the kid who'd nabbed the motherboards. That was the brand he used most often. But he had another pretty well-known signature, the one he used to market his services as an antique automobile restorer. That one was scrupulously clean.

The Dealer's preference on the bid would have been to use an anonymous identity. Then, if he won the bid, he could stash the cash and get on with his life, leaving the poor sucker who'd given him the job well-stiffed. That would have been a Deal. But the RFP clearly stated that only a brand with an extensive, positive reputation would win. An anonymous identity was out.

And after staring at his screen for a while, the Dealer had to confess that his reputable criminal brand wasn't any good for this task either. All the contracts that he'd ever undertaken with that brand contained vague, slippery wording that law enforcers couldn't use against him in court. Anyone with a brain would quickly recognize such a brand, maintained specifically for shady, if not necessarily illegal, deals. The Dealer shook his head. If he used that identity, and if the customer understood what it meant, he'd lose right there. He couldn't accept such a big risk of losing based on the brand, when he had such a good shot at winning otherwise.

It was really a shame. The Dealer had lined up some low-ball pricing vendors for several of the components.

He could have just about doubled his profit if he'd been able to use the criminal brand and cut some corners (after all, how much would his fencing customers care about how he'd stiffed a non-criminal firm? Not in the least). No, he was stuck. If he was going to win, he'd have to use his best signature, and that meant he'd have to use the right components. He told himself it was still all right. After all, even with top-quality materials, he'd still make a handsome profit, considering that his design innovation allowed him to build a substantially less expensive machine anyway. He could, and would, skim a substantial part of that cost savings as his take. Not quite a Deal, but certainly a big win.

Choosing his car-mechanic brand, the Dealer filled out the form, submitted his truck plans, and included the sims he'd run: the sims weren't required, but he was pretty sure they'd clinch the deal if anything did.

"You are a devil, Viktor Gudonov," Lou told his old friend on the screen.

"So you liked my present," Viktor replied, beaming in delight.

"You have to stop sending things like that. Someone is going to get hurt. Probably me."

Viktor waved the objection aside. "I haven't sent you a proper birthday present in four years, and now you complain. Old man, you are getting to be an old man."

"And you are getting to be an actuarial nightmare. Last I heard, Russians were supposed to die in their seventies." Viktor was ninety-eight. Lou continued, "I hope your insurance company appreciates the dividends they're making on your carcass."

"I pity your children, having to pay for *your* carcass." Viktor laughed. "Did you like the explosive?"

"The duodec? Cool stuff, no doubt about it. I have this feeling we still haven't really tapped its potential, though. Despite the money we've won." Viktor and Lou had designed a duodec pattern that could bring down a chunk of ceiling in that *Shiva*, which had been quite valuable for Angel One. The prize had been a handsome reward.

"My feelings exactly. I think we ought to get together and work with it more seriously, to see if there's some fun we've been missing."

Lou stared at him in astonishment. "Get together? Like physically get in the same room together?"

"Not a room, an open field. A large open field. No sense knocking down a building if we can help it."

Lou looked out the window. Spring had come to most of America, but here in Rochester, New York there was still the odd spot of snow on the ground. "Viktor, even the fields just around here are too cold for me right now, and I know what the temperatures are like around your house. I wouldn't survive it. My teeth would freeze together."

Viktor clucked his tongue. "Tsk, Lou, maybe you really are getting too old. I'll have to find a younger partner." He looked wistfully into the distance. "A young woman, perhaps, no older than seventy, with a—"

"With a background in explosives. Sure, Viktor. I'm sure there are some around, but let's face it, the art of explosives isn't what it used to be. The Cold War has been over for a very long time. Today's terrorists just aren't up to snuff. Thank God."

"Too true, too true. I suppose I shall be cursed with you as my partner for the rest of my days." Viktor's broad face took on a mournful look.

Lou snapped his fingers. "I know where we could go. Let's buzz on over to Vegas."

Lou had the satisfaction of seeing his comrade's face twist in surprise. Lou didn't get to surprise Viktor as nearly as often as Viktor surprised him.

Viktor said, "Lou, when I said there might be some fun we're missing, I didn't mean gambling, games, and dames. Or are you thinking we could check out practice charges on the Luxor Hotel? I confess the idea intrigues me. Certainly, if we could bring down a beautifully stable structure like that pyramid, we'd have something."

"Viktor, no!" Lou chided him. "I agree it would be a great test, but we'd have terrible trouble getting the building cleared first. Forget that. We'll meet at the Vegas drop port. And then . . ." Lou enjoyed watching Viktor lean forward just a smidgen, in eager anticipation. The old KGB agent still didn't know what he'd planned. Score one for the CIA. "We'll tool on over to Fort Powell. Trust me, there are plenty of open fields around the base where we can blast to our heart's content. Shucks, there are whole mountains in the neighborhood that have no purpose except to serve as testbeds. Plus, there's an added bonus."

Viktor's eyes brightened with excitement. "Of course, the Angels!"

Lou shook his head doubtfully. "Yeah, that's where the Angels train all right, though that's not exactly what I was driving at. Not only are the Angels there, but so is all their equipment. In particular, there's a complete set of gear available for inspection by specialists such as ourselves."

"So we can see exactly what equipment we'll have to work with," Viktor said, finally up to speed.

"Exactly."

"I like it, old friend. In fact, it is such a good idea, why didn't you suggest it for *Shiva IV*?"

Lou glared at him. "Don't you ever stop complaining, Viktor? I come up with a great idea, and now you're giving me a hard time because I didn't think of it five years ago?"

"Someone has to keep you on your toes," came the huffy response.

Lou heard the muffled whine of his grandson's van coming down in the back. "My great-great-granddaughter, Lanie, does that for me. I don't need you."

Viktor raised his hands to his forehead. "Of course! Lanie! You're right, you don't need me. Well, you don't need me for that, anyway. Please tell me, how is the delightful bride-to-be?"

"She grows more wonderful by the day," Lou said, and mist filled his eyes. "I wouldn't hold my breath on her marrying Illya, though. Indeed, I think she's forgotten the crush she had on him when she was five." Six years earlier, Lou had journeyed to Murmansk to visit his ex-nemesis, now his closest friend. Viktor's family, Lou had known, wasn't quite sure how to respond to a man Viktor claimed as a great friend, but of whom Viktor told many tales, most of which involved death by violence for Viktor's associates. To help break the ice (so to speak), Lou had taken Lanie with him. Ice-breaking was one of Lanie's talents. She was effervescent and had no trouble bringing smiles even to the face of Viktor's dour brother. And Lou had figured that the experience would be interesting for Lanie as well. Lanie had quite fallen for the fair-haired Illya, who was twelve at the time. And Illya hadn't minded having Lanie tagging around after him.

Viktor shook his head sadly. "She has forgotten my Illya! Astounding! Incomprehensible! And also, a great loss for the CIA-KGB détente. She could have been Juliet for my Illya's Romeo. Maybe they'd even beat the classic ending and live happily every after—a couple of smart kids like that."

Lou shook his head. CIA-KGB détente?! The CIA and KGB were both long dead, but still they lived on in Viktor's romantic heart.

Viktor's eyes widened, and he leaned toward the camera. "Well, perhaps they'll have another chance," he said in a secretive hush. "Illya is coming to America next month."

Lou blinked. "Really? To do what?"

"He's going to Colorado Springs, of course. To the Space Force Academy."

Lou gave Viktor a big smile. "That's wonderful, Viktor. Space Force. So he's going to follow the family

tradition of defending the *rodina*, hmmm?" Viktor's son
had been in the Russian Navy, and his granddaughter had married a missile commander in the Earth
Defense Space Force.

"Illya most certainly is going to follow our proud
tradition. If he cannot take down *Shiva*, no one can!"
Viktor's nostrils flared, and his fist came down on the
table, out of sight of the camera, but with a bang that
Lou could not mistake.

Back in Lou's own office, an eleven-year-old tornado
charged through even as Lou heard an irritated mother
cry out, "Lanie! Let Pops talk to his friend in peace!"

Lanie wrapped her arms around Lou, and Lou smiled
lopsidedly into the camera.

Viktor gave him a wink and a small wave of his
massive hand. "See you in Vegas," he said.

"Check," Lou replied, and the screen went dark. Lou
lifted his youngest descendant up and hauled her into
the rec room.

The Earth Defense Ship *South Hampton* fired its
engines one last time. It stopped dead adjacent to the
supply ship. Missile Commander Vinogrado stood
patiently at the docking bay, watching his younger
comrades pace impatiently while eagerly awaiting the
next load of goodies.

Vinogrado couldn't believe his fortune. The EDS
South Hampton was one of the newest ships in the fleet.
With its boron-hydride fusion engines it could maintain
a continuous half-gee acceleration, leaving the old ion
drive ships far behind in its alpha-particle wake. The
new engines were the only reason the ship was here,
reloading its missile bays— the ion drive ships couldn't
keep up with *Shiva*, and so the few survivors that had
participated in the missile attack for the Angel One
Assault had been left behind. The missile attack that
would now presage the Angel Two Assault had to be
conducted solely by the ion drive ships of Moon Fleet,

plus the handful of boron-hydride ships that had
survived the first assault.

And he, Anatoly Vinogrado, was back in action again.

Actually, Vinogrado knew that luck had played little
part in his getting this choice assignment. After all, he
was one of only a dozen people who had ever gotten
a missile past *Shiva*'s defenses. Whether he had been
lucky on that or not made little difference. Any skipper
would've given an arm and a leg up to the knee to have
such a powerful totem aboard his ship. Maybe lightning
didn't strike twice, but perhaps a missile commander
could.

The hatches whirred open, and the cargo started to
pour through. As Vinogrado helped with the loading
process, he couldn't help examining the sleek jet-black
missiles with a critical eye. There was something
different about these missiles from his last batch of
HellBender Mark VIIs. Something was wrong.

Finally a missile came through with its labeling facing
up. A huge smile swept Vinogrado's face. These weren't
Mark VIIs, these were Mark VIIIs! What had they
changed in the enhancement package? He couldn't wait
to get back to his station to hook in and read about the
new weapon. He had no idea at all what might have
caused the bosses at home to rush a model change
through during the Month of *Shiva*, but he was pretty
sure it had to be something devious.

He licked his lips in anticipation.

Chapter Seven

T minus Eleven

Paolo tapped on his desk idly. He watched the clock. He ran some links on the Web without really reading the pages. He did his best to avoid thinking about what he would do in . . . two minutes and twenty-seven seconds.

He would turn his back on a friend. Tough love at its finest.

It was probably the price of being a successful boss. But it still didn't seem fair, somehow. It seemed as if every day he woke up just to knock down somebody's world.

Just three days ago he'd clobbered the tailriders looking for him in the 'castpoints. He'd tried to follow the trails of some of the losers, to see if anyone had really been ruined, to see if he could prop them up for a short while, just enough to get back on their feet. But his search had been unsuccessful—after all, tailriders wanted to keep their anonymity, too.

Today would be worse. Jeff would not be destroyed outright by the outcome. But Jeff had been a personal project of Paolo's, a whiz kid from a broken background.

Sometimes Paolo treated Jeff more like his son than Fernando. Though that wasn't entirely Paolo's fault. At least when Paolo sent Jeff email, Jeff replied.

Paolo considered pouring himself a short tequila. It would help with his task, he knew. But he was sure Jeff would have already taken enough short drinks for both of them. Better if one of them kept a clear head.

Paolo considered handling the situation with a simple email. But it would be unethical, somehow, to deliver this news so impersonally. Even if he could not make the trip to Detroit to confront Jeff in person, Jeff at least deserved a face-to-face conversation.

Luis spoke, "I am connecting now," the calm computerized voice asserted.

A moment later the screen brightened. Paolo spoke softly, "Jeff."

Jeff wiped his hand across his eyes, then smiled wide. "Paolo!"

Staring at Jeff, Paolo found himself unable to go on with his prepared speech. Jeff looked a wreck. His eyes bulged feverishly from a face too drawn, too gaunt to be healthy. It took several moments for Paolo to figure out the most disturbing thing about Jeff's eyes: they didn't blink.

Jeff had become a marathon runner after joining Paolo's forecasting team, a largely successful effort to fight a weight problem he'd had since childhood. But things had changed. Now, Jeff was actually worryingly thin . . . and also soft. Paolo suddenly recognized the symptoms. Jeff didn't have an alcohol problem, Jeff was tripping on Golden Euphoria.

Paolo heard a giggle in the background, and for just a moment a lithe, naked teenage girl darted across the edge of the screen. Jeff still didn't blink. "Paolo, what can I do for you?"

Paolo shook his head. Somehow, it was easier now. "You haven't submitted your analysis of the docking bay photos from *Copernicus*."

Jeff nodded. "Oh, yeah, I knew I forgot something; I'll get right on it." More giggling came from behind him. "Anything else?"

"You're also bankrupt." Paolo didn't mean it literally. Between stock options and bonuses, Jeff had earned over five million Masterbucks with Paolo's team. Paolo had no idea what had become of that considerable wealth, though if Jeff were on Golden Euphoria he could assume the worst. Nonetheless, that was not the bankruptcy issued at hand.

Paolo was referring to the token economy he'd set up inside his team, for their private 'castpoint. Every forecast Jeff had made lately had gone wrong. Jeff had backed every forecast with huge stakes. His account had nose-dived into the ground.

Jeff nodded vigorously. "Yeah, I've been meaning to give you a buzz about that. It's been a really remarkable run of bad luck."

Paolo just grunted. A monkey tossing a coin would, on average, have done better than Jeff had done in the last forty-five days. Reliable forecasting might rely heavily on statistics, but luck did not enter the equation.

"I was wondering if you could, uh, give me a grub stake, like when I started." He shrugged. "Basically let me start over again."

Paolo lowered his eyes. In the silence that followed he could feel Jeff's growing awareness—it wouldn't be that easy. The taste of Jeff's first thoughts of fear upset him.

Despite everything Paolo had seen and heard and learned today, he could feel compassion driving him into a bad mistake. But Paolo had had a similar experience years before. Jeff's best chance of recovery came from the world of harsh reality, not the world of simplistic compassion. "Oh, I'm letting you start over again, all right." He took a deep breath. "You're fired, Jeff." Paolo looked at his computer's vidcam. "Luis, please record the event."

"Of course."

Jeff was still smiling in disbelief. "But you can't do that. I'm the only ceramic laminate expert you've got."

"An expert who is consistently wrong is a liability, not an asset. You've hurt our forecasts too long, too much. And right in the middle of the time when our best is barely good enough."

Jeff stared at him open-mouthed.

Paolo felt himself losing control. "*Shiva's* coming, goddammit! How could you do this to me, to say nothing of yourself, now of all times!" Paolo looked away and focused on breathing. Finally he felt enough control to continue. "Ditch the drugs, Jeff. Get yourself together. And call me in a year. You promise to call, right?" Paolo was still looking away from the screen.

The moments passed. Paolo turned to look at his ex-employee, ex-protegé, ex-friend once more. An ugly expression now darkened Jeff's face. He leaped up; the camera wobbled a bit as it tracked him. "I'll take you to court, damn you!"

Paolo felt himself turn to stone. "Even in your country, Jeff, the courts would hand this straight back to the arbiters. The Sowell rulebook specified in our contract is quite clear. Check out the Personal Responsibility clause. You can leave me any time . . . and I and my team can leave you. We are leaving." He looked away. "Close this connection, please." The window folded on a face now red with rage.

Paolo noticed with a sense of distance that his own hands were shaking. It had gone as badly as his worst fears. Jeff's response was to lash out.

Fortunately, Paolo had already taken the appropriate precautions—Jeff's capabilities to use the team brand had already been revoked. He could no longer access the private 'castpoint. Paolo had learned the importance of defensive preparations from a similar, bitter experience a few years earlier. Another young team member had begun to wallow in his sudden success. The kid had gotten to the point where he couldn't forecast the current time, much less a *Shivan* countermissile. Paolo had tried compassion that time; the kid hadn't pulled out of it until Paolo dropped him cold.

Paolo realized there was one last way Jeff could cause him grief. "Luis?" he called out.

"Yes?"

"Put the courtesy filters on Jeff's brands, would you?"

"Filters activated."

"Thanks." He had this feeling he was still forgetting something. But it was time to get on with business. Many difficult problems awaited him, though they would be a joy in comparison with the task he had just performed.

The Dealer stood straight and proud, staring out the glass wall of Cafe Deco, down upon the city of Hong Kong. Off to the right, he could see the Peak Tram glide away from the Galleria beneath the restaurant. The tram was a curiosity now—most people came to the Peak Galleria by air—but for a handful of people like himself the tram still had practical application. Fortunately, dressed in a black double-breasted suit, he had looked like just another tourist taking the tram, journeying through history for the sake of the amusement.

Now, claiming his reservation at the cafe, he stepped into his proper element. Soon he would be the tourist he seemed to be, someone who took tram rides only for their historical flavor. Soon he would take his chance in the big leagues.

The future seemed so clear now that he had won the contract for the custom skytruck.

It seemed only proper that he celebrate in the proper style. So he had bought the suit, and he had come to this exotic place, in this most impressive of cities, for dinner. For just a moment he regretted the missing element of this evening of success—the beautiful, charming woman he should have on his arm—but that was for another day. After he'd made the bucks he could pick and choose, and find the woman of his dreams. Yes, next time the right woman would accompany him as well.

Tomorrow he would have a great deal of work to do. He would have to order all the components for the skytruck. And he would have to start the laborious job of putting it all together. It would not be a difficult assembly project—he'd selected components that, for the most part, fit together with standard connections—but there could be no doubt but that this was serious work. It was also careful, meticulous work, a kind of work that he was good at but did not enjoy, at least when it was part of a job.

His eyes widened as he realized the correct solution. How embarrassing not to have thought of it sooner! He was, after all, the Dealer.

He would put up a contract on the Web for an integrator, someone who, for peanuts, would put the truck together for him! It would be best if he got someone in Nepal, to reduce costs of transport once it was built . . . on second thought, it should be someone here in Guangdong, someone he could supervise, so he could do his own quality control. He didn't know anyone offhand—let's face it, almost everyone he knew was a crook, he wouldn't trust them as far as he could throw them with something like this, with his reputation at stake—but he was sure he could get a half dozen offers from the right kind of craftsmen once he posted the contract in Wan Feng Emarket. The Dealer would do almost no work at all and skim the bulk of the profits. At last, he'd turned his design insight into a Deal.

His right hand reached unconsciously for his palmtop, to browse the Emarket to find the best place for his posting. He closed his hand and forced himself to relax. Tonight was for celebration, not work.

The piano in the darkened background of the restaurant produced a mellow, soothing rhythm. He heard the swish of a long dress to his right, and he turned. The hostess smiled at him. She was wearing a metallic blue cheong-sam as long as it was tight, with a slit running to her thigh that alternately displayed and concealed the curves of her left leg. She was dressed as elegantly as he. When he looked into her eyes, he could see that she recognized him for what he was— a man on the move, someone who was making his own way, but making it with speed, and sure confidence. Her eyes looked into his so warmly, his own temperature rose. "Your table is ready," she said in a lilting voice that broke his heart.

"Thank you," he replied, and followed her to a table that had a view almost as excellent as the one he'd commanded standing by the glass.

He ordered champagne, a ridiculous homily to his success, particularly with the outrageous prices charged here. He didn't even like champagne. But by now he'd risen beyond mere happiness. He'd been happy when he entered the restaurant. When he'd figured out the last piece of the skytruck contract, how to turn it into a real Deal, his feelings had expanded into a glowing sense of elation.

He sat back in his chair, savoring this time. He was back at the top of his game. He'd never run a better scam.

"I'd like a chocolate malt, please," CJ said to the cashier behind the counter of Centuries Restaurant. The cashier no longer stared in astonishment at the request. CJ had been getting a chocolate malt for her breakfast meeting with the team since the beginning of the Month of *Shiva.*

CJ heard Axel's voice grow loud with anger in the corner booth where everyone was assembled. She accepted her malt from the cashier and turned to the voice.

The tall back of the booth gave the table privacy,

which now meant that the Angels couldn't see her as she approached, quietly, as if she were sneaking up on a minitank.

"It sure took you long enough to get me the duodec," Axel was saying, presumably to Lars since he carried the bulk of the explosives along with everything else.

"It sure took you long enough to plant it," Lars retorted. "And being perfectly honest, you were sloppy."

"What?! Me, sloppy?" CJ watched Axel rise to his feet; his back was to her, however, so he still didn't know she was there.

"That is correct, Axel. You. Sloppy. One word." Lars rose to his feet as well, to stand at the opposite end of the table. CJ froze as Lars' eyes fell upon her. Then she moved smoothly into a smile, and skipped to the edge of the table so everyone could see her.

Her eyes danced as she said, "You guys leaving already? I just got here." She pointed at the clock. "And I'm on time, too!"

She looked around the table. Lars and Axel struggled to mask their anger, but their clenched fists gave them away. Roni was calmly eating his rye toast slathered with strawberries. In Israel, he'd told her, everyone is blunt all the time. It must have sounded like home to him.

Akira, motionless except for his eyes, was rapidly shifting his glance back and forth between the combatants. CJ suspected he was deciding just which one to cripple if a fight started, and exactly how to cripple them to minimize the damage while assuring order was restored. He could do it, too—no one doubted that of all of them, Akira was the best at hand-to-hand fighting. If he decided to stop the fight, someone would find himself in spectacular pain for five minutes. After the five minutes passed, however, the world's finest doctors would find no indication that any harm had ever been done. Rubber hoses could learn from Akira.

Axel gave her the lopsided grin that CJ always thought was a leer. "We, ah, were just having a disagreement. Nothing serious." He sat awkwardly back down, though he was still too angry, CJ observed, to begin eating right away.

Lars cleared his throat. "Yes, a minor disagreement. Which I shall shove down his throat in due course." He sat down with a glare that faded quickly into a twinkle of laughter.

CJ rolled her lips. "I see. Well, I'm so glad everyone's having a good time." She hooked her foot around the leg of a chair at an empty table and twirled it into place by the big Swede. She sat down and took a slurp of her malt. "Lars, you weren't ragging on Axel about the problem we had getting through the missile bay door in yesterday's sim, were you?"

Lars' blue eyes were all innocence. "Only after Axel sought out the compliment."

CJ raised an eyebrow. "Axel, you wouldn't criticize your teammate, would you?" She looked at Axel with a face that mirrored Lars' innocence.

A tough kid from the south side of Chicago glared back at her. For the most part, Axel had buried his past, but in moments of stress, the kid was still there. CJ wondered if the assault on *Shiva* would bring the kid out again. Perhaps not; perhaps it was the training and the waiting, and the training and the waiting, that stripped him of his armor.

CJ changed the topic. "I spotted a twitch yesterday," she said.

Axel laughed, not pleasantly. "One of Morgan's, right? I'd've thought you'd have found out everything about Morgan by now."

Roni put down his toast and stared at Axel like he was a loathsome but interesting insect. Apparently, that kind of innuendo didn't fit his sense of forthrightness. "Listen to the Boss Lady and learn, Axel." It didn't quite sound like a threat.

CJ clucked her tongue. "Recognize that sound?"

The whole team fell silent as they tried to figure it out. It was a guessing game, to see who could recognize a mannerism first, and whose mannerism it was.

Akira spoke. "Axel, you are correct that this is a Morgan mannerism. I haven't quite figured out when and why he does it, however."

CJ looked into the eyes of each member of the team, silently asking the question. They all shook their heads. "No one knows? Well, watch for it. When Morgan clucks his tongue, he's making a hard decision, the kind of decision where you can't know the right answer till it's too late."

Lars and Akira sank back into the cushions of the booth, memorizing the snippet for future reference. Axel looked off in the distance, and finally resumed eating. Roni just smiled at her. "A good thing to remember," he commented.

A few moments later, Axel spoke again. "That was a good catch, CJ." Axel was back to normal.

But a few minutes later CJ realized he wasn't quite back to normal. And neither was anyone else. They all stopped eating before finishing their breakfasts. As one pair of eyes after another turned on her, she waved her hands. "If you guys are done, get out of here. You're all packed for tomorrow, right?"

A wave of tension passed around the room, and CJ knew what the problem was. She shooed them off. "Go, go. I'm going to take my time."

They rose as a team, and straggled out as individuals. CJ stared at the bottom of her chocolate malt. Normally, she pointed the straw into the corners of the cup, to suck out the last drops. Today she just put the cup back on the table and rose to leave.

Even with her stomach full, she had butterflies. She understood Axel's anxious desire to lash out. In the morning they would board a roton that would take them to the *Argo*. There was little chance they would ever come back.

Jessica watched carefully as Granma grabbed spices out of the cupboard and sprinkled them, with hardly a hint of care or order, onto the steaming vegetables. "I wish you'd let me videotape your cooking," Jessica told her. "I'm telling you, we could get rich selling the video on the Web." Jessica believed they would, too, though she was uncertain which reason would drive people to buy the video: would they want to learn how to make the remarkable dishes like Granma made, or would they want the entertainment, because Granma was such a stitch when doing combat with zucchinis?

Granma grunted. "You don't need a videotape, girl. I gave you the recipe five years ago." Lemon pepper made a high-speed assault on the T-bones as they grilled.

"But, Granma, you don't follow the recipes yourself. What good are they? The only real way to capture your genius for posterity is videotape." Jessica stepped out of the way as Granma whipped past to claim the butter from the refrigerator.

"You still wouldn't eat right," Granma asserted.

Jessica threw up her hands. "You're probably right." She took three steps and threw herself onto the sofa, conveniently located next to the kitchen in the tight little studio apartment. "Since you won't let me help, I'm going to sit back and relax."

"'Bout time," Granma grunted. "Now, while you're sitting there, why don't you just pop open that palmtop of yours and do some quick currency exchange. I don't want you to be stranded, penniless, the way I was the last time."

How could she get her grandmother to stop living in the past? Somehow she had to stop the woman from telling once again the story of how, after the Entitlement Crash, Granma had moved what little money she still had into untraceable electronic securities, and hadn't looked back since. Jessica smacked her forehead with her hand. "Granma, I have a confession to make."

Granma stopped in her tracks and stared at her. "You didn't let that blasted boyfriend get you pregnant, did you?"

Jessica clenched her fists to avoid screaming. "No! 'Course not. I'm talking about the money." She sat up. "I don't really have any money in Swiss francs, Granma. Most of my money really is in Masterbucks. I just keep some money in dollars for the supermarket and stuff." This statement was almost true: Jessica kept half her money in Masterbucks and half in dollars. Jessica didn't trust the corporate currencies any more than the government's. They were both controlled by the same simple equation: if the currency owners corrupted their money, with inflation or massive debt, everybody'd move to safer currencies as fast as you could count—probably faster. A debt scare had finished off the Samsung baht a few years earlier, leaving only four major currencies in the world. The surviving currency owners probably wouldn't forget the consequences soon, but why take chances?

"Well, I'm glad you're smarter than I was. Or your silly father." Granma shut off the burners. "*Voila!* Dinner is served."

"Thank heavens. You fill this place with such good aromas, Granma, my stomach is growling at me." Jessica jumped up from the couch and started setting the table.

Granma dished the plates, and they sat down. "Well," Granma confessed, "They seem to be treating you fairly well, anyway, even if it is the government. This place is nice, but not so nice that you're soaking us taxpayers."

Jessica almost choked. "You, pay taxes? Since when?"

Granma smiled; her dentures were pearly white. "I've been working a bit in the electronic markets. Not much, but every once in a while something comes up that calls for my talents with legacy SQL databases." She grumped. "And you can't avoid taxes when you work in such a public forum." The marketplaces paid a small percentage of all transactions to the governments where the market operators resided.

"Come on, Granma, I know enough history—you taught me enough history—to know that the taxes today are only a fraction of the taxes before the Crash. You can't fool me. For someone who lived through that, what we pay now must seem like a relief." Jessica chewed another heavenly bite of steak—how did Granma bring out such flavor!?—before continuing, "Besides, most of the money goes to Earth Defense, and even you have to admit that that is a good cause."

Granma almost choked. "Government and taxation is the most evil thing on Earth."

"Come on, Granma, even you can see *Shiva* is worse, even more evil than the government."

Granma stopped eating for a moment and pondered the question. "Maybe," she replied, not entirely convinced.

Paolo watched the webcast idly. The reporter was showing the preparations underway for the next step in defense from *Shiva*. Tomorrow, the Angel Two team would climb on board a roton and lift off to orbit. Ninety-four percent odds said they would never come back. Paolo thought he detected just the barest hint of tension in the reporter's face—his smile was too wide, too fixed, even for a reporter. The reporter knew as well as anyone that this Angel team was the last chance to stop *Shiva* before it started vaporizing cities.

The news report moved from the launch site to cover a vast assemblage of people milling about by a large lake. He recognized Lake Mead when the skycam brushed passed the Hoover Dam. The place had a carnival-like appearance—so many wild styles of clothing, so many people with their arms in the air, rocking as they sang their chants of prayer and anticipation.

But after watching for a few moments, Paolo discerned the deeper truth. The brightly enthusiastic folk might be the ones attracting the attention, but lots of the others were huddled together in the miserable clusters around which the jubilant ones wove their chaotic Dance. Only the truest of believers chanted; the others knew, just as well as Paolo himself knew, that unless the Angels getting ready to lift off succeeded, in eleven days their religion would be put through the severest test a set of beliefs could encounter. And if their religion were wrong, nothing could save them.

Yes, the moment of truth was coming, and everyone knew it, even if they could not admit it even to themselves.

He at least had something he could do about it. He turned back to his analysis of his team's preparations and predictions.

Later, the wallscreen chimed softly with the arrival of new mail. At first Paolo ignored it, intent on deciphering the meaning of the latest, and most bizarre, forecast made by Crockett II, the newest and most experimental of his team's genetic programs. Crockett figured the Gate was located one hundred kilometers down-axis from the center of the sphere, roughly where all sensible assessments of the ship said the primary fusion engines had to be. Either Crockett had uncovered a change in *Shiva* structure of devastating importance . . . or it was going to take a lot of debugging to find the problem.

As part of the testing, Paolo wiped Crockett's knowledge of *Shiva V*, and fed the program with comparable data for *Shiva III*. When Crockett made the same prediction for *Shiva III*, that the Gate was down-axis, Paolo knew for certain that debugging would be the order of the day. It was just as well; getting Angels from the docking bay to the ship center was hard enough, getting them all the way to the engine area was unthinkable.

Having reached a stopping point, Paolo turned his attention to the earlier chime. "Luis," Paolo said to his computer, "show me the new mail."

Luis opened a small window. "One message from Jeff, requiring filtering," the computer explained. "I have returned a recommendation that Jeff word his request more carefully." Paolo looked in the small window to see what parts of Jeff's email had survived the courtesy filter. He was not really surprised to see that only the sender's name and date of transmission had made it; even the subject line must have been a blaze of pure rage, for Luis had excised that along with the entire body of the message. Paolo just shook his head. You'd think people would figure out, in this day and age, that flaming on the Web served no purpose at all: people just filtered you out, shutting their eyes to you with a perfection not possible in other mediums. For all intents and purposes, angry and rude people had simply ceased to exist on the Web.

Despite this, it must have given Jeff a lot of satisfaction to scream digitally at him, even though Jeff had to know, if he thought about it for even a second, that he was shouting in an empty closet.

Luis spoke again. "You also have some unsolicited mail."

"Great! Show me." Paolo kept a 75-cent fee on his mailbox for information from unknown brands; anyone in the world could get his attention briefly by paying the fee. Seventy-five cents was high enough to prevent the kind of random spam he'd heard was common before the Crash, but low enough so that if someone were really sure they had something interesting for him, they could get the message through. And of course, if the message really *was* interesting, he returned the fee. Advertisers had gotten very smart about figuring out which things he really would be interested in seeing. So on those rare days when Paolo got unsolicited mail, it usually meant he had a treat in store.

But when this message popped up, it just about burned his eyes out. *You BASTARD!* The first line shrieked at him, and got worse from there. Paolo closed his eyes with a sigh. Jeff had clearly sent this email, using an anonymous identity. "Luis, close it for me." Jeff had been so angry that he was willing to pay Paolo for the right to send hate mail.

For just a moment, Paolo considered letting Jeff continue to send email at seventy-five cents a pop, just out of morbid curiosity to see how long it would last. But he didn't want the hassle. On the other hand . . . "Luis, set the unsolicited mail fee to seventy-five Masterbucks, please."

"The new setting is in effect."

Well, Paolo thought, he'd indulge his morbid curiosity, but for higher stakes. If Jeff were willing to pay seventy-five bucks per message, perhaps Paolo was giving him a real therapeutic benefit by letting him blow off steam.

"Luis, keep the fee there for thirty days." That should be enough time for Jeff to lose interest.

Another sound interrupted Paolo's stream of thought. This time his palmtop tinkled for him, a sound easily interpreted as a computer sharing a private bit of humor. Paolo smiled, for the sound made him think of Sofia; time to phone home.

He turned from his screen; through his window he could see dusk fall over the lands of the house of Ossa. Stars began to twinkle. Yes, it was time. "Luis, where is Sofia?"

An unusual pause preceded the answer. "Perhaps she is in her Zen room."

"Ah." The Zen room was disconnected from the house computers, consequently Luis could only guess.

Paolo headed out the door humming quietly. Twelve years earlier, during the WebEveryWhere initiative, his beloved Sofia had railed at him for never calling her from his forsaken remote sites. He'd been exhausted at the time of the argument—he'd just gotten back from the damned jungle—but he'd had enough wits left to offer the obvious solution. He'd pulled out his palmtop and set a recurring alarm to tell him to call his over-wrought spouse every day. The alarm had had no expiration date. So even after Paolo had finished that project and returned home, it continued to go off at the specified moment. Indeed, even though he had discarded that old palmtop and changed machines and software half a dozen times, the reminder had survived every upgrade.

The digital information had remained intact, but its human interpretation had changed ever so slightly. After all, Paolo worked at home now. Merely calling her would have been silly when his presence offered so many better opportunities.

Paolo slowed to a creep as he came to the Zen room. The door hung ajar, telling him the situation—his entrance was permitted, though only for important matters. Paolo decided that their daily phone call was important enough. He eased the door open.

The light of the Zen room, set to simulate candlelight, flickered with crimson and orange pulses that cast darting shadows. Sweet burning incense hung in the air. Paolo sang softly, "Sofia. It's time for me to call you."

She turned to him from the touchscreen on her desk. "Of course," she replied, though her voice seemed a bit tense. He took her head in his hands and kissed her—*this* was the new meaning of his twilight alarm.

Sofia returned the kiss, but it was brief, too brief for a true Sofia kiss. Then she turned away. Paolo exhaled slowly just beneath her ear. Normally his breath would have come back warm and moist, rich with the scent of Sofia's perfume. Somehow, though, this time the breath seemed cold and dry. Paolo stood up slowly. His voice barely rose above a whisper. "What's wrong?"

"Nothing," Sofia said unconvincingly, her eyes fixed on her touchscreen.

Paolo looked over her shoulder to see the focus of her attention. The touchscreen was the color of green felt, with playing cards arrayed around the table. One hand lay open, with aces and diamonds and clubs, but no spades. "Engaged in a game of bridge, I see," he continued, feeling stupid.

"Yes." Sofia's voice sounded irritated. "You're winning."

Paolo opened his mouth, then closed it again. "I am, am I? I didn't even know I was playing."

"Well, I named one of the computer positions Paolo," she explained. "You aren't playing very well, but you're still winning." Sofia's nostrils flared. "And you're winning because Mercedes can't make an intelligent bid to save her soul. I swear she's on your side, even though she's supposed to be my partner."

Remembering that this room was unwired, Paolo knew Mercedes was not playing a hand in this game any more than he was. He thought he'd try something lighthearted. "Sofia! Be glad that Mercedes and I aren't really playing. Neither of us is up to playing your kind of game, you know." Sofia held a Diamond Master card.

"Umph." The last of the cards flipped into the center. Scores automatically adjusted on the screen. Paolo could see Sofia's little hand clench into a fist.

Paolo spoke very gently, exactly the way a person of good sense would speak to an angry baby gorilla. "Uh, sweetest Sofia, could you rename those players so that Mercedes and I are not involved? Please?"

"What difference would that make?" she asked, eyes still fixed on the screen as the computer dealt another hand.

"Please, just humor me," Paolo said.

"After this game," Sofia compromised.

"Thank you, love. I'll leave you to your, ah, game."

"Umph," was her sole reply.

Paolo escaped from the room as quietly as he could. He was not as quiet as a cat, but he did his best.

When he reached the hallway he exhaled loudly and gasped for breath. He could feel a cold gray anger spreading through his mind. Why did Sofia have to be going crazy now, when things were getting so scary anyway? Then he closed his eyes and worked the anger, kneading it with his own understanding. Why shouldn't Sofia be a little crazy too? The last battle was nearly upon them, and all they could do was wait and play bridge. Sofia had as much right to a little anxiety as the newscaster, or the people featured on the newscast. By the time he was done going over it in his mind, the mix of anger and understanding had leavened into a soft compassion. He felt like himself again. He wondered how many times he'd lose it before the final hour. As for Sofia, he just hoped she didn't kill anything. Since he was the closest, he'd inevitably be the target.

"I can get out of this chair perfectly well on my own," Morgan snapped at CJ. He lifted himself, switched one handhold to the reclining lounge chair on his deck, swung himself around, and rolled onto his back. He took a deep breath.

"At least let me pour you a drink," CJ replied. She knelt next to the pitcher and glasses sitting on a tray on the deck. Morgan watched her, feeling his mood swing like a giant pendulum coming loose from its hinge. In eleven days he would cause the death of the woman now offering him a strawberry margarita. And she knew it!

He raised his hand and accepted the drink.

CJ pirouetted and fell into the lounge chair with him. He did not understand how she managed to not spill her own drink, nor how she managed to snuggle into such a small space with him without jostling him enough to make him spill his. She was a genius of physical agility! His heartbeat steadied again. Perhaps she would not die after all.

She pressed upon him, mapping herself to his contours. Her neck twisted. She looked up and gasped. "The stars really are a lot closer here."

Morgan smiled invisibly in the darkness. He relaxed into CJ's warmth. "I often think that if I could just reach up a little farther, stand on my toes, I could touch them." Morgan's ranch lay at six thousand feet altitude, on the edge of the Colorado Plateau, with nothing but the crisp clean Arizona sky above. For anyone raised in a city the night sky sparkled, a festival of resplendent fireworks that never waned. A story came to his lips unbidden. "You see the band of haze crossing there?" He swept his hand in an arc. He could feel CJ nod her head against his shoulder. "The first time Elisabeth saw it, she apologized to her guests for the cloudiness of the sky that evening. She had just come from L.A., of course, and hadn't quite gotten used to Arizona." He chuckled. "She had to apologize again a few minutes later when she realized that the haze wasn't clouds at all. That band of soft light is the Milky Way."

Morgan could feel CJ's cheeks widen in a smile. "That's a funny story," she said.

He looked down at her. Her eyes were closed; the miracle of the stars was not in tune with her mood. But he suspected that listening to him talk, about anything at all, would make her happy.

"We bought this place from a software guy," he said.

"A software guy on a ranch in Arizona?" she asked.

"Yep. It's not really that unusual these days—I mean, you can do software in the middle of a jungle—but the guy we bought it from wasn't the guy who built the first house here. That was over fifty years ago, and that was a software guy too." Morgan ran his fingers through CJ's hair. It was too short to be a girl's hair, in Morgan's opinion, but too soft and fine to be a boy's. "That guy who built the first house had been a VP in a big software company back in the Valley. He'd gotten burned out, and built a house here for the solitude. He was weary to death of dealing with people." Morgan paused. "Here there wasn't anybody but coyotes to bother him. Well, maybe his wife made him clean corrals, but what's a few horse apples compared to flame wars?"

"So you came here for the solitude, too," CJ guessed.

Morgan shook his head. "In fact, no. The guy the VP sold it to, and the guy after that, were both burnouts too. But Elisabeth and I actually bought this place for her bird experiments. We broke with tradition." He laughed harshly. "And then the first *Shiva* came and blew away Beijing while Elisabeth was attending a seminar there." Silence hung there for a moment. He shrugged. "Now I'm following the tradition, too."

CJ burrowed deeper into his side. "They all recovered, didn't they?"

"What do you mean?"

"I mean all those other people, they recovered, and went on with their lives, right?"

"Yes, but—"

CJ put her right index finger on his lips. "Shh. You will, too." Her finger brushed delicately across the lines of his face. "When I come back."

The silence hung heavy for a moment. Morgan said thickly, "Of course."

CJ's finger worked its way back to his left ear, tickling him. Blast it, the woman made it hard to stay focused on important things. But another part of his mind had to ask, was death really the important thing? Or was life? Somehow, his values had gotten twisted.

CJ spoke. "You know why I want you so badly, don't you?" Her voice had an edge of wicked laughter.

"Because you're infatuated with an old guy everybody thinks is a big hero."

She chuckled. "That too. But that's not what I was getting at. I want you to personally care, desperately, about getting me back. Maybe that will make the difference."

"I . . . wish it could be that simple." He breathed a deep sigh that turned into a sob before finishing. "You know, if you come back, it won't help me a bit."

CJ laughed at that, a low, wicked laugh that the goblins of the night could not help but hear and dance to. She nibbled his ear. "We'll see about that."

Morgan shook his head. "You don't understand. One of the reasons for getting someone out alive is so they can take my place." His voice choked. "But," he continued softly, "if I get you out, it won't help me, because I'd do anything to prevent you from living the way I do, dreaming of sandstone corridors smeared with blood and smelling of death."

"Love, we'll cross that bridge when we come to it."

"Oh, God, no," he moaned, closing his eyes tight. He turned his face to her and, guided by the warmth of her breath, brought his mouth down upon hers. The glittering stars watched in silence.

The Dealer walked along the pier, staring at the blazeboats resting quietly in the water. His dinner repast had been excellent. The champagne had been silly. Not as silly, however, as the champagne had made him, he feared. Still, he was enjoying he state he now found himself in, just a little bit out of control. He burped quietly—considered good manners in the old days of China; now he was glad there was no one near enough to hear or see.

The blazeboats were the latest rage among the young rich of Hong Kong, among the foolish children of the people who had earned the wealth in the first place. Now, in his elevated state of mind, the Dealer understood the roots of true wealth.

Expertise was the key, he realized. Karl Marx had almost gotten it right with his labor theory of value. But it wasn't quite the labor that counted, it was the cleverness—the expertise that put it all together—that made the difference. The Dealer's latest scam on the truck put it all in perspective for him. His expertise had been the secret weapon he'd used to pull off the deal.

Expertise. He'd read about expertise somewhere else recently, he recalled.

He strode along the edge of the water, trying to place the reference. He saw a slender, striking woman, barely visible from this distance despite metallic moonglow scattered from her silver dress; she laughed, and then he saw, just barely, the fellow in a black suit who accompanied her.

Expertise. The thought nagged him: where had he seen something important about it just days ago?

He came to the end of the dock and turned back up the street into the city. The skyscrapers rose everywhere. He looked up and saw, several stories in the air on one of the newest behemoths, a modest sign: Wan Feng Emarket and 'Castpoint.

Then he remembered. Reggie Oxenford had talked about expertise, that's where he'd read about it. The Dealer sort of remembered what Reggie had said:

Use your expertise to buy forecasts. Make a profit. Make a big profit. What could be more noble, more honorable, more just, than doing well by doing good?

What a delightful little silver lining. Doing a good deed as well as getting rich. Kam Yin almost laughed. Reggie had nailed another reason for the Dealer's feeling of triumph, one that the Dealer hadn't even thought about till now.

In getting this military cargo up to the top of Everest, whatever it was, the Dealer was not only making a profit, he was making a contribution to his whole planet. The cops wouldn't be chasing him for this one. What a relief!

But wait! The Dealer stopped, dazed, as he realized that Reggie had answered another question for him. The key to the 'castpoints was using your expertise. Forget the old-fashioned scams he'd been trying. The real money was in the knowledge, the quick insight. He was sure he could become a major contributor to the next assault on *Shiva V*. He didn't know exactly how his expertise could make a difference, but at this moment that seemed a minor detail. He would go to Fort Powell, immediately in the morning, to study the equipment the Angels used, to lard his cleverness with the knowledge he would need to be a true expert.

The Dealer had wandered back to the populated section of town. Clusters of people milled around everywhere. But now he didn't care about his audience; as he realized how to suck money out of the EDA 'castpoints, he gave a little whoop and threw his arms in the air.

His exultant whoop ended abruptly. Suddenly he felt sober, and not quite so proud as he had a moment earlier. His arms fell to his sides even as he continued to stare into the sky.

A bright ball of light hung in the heavens, a light that had not been there a month earlier. He recognized the newborn planet: *Shiva V* approached with a determination almost as unwavering as his own.

"I am ready," he whispered defiantly. "Come to me, and join your ancestors in oblivion."

Chapter Eight

T minus Ten

The Dealer sat back in his chair, trying to get comfortable. The chair itself really was quite wonderful. The plush leather seat had a tall reclining back that curved around him like the chrysalis of a silkworm. Back in his own closet-apartment, the Dealer would have considered it a luxury beyond imagining. But here in the roton, two hours into the trip, the Dealer thought the chair an exquisitely designed torture device.

They had just landed in the St. Petersburg drop port, farther from his destination than when he had started the trip. Traveling through St. Petersburg was a funny way to get to Fort Powell in the United States. But from St. Petersburg the roton flew directly to the Fort. Most other flights went to Las Vegas, where he'd have had to rent a skycar. This circuitous trip through Russia actually got him there faster, and cost less besides.

A big man with broad features lowered his bulk laboriously into the chair two seats over from him. The fellow looked like a typical Russian. His face was set in an impassive expression of perseverance, the reflection of a thousand years of the pain only Russian history could produce. Well, in a way history was looking up. At least the Russians wouldn't have to defend Moscow anymore. Sadly, *Shiva*'s destruction of that capital had upset the Russians far more than the destruction of Beijing had bothered anyone in Chan Kam Yin's homeland.

The Dealer's stereotyping of the guy lasted only a few moments. Then the stewardess stepped up to the Russian, and he smiled. A ruddy charm broke through his stoicism, and the stewardess responded to the warmth. Suddenly Kam Yin felt a sense of envy for the Russian's self-confidence. A charming smile was not one of the things Kam Yin had ever learned. He suspected he would live his whole life crippled by its absence. He would have to depend on cunning to achieve his goals.

The Russian caught him staring. A dark sorrow rippled the wrinkles around his gray eyes, then disappeared. The Russian smiled even more broadly. "It's a good time to be going to Fort Powell, eh?" he asked in English, the language of the Web and the best chance random people had to talk to one another.

Kam Yin opened his mouth and suddenly realized how much embarrassment he would now suffer. He could read and write English quite well. And he'd watched enough vids on the Web to be able to understand the speech moderately, though the slang still left him puzzled sometimes. But this was the first time he'd ever had to speak it. With more courage than the Russian could possibly grasp, the Dealer replied briefly, "Yes, I wish to see the armor suits."

The Russian nodded wisely. "They are most impressive. A marvel of engineering."

A bell clanged, and Kam Yin could feel the vibration as the roton quickly whirled to life and started to rise. The gentle pressure pushed him into his plush chair for a moment. He closed his eyes.

"Are you an engineer?" the Russian asked.

Kam Yin opened his eyes once more, then suddenly realized that the question had been asked in his native tongue. He must have shown his surprise, for the Russian laughed, a deep vibrant sound that belonged in a cathedral. The Russian spoke again. "Would it be okay if I practiced my Cantonese with you? I don't get much chance to use it anymore. It has been a long time since . . ." He shrugged. "It has been a long time."

Kam Yin gave him a wary smile. "Of course." He paused, then answered the original question. "Yes, I am an engineer, more or less."

The Russian nodded. "Learning about the suits first-hand is important for anyone planning to work the prizeboards during the Assault."

"Exactly." How did the Russian know his business? Could he be a tail, someone watching him for the computer company, watching for a slip? The Dealer sat very straight, at a peak of alertness. He concluded there was a much simpler explanation: just about anybody going to Fort Powell during the Month of *Shiva* had to be interested in the prizeboards. Including, the Dealer realized, this Russian. "What about you—are you an engineer as well?"

The Russian shrugged. "More or less. I'm here to learn to about the Angel's gear, too. But explosives are really my specialty."

Kam Yin nodded. So this man would not be one of his competitors for the prizes. Indeed, the Dealer realized as his eyes narrowed in thought, the Russian might even be an ally someday. Since the Russian's confidence suggested he knew what he was about, cultivating the relationship seemed cautiously profitable. "I haven't had much chance to work with explosives."

The Russian rubbed his nose. "The Republic of Guangdong is a bit crowded for playing with duodec. I think you'll be surprised by the vast spaces around Fort Powell. They're both empty of buildings and barren, just the kind of wasteland the Americans romanticize about."

Kam Yin laughed, as much to hide his nervousness as because he enjoyed jokes about Americans. "I've seen the pictures of Fort Powell on the Web," he said. "I don't think I'll be shocked."

The Russian raised an eyebrow. "I see. Well, I'm glad of that," he muttered as he closed his eyes. A few moments later Kam Yin heard him snoring softly. The Dealer snorted, and closed his eyes to try to get some sleep himself.

The Dealer awoke with a start. Looking groggily out the window into the bright light, he remembered suddenly where he was. He fumbled with his seatbelt, and once free, leaped to his feet, sure that the ship had landed and that if he didn't hurry they'd take off again with him still on board.

A stewardess appeared from nowhere and whispered, "Please get back into your seat. We'll be landing in a few minutes."

"Oh." When you do something foolish, always stand up straight. He stood very straight indeed, then settled his thin body back into his chair, smashing his already damaged right kneecap into the seatback in front of him once more for good measure. He looked over at the Russian. The man's nostrils flared, and the Dealer heard a chortling sound, but the fellow was just snoring, not laughing at the Dealer's mistake.

They landed without further incident.

The Dealer unbuckled his seat belt and rose to find the Russian standing in the aisle already—the fellow could move his bulk quite quickly. The man slapped the Dealer on the shoulder. "Now we'll go see some fun stuff, eh?"

The Dealer nodded solemnly. He had finally concluded how he felt about the Russian. He disliked the man, for a reason that cost him a lot to recognize: the man made the Dealer feel like a nervous kid again. How disconcerting. And how irritating. The Dealer thought he'd outgrown that sort of adolescent anxiety ages ago.

They stepped out onto the ramp, and the sunlight hit Kam Yin like a hammer to the face. He held up his arm and squinted while water ran from his eyes. He heard a little girl scream, "Uncle Viktor!"

The Russian gave a whoop of delight. "Lanie!" He waddled down the steps with his surprising speed and lifted the child, a slender green-eyed imp with long red hair, into his arms.

The Dealer saw another man at the bottom of the ramp. This person was looking up at the Russian with a brooding frown. The hint of a smile tugged at the edges of the man's lips, marring the effect of the frown. The man spoke. "Careful, Lanie, Uncle Viktor isn't strong enough for a lot of horseplay."

The girl—Lanie—laughed gaily. "Sure he is, Pops."

Viktor glared at the other man. "I will always be strong enough to carry my favorite girl, Lou."

"Your head will always be thick enough to try, you mean."

The Dealer stepped away, shaking his head. He looked out to the terminal, a good hundred feet away. He couldn't help looking beyond the terminal, too, and seeing . . . a vast desert wasteland. For mile after mile, there was nothing but an occasional patch of straggly brown plants, more sticks than anything, with the occasional cactus. In the farther distance sharp craggy brown mountains stood scattered at random, as if flung from a giant's hand. It was breathtaking.

It was also hot. And dry. The cool sense of air-conditioned comfort from the ship evaporated, and he could feel his lips begin to chap as the kiln-like air sucked the last bit of water from his pores. He licked his lips, realizing the gesture's futility even as he did so.

Out of the corner of his eye he could see Viktor

eyeing him. "You might want this," he said, tossing a Chapstick at the Dealer. "I have a spare."

Kam Yin caught the small cylinder awkwardly. "Thank you," he offered. He applied the soothing cream to his lips, just in time, it seemed.

Lanie and Lou looked over at him. Viktor waved a hand. "Lou, Lanie, I'd like you to meet my new friend, uh," he waved his hands in the air theatrically, "uh . . ."

The Dealer smiled; he was finally one up on the Russian. "Chan Kam Yin," he said with a bow. He continued, very hesitant because he knew his English was so poor, "Pleased to meet you."

The Russian continued, "Chan Kam Yin is an engineer, come to see the Angel exoskeletons."

Lou nodded approvingly. "Good for you."

Viktor asked Kam Yin, "Does it look like the pictures on the Web, my friend?"

Once more the Dealer scanned the horizon. "It is different," he admitted. "Being here, it is . . . more big."

Lou smiled, and spread his arms. "Yeah, parts of America are like that. You should see Montana. They call it 'Big Sky Country,' and they mean it."

The Dealer watched Viktor put a finger to his nose and mouthed the word, "Romantic." Yes, the Americans did romanticize their wastelands. How quaint.

"Very beautiful," the Dealer murmured.

Viktor shook his head. "Very barren," he sniffed, "unlike my home. You should see it. The frozen tundra of Murmansk gleams with a purity and grace not to be found anywhere in America south of Alaska."

Lou snorted. "Beautiful Murmansk, where the popsicles and the ice cubes play."

Viktor dismissed the matter with a wave of his hand. "Kam Yin, we need to get you speaking your English more. It is quite good enough, you know, and there's an old rule to languages: If you're not sure how to say it, say it loud. Mumbling doesn't help."

Kam Yin bowed his head, and thought to leave before the old fool completely embarrassed him.

But Viktor continued. "I know just how to improve your language skills. I'll teach you the same trick I learned when I was your age."

Lou rolled his eyes. "Viktor, you can't be serious. Your friend here doesn't have the training to survive your idea of a learning strategy."

Lanie grasped Lou's arm. "What's Uncle Viktor's plan?" she asked disingenuously, knowing it would be something juicy from Pops' disapproving tone.

"I know a special drink that improves the language skills," Viktor announced proudly.

Kam Yin was intrigued. "A learning chemical?" There had been a lot of claims of such things lately, but nothing that had passed the scrutiny of the Lloyd's-Glaxo certification test.

Viktor blinked his eyes. "It only works for improving your spoken language skills," he warned. "I can get it for you right here, in the terminal."

"That would be wonderful," Kam Yin said. Imagine, advanced learning chemicals right in the terminal! America was certainly living up to his expectations as a most amazing place.

"Viktor, you have got to mix it with orange juice this time," Lou muttered darkly. "He's just a boy, for heaven's sake."

Kam Yin didn't understand the reference, but he was sure that he would figure it out with the help of the learning chemical.

Paolo sat in the breakfast nook sipping his orange juice, staring out the window. His face held no expression, his mind held no thoughts. Soon he would send his mind into overdrive, to do his best to help Earth Defense again. The closest he could come to a well-formed thought right now, though, was to hope that someday this wouldn't be necessary anymore.

Sofia came up behind him, too quietly to be heard, but he could feel her warmth even before her hands reached out to travel the muscles of his neck and shoulders. Tension he hadn't realized he had melted away as her massaging hands lured him into relaxation. "Paolo, did you—"

"Yes. What about—"

"Taken care of." She worked his neck for a moment; his head lolled. She continued. "Will Mercedes—"

"Of course."

"You called."

"Would I—"

"In a heartbeat, darling." She bent over and kissed him. "Glad that's settled." She glided out as quietly as she had come in. Paolo guess she had worked through her snappish mood. Thank heavens.

"Exactly right," she called back at him from beyond the nook.

"Viktor, I can't believe you." Lou panted with exertion at the heavy load he had slung across his shoulders. "Did you pour a whole fifth down this poor kid's gullet?"

Viktor grunted. "Not hardly. I drank most of it. It was very hard to get the boy to loosen up enough to take his medicine."

Lanie's palmtop beeped. "The door's open." She looked with urgent concern at her uncle. "Really, Uncle Viktor, please let me help Pops carry him the rest of the way."

Viktor's face had turned bright red with the exertion as he helped Lou carry Chan Kam Yin to the room. Viktor grunted. "I'm all right. And you're too little."

Lanie pouted. She put her hands on her hips. "I am not. I'm stronger than you are."

Viktor laughed at that, but not with his usual overpowering strength.

Lou led the way into the motel room. "Listen to the girl, Viktor. She's tougher than she looks. You should see her play soccer." He paused to take a breath. "Besides, though it would serve you right to drop dead carrying a burden of your own making, I need you alive for the assault on *Shiva*." He started moving again.

Chan Kam Yin snored softly, his head lolling to the left at a precarious angle. Lou had to wonder if the human neck could really twist that far. The evidence said yes. Amazing.

Viktor rasped out, "We're almost there."

Lanie threw up her hands. "I've got the lights on." Lou blinked as the room suddenly became as bright as high noon.

"Could you turn that down a little?" he asked.

Chan Kam Yin groaned.

Melanie apologized, "Sorry." The lighting settled into a mellow background glow.

With a final effort, Lou wheeled and half-threw, half-dumped, the boy onto the bed. Viktor removed the kid's shoes while Lanie carefully tucked blankets around him.

Lou sagged into a chair. "I'm way too old for this. Viktor, why did you accost a perfect stranger like this? I'm sure he's a nice kid, but—"

Viktor plunked down on the floor. His words came out garbled, but recognizable. "No, he's not a nice kid, Lou. That's the point."

Lou stared at him.

Viktor explained. "He's an angry, street-smart kid with a con on his mind. I know the type. I used to train kids just like him to be terrorists."

Lou threw up his hands. "So you're back in the terrorist training business? For who?"

Viktor shook his head. "Of course not. I just wanted to try to help one do something better." He lay back, spread-eagled on the carpet. A gasp arose from his heaving chest. The flush finally started to fade from his face. "And I think I succeeded."

"By getting him drunk?" Lou demanded. "And by making my Lanie watch?"

Viktor chortled. "Lanie played an important part in the victory, Lou. She's young enough, and charming enough, so that Kam Yin didn't feel intimidated. She's the one who got him talking about his childhood."

Lanie looked sad. "He's had a terrible life," she said. She paused to reflect. "But it's certainly been interesting." She looked up at Lou. "Pops, I really had fun getting him to talk. He really does know a lot of English." She smiled smugly. "And I do think he uses it better now than when we first met him. Uncle Viktor was right—vodka really does improve your speaking if your main problem is just that you're worried about how bad it is."

Lou grunted. "Well, it's the strangest good deed I've ever seen. Can we go now?"

Viktor dragged himself slowly to his feet. "Of course. Lanie, thank you once again for a job well done."

"Nothing to it, Uncle Viktor. I wanted to thank you for agreeing to teach me explosives. We start tomorrow, right?"

Lou leaped from the chair. "You promised Lanie *what*?"

Viktor stretched and moved sluggishly for the door. Lou came up to him with his hands curled in a position well-suited for wrapping around the Russian's neck. Viktor shrugged. "I told you I wanted a younger, more exciting partner for the business, Lou. And this keeps it in the family, as it were."

"*No!* You will not turn my grandkids into pyro-maniacs!"

Now Lanie gave Lou her world-famous pout. "I won't be a maniac, Pops. You know better." She smiled mis-chievously. "And it'll be fun. You know I've always been interested in your work." She squeezed past Viktor into the hall. Viktor followed, with Lou right behind.

Lou shuddered as he thought back over the preceding eleven years. He realized with horror that Melanie really had always been interested. He remembered how pleased he'd been at the family get-togethers for the

Fourth of July, when Melanie showed great caution, but
never fear, when he would set up the fireworks. "The
answer is still an absolute, utter, resounding no," Lou
said again, this time without shouting.

Melanie recognized her opportunity. She wrapped
herself around Lou's right arm, stood on tiptoe to put
her head on his shoulder, and said dreamily, "Thank you,
Pops."

Viktor closed the door to the boy's room and whooped
with laughter. "She's got your number, Lou."

Lou marched down the hall muttering to himself. It
was going to be a very long couple of days.

The Dealer rolled over in the unfamiliar bed and
flung out his arm. His hand knocked against the lamp,
pushing it onto the ground with a painful clatter. He
groaned to life, his head splitting, his mouth as dry as
the Nevada desert. Viktor had given him vitamins to
counteract the effect, and it wasn't the worst headache
he'd ever had, but it was still impressive.

The Dealer never would have picked vodka as a drug
to enhance learning. But as nearly as he could tell,
Viktor had been right—all he needed was a little less
anxiety, and he was fine.

Chan Kam Yin remembered the stories Viktor had
told while drinking, of terrorists and terrorism in the
days of Communism. He shuddered at the thought of
what a terrible life Viktor must have had. Still, Viktor
had come out of the ordeals with a good friend. Lou
was the nicest person the Dealer had ever met . . .
except for Lanie, who was just a kid. The Dealer
wondered if he would ever have a friend like that.

In one sense he did have such a friend. He remembered, with a foolish glow in his heart, that they'd
exchanged brands with him. He could reach them
anytime on the Web.

He rolled over again and went back to sleep. This
time he dreamed in English.

✧   ✧   ✧

Morgan looked up at the black stealth roton resting quietly on the McCarran landing pad. It was a heavy lift roton, and the size difference impressed him. Normally, such a vehicle did not carry passengers. Not unless the passengers were very special, like today. Solomon stretched her wings. "Big Bird," she commented. Then she whistled. "Where's CJ?"

Lars squinted into the sun and growled. "Yeah, where is the Boss Lady, anyway?"

Out of the sun came the answer. "I just *had* to get a last chocolate malt," CJ said as she strode up to the little group. She stepped out of the sun, and Morgan watched along with everyone else as she licked her lips in sheer, sensuous delight. "Double chocolate, extra malt. Yummy!" She bent over and looked into Morgan's face, eye-to-eye. "I can't believe how easy that last sim was, Morgan. Tell me the truth. Did you let us win? Or are we really that good?"

Morgan wrinkled his nose. The Angels gathered around. No one smiled; no matter how light and joking the question might be, the answer was important. He told the truth, grudgingly. "You're that good," he whispered. He continued more strongly. "It's just realistic. Remember, no Angel Two team has ever failed. This is our best guess of what's likely to happen." He grunted. "Except the pain. Real broken bones and sword wounds are going to hurt a hell of a lot more than anything you've experienced so far."

CJ rubbed her left shoulder where the electroshocks had fried her in the last sim. "I just don't believe it. I think you made it hurt worse, so we'd be pleasantly surprised."

A man in a captain's uniform stepped up. "If you would please come with me, you can board now."

CJ nodded. "Okay, guys, let's go." She bent over and kissed Solomon on the beak. Solomon, flapping her wings enthusiastically, whistled the song "Jump." CJ bent further to kiss Morgan, shifted her eyes around to see the rest of the members of the team, and thought better of it. She stood up. "Back in a couple of weeks," she said with the airy style of a teenager telling her parents she was off to Spring Break.

Morgan saluted the team; they saluted back.

Solomon abruptly changed keys. She sang "The Battle Hymn of Humanity." Her voice swelled into a symphony, and she sang beautifully.

The hymn had been written by Isaiah Southworth, a young American composer studying in Moscow. Southworth had been caught on the edge of the blast when *Shiva I* destroyed the city. He had written the hymn lying on a cot in a tent outside a half-ruined hospital.

The symphony opened as an epic of despair fully understood only by the Russian soul. It closed as an epic of triumph best appreciated by the American heart.

The third-degree burns that covered half of Isaiah's body killed him shortly after he completed his masterwork. Russian doctors certified he had died before *Shiva*'s own destruction. However, the two nurses who carried him away asserted vehemently that, as the light of *Shiva*'s disintegration split the night, he had smiled. Romantics around the world agreed that he had, one way or the other, witnessed the finale that affirmed his music.

All the Angels were romantics.

The music faded. One by one, the Angels disappeared into the darkness of the shuttle door.

Morgan turned his wheelchair and headed into the building. For the next ten days, CJ and the Angels would be switching ships and changing orbits, till they were in position to coast into *Shiva*'s dock. And then . . . and then, Morgan thought grimly, he would figure out a way to get her back again.

Chapter Nine
Angels Eve, T minus One

One window on his wallscreen showed *Shiva* in closeup, from the telescopes on the moon. Another showed *Shiva* as everyone else saw it, a view from the vidcam on his deck. A great tentacle of cloud swept across the moon; *Shiva* was alone in the sky. For a moment Morgan wondered how many billions of others were looking at the ship as he was, this night.

The third window on his wallscreen showed four young men and a child of a woman, all their attention focused on him.

Morgan barked at the Angels, "What's the difference between real *Shiva* robots and sims?"

The Angels answered in unison. "They're stronger than sims. They're faster than sims. And they *really* want to kill us."

"What's the difference between the Angels and the robots?"

"We're smarter than they are. We know we have to win."

196

Morgan nodded in mute satisfaction. "The robots have the stupidity of the casually brave. They waste themselves to no purpose." He looked each member of the team in the eyes. "You will not be wasted. That, above all, I promise."

His Angels stood very straight. Even from two hundred thousand miles away, he could see that they were radiant in their quiet pride and power. They would need it.

"Dismissed. I'll see you after you've docked." The images of four of the Angels winked out. One did not. Morgan was not surprised. "CJ," he said lovingly, "go join your team."

"I will," she said quietly, then smiled widely. "I just had to make sure you knew that I'm going to come see you again after we get out."

Morgan knew he shouldn't say anything—how he knew! "When you get out, I'll take you on a date," he promised. "A raging water date."

Her eyes widened. "Back to Topock Gorge," she asked excitedly.

"Of course not. Been there, done that. I was thinking of Fiji. We'll buy a boat and sail the islands."

"Cool!" She lowered her eyes. "I have to go suit up now."

"Yes, you do."

CJ raised one eyebrow, blew him a kiss, and blinked out of existence.

After a moment of frozen silence, Morgan slowly raised his lips to his fingers and blew a kiss back.

Sofia led him by the hand, out into the lush darkness of the garden. Paolo remembered how dangerous the garden had seemed in the daylight when he had entered it alone. Now, lit only by the shadowlight of a dwindling moon and a growing *Shiva*, the garden felt comfortable and safe. The difference was Sofia's guidance, the warmth of her nearness, the firm strength of her hand.

They came to a loveseat surrounded by thickets. Paolo put his arms around Sofia, and they sat down together, laid their heads back, and looked up to the cloudless sky.

Sofia huffed, "It washes out all the stars."

Sofia's "it" was, of course, *Shiva V.* Though close enough to suggest its immensity, it was still too far to make out details in its armor. At the moment, it looked like a fairy jewel, a shiny alabaster bauble in a child's treasure chest.

Paolo squeezed her tight. "It will not be there for long, of that, I can assure you." He did not mention that it might not be there because it would soon be here.

"I know, darling." She turned to him and kissed his cheek. "Kill it for me, please, darling?" In the tone of her voice, all wrapped together in that moment, were all the emotions ever devised by a woman: love, hate, teasing, fear, yearning, puzzlement, and a host of others too subtle ever to be named or understood by a mere male.

But Paolo knew they were there, and responded to them, as men do. "We will kill it," he promised.

"And their homeworld. Destroy their homeworld, so they never come again." Sofia shuddered in the darkness.

Paolo exhaled slowly. There was a limit to his willingness to embrace a lie, even to comfort his beloved. He felt a shiver of tension rise up his back, knowing what Sofia needed to hear, knowing he could not say it.

And then he was calm—unnaturally calm, calm beyond quiet. The shiver of fear disappeared, and a tranquil certainty he had known once before filled him, and he was not himself. He became, for that moment, someone else, someone looking back upon this moment from a distant future, someone who knew the truth as it had already been writ. "I will not destroy their homeworld," he said at last from that distant place. "The fate of their star is for Mercedes to decide, and for the people who will join her."

"As long as we keep it in the family," Sofia replied, pressing her head into his shoulder.

Jessica stepped from her cocoon, wobbled a moment, and walked quietly out of her office, out of the hall, out of the building, into the night sky. She discovered the nighttime had drawn a crowd. As nearly as she could tell, everyone at Fort Powell was out here, staring into the sky.

She did not have to look up to see what drew their attention. *Shiva* hung there, a most beautiful harbinger of death. Seeing the others standing there transfixed, Jessica considered going back inside. But she peeked up for just a moment, and could not take her eyes off of it.

A deep male voice made her jump. "Gorgeous, isn't it?" General Samuels said, wistfully.

"Gorgeous," Jessica agreed. They stood quietly for a moment, staring at the now-angelic orb. "Why are they so determined to kill us?" she asked of no one in particular.

She should have known, the General would somehow respond. He shook his head. "There is a more interesting question, Jessica. Why is their determination so half-hearted?"

Jessica turned to look at him with upraised eyebrows. "It doesn't seem very half-hearted to me, General."

Samuels shrugged. "And most people sleep better, believing this is a full-out effort on the *Shiva*'s part. But really, Jessica, suppose you wanted to destroy us at all costs. Would you drop a *Shiva* into orbit before blowing up cities? Why bother with individual cities?" He pointed into the sky. "Our calculations suggest that when a *Shiva* comes through our Oort Cloud, it is traveling at eighty percent the speed of light. If they didn't care about anything except destroying us, it wouldn't slow down, Jessica. It would just charge right through the system, and hit Earth head-on at full speed. There wouldn't be anything left except molten rock." Samuels spread his hands. "Nothing left at all."

Jessica shivered. "So they want us—or at least our planet—for some purpose of their own." She shook her head. "What could it be?"

Once more Samuels just shrugged. "The 'castpoints have a lot of theories, all with low probabilities." He smiled. "My own personal favorite explanation is the 'Galactic Sierra Club gone amuck' theory." He gave her a short laugh, which subsided when she just stared at him.

"What's a Sierra Club?" she asked, puzzled.

The General deflated as she watched. "It was an organization I belonged to in my youth that . . . ah . . . well, never mind. Some jokes just don't span the generations very well, I guess."

To cheer him up, Jessica decided to offer him the most ridiculous explanation she'd heard. "My grandmother thinks the *Shivas* are manufactured by a machine, originally built for a big government by the lowest bidder. The original purpose was for wiping out competing governments, while keeping most of the people alive to serve the *Shivas*' government. Granma says the good news is, after becoming operational, the *Shivas* almost certainly destroyed the bureaucrats who spawned them." She gave the General her warmest smile.

But he didn't find her story any funnier than she'd found his. He nodded quite seriously. "A variant of Saberhagen's Berserkers," he said. He watched her eyes nervously, wondering if she'd understand at least that reference from long ago.

"Right, I've heard of the Berserkers," Jessica said. The General visibly relaxed, knowing he wouldn't have to explain that one. They laughed together.

Samuels tilted his head back to *Shiva* V. "You think it's beautiful now? Wait till we blow it up. *That* is a sight of corruscating splendor," he said with a confidence she knew he could not feel.

"Why General, you're a poet." She batted her eyelashes at him, then continued, "I can't wait to see it," she replied with a burst of verve she knew that he knew she could not feel, either.

The Dealer sat alone in his apartment and looked out his tiny window at the bright, terrible face of his greatest opportunity. By this time tomorrow, he would be a rich man.

He considered emailing to thank Reggie Oxenford for giving him the insight. Now the Dealer not only knew he would soon become rich, but he would become rich helping, more or less, to save the world. It was a good thing to believe, looking up into the sky at a terror so cold and alien.

Yes, the time for scams was past. Or at least his next great scam was put on hold for a couple of days.

Reggie stepped off the roton with a gratefulness even greater than usual; all the time they'd been in orbit, he'd kept expecting the ship to get hit by a missile from *Shiva*. It was a silly thought, of course, but with the enemy vessel so close, so big in the tiny viewplates of the roton, it was hard to avoid.

He walked to the edge of the landing pad and looked up into the night sky. Deadly beauty gleamed back down.

A silken voice of lace and satin spoke, "Taxi, sir?" The voice ended in a mocking tone. He saw from the corner of his eye that the speaker was throwing him a salute. Mercedes' eyes glowed in the night, almost as bright, in his opinion, as the light of *Shiva*.

Reggie shook his head. "You are outrageous, girl." He held his hand out to her, and Mercedes stepped close. Reggie continued, "Take me to milady's apartment," he said with appropriate haughtiness.

"No way, mister." The tone was still laughing, but the message was serious. "This here taxi service takes you

to your motel." Mercedes stepped closer, so close, but
not touching. " 'Milady' has to work tomorrow, and she
needs to be undisturbed."

Reggie sighed. "I suppose I can understand that."
Unable to restrain himself in such close proximity, he
reached suddenly around her head, grasped her hair in
his hands, and pulled her in for a kiss. "For luck," he
explained.

She responded with surprised pleasure, then stopped.
They stood together, holding hands, looking up into the
face of night.

Chapter Ten

The Alabaster Hall

True love was a rare thing, and Anatoly Vinogrado understood just how incredibly lucky he was to have had two loves in his life. His first love was, of course, his wife. But his new love, his new mistress, was every bit as special to him. He loved his Mark VIII Hell-Benders.

He'd loved them when he first ran the sims of them in action, so fast and agile. Now he loved them even more, watching them in their elusive grace, driving home to *Shiva*. Somehow, *Shiva* was having trouble tracking them—he could tell from the subtle errors in the countermissile fire, their slowness to retarget as the HellBender evaded. Time after time, Anatoly's new babies got closer to *Shiva* than ever before.

But still not close enough. Anatoly sighed. Well, even true love did not promise perfection.

Shiva knew that it faced something terrible and new. It had fired a huge flock of Hydras in the direction of Vinogrado's task force. *Shiva* hadn't found the fleet yet—

if it had, the fire would be aimed at them, not merely in their general direction—but if it did . . .

He focused on getting his HellBenders ever nearer, ever deeper into the defensive envelope, into the plasma tube beneath the ragged hole he had made with his last hit. At last he conceded defeat: *Shiva* had more layers of defensive fire protecting that cratered opening than it had for half the rest of the ship. Anatoly would have to try a different tack.

He turned to targeting the ring of small hemispheres encircling the tube, the proximity antimissile batteries. If he took a chunk out of those, maybe someone else would get another hit on the tube itself.

Two of his missiles jigged onto his newly designed tactical course just in time to avoid destruction. One of those died shortly thereafter.

From the corner of his eye, Anatoly saw a Hydra on his screen suddenly change course, zeroing in on his task force flagship. *Shiva* had found the fleet at last. Anatoly didn't have much time left.

His surviving HellBender dodged another counter-missile. Enemy laser fire grazed it, but it was too close now, and a flash of light blossomed on the screen as the missile struck, halfway between two of the counter-missile batteries.

"Victory!" Anatoly shouted to no one in particular, raising his fist in defiance of the seemingly invincible *Shiva*. He had just set a new world record—he was the first person in history to get two scores against the goddess of destruction.

Examining the results of his hit, his practiced eye suggested he might have wiped out six of the counter-batteries, not just the two closest to the blast. A good score, indeed.

Another flash lit the screen, but this time it was not good news. The cruiser *Phnom Penh* disintegrated as a pair of missiles struck home. Then Anatoly stiffened; three Hydras veered toward his own *South Hampton*.

There wasn't really any chance of surviving a three-Hydra salvo. He would have to hurry.

Anatoly punched buttons to fire again, and found he couldn't: his missile bays were empty. He was out of a job.

But someone else on some other ship had noticed the weakened counterfire in the area where he'd nailed the countermissile launchers. And someone was trying to exploit the weakness. Anatoly could see missiles streaking toward the plasma tube from the undefended angle. If they could keep it up long enough, they'd surely get another hit.

He watched idly as the *South Hampton*'s countermissile fire nailed one of the Hydras. His mind turned to the future. His son, Illya, had just been accepted to the Space Force Academy in Colorado Springs. There had never been any doubt that Illya was a bright kid, incredibly bright. Indeed, Anatoly's wife Aleksa frequently compared Illya to her own grandfather, who, while he might be a rickety old codger, was probably the smartest man Anatoly had ever met.

Anatoly raised his fist once more. "My son will finish what I have begun," he promised the distant monster. "You will be sorry you ever—"

Five submissiles from a Hydra struck the *South Hampton* as one. The light radiated so brightly as to be completely painless.

CJ floated in the pitch blackness of the windowless ship, hardly daring to breathe. She could tell the other members of her team shared the same fear of sound she felt, for she could not hear them breathing, either. She wondered if the others had died somehow; she wondered if instead she had died and this was the afterlife. Or afterdeath.

The blackness clung to her. As she started to feel like she was suffocating, she heard a hearty laugh. "Is anyone still alive?" she heard Lars' booming voice.

CJ cringed, then forced herself to be calm. "It's funny, Lars, isn't it, that your voice makes me nervous, because I'm afraid *Shiva* will hear."

Axel's voice came from the other side of the cylinder. "You can say that again, CJ. Lars, I know that, in space, no one can hear you laugh, but could you keep it down anyway?"

Lars chuckled again, but this time the sound was muffled, like he was holding his hand over his mouth. "Do you really like the silence better?"

A rush of acceleration pushed CJ deep into her shockweb. CJ could not see, but knew that the huge concrete ballast had been thrown off, leaving the *Argo* almost motionless relative to *Shiva*. A tiny push, delicate compared to the last one, came next, followed by a thin whining sound as the grappling hooks reached into the docking bay. CJ knew the hooks had found purchase when she was pressed once again into her shockweb, ever so gently. A muted clang announced the ceramic-on-ceramic collision of the *Argo* with the enemy ship. A soft glow, the glow of a thousand Midwest lightning bugs, filled the room as chemical-powered lights came up. The left side of the *Argo* became the floor as the *Argo*, locked now inside *Shiva*, took on *Shiva*'s gravitational force, induced by the smooth and constant deceleration of .85 gees as it approached Earth.

CJ spoke at last. "Okay, folks. We're here. Axel, do your stuff."

"Check," Axel said with his leering grin. He swung down into the chair by the touchscreen.

Everyone sat up to watch Axel work the controls. On the screen they could see the lock-picking arm of the *Argo* swing out to the docking bay's optical verifier.

Back on Earth, CJ knew, a 'castpoint and prizeboard were working at full speed as the various experts of Earth vied to determine the best method of attack. The problem was actually straightforward, since the lock's mechanism had not been changed since Angel One's assault, merely the codes. And no one planned to sit around trying to figure out the codes.

Instead, the lock-picking hand snapped the lid off the lock, and a long finger dug into the bowels of the mechanism. Axel worked the finger using analyses coming off his screen, forwarded by MacBride from the 'castpoint.

A tiny tremor shook the ship as an outer wall slid over the dock's opening, to seal the dock for pressurization. Then the first blast shield separating the dock from the interior of the ship revealed its true nature, by sliding back into a hidden recess.

Roni clapped his hands. "Let the games begin." Lars was already heaving the heavy rear hatch of the *Argo* out of the way. Akira slid out, graceful as a ghost, and started setting up the drilling system on the outer docking bay door. Axel squeezed out after him—the *Argo* fit the *Shiva* docking bay like a hand in a glove, filling the bay with as much gear and as many people as Earth engineering could cram in.

Lars went to the front of the *Argo* and rolled the forward hatch back. Roni and CJ rolled gear forward, which Lars lifted over the lip of the hatch and onto the *Shiva*'s floor.

By the time CJ stepped down from the hollow ceramic crate that had brought them here, Akira and Axel had completed their efforts: the redundant pair of X-ray lasers that supplied their link to the outside world was in operation, peeping through a pair of tiny holes in the outer door.

Five minutes later everyone was encased in their exoskeletal armor frames. They climbed onto their bikes and started down the Alabaster Hall.

Jessica rubbed her temples. The headache was worse than it had ever been during the exercises, but she could take no chance of dulling her perceptions, even with as mild an analgesic as aspirin.

From the start of the lock-picking operation to the moment when Morgan turned away from the screens to take a break, hardly half an hour had passed. Yet she was trembling from the tension. She cracked the hatch on the cocoon and stepped out for an orange juice.

With the juice in her hand, halfway to her mouth, she broke into an uncontrolled, almost hysterical laugh. Her heart had just about stopped when all the feeds from the *Argo* had shut down moments earlier.

A twist of the doorknob made her turn: the General walked in, looking sympathetic. "You all right there?" he asked in a worried tone.

"You didn't warn me about the blackout," she snapped in accusation.

The General stopped, then nodded. "You mean when *Shiva*'s outer air lock door closed."

"Right." Jessica brought her hands up to cover her eyes. "When the door closed, and shut off all our comm, I was suddenly blind. I thought for sure the Angels were trapped in there, without help, and Morgan and I would both just twiddle our thumbs till the missiles hit us."

"I am very sorry. I think, though, you'll find the comm system reliable from here forward."

"Right." She took a drink of her orange juice. "Well, I need to get back into the cocoon. Um, could I ask you for a big favor?"

The General looked at her in surprise. "How can I help you?"

Jessica looked away. She could feel heat on her face. "Could I keep a screen open to you in your office? So I can ask an occasional question."

Samuels smiled in sympathy as he replied to her real concern. "Of course, Jessica. It is very lonely, working on this all alone. Morgan, of course, is in constant communication with the Angels, but for you, the problem is even harder, at least in that respect."

"Thanks." Jessica stepped back through the hatch of her cocoon. Her head still hurt, but she definitely felt better.

The Dealer watched the sloping walls of the Alabaster Hall slide by. His touchscreen was mostly filled with the view from a camera affixed to Roni Shatzski's frame. The scene commanded the Dealer's most complete attention: now that he was into the assault for hard money, it all seemed much more real.

He had never before understood why they called the first part of the path the Alabaster Hall, but now, as he stood like a speck of dust on its floor, it was obvious. The first twelve kilometers of hallway from the docking bay weren't really halls in the same sense as the corridors deeper inside the ship. It was more of a tunnel through the ship's armor. Consequently, just as the armored hull of the ship looked like alabaster, so did the walls of the tunnel. The builders must have constructed the interior of the ship out of a more forgiving, more workable material. That would explain the sandstone appearance of the halls deeper inside *Shiva*.

Though he sat in impassive silence, the Dealer was almost as charged as the Angels. This was his big chance. He had to be there, totally focused, because he couldn't tell when the Angels might run into a requirement for his expertise. He had to be fully informed on the situation the moment opportunity arose, lest someone else beat him to the punch. Meanwhile, he'd blanketed the Earth Defense 'castpoints and prizeboards with detectors. Anytime anyone posted a new prize or forecast, his detectors awoke—but they didn't just pass the alert on to him. The Dealer had set filters on the detectors, to ensure that he only received an alert if the new prize or forecast were something that might interest him.

Of course, he'd set the filters to be "weak." So if any doubt existed as to his interest in a new event, his filters passed the alert to him. Consequently he could be confident that he didn't miss the great opportunity, whatever it might be . . . but it also meant that he was personally screening a fair number of postings. It was frustrating to see so much money, so many possibilities, just flowing by, but he bided his time, waiting for the chance that, like the skytruck for Everest, he alone could fulfill.

And he watched the action. Though he had envied the Angels their beautiful, expensive equipment when he was in America, the feeling had fled. Studying the immensity of the enemy starship from the safety of his apartment, he wished that somehow the Angels could have more and better equipment. Marvelous as the machinery had seemed, now it looked clumsy and forlorn. He swallowed hard, realizing that if that frail equipment failed too soon, the prizeboards would shut down prematurely, and his chance might never come. He hoped desperately for the Angels' survival.

CJ swerved her bike from the right-hand wall to the center of the hall, coming up adjacent to Lars. Lars smiled, tossed her a sapphire rod, and reached back into his cargo trailer for the next one. They used sapphire for these blocking rods because it was harder than any comparable metal—a necessity for jamming the monster airlock doors.

While CJ made the pickup, Axel accelerated to leapfrog in front of her, his rod at the ready. On the left-hand wall, Roni and Akira played essentially the same game, practiced to perfection in the last month.

The blast shields of the hall were half a kilometer thick, spaced half a kilometer apart. For each shield that slid back into the left side of the hall, the next one slid into the right. On the side of the hall that a shield slid across to, there was a shallow recess, perhaps a meter deep: the shield extended into that recess to lock into place.

But if, after the Angels were through, the shield closed all the way into position, it would snap the fiber-optic cable trailing out to the comm lasers. To prevent this disaster, each blast shield had to be jammed open. So the Angels dropped the sapphire rods, each slightly more than a meter long, into the recesses, wedging the blast shield open. CJ looked over her shoulder as the shield they'd just passed slid across, then froze open the few millimeters required. She smiled in satisfaction.

Hell's bells, this damn ship was huge. "Morgan, there's a really big problem with all the simulations."

"Which particular big problem are you referring to?" Morgan's voice came to her from half a million miles away, several seconds later.

"All those tenth-scale models just don't prepare you for the size of this thing."

"The size of *Shiva* won't kill you, CJ. The robots will."

He was right, more or less.

Morgan's next message came through with the slight echo, the sense of loudness, that indicated the message was being broadcast to all the Angels. "Okay, folks, you're past the last blast shield. Half a klick ahead there's just an airlock cover, like the one that closes over the docking bay. When that cover slides open, you'll be in contact." CJ heard Morgan cluck his tongue across time and space. CJ perked up. Morgan was uncertain about something. But of all the parts of an Angel assault, this part was most standardized.

What change in SOP could Morgan be considering?

No! a voice screamed in Morgan's head. *Get her out of there!*

But no one listened, least of all Morgan himself. It was too late to extract CJ from *Shiva*, even if she would let him. Though they had wedged the blast shields wide enough for the hair-thin cabling to go through, even the tiny CJ could not squeeze through those gaps. Morgan had a glimmer of a plan for getting her out, but the shortest path to his great hope lay through *Shiva's* control room.

As he watched her roll through the final shield, a single thought took hold of his mind. Shake his head as he might, he could not throw the realization aside: only one more wall, hardly a meter thick, separated his magnificent CJ from *Shiva's* first deadly reception committee. His heart started pounding hard and erratically. He was glad no one had him wired up like the Angels, or they'd have paramedics standing in the hall for him, which was the last distraction he needed. Via the vidcams that watched him as well as the Angels, the whole world could see the tension lines cross his forehead, but at least his heartbeat and adrenaline levels were private affairs.

He stared at the pristine smoothness of the airlock cover, coming up so fast. Soon it would open, and something terrible would face his team. He clenched his fists; his fingernails dug into the palms of his hands. He desperately wanted to know what, and how many, and—

A soft chime sounded as his detectors sniffed a new offering on the Angels' realtime prizeboard. Somebody wanted one of the Angels to throw a rod against the cover while another Angel listened on the floor. The prize-holders were willing to pay Earth Defense a thousand dollars to do so.

The thousand dollars was an infinitesimal handful of change for the Earth Defense budget, of course, but you'd only make such a serious offer if you could get some serious insight from it. And whoever offered the prize claimed they could glean the insight that struck to the core of Morgan's most desperate concern—they thought they could tell him what lay beyond the cover.

Could they really do it? The offerer's brand had links to past successes; Morgan's forecast-assessment team traced the links and found a solid reputation.

There was only one way to find out if the anonymous someone, somewhere on the Web, could answer his prayers. He clucked his tongue again as he thought about it.

Along with CJ and several billion other participants, Selpha listened as Morgan pondered the prize she had offered. She allowed herself a small smile; she was pretty sure she knew what would follow.

It was delightful to have the resources to offer Earth Defense and the Angels a prize to gather information for her and Peter. It made a big difference in their ability to make good forecasts.

The idea had been born in her mind as Peter listened dreamily to the sapphire rods clatter into the blast shield recesses. He was smiling as he listened. "So pure and clean, I can hear for kilometers," he said with a sense of rapture.

Since learning of Peter's gift, Selpha had studied acoustics intently. And when he said that, she suddenly put several different little facts together.

Sapphire was not only an exceptionally hard material, harder even than ceramic armor, it was also one of the most acoustically perfect materials known to man. Float a cylinder of sapphire in a vacuum, tap it gently, and it will ring for days. Selpha could not have designed a more ideal sensing device for her son.

And *Shiva*'s alabaster armor, while not as acoustically pure as a sapphire crystal, was nonetheless a "clean" material. Quite possibly, Peter was not exaggerating when he said he could hear for kilometers. So if they threw one of the rods against the last alabaster wall, producing a sharp sound, Peter might be able to figure out what lay beyond. And since the Angels consistently met the first enemy resistance there, the information could be tremendously valuable.

CJ held her breath as Morgan spoke, though the pause hurt her bicycling rhythm; she wanted to make sure she missed no part of the order. "Lars, grab one of your spare rods. When I say 'throw,' pitch it with full force against that last wall. Akira, when Lars throws, I want you to hit the deck and listen to the sound through the floor. Or rather, I want you to press your microphone to the floor. Got it?"

"Got it," Lars and Akira said in unison.

"Good."

A minute passed, and CJ saw the last wall looming in front of them. In just a second it would start to open, as it sensed the approach of whomever had opened the docking bay door. Morgan yelled, "Throw!" and Lars' rod hit the wall just before it started to slide.

Selpha watched as Lars threw the rod. She watched Peter's expression as the rod clanged against the shield. Peter nodded his head. "There are a lot of them, Mom." Selpha was already punching in a new forecast for the Earth Defense 'castpoint as he described what he had heard.

Mercedes paced back and forth in front of her wallscreen. She was glad she had been firm with Reggie, refusing to work in his penthouse or to allow him to join her here. She hated the idea of him seeing her in this agitated state.

The swift race down the Alabaster Hall lent very few opportunities for interesting forecasts: they already knew how many blast shields there were, because Angel One had crossed through them all less than a month earlier. And when that last portal opened, the action would follow too fast and thick for even the Angel Controller to make a difference, much less the 'castpoints—the Angels would have to rely on their own instincts in the heat of battle. So there wasn't really any chance she would have anything to do in this phase of the assault, but—

Blake Gosling, the head of the Earth Defense-endorsed Forecast Spec team, appeared in a corner window of the screen. He smiled. "You're on, Mercedes. Check this out." Another window appeared on her screen, with a forecast sketch. The sketch predicted that there were between twenty and twenty-five robots at the entrance to the hall, over half of them were mini-tanks, and there were no Destroyers.

Mercedes whistled. "White-hot," she said.

"Very," Blake replied. "Hurry," he said as he shut down his feed.

The forecast sketch had already been posted to the 'castpoint, and the person who'd submitted the 'cast had already planted fifty thousand dollars on the forecast's correctness. Mercedes stamped the sketch with her brand, and all around the world trading on the new forecast began, even as Mercedes said, "Trillian, work mode."

When her central server, Trillian, went into work mode, the big window of the scene in *Shiva* shut down. Four tamperproof vidcams around the room went into operation, recording her every action.

In the "sketch" format generally used for forecast submission, the 'cast was easy to understand but difficult to quantify for judgment. Consequently, the sketch contained plenty of room for heated argument about whether the forecast had been right or wrong. In the end you could force resolution with an arbiter, but that was expensive and wasteful. It was much better to write a precise specification, with little ambiguity, as part of the forecast, and judge right/wrong based on the spec.

For the realtime Angel forecasts there wasn't always enough time to complete the spec before the forecast became history. So instead of insisting that the spec be complete before trading began, they posted the brand of the person who would write the spec. Professional forecasters could then follow the links on the brand to see how this particular spec writer had quantified forecasts in the past. They could get a feeling for how this 'cast would be quantified even as trading proceeded.

Actually, real professionals would read the histories of all the brands in the endorsed Forecast Spec team before the assault began. Mercedes was already famous in large parts of the world, just by being a part of the team.

Though this forecast would be resolved very, very quickly, it was also pretty easy to transform into a spec. Her hands were shaking as she finished her first draft. She stopped and forced herself to take her time. Aside from her summer jobs, small subcontracts from Blake and associates, this spec would be her first professional work. She needed to make it good. Out of the corner of her eye she noticed that the trading on the 'cast had reached a furious intensity. She forced herself to look away, back at the spec.

MacBride watched the buying on the forecast with awe and terror. Awe, because someone had made a remarkably detailed prediction of what they faced beyond that last airlock. Terror, because it was the biggest enemy force ever assembled at the end of the Alabaster Hall.

Morgan remembered coming to the end of this hall in *Shiva I*. He and his friends had been ready for anything . . . well, as ready as they could be with little more than their bare knuckles for fighting. Morgan had correctly surmised that, to get into *Shiva's* docking bay, you had to go without metal, without anything that could be spotted by a simple magnetic detector. So they'd left their guns and most of their knives at home—

Anyway, at the end of the hall, they'd run into a handful of repair mechs. The mechs' sole interest had probably been in repairing the damage the invaders had done to the outer airlock to force entry. It had been so much easier then—

The odds on the opposing-strength forecast firmed up. The 'cast was too detailed and too strongly supported for Morgan to ignore it. Normally the Angels just rushed the robots at the end of the hall, but this time they had to use a different strategy.

The lock was opening! He silently, swiftly blessed the person who had made the 'cast, whoever it was, for averting disaster. Then he barked out the orders that he hoped could save the team.

The airlock cover started moving. CJ gripped her spike more tightly and started to sprint.

"Freeze." CJ heard Morgan's voice reach its most quiet, most authoritative form. She skidded to a halt, the last to succeed in obeying the order.

"Unfreeze. Expect twelve Mark II minitanks and eleven roboguards. Barricade now, left side."

Twelve minitanks! She couldn't believe it. But if it were true, they were in deep shit. Already.

Lars wheeled the cargo trailer into position as the center of the barricade. Axel popped the 40mm pellet launcher into its stand on the top of the trailer. CJ waved Roni to the far right side, to outflank the enemy as they charged the barricade.

Morgan's voice continued. "Full fire." They wouldn't try to use the spikes against this massive opposition; instead they'd use up ammo at a disastrous rate. But the ammo wouldn't do them any good if they were dead.

Earlier, the blast shields had opened far too slowly for CJ's tastes. She had wanted them to pop wide so she could rush through. Now this door opened at the same speed, yet it felt as though it opened far too fast.

The door slid from left to right, from the barricade toward Roni. Soon the opening was wide enough for a roboguard to come through. Sure enough, the first enemy robot ran toward them on its two legs, its armored breast plate shining, its arms reaching out to kill.

"Viktor, Viktor!" Lou half-screamed at his friend through the touchscreen. "You having a heart attack?! Talk to me!"

Viktor dropped his hands away from his face, and Lou was shocked at the sight. Viktor's bloodshot eyes looked back at him in forlorn apology.

"Viktor, there's a damn army on the far side of that blast shield. We need to design a minefield for them." Lou thought about using the clever trick they'd developed earlier for dropping a section of the ceiling, but the alabaster armor now hanging over the Angels' heads was too tough for that.

Viktor choked out, "You help them on this one. I'll be back in a few minutes."

Lou had no idea what was wrong with the old fool, but the Angels didn't have time for it. Lou started working out a plan. He felt half-crippled without his friend by his side, but hell, he'd worked alone for twenty years when he was a kid. And then he had been fighting *against* Viktor. He could do it again.

The minitanks would be the problem here, particularly the Mark IIs, which were almost impossible to kill even with the 40mm ammo. The pistols were actually more effective against the Mark IIs—the pellets ricocheted off the floor more reliably, giving you a chance to hit the vulnerable underbelly. Mines were the right answer.

The minitanks were physically broader than the guards; they'd be the last things through the opening. That gave him a chance to plant the mines with a higher chance of nailing the tanks and not wasting them on the easier targets.

Feverishly, Lou laid out a plan and posted it to the 'castpoint.

The headache now felt like a series of low-yield nukes going off in her head, but Jessica hardly noticed it. She watched the new prediction take form on the 'castpoint, that Roni could lay a minefield in the right-hand side of the hall and take out at least one-third of the minitanks. There wasn't any time for watching a bunch of traders reflect on the correctness of this plan, but she knew Morgan would go with it. "Hurry the mines," she whispered.

CJ might have had the fastest reflexes in history, but she was still busy organizing the barricade when the first roboguard appeared. So Akira scored the first kill: a pair of pellets from his pistol caused the guard to stumble, and a third shot went home under the exposed lip of the breastplate.

Two more roboguards crowded through the opening.

Morgan's voice once again came through. "Roni, duodec. Ten one-centimeter charges, pressure caps. Plant 'em on the right side of the hall in two rows."

Roni snapped his gun into its holster and built the mines while the others stood off the growing collection of adversaries. CJ nailed a roboguard, and Axel opened up the 40mm on the four minitanks skittering toward them. Two of them fell, both Mark Is. The other two, both Mark IIs, accelerated.

Mercedes read her spec one more time out loud. Even without anyone in the room to hear her, she had found that if you read it out loud and it didn't sound funny, it was a pretty good spec. No passage tripped her ambiguity sensors, carefully honed over the last four years of college, and she touched the button to publish the spec. "Trillian, view mode," she ordered.

Once again a scene from *Shiva* filled the bulk of her wall. But the last view she'd had was of a quiet hall with just the five Angels. What she saw now made her gasp in horror. Whoever had made the opposition-strength forecast had been hideously correct. Now her screen looked upon a wild chaos of combat. Somehow the forecast she'd been working hadn't helped at all, or so it appeared. It seemed impossible for anyone to survive. She watched with a helpless feeling of doom as the door slid completely into the wall, and a last group of minitanks rushed the Angels. She wasn't sure what to think when the whole right side of the screen lit up with a series of explosions, leaving her with sunbursts dancing in her eyes.

Jesus, there were a lot of the bastards! CJ screamed in primal fury. Lars was making mincemeat of the roboguards with the 40mm, but the minitanks just kept coming. She angled her pellet gun down and got off a good shot, killing one of them. Akira and Axel each scored one as well. One skittered past, zeroing in on the trailer, with all their spare equipment and their heaviest gun. With a swift motion, it smashed one of trailer's wheels into junk and started to climb. CJ dropped her gun and flung herself at the thing, charging low to stay out of Lars' fire. She grabbed its arms and pulled back, with both the strength of her fiercest determination and the amplified strength of her frame.

Tipped up in a climbing position, the minitank was awkwardly positioned. It reached for the 40mm gun tube, didn't quite reach it, then steeled itself for another pull. It was far stronger than CJ and her frame; in a moment it would be free.

Lars pointed the gun at the minitank, but paused: CJ was braced behind the tank, and it was fundamentally impolite to shoot at your teammates.

"Lars, shoot the damn thing," CJ yelled in fury.

Lars pulled the trigger, and a burst of shells hollowed out the minitank. With a range of inches, the force of the hits threw CJ backwards, but she was able to hold the shell of the minitank in front of her. The tank's own armored back protected her from the gunfire till Lars trained his weapon on another target.

Another minitank ripped the front right wheel off the trailer and started climbing up for the gun.

CJ threw the shell of the dead tank from her. She was about to charge the one climbing the trailer when she saw, out of the corner of her eye, another whole wave of minitanks coming through the doorway. Axel and Akira were still engaged with a pair of tanks from the last wave. Roni was out of position, on the flank where she had sent him. There was really no stopping this next collection. They were already beaten.

Then she was thrown to the floor by a series of four blasts. Looking up, she saw that everyone and everything was surprised by the explosions except Roni, who hopped around the dead minitanks and calmly shot a fifth one dead with a ricochet hit.

The minitank on the trailer had been thrown down on its back, but it held the 40mm gun in its hand. The minitank squeezed the weapon, shattering its breach. But while the tank concentrated on the gun, Lars leaped lightly to the top of the trailer to thrust down with his spike. The minitank lay motionless.

Akira got a good shot into the last minitank as Axel blocked a blow from the tank with his spike. The spike survived; the tank did not.

CJ looked around wildly for more opposition. Then she heard Morgan's voice. "Relax, CJ." With billions of people listening he couldn't say, "Relax, love," but the feeling came across in the warm glow of his voice. She could feel his breath on her shoulder, and she shuddered. Morgan spoke again. "You won the first round. Time to assess the damage."

CJ rose to her feet, still blinking the sweat from her eyes with a sense of astonishment. "We're all still alive," she muttered in wonder.

"Yes," Morgan said simply. "Against all odds. Well done."

Chapter Eleven

A Crack in the Wall

Jessica shook uncontrollably. She planted her feet on the wall beneath the forward screen of the cocoon and pushed. She thrust herself into her chair, relaxed, and pushed again, until she had control of herself again. Too much adrenaline, not enough outlet. It reminded her of how she'd felt on the last night of her normal life, before the arrival of General Samuels, when she'd beaten the simulated *Shiva*.

She watched as the Angels took inventory. Everyone was still alive, despite the most vicious trap ever set in the Alabaster Hall. It seemed like a good omen.

For just a moment she studied the scene as herself, as Jessica. Then she flipped back into Morgan-simulation mode and started planning the next steps. Normally, you'd just drop a few booby traps at this doorway to prevent the repair mechs from scrupulously doing their job by going back up the hall and removing the rods so the blast shields could close. But the size of the welcoming committee this time suggested a more aggressive form of defense. Would Morgan hold one of the Angels back, keep him posted here as a guard? Maybe Axel?

No, no, of course not. Morgan had a much better option. He'd blow the roof, cause a cave-in, and boobytrap the debris. That would keep the repair mechs busy plenty long enough for this assault to succeed. Or fail.

Dragon's teeth! That had been one serious encounter with the minitanks. His heart had sunk when that last squad of enemy machines had charged out: what were the chances of anyone surviving a whirlwind of destruction like that?

But they'd come through it all right. In fact, no one had gotten killed; as nearly as he could tell, no one was even hurt. He wasn't sure, but he suspected that might be a first for the Angel teams. And against the toughest opposition yet, no less.

The Dealer smirked. The tailriding suckers who'd bet that none of the Angels would get off the ship were probably shaking in their shoes by now. He glanced down the screen of 'casts . . . yes, the odds were changing as he watched. He was very glad he was out of that kind of ride and into something better.

Three different 'casts had been placed on how they would repair the damage to the trailer. One plan seemed obviously better than the others, and he bought into it, though as with all the obvious choices, the odds meant he wouldn't make a lot of money off of it. His great opportunity still lay down the road somewhere.

Paolo's heart filled with pride to the bursting point. "Sofia," he cried, "There's something you have to see."

"Be with you in a minute," her voice came from somewhere deep in the bowels of the house. A few moments later she appeared. "What's up?"

"Take a look at this." Paolo pointed at a forecast in the 'castpoint.

Sofia looked at the forecast. It took a few seconds for her to pick out the special feature. At last she smiled. "That's Mercedes', isn't it?"

"Yes, that is our daughter's brand. She wrote the spec—" he pointed at Mercedes' carefully crafted text, "and let me say, as a professional in the field, she did a very good job with it."

"That's marvelous." She hugged him. "Did you take a position on this forecast? It seems only fitting that we should support our daughter."

"I'm afraid it wasn't a 'cast we're expert in. Not even the Predictor can predict everything, you know."

"Oh, I know." With a swift, darting motion, Sofia's finger found Paolo's ticklish spot, in the small of his back. Paolo jumped. "Yikes! Why did you do that?"

Sofia's smiled turned wicked. "To show the Predictor just how surprisingly unpredictable the world can be," she replied smugly.

Lars stood from his labors over the trailer's front axle. He slapped his hands together with the satisfied sound of a job well done. "Just like new," he announced. "Well, more or less like new."

CJ stared doubtfully at the results. "Great job, Lars." Sometimes being the team leader meant congratulating people on a job not so much done well as done at all.

And the axle bracing seemed liked it would hold until they got to the center-level slidechute, anyway. If it did hold that long, they'd get their trailer as far as Solovyev, the record holder, had gone.

Roni took off to scout ahead. CJ watched him depart, then looked over her shoulder. "Axel, let's blow this banana stand."

"A pleasure," Axel replied, pressing the button. The force of the explosion shook the floor. The chunk of ceiling brought down by the blast shook the floor again.

Akira surveyed the results as he threw a few last traps into the rubble. "Nice work, Axel. But you are not permitted to redecorate my house."

Axel sniffed. "I'm sure I could transform your place with subtle yet delightful enhancements."

"Mount up, everyone," CJ ordered. She climbed up to sit on the trailer, pellet gun in hand. A roboguard had totaled one of the bikes before Lars had turned the enemy into broken china, so they were a bike short. Lars would have to pedal for both of them; fortunately, for Lars this wouldn't be a big problem.

"We're outta here." CJ leaned over and patted the shoulder of Lars' armor frame. "Giddyap."

They started rolling, counter-clockwise around *Shiva*, toward the radial corridor that would take them deeper into the ship, to the slidechutes.

Lou paced one more time across the rec room, kicking another of Lanie's talking dolls across the pale green carpet. The doll landed between the two big, red recliners close to the small wallscreen. His breathing was still a bit ragged from the tension of battle. Now, to top it off, the exertion of the pacing was wearing him down. In short, he was getting too old for this sort of thing. He looked at his hands; they shook, and purple veins stood out on the mottled, wrinkled skin. Lou considered that if he didn't keep moving he'd probably fossilize in place. His son would take a petrified finger and place it on the mantle as a remembrance. Clenching his hand into a fist, Lou shook himself and marched back into his office.

He found Viktor's broad face on his touchscreen. Viktor began to speak, but Lou spoke faster and louder. "Viktor, what the hell happened to you? We almost lost 'em."

"It killed Anatoly, Lou," Viktor explained. "My grandson-in-law was with the fleet that set up the diversion for the Angels. His ship is gone. There were no survivors this time."

Lou closed his eyes. "I'm really sorry, Viktor." In the moment of silence that followed, he could hear wailing in the background.

Viktor shook his head. "I am sorry I let you down." He sat straighter. "This makes our job even more important."

"Very true," Lou said. "But that doesn't make it hurt any less."

"We thought we'd be better prepared for losing him, after the last time, when we thought he was dead." He smiled through tears. "We were wrong."

Lou searched desperately for something to say, to cheer his old friend and older enemy. "Listen, when this is over, I've been thinking I should bring Lanie up to visit."

Viktor's visage filled with astonishment. "Just to cheer me up, you will suffer the desolate winds and inhuman cold of Arctic Russia? To lighten my heart, you will bring the light of your life to this land where darkness rules?"

Lou knew he couldn't let it sound like a charity journey. "Since when have you had a heart? If you had a heart, it would have stopped by now, and you'd be dead. Nonsense, Viktor." He waved his hand. "I've been thinking for a while that Lanie should come and visit so she can appreciate the depths of human madness and the grotesque alien conditions to which humans can adapt. After all, the real reason your ancestors settled up there was to conduct a survival experiment, right? Figuring that if they could live in Murmansk, then living on the Moon would be easy?"

Viktor waved a pudgy finger at him. "You are a wily fox, old friend. I will hold you to your promise to visit." Lou heard another wail from another room in Viktor's house. Viktor glanced over his shoulder. "In the meantime, it looks like our heroes are okay for the moment, and I must attend my family. I'll get in touch in a couple of hours."

Lou nodded. "A couple of hours it is. I'll keep an eye on the Angels, make sure they don't get into any trouble we can't get them out of."

Viktor's image on the touchscreen turned dark. Lou closed his eyes and leaned back in his chair. He considered taking a nap, decided against it, and fell asleep.

Peter sat frowning, pressing the replay button again and again. The movement seemed so mechanical Selpha wondered if he were really listening, or if he were trapped in some compulsion of his own. She had worked with her son long enough, though, that she didn't think it was just a meaningless fixation: she thought she could tell from the way his frown changed shaped, his mind was actively engaged.

Selpha listened to the swatch of sound he repeated. It started after the Angels had killed the last enemy robot, as they stepped from the Alabaster Hall into the sandstone corridor. It ended after the explosion that brought down the ceiling. She couldn't hear anything interesting at all.

At last Peter stopped the playback. His face relaxed. "There's a crack in that wall," he said.

"Are you sure?" Selpha asked. She knew that he would say yes, that he was quite sure, but the length of his hesitation before he made the assertion would tell her his real level of confidence.

The hesitation did not last as long as she had expected. "I'm quite sure. There's a crack in the wall."

"Thank you," Selpha said, and turned to her terminal.

Mercedes watched Blake laughing as he earmarked another forecast for her attention. Mercedes found herself joining him. She looked at the sketch. "There's a crack in the wall?"

Blake shook his head. "I don't know how they could possibly have figured that out. And I can't imagine who could use the information for anything even if it were true."

Mercedes continued the commentary. "And there's no chance at all that this forecast will get resolved. Nobody is going to go back there with a sledge hammer to see if it's true. I predict that in forty-eight hours this forecast will get scrubbed from the point, unawarded." She shrugged. "But you're the one who taught me that even the most obscure, irrelevant forecast can supply valuable insight to someone, if the forecast is disseminated widely but filtered effectively." She cleared her throat. "Ours is not to question why, ours is but to write, not lie."

"Ouch! Hoist on my own petard," Blake said, recognizing his own words. He shrugged. "Well, no matter how useless this 'cast is, writing the spec will be good practice." He smiled wickedly. "That's why I'm giving it to you."

"Thanks." Mercedes sighed, but just for effect. She was perfectly happy working some live forecasts that weren't life-threatening. "Trillian, work mode."

Normally, the forecast would have penetrated Paolo's filters as a low-priority notification—the 'cast had a slight relevance to his analysts. Instead, however, it jumped to his attention because he'd put a priority acceptance on anything with his daughter's brand on it. He read the 'cast, passed it around his team, and went back to work on Crockett II's deductions. A couple of minutes later, thunderstruck, he realized the meaning of the forecast.

No one had ever found, or even suggested there might be, a flaw in a wall before. Indeed, to the best of his knowledge, no one had ever found a defect of any kind in any of the ships, aside from the damage created by the bombs set off by the Angels themselves.

There was a perfection in the manufacture of the *Shivas* that still made the best of human engineering look like a backwater hack job. A fracture in the wall would constitute a remarkable change in *Shiva* engineering.

But what if the fracture were intentional? Or, more likely, what if the fracture represented a change from the original construction of the *Shivas*?

One of the surprises in *Shiva V* had been the layout of the corridors at the end of the Alabaster Hall. In the previous *Shivas*, there had not only been a corridor running the circumference of the ship to the clockwise and counter-clockwise directions. There had also been a corridor running straight down the radius, toward the central axis and the slide chutes. The recon bots and birds that preceded the Angel One assault had been rudely surprised to find they could not go straight down that hall. What had been the shortest path in *Shiva IV* simply didn't exist in *Shiva V*.

Now Paolo thought he understood. The repair mechs on board *Shiva V* had sealed off that corridor! They'd done a great job too, by human standards. But even a great job by human standards did not reach the inhuman standards of *Shiva's* original engineers. Though the improvised seal had no visible seam, beneath the surface the welding of the new section of wall had left behind an imperfection. That imperfection had all the characteristics of a "crack," a fracture in the ceramic latticework.

Shiva could only have decided to seal that corridor because it knew that the corridor exposed a weakness. It was another indication that supported the oft-posited theory that the *Shivas* were in communication, that each *Shiva* learned from the experiences of the previous one.

But from Paolo's point of view, another point was even more important. For his predictions of the layout of the ship, he had to know where the corridors were even if they were sealed—all his team's algorithm's were set up

to analyze the unsealed layout. To succeed, Paolo had to
know if there were other sealed corridors. He had to know
if there were other cracks.

He turned back to his wallscreen and laid out several
new items. First, he wrote a forecast on the 'castpoint
asserting that the wall fracture was really a sealed-over
corridor. Second, he posted a prize on the board for any
other fracture forecasts that proved correct. Third, he
bought into the original prediction that the crack in the
wall really existed. After all, his identification of why and
how such a crack could be there was supporting evidence
that the crack existed, and significantly increased the odds
that the forecast was correct.

Paolo sat back with satisfaction. This had been a very
good little piece of work.

Jessica muttered the demand repeatedly, but no one
could hear. Finally she shrieked it, though she knew that
even this would not make a difference, "Morgan, ask
if there's a crack in the control room wall!"

The situation seemed obvious to her, now that
someone had figured out what had happened to the
third corridor from the hall. The original forecasts had
been right: the Gate to the control room was in its
standard location—but the Gate had been sealed the
way this corridor had been sealed.

Of course, right or wrong, the stakes were huge. They
had to buy the best assessment they could get, probably
with a direct subcontract to the person who had made
the forecast in the first place.

Why wasn't Morgan acting?

CJ was still alive! Alive! The pleasure of the thought
rolled with thick sweetness in Morgan's mind, like a
chocolate caramel yielding its rich flavor across the
tongue. Everyone was still alive.

More than anything, Morgan wanted to whisper in
CJ's ear. He needed to tell her he loved her. But with

over four billion people watching and listening to every word he said, it was quite impractical. He smiled unhappily, remembering how pre-Crash politicians had complained about the public microscope. Those bumpkins had had no idea what real scrutiny was like.

He considered shutting down the cameras so he could talk to her. But the cameras had just saved her life, and would have to save her again. He had no idea what little tidbit picked up as they sped down the halls might make the crucial difference. The cameras must remain inviolate.

Still, he couldn't keep it all bottled up. He spoke softly into the microphone. "CJ?" he asked with all the tenderness he could express. He knew it could not carry the full weight he desired, but he had to try.

He could see her in the view from Akira's vidcam, sitting astride the trailer while Lars sweated for both of them. She looked queenly, perched upon a throne held aloft by her subjects. She turned to the camera, knowing that he would be watching. Her eyes glowed, a reflection of the tenderness in his voice. Her smile caressed him. "Me too," she replied. She turned back, to face the future.

It was so little, but it was enough. He could concentrate again.

Jessica activated her connection to the General. "Samuels," she said in an urgent voice, "Morgan's losing it. He loves that girl, and he's losing it."

The General looked at her with harried concern. He was closer to showing stress than Jessica had ever seen. "Explain," he snapped.

Jessica ran through her deductions about the control room entrance. Then she voiced her concerns about why Morgan had missed the possibility.

Samuels nodded. "Right or wrong, we need to pursue your analysis."

Jessica pressed on. "So you'll tell Morgan to

subcontract with the original forecaster to see if the Gate is sealed up?"

The General shook his head. "Way too distracting if I bring it up."

Jessica considered this, puzzled. "So you want *me* to tell him? He doesn't know me from Adam."

Samuels made a dismissive wave of his hand. "Personal suggestions are inappropriate in the current context. No, Jessica, I want you to drive this matter to a conclusion. And then use the obvious method to tell Morgan about it." Samuels explained further.

Jessica laughed. "Of course. It is obvious, isn't it?" She pursed her lips. "I can see I still have a ways to go."

"Don't worry about it, Jessica. Just hurry."

Selpha studied her screen with surprise, pleasure, and a certain amount of disbelief. Earth Defense had just asked her to do a special analysis for them. Seeing the request, the merits of the analysis were obvious.

Was there a crack in the wall where the Gate should have been? Given the new forecast on the 'castpoint derived from Peter's forecast, the question and conclusion were obvious.

Earth Defense wasn't even demanding that she be correct with her results. They were just asking for her best judgment, her expertise, and her confidence level in her results. The contract would take her a considerable distance toward her goal, and she couldn't lose. It gave her a light, airy feeling as she endorsed the contract.

"Okay, Peter, we have a very special job to do," she said in her most gentle, patient voice. She hyperlinked through the Web-stored recordings of the Angel One assault, to last battle where Hikmet had died. The visuals were so violently ghastly, it was hard for her to concentrate while they ran. Peter wouldn't have to deal with the sight of the horrors, of course, but the audio was almost as bad. "I know this is going to be very hard, Peter. I know it is very noisy, and it'll be hard to understand. But it is really important that we listen very carefully, and see if we can tell if any of these walls are cracked like the other one was. Can we do it, Peter?"

Peter bobbed his head. "Okay, Momma."

Selpha handed control of the recording over to Peter, almost as worried as she was hopeful.

Paolo shook his head at his own inadequacy. Aargh! How could he have missed it? Now that the 'cast was up, it seemed obvious. And it was in his field of expertise. He should have been the one to post that 'cast. Blast it, he himself had made the deduction that led to this next natural conclusion.

On the other hand, with a couple billion active participants, it really shouldn't surprise him if, even in his own field, people regularly beat him to the punch. His failure to draw the obvious conclusion beautifully illustrated the flaw in the Web's foolish gossip about the Predictor: even if you were a thousand times more likely to root out good forecasts than anyone else, you would have less than one chance in a thousand of being the first one to invent a new analysis. Of course, Paolo, thought with a determined smile, he had better than a mere thousand-fold improvement on the average. Nonetheless, the principle still stood.

Paolo alerted the rest of his team to the new forecast. They just had to come up with a good analysis of this issue, not only for profit, but also to save the Angels from a terrible mistake whichever way it turned out.

He looked at the preliminary results coming in from his team and felt a touch of sorrow. It would be a lot easier for everyone if the forecast were correct, and the Gate was just in the same old place, just a little harder to open. But according to his own preliminaries, it wasn't true. Even adjusting the analysis to assume that the third

corridor from the Alabaster Hall had been sealed—an
assumption that went beyond the confidence level they
could assign to the proposition—other anomalies in the
construction of this ship suggested that the entrance had
been relocated along with the innermost ring of robot
repair bays.

Preliminary results weren't enough for something this
important. Every reducible doubt had to be removed.
Paolo shot off a consulting request to the brand that
had first theorized about the fracture, to see what
additional information he could buy to fold into his
analysis.

Selpha's eyes glowed in satisfaction. Now that someone had posted the sealed-entrance forecast, requests
for information were pouring in from all over the world.
She had over a dozen consulting contracts in her hand,
all asking for her best answer on the same question that
Earth Defense had asked: Was there a crack in the hall
where Buzz Hikmet had died?

Unfortunately, Peter's analysis was inconclusive almost
to the point of uselessness. Consequently Selpha felt she
couldn't charge a lot for the answer—better to set up
a quality relationship with these people, in preparation
for future contracts—but still, it was almost free money.
She sent to each requester the same careful assessment
she had made for Earth Defense.

Upon completing the contracts, she realized there
were probably other people who would be interested
in the results. She posted her assessment as a simple
document on several of the EDA-related eMarkets. In
the next half hour, she sold almost seventy copies to
people and companies around the world. She still kept
the price low, though, for her summary conclusion was
not very exciting: amidst the noise and vibration of the
battle, she could find no evidence of a crack in the wall
from the Angel One recordings.

✧   ✧   ✧

Jessica drew a deep breath. She watched as the odds seesawed wildly. The trading volume started to stabilize the assessment, but as the volatility waned so did the early enthusiasm for the 'cast. The odds favoring a sealed Gate in the usual location fell below fifty percent, and only leveled off around thirty-five percent.

A soft ping announced the activation of her window to General Samuels. "Don't be disappointed," he said. "You had a brilliant insight, and we had to pursue it."

"I probably shouldn't have bothered to post the 'cast at all, after the initial report from fracture analysts."

"No, posting it was the right thing to do. With as much uncertainty as they had, it only made sense to pursue the matter further, to see if anyone in the assembled multitudes could make a better assessment." He shrugged. "Actually, it looks like the assembled multitudes *did* make a better assessment, just not the one we'd hoped for." He raised his fist, thumb extended upward in a sign of upbeat confirmation. "Keep at it."

Jessica smiled wanly. "Back to work," she said. She turned her attention back to the seven screens that represented Morgan's world.

Chapter Twelve

The Weapons of the Destroyer

CJ and her compatriots raced counterclockwise around the ship. According to the 'cast, it made little difference if they went left or right at the end of the halls—the forecasts predicted that the distance to the slidechutes was the same either way. A weak prediction held that there were fewer robot storage bays counterclockwise, hence a slightly smaller range of opponents. But the most important feature of the counterclockwise direction was that this was the way Angel One had gone, and they had won through. Angel Two would try to build on that success.

CJ and Lars came to the intersection with a radial corridor that shot straight inward, toward the ship axis. A trio of recon pyramids already lay scattered in the intersection like a child's jacks, thrown earlier by Roni as he turned the corner. CJ looked into the mirrored, curved faces of the pyramids to make sure nothing lay around the corner, to ensure that nothing had gotten between them and Roni. With only the barest pause, she and Lars swept around the corner. Akira scooped up the pyramids on his way past, tossing them casually to CJ, who stashed them in the trailer. Lars lazily threw a laser relay against the ceiling. Their link to the Web remained unbroken.

Half a klick ahead, CJ could make out Roni moving in a staccato rhythm—a quick burst of speed from the bike, followed by a long, perfectly motionless pause as he surveyed the shipscape before him: the next chunk of the hallway, the openings to the various rooms nearby, and the other corridors along crossing the main hall.

These damn hallways were so boring and dull they made CJ crazy. She knew she should be thankful for the empty simplicity of the passage, but it was not in her nature.

Roni stopped again. This time he put his ear to the wall. From CJ's position it looked like a shadow hung in front of Roni, probably a doorway. Roni listened a moment, then went past the doorway and turned. CJ was not surprised when Morgan cleared his throat.

"Expect a dozen or so repair mechs," Morgan advised.

Lars slowed down. CJ hopped to the ground. Everyone unlimbered their spikes.

Morgan spoke again. "Axel, knock on the door."

Axel smiled. "No problem," he said, and slammed the wall with his staff.

The door opened. Half a dozen repair mechs straggled out, blades in hand. Much simpler targets than the roboguards they looked so much like—without breastplates, they would be quick kills.

"Akira, Axel, CJ, take 'em." The two opposing groups charged each other. In a moment, each of the three Angels had taken down an opponent, retreating as they did so to avoid the outflanking maneuver of the other three mechs.

Axel grumbled, "Too easy." He turned with CJ and Akira to the remaining three mechs.

A heavy footfall came from the doorway, and all the Angels looked to see what it was. Axel jumped back, exclaiming, "Holy Christ. It looks bigger here than in the videos."

A Destroyer stepped beneath the arch of the door, weaving slightly as it turned to face the center of the Angel team. It stepped into the corridor, waving its heavy-barreled gun at chest height. The machine's oversized broadsword, socketed directly to its shoulder and elbow, hung limply at its side.

The thing had not seen Roni on the far side of the doorway. Roni exploited the error, jumping the Destroyer from behind. Roni lunged twice, the point of his spike probing for an opening in the robot's close-meshed armor plates. The Destroyer swiped casually back with its right hand, knocking him down the hall. Then it stopped weaving and stood very still. The gun came up, clicked once, and started to fire, straight at CJ.

As the gun steadied on her, CJ was already leaping, up and forward and toward the center of the hall. The bullets missed her. She heard an explosion and glanced back to see what had happened.

The stream of bullets had torn into the trailer, with all their supplies. Secondary explosions, from the caseless ammo stored there, had turned the trailer into a fireball. Lars had been thrown against the wall by the force of the blast; CJ couldn't tell if he was dead, hurt, or ready to play. She realized that the Destroyer hadn't been aiming at her at all; she had merely been in the path of the Destroyer's true focus.

Jessica's heart leaped in her throat. What could they do? They hadn't managed to kill even one of those things in the Angel One assault. Everyone had known they would face Destroyers again on this round, but not this soon—Angel One hadn't seen any of the things till they'd gotten to center level.

Now the team was split by the Destroyer: CJ and Roni were down the hall from it, while Axel, Lars, and Akira remained out-axis.

Jessica reviewed the events of the earlier assault. After being hacked horribly by the first Destroyer, Angel One had dealt with the problem by retreating toward the center of the ship. This was not an option for Angel Two, unless they could find a way to circle through the corridors and regroup. Jessica prayed Morgan didn't share her own rising panic.

The Destroyer started to weave again. That was strange; she couldn't remember seeing them do that in the recordings from the first assault. The broadsword still hung limply at its side. Jessica choked down her terror and peered intently at the Destroyer. Something was wrong with it. Inspecting the thing from the safety of her cocoon, she then saw that the left leg was only partly armored.

She slapped herself on the forehead. "Of course," she muttered. "They were building this one. It's not done yet."

"CJ," Morgan commanded, "the left leg is weak. Destroy it."

CJ drew her eyes away from the machine's weapons and saw the missing plates. She hurled herself forward as the gun barked again, against whom or what she had no idea. She thrust the tip of her spike into the space between the plates, just above the knee, and twisted.

The Destroyer fell over as its leg collapsed. Its gun burst into action again, this time firing wildly into the floor. The chattering ceased; CJ heard the gun click repeatedly. "It's out of ammo," she cried triumphantly. "Kill it."

Axel and Akira joined her within moments; Roni arrived a second later. The damn thing had too much armor to be an easy kill, even lying on the ground, weaponless. One of its hands reached out and grabbed at the calf of Axel's leg. A sharp crack of sound announced the shattering of his armor frame. CJ thrust with desperate ferocity to stop the machine before it crushed Axel's leg as well.

Another spike suddenly jammed its way into the Destroyer's shoulder socket. CJ heard a grunt of pure effort, and saw Lars' face, focused and deadly. He heaved, and the Destroyer's arm popped from its socket. The hand that had been crushing Axel's leg, detached from its owner, sprang open.

CJ dropped her spike and grabbed her pellet gun. "Here," she told the Destroyer sweetly as she thrust the barrel into the exposed shoulder socket. "Enjoy." She pulled the trigger, and the Destroyer rocked gently as the pellets bounced around inside its case. She ceased fire. The Destroyer lay still.

Axel hopped over and clasped Lars on the shoulder. "Thanks, big guy. Remind me never to shake hands with one of those things." Axel turned, took one step, and collapsed on the floor as his leg gave from under him. "Damn," he muttered. "I guess it's broken."

CJ knelt over him. Akira was already picking up the two longest shards of the shattered frame leg to use as a splint. In less than a minute they had Axel standing again, though, as CJ said, "It's gonna be a little hard for you to run until we get back."

"Check, CJ," Axel said with a smile that started and ended with his mouth; his eyes said he knew better.

Roni exclaimed, "Look here." He pointed through the door.

CJ stood up from the defunct Destroyer to peer around her tall companion. "Looks like the academics back home were right. They really do build all these things out of the same old robot parts." Laying on a table was a chameleon of a machine. The top half was a Destroyer. The bottom half was a repair mech.

❖   ❖   ❖

Paolo whistled appreciatively.

Sofia called from another room. "I heard that. Are you looking at pictures of naked women on the Web in there?"

"Sweet Sofia, you know I only have eyes for you," he yelled back.

"Then what was that wolf-whistle about?"

"They found a half-built, deactivated Destroyer. We could learn incredible things from it." They might even learn how to kill one of the blasted machines, though he wasn't going to hold his breath.

"That's just wonderful, darling. I guess." Sofia sounded quite doubtful; Paolo suspected she might have been happier if he'd been looking at pictures of other women. Sofia could compete quite successfully against another woman for his attentions. But a half-built Destroyer presented a more complex problem.

Paolo turned back to his team conference and their private 'castpoint. He was fascinated on a personal level with the analysis of the enemy robot. But whatever treasures it might reveal, they were not directly relevant to his field of expertise. For him and his team, the most interesting bit of information had already been revealed. Namely, this room was a machine shop, a repair station for *Shiva* robots. They would feed this bit of information into their analysis, and see if it helped them forecast other bits of the ship layout.

Morgan shook his head. Finding a Destroyer to study was the kind of marvelous opportunity you desperately wanted . . . until the opportunity arose, at which point you realized you faced too many choices to exploit any one of them fully. Which dangerous course should they pursue?

He looked through the vidscreens at the machine stretched on the workbench—the *Shiva* version of an operating table. There lay the captured, virtually intact Destroyer. It was a prize of incomparable value. It was a prize that could easily get his CJ and his team killed.

On the one hand, over a thousand prizes had been posted already from people around the world, requesting that the Angels stay and examine the machine. On the other hand, every minute they stayed, the likelihood that reinforcements would show up grew exponentially. The dilemma was neatly captured by the odds now appearing on forecasts about how soon the team would be destroyed if they stayed, while other forecasts blossomed with other odds on their pathetic chances if they didn't learn how to destroy the Destroyers.

He looked at his watch. With a visible clenching of his teeth, he muttered to himself, "Fifteen minutes, not a minute more, not a minute less, no matter what."

The Dealer stood up and started pacing, the touchscreen in his hands. He'd put his money up on the prizeboard along with a lot of other people, and Earth Defense had listened to their united plea. He had fifteen minutes to figure out how to destroy the Destroyers. What an opportunity! If only he could figure out how to exploit it.

He watched the Angels crowbar the plates off the machine, exposing wiring and objects of varying sizes and shapes. It made him impatient. The internal wiring would be interesting, but didn't strike to the heart of the question. What was the machine's weakness? How would Sun Tzu take down a Destroyer?

One of the Angels levered the Destroyer's gun out of its socket. It rolled, exposing the wiring that led into the firing mechanism from the Destroyer's midriff. And the Dealer shivered as an electric shock of excitement rushed through him. He knew the answer. He would use the Destroyer's own gun to destroy the Destroyer. Of course.

❖   ❖   ❖

CJ clapped her hands. A giddy, little-girl quality filled her voice. "Morgan, you really believe we can patch up this gun so that we can fire it ourselves?"

"Everybody here seems to think so," Morgan replied. "Hook it up and find out."

Akira had already bent to the task, splicing optic fibers to the gun leads. Axel pulled out his pellet pistol and stripped it down, extracting the trigger mechanism. In a minute and a half they were done.

Axel smiled. "I have got to check this out," he said, standing up with the gun in his hands.

CJ plucked it from his fingers. "Naughty boy, Axel. Don't you know that it's ladies first?" She held the weapon awkwardly. "I can see this isn't going to be all fun and games. We could really use a shoulder stock on it."

Lars roared, "Next time we'll put in our order early."

CJ shrugged. Then in a sudden motion she raised the weapon, aimed at the far wall, and pulled the trigger. A single shot produced a trio of violent noises that echoed in the room: first, the sound of the gun firing; second, the sound of the bullet blasting a hole in the ceramic wall; and third, the sound of CJ landing on her back as the recoil knocked her from her feet. "Wow," she said with delight, her enthusiasm unimpaired. "So many guns, so little time."

Lars bent over her. "Perhaps you should let someone built like a Destroyer handle the Destroyer's gun, Boss Lady." He held out his hands. CJ reluctantly handed it over. "Thank you," Lars said with warm mirth.

CJ stood up. "At least we have confirmation, those guns must be shooting depleted-uranium ammo. Couldn't have knocked me down, otherwise."

Axel pointed out the door. "You know, there's another gun just outside."

Roni shook his head. "It's empty. Do we know how to reload these things? Or where to find ammo if we do?"

CJ waved her hands, brushing the questions aside. "Have faith in the Web, guys. If we have the gun, somebody'll figure out how to use it." She glided toward the door.

Roni thrust his hand against her chest. "Just a minute, there, Boss Lady. I'm the recon guy here. And now that hall is a recon objective." Keeping CJ at bay with one hand, he tossed a pyramid through the door into the hall with the other. "You always have to make sure there's no—" A sudden burst of gunfire interrupted Roni's lecture and turned the pyramid into powder. A pair of Destroyers stepped around the corner, weapons trained. The noise of a hail of gunfire rattled the room, and—

The Destroyers disintegrated, leaving behind spumes of powder as fine and harmless as the remnants of the pyramid. Lars leaned over and theatrically blew the smoke from the tip of his barrel. "Now *that's* the way to fight a Destroyer." He held the weapon high. "This here is a monster gun, folks."

Morgan's voice interrupted. "Expect four minitanks."

Everyone but Axel leaped to the inner side of the wall; Axel was still hobbling out of the way when the tanks came through the doorway, two at a time. The tanks really didn't have a chance, even though Lars had stowed his handheld cannon; the Angels were ready. The battle lasted less than a minute.

Roni threw out another pyramid. This time no one fired on it. They stepped into a clear hallway.

The Dealer listened to the Angels chatter about the Destroyer gun with a sense of pride. It was his idea, after all, that got them so excited.

And CJ was right about the gun in the hallway. Somehow, they ought to be able to make use of that one as well. But how would you reload those things?

Chan Kam Yin flickered through the vid footage of the guns, freezing half a dozen frames in their own windows for closer scrutiny. The magazine on the weapon looked like an old-fashioned drum magazine, the kind you saw in black-and-white American gangster movies. But the unit was completely sealed. He needed a way to make a hole in it big enough to load ammo but small enough, and out-of-the-way enough, to not interfere with the weapon's action.

He figured out where he wanted to cut out a section of the device. Now the question was how. The Angels didn't have a machine shop for working ceramic parts. Should they burn a hole in the ceramic case with the new molecular acid? You sure couldn't use explosives for such a delicate operation.

Or could you? He knew just who to ask.

Lou heard someone snoring while the chime on his touchscreen rang insistently. As his irritation with the twin noises rose, so did his level of awareness; he finally recognized that he was the person doing the snoring.

As he reached consciousness, the snoring stopped, but the chime remained. He slapped his hand down irritably to make the connection. "Yes?" he asked thickly.

Viktor's broad face filled half a window. A much younger, Oriental face filled the other. He felt like he ought to recognize the Oriental. Then his eyes lost focus; he still wasn't awake yet.

Viktor waved. "Conference call. You remember Chan Kam Yin?"

Lou blinked, scrunching his face around to try to get some blood flow. "Oh, yeah, Kam Yin, hi." He stretched his arms. "I'm still coming back to life. Sorry."

"Sleepyhead," Viktor chided him. "You need to exercise more."

"You come over here anytime, Viktor and we'll run a marathon and see who finishes first," Lou retorted. He leaned forward. "How're our Angels doing?"

Viktor nodded his head. "Pretty good. One broken

leg, but they took a Destroyer apart and figured out how
to use its gun."

"Great."

Viktor agreed. "They are doing very well, indeed. But
we want them to do better. Kam Yin, could you explain
for Lou your idea for reloading the second gun?"

Lou listened to the boy explain the problem in his
halting English. Lou could feel a sense of impatience
every time he thought about the Angels' plight while
he sat here waiting for the explanation to rattle to a
conclusion, knowing that Viktor had already heard this
explanation and could get through the essentials ten
times as fast. But he understood Viktor's purpose. And
he supposed that teaching the younger generation was
a never-ending task, a task that shouldn't be cut off, even
with *Shiva* closing on them at meteoric speed.

Kam Yin finished, "How do we open the ammo case?
Viktor says he can open the case with duodec more
safely than molecular acid."

Lou laughed. "Surgical duodec, Viktor?"

"With the right thin bead, we can make a clean
fracture in the ceramic," Viktor replied huffily. "Try that
with acid."

Lou nodded. "He's right, Kam Yin, despite his
prejudices. Let us draw up a plan for you and get back
in about fifteen minutes, okay?"

Kam Yin nodded. He looked uncomfortable. Finally
he blurted out, "What sort of contract do you want?"

Viktor waved the matter aside. "Our first recommendation is free. The second one, though, Kam Yin,
will cost you."

Kam Yin looked surprised. "Thank you," he said, and
logged off.

Lou frowned. "Our first recommendation is free?
When did that start happening, Viktor? Particularly for
a person you yourself described as a con artist? "

"Lou, Lou, we are trying to help this boy grow to
be a better person. I'll bet no one has ever helped him

for free in his life. We're setting a good example." Viktor closed one eye and peered at him from the other. "Besides, what's an old miser like you need more money for, anyway? At least in the good old days we could shoot people for being as tight with a nickel as you."

"In the good old days your whole country had only a handful of nickels, Viktor, and the State owned all of them."

"It was not perfect," Viktor conceded.

"An amazing concession. And now, let's lay out a det charge."

Morgan's voice finished, "You see the schematic on your left windshield?"

CJ gurgled with joy. "You bet, Morgan. Axel, can you lay a line of duodec that precise?"

"No problem, Boss Lady."

"Okay, let's break for a minute. Akira, you copy?"

Far down the hall she could see Akira come to a halt. "I await your pleasure. But please ensure that our delightful Axel acts with speed as well as care."

"I love you, too," Axel replied, ending the words with a kissing sound. He dismounted and knelt over the empty firearm.

Lars asked, "You have some duodec?"

Axel said, "Of course. I never leave home without it." He set to work.

Despite Akira's jibe about speed, Axel had a delicate task that would take several minutes. Waiting as patiently as she could, CJ rocked back and forth on her heels, dimly aware of her own inability to stop moving. She studied the disposition of their team with a sense of frustration. The layout's imperfections bugged her, but she could not think of any way to improve it.

The destroyer that had blown away the trailer had also nailed another pair of cycles, drawing them down to just two wheeled vehicles. Axel rode one of them— he had to ride, to keep up—and CJ had put Lars on the other one, carrying the weight of the last of their supplies salvaged from the trailer. The bottom line was that the team could move no faster than she could walk with her suit amplification set low to conserve power.

Meanwhile, she'd sent Akira out as recon, holding Roni back to use the second destroyer gun once they had it operational—Axel couldn't handle the recoil with his injury, and though CJ enjoyed joking about wanting the gun in her own hands, she knew that neither she nor Akira was big enough to handle the damn thing properly.

Overall, the situation was good compared to the situation of a typical Angel team, but CJ wanted more. Standing here in the quiet hall, unable to act, the fear caught up with her. She could feel control of the situation slipping away from her . . . as it had ultimately slipped away from every other Angel team in history. She shook her head violently to dispel the thought. Lars spotted the motion, and she could see the concern in his eyes. "It's nothing," she told him before he could speak.

A soft sound of cracking ceramic caught her attention. Axel stood up, gun in hand. "Got it," he said with pride. "Now all we need is some ammo."

MacBride's voice answered. "There's a storeroom two rings out from the slidechutes. You should find ammo there."

Roni took the gun from Axel. "Great."

CJ shook her head. "But is it great enough, Morgan? Will the welcoming party at the slidechutes let us break into the storeroom without trying to stop us, just two rings away?"

In the silence that followed, she could imagine Morgan shrugging his shoulders, thousands of miles out of position to help. Worse, she could almost hear him trying to figure out how to protect her, rather than worrying about reaching the goal. If Morgan tried to keep her out of the pending danger, she would have to . . .

With an effort, CJ regained control of her dark thoughts. She straightened, she smiled, and she forced her normal attitudes to wash back through her mind; it felt like fresh rain. "Why's everybody standing around? Move out." She hurried, too fast, feeling Lars' eyes still on her.

Chapter Thirteen

The Slidechute

CJ could just barely make out Akira, moving slowly forward in the distance. They'd built the armor frames to have the same sandstone texture and color as *Shiva's* halls, and the camouflage worked pretty well, at least for human eyes. She felt less confident about how well it worked against the eyes of *Shiva*.

Straining to see, a motion close to Akira startled her. Then she realized it was Roni. Once again she wondered how Roni did that, disappearing in the middle of the damn hall. Well, that was why he was recon, not somebody else.

Akira jumped catlike to Roni's shoulders and went to work on the ceiling. Then Roni muttered, "Shit. They see us."

CJ shouted to Lars and Axel, "Move!" She dialed her suit to full amplification and started loping down the hall, keeping up with Lars and Axel quite nicely even though they rode bikes.

CJ heard Roni grunt with effort as he pushed Akira closer to the ceiling. She could see Akira's hands now as a blur of speed, laying out the lattice of duodec.

Morgan's voice murmured in her head with the analysis. "Eighteen Mark II minitanks in the first squadron." Eighteen of them! Christ! She could see them beyond Roni and Akira, moving as fast as she was, a swarm of monstrous beetles that covered the floor of the hall. It was going to be too close a race.

CJ wanted to tell Lars to open fire with the monster gun, but she knew she couldn't do that quite yet. They needed that weapon to kill the Destroyers they would surely encounter on the center level, and they didn't know they would really find ammo in the storeroom yet; they didn't even really know that the reloading system would work. Even if it meant spending blood and lives, they dared not spend the ammo.

CJ snapped, "Axel, when we get there, get that damn storeroom open. I wanna see if we've got ammo or not. I don't care what else is happening, you get that room open."

"Check, Boss Lady."

She wasn't going to make it in time. The lead minitank swung its sword back, preparatory to cutting Roni in half. CJ fired a burst from her pellet gun, not to kill the tank—the angle was wrong—but to slow it down. And for half a second, the minitank hesitated.

Roni fell away from the tank as Akira jumped forward, off Roni's shoulders, into a spin that brought him down with a crashing kick to the minitank's swordarm. The sword snapped off. The three minitanks right behind leaped on Akira. The ceiling exploded. Huge chunks of roof rained down on the minitanks. CJ, Lars, and Roni fired at the exposed bowels of six more minitanks trying to scurry over the debris. Axel slewed his bike in a three-sixty, stopping with grace and precision adjacent to the storeroom lock. His hand snapped out; his electronic lock-picker slapped down, covering the lock. A thousand experts on Earth joined Axel in his private assault on the lock.

The muffled sound of a pellet gun came from the bottom of the pile of debris. Akira still lived, buried under the minitanks.

Another minitank made it across the wreckage unharmed, grabbing Axel. Roni hooked the minitank with his spike and heaved. Armor plate cracked as the minitank's sword struck Axel in the abdomen. Axel jerked but did not collapse in two pieces; the minitank's blow had been twisted to an off-angle by Roni's efforts. Axel continued to work the lock.

Roni swung his spike up into the minitank. It jerked to a stop.

CJ slid under an overhanging ledge of ceramic debris, feet first, like a baseball player sliding into second base. A minitank, seeing her so helpless, started climbing down from its perch to get her. The tank didn't realize that this had been CJ's hope, to entice the minitank to expose its belly. CJ fired, blowing the tank's undercarriage apart. More minitanks approached her. They were all easy targets from her new vantage, but there were too many of them. She killed three more. A fourth grabbed her arm, smashing the pellet gun against the rock.

The storeroom door popped open. Axel whistled. "All the ammo you can eat."

Lars dropped his pellet gun. The arm of CJ's frame fractured into a dozen pieces. A minitank swept an arm underneath Roni's legs, flipping him onto his back.

Lars and his monster gun fired. Trails of ceramic dust followed the stream of bullets from his weapon, and the raging sound echoed down the hall. Confident he could reload with the ammo Axel had just found, he kept shooting till he was dry.

Silence filled the room.

A voice spoke over the radio, "Is anybody left out there, or do I have to deliver the football all by myself?" It was Akira.

CJ shouted with joy. "Akira!" She pulled herself out from under her ledge, by which time Lars and Roni had already dug halfway through the pile.

They reached Akira half a minute later. CJ asked, "You okay?"

Akira smiled. "I am much better than the three minitanks you just removed." Blood bubbled from his mouth. He coughed. "Perhaps not that much better, however," he conceded.

Lars and Roni lifted him gently from the rubble. He tried to sit up, sank back down. Roni spoke to him sternly. "Damn it Akira, you can't die on us yet. The recon guy is always the first one to get killed. Don't you dare try to hog my spotlight."

CJ felt a moment's burst of anger. She barked at Akira, "Why'd you jump on those tanks like that? Did you feel the need to commit suicide?"

"They were about to strike Roni. You need Roni to fire the second monster gun."

CJ didn't let go. "Roni can take care of himself. Where'd you get the idea you should sacrifice yourself for him?"

"MacBride told me."

CJ rocked back on her heels like she'd been hit in the face. How did Morgan dare think of ranking the value of each individual team member and discarding the lesser ones?

Of course, he was right. Damn him anyway.

Jessica stood outside her cocoon, staring into it, reluctant to take the next inward step that would transport her from the nice little office to the terrible world of *Shiva*. She'd just gone to the bathroom—one of the things they still hadn't integrated with cocoon technology—and she was grateful for the break. She raised her arms and stretched, in a mirror-image of the motion she had taken upon stepping out of the cocoon in the first place. Her fingers and toes tingled at the effort.

She stepped inside and rooted around till she was comfortable, studiously keeping her eyes off the screens and windows to *Shiva*. She knew what she would see if she looked, unless something terrible had happened during her break. Of course, terrible things during the break were probably the rule, not the exception.

The Angels were taking a break too, before hop-running the slidechutes. Of course, for the Angels a break was a bit more work-related than for others. During their break, they reloaded the monster guns. And worked on their injuries. And tried to keep Akira alive.

Jessica shook her head, thinking about the nutcases they'd sent to *Shiva* to save all humankind. Axel had a bruise across his chest the size of Texas. His response, when CJ asked him how he was, had been straight from a teenager from the rough side of Chicago. "Enough with the foreplay, CJ," he'd said with a smile.

When Morgan asked the same question of CJ, she held out her right arm, with a ring of purple bruised flesh where the minitank had grabbed her. As she clenched and unclenched her hand, she explained, "You know, it hurts a lot less than your blasted electroshocks in the sims."

Nutcases. The 'castpoint gave CJ roughly even odds on having a hairline fracture to the ulna in her forearm.

Roni had a puncture wound in his left thigh, but you couldn't tell when he walked. Of course, he was being careful not to run.

She heard General Samuels' voice, soft and concerned. "Jessica. How're you holding up?"

She looked up; he was on the screen to her left. "Okay, I guess. But I don't think I could have told Akira to take on those minitanks to protect Roni."

Samuels glanced offscreen, no doubt at a recording of earlier events. "But you predicted correctly that Morgan would tell him to do so."

Jessica nodded. "Yeah. But telling him to do it myself . . ." She shuddered.

Samuels nodded sympathetically. "Nonetheless, things are going pretty well so far."

Jessica shuddered again. "I know. That may be the most terrifying thing of all, that this is what it's like when it's going well."

CJ held the fractured axle of what had recently been Axel's bike, staring at it forlornly. *Shiva*'s robots went after the bikes and trailers with a methodical determination, as if they considered the machines more dangerous than the people who manned them. CJ sighed. At least she still had one bike left for Axel, which was more than Angel One had had by the time they reached the slide-chutes.

She looked up at the sound of coughing. Akira was sitting up now. CJ knelt next to him and handed him the axle to the bike. "Morgan and the Web will help you patch the bike together," she told him with a voice that sounded grotesquely perky, even to herself. "Then you can catch up with us."

"Excellent," Akira replied. A spasm of coughs racked his body. "I'll be with you shortly."

"Don't sweat it if it takes some time," CJ continued. "As a worst case, we'll pick you up on the way back out."

Amusement danced around Akira's eyes, though the rest of his face remained as impassive as ever. "There are ten billion people in the world, CJ, but only you could believe that." He shook his head. "Worse. When you say it, even I believe it." He saluted her.

Morgan's voice interrupted. "Go," was all he said.

CJ stood up. "Okay, let's do it!" She stepped to the lip of the forty-five-degree chute, looked to make sure everyone was ready with her, and hopped onto the slide.

Her practice with the ice slides in Nevada had not been enough to prepare her, she learned instantly. She lost her balance . . . but her speed and training saved

her from falling down. Her arms compensated as she
knelt low and accelerated down the slope.

Despite the throbbing of her arm, despite the quiet
understanding gnawing at her that Akira was as good
as dead, CJ could not help enjoying the slide. She hadn't
really believed the stories Morgan told, or the video
commentary by the other Angels who had taken this trip
before: the slides were perfectly frictionless. Actually,
after watching hundreds of tapes and running thousands
of simulations, the physicists had concluded that there
was, just barely, the tiniest bit of drag from the floor.
Now CJ doubted the physicists, not Morgan.

She'd had a tiny, tiny bit of rotational energy as she
stepped onto the slide. She had to use her hands
outstretched behind her in a "V" to prevent the slight
initial rotation from spinning her around. She could see
out the corners of her eyes how the others were doing.
Lars, with his monster gun in one hand, was having
more trouble than she was, though Roni seemed to be
doing just fine. Axel, however, was in real trouble. He'd
chosen to try to ride the bike down, and he just couldn't
get enough control. So he'd lost all control now and was
spinning helplessly as he accelerated down the slide.
"Look alive, Roni! If the bad guys show up down here,
it's just you and me."

Roni grunted assent.

The next floor arrived all too quickly. CJ sprang from
the slide as she reached the bottom, and this bit of the
training worked perfectly: she landed on her feet well
clear of the other Angels sliding in behind her, with her
spike at the ready.

As the Web had predicted, no minions of *Shiva*
waited for them. Which was fortunate, because her
prediction had also been right: Lars and Axel landed
in a heap at the bottom.

By the end of the third slide, they'd gotten the hang
of it. Axel was leading his bike down, sliding on one
leg. He was still clumsy getting off the slide . . . but

then, he was clumsy with only one leg fully operational anyway.

From somewhere on the Web came the suggestion that they rip Axel's shirt into pieces and string it across the bike to make a stall chute. Axel slid down this time in a sitting position, with the bike dragging air behind him. It worked beautifully.

Soon CJ lost track of the slides they'd run, the chutes they had yet to slide. All she knew was that it was as close to joy as she would get on this ride, and she rode it with gusto.

It could not, however, last. Eventually Morgan informed them, "Okay, folks, this is it. Next stop is the center level." As one, the Angels stopped. No *Shiva* had ever tried to ambush Angels on the slides to the center. But every *Shiva* had set up a welcoming party at the center level itself. This was where Angel One had first encountered the Destroyers. No one doubted that this time the opposition would be deadlier still.

CJ peered down the last chute. As with all the other slides, she could not see much at the bottom: the floor to her level, and the ceiling of the level below, blocked the view. She could see where they would land, but an army could lurk a sword's length away and stay hidden. She knelt down beside the chute, pulled out a recon pyramid, and placed it gently on the slope. It slid away with growing speed, till it reached the bottom.

A huge roar echoed up the chute—the sound of Destroyer guns chained together in terribly harmony. CJ muttered, "Sounds like there are a thousand of them down there. It's a real hornet's nest."

No speck of the pyramid remained large enough to see. Her teammates stood about silently, uncertain what to do.

CJ just knelt there, until finally she had an inspiration. "Hey, Morgan," she yelled, as if shouting made a difference. "You think we could get them to empty their magazines?"

She heard a sound that might have been a laugh, muffled by a hasty grunt to disguise his appreciation. "By all means try it."

Still kneeling by the shoot, CJ cocked her head. "Axel, toss me another pyramid if you would, dear."

"Comin' at ya." A pyramid flew through the air to her waiting hand.

Once again she gently pushed a pyramid down the chute. This time a single gun fired, a single shot. A half dozen shards of mirrored glass flew in the air. A sword flicked into view, swept them away, and disappeared again. The sword identifiably belonged to a minitank Mark II.

Morgan spoke first. "Well, it was a good idea." He clucked his tongue. "In fact, it probably helped us a good deal."

CJ didn't see how he'd drawn that conclusion, but if he was happy, she was happy. She stood up and unsnapped her spike. "Time to rock?"

Morgan responded sharply. "No. Take a rest while we think about this."

Axel popped open the top of his water bottle. "Sounds good to me," he said, dropping to the floor.

Selpha watched as Peter once again listened to the first burst of fire at the base of the slidechute. To CJ it might have sounded like a thousand Destroyers, but Selpha knew better, and she was pretty sure that Peter could prove it.

"Eight," Peter said at last.

"You're sure?"

He responded instantly. "Yes." His hands flew about in a pattern only he understood. "Lots of other stuff, don't know what."

"Thank you, Peter." Selpha turned back to her touchscreen. Someone else had already posted a forecast that there were eight Destroyers at the bottom of the chute. The odds were still good, though, so she bought in.

She didn't do anything with Peter's comment about lots of other stuff. Everyone already knew that, after all.

CJ was not surprised by the plan that evolved during their rest break. In the end Morgan made a proposal, and the Angels accepted. The proposal would not win the award for best idea of the century, but it was, she admitted, better than a simple charge of the Light Brigade.

They practiced the maneuver a dozen times, using the last few feet of the slidechute from which they had just emerged. Each time Lars and Roni slid head-first down the chute and bumped their heads against the floor. Each time CJ covered her mouth so no one could see her laughter. When the bumps had finally gotten as refined as seemed likely, CJ called a halt. "Guys, it looks like you two are about as good at this as you're going to get. Morgan, in the future you may want to make the Angels practice this a bit more ahead of time."

"You can count on it," Morgan replied grimly.

Lars and Roni flipped to their feet, Roni with a graceful arc, Lars with an irritable grunt.

Lars said, "I've spent so much time upside down, it's starting to look right-side up to me."

Roni chuckled. "That's the way it's supposed to be."

Lars grunted. "Let's get this over with." He lay down on his back, his head just an inch over the lip of the slidechute, his right shoulder by the left edge of chute. Roni took a similar position on the opposite side. Axel took a kneeling position at Roni's feet.

CJ stepped to the middle of the chute, pyramid in hand. "Here we go," she said as she let the pyramid slip from her hand and begin sliding. She dashed over to Lars and, in a swift synchronization with Axel, pushed Lars over the edge as Axel pushed Roni.

Headfirst, guns poised, the two Angels slid upside down into the killing zone. CJ and Axel gave them a three-second head start. Then, spikes in hand, they followed.

The following moments seemed like the longest and loneliest years of CJ's experience. The earlier slidechutes had been a joy-ride; now, all she knew was that, no matter how terrible the consequences, she could not stop until she came face-to-face with the enemy swarm.

Destroyer guns opened fire. The pyramid in the center of the chute dissolved. Then the sound of Destroyer guns came to life again, much closer—it was Lars firing this time. Roni echoed the roar on the far side.

CJ shouted, "Yes!" The pyramid had distracted the Destroyers, and now the Angels were getting in the first deadly shots of the battle.

Her scream of victory was drowned by the bellow of more guns. She could see chunks of slidechute flooring jump up as streams of bullets trained on Lars and Roni.

And the two Angels were easy targets: the recoil from their gunfire had eaten their forward momentum; they were now sliding very slowly back up the chute. The streams of bullets reached their bodies, and—

CJ reached Lars first and shoved him forward, out of the spray of death. Pushing Lars forward drove her backward, till she stopped for a moment on the slide, then accelerated down into the focus of fire herself.

The roar of machine guns ceased. Everyone was out of bullets.

Having pushed Lars ahead of her, he was now accelerating away, into the middle of a circle of mini-tanks. CJ knew he didn't have much of a chance, upside down, of defending himself. She jumped from the slidechute surface, screaming, hoping to distract the tanks. The screaming failed to attract their attention, but her landing on the middle one could not be disregarded. The minitank sagged to the floor beneath her, and her spike swept out at the one farther from the wall, sweeping its blade arm away from Lars.

The minitank against the wall did, however, strike

true. Lars grunted as blood sprayed from the right side of his chest. He twisted, trying to get up and away. CJ turned to the minitank, wedged her spike beneath it, and flipped it with the smooth technique she had practiced a thousand times in SimHell. A second swift motion later, her spike thrust home. The tank ceased to move

Lars had his spike out and managed to block another blow from the minitank farthest from the wall.

The tank upon which CJ stood heaved itself up. Another person might have been knocked off balance, but CJ simply flipped lightly off, landing with pellet gun in hand. The loss of her weight left the tank suddenly extended to its full height, its belly far from the ground. CJ's blast of pellets ricocheted from the floor into its belly. It collapsed in a heap.

Lars blocked another blow from the third of their foes, got his spike underneath, and flipped it into position for an easy kill, just as CJ had done the other one.

CJ looked up to see what she faced next, faintly surprised that she hadn't already been struck down while protecting Lars from the closest three tanks. Her mouth opened in wonder.

Through the still-settling dust she could see the carcasses of more than a dozen minitanks chewed up by machine-gun fire. A few roboguards lay scattered in the carnage as well, and the huge chests of dead Destroyers poked out of the rubble here and there as well. Almost nothing moved.

Except at the far side of the chute, she quickly realized. Axel rose unsteadily on one leg to face a Destroyer that reached for him with both hands and a blade. CJ was too far away to help, even if she'd had any idea how to make a difference—neither her pellet gun nor her spike would make a dent in a fully armored Destroyer. Nonetheless, CJ ran toward them, spike held high.

The Destroyer swung its weapon, and Axel successfully blocked—but the blow shattered his staff and knocked him against the wall. Off-balance, he promptly slid sideways to the floor on top of Roni, who did not move. Axel held up his arm in a futile effort to block the upcoming blow.

Out of the corner of her eye, CJ saw a blur of sandstone on wheels hurtling down the slidechute. As the blur reached the bottom, the sandstone apparition leapt from the bike and arched forward. Akira!

With the perfection of a ten-point high-dive, Akira straightened out and crashed helmet-first into the Destroyer's throat.

The hit did not snap the Destroyer's neck, as it would have done to a human being, but it did knock the robot flat on its back. CJ recognized this position, as did Lars, who had risen to his feet and staggered after her. Even as the Destroyer sank its blade into Akira's stomach, Lars wedged his staff into the Destroyer's gun mount socket and heaved. CJ was already in position with her pellet gun: as the destroyer's gun popped out, she buried the nose of her pistol in the exposed socket and fired. The Destroyer shuddered and stopped.

Akira rolled off the robot, panting painfully. "I thought those things were supposed to be tough," he gasped.

"Roni!" Axel wailed. CJ jumped up and ran to his aid. She slowed as she reached them, as she saw how little difference she could make.

Roni was still lying upside down on the chute. CJ knelt to pull him down, off the chute onto the level ground, then realized it would be a mistake. A stream of bullets had cut him practically in half. If she tried to move him, his lower abdomen would be left behind.

Roni looked up at her. His eyes bulged with pain. "Akira still alive?" he asked.

CJ nodded.

"Good. Tradition preserved," he said. He shuddered and lay still.

Akira coughed, hideously. CJ stood up, exhausted, and went to kneel beside him.

Akira raised an eyebrow. "Roni's gone?" He asked.

CJ nodded to him, as she had nodded to Roni. There was nothing else to do.

"Well. Glad he got what he—" Akira exhaled sharply. He did not breathe again.

CJ blinked, again and again, to keep the tears out of her eyes. She sat back, huddled into herself. Axel and Lars came up on either side and hugged her.

Chapter Fourteen

The Shootout

The Dealer permitted himself a small smile. The Angels had set all kinds of new records. This was the first team ever to get everyone alive to the center level, even if two of them had died pretty much immediately upon arrival. And this was the first team to still have a wheeled vehicle operational at the bottom of the slidechute. That was a pretty big achievement. It meant they would use less of their limited compressed-air packs to get to the ship center. They'd be stronger in the last, most terrible battles.

The smile reflected his belief that he was, in large measure, responsible for their success. The monster gun—*his* gun—had made the difference. It was *very* cool.

Jessica closed her eyes, but the hideous images stayed with her. The Angels had set all kinds of new records. This assault was going extremely well. How horrible.

Ghastly as the sight of the Angel One deaths had been a month earlier, at least she had not known them personally. In contrast, Akira and Roni had always had friendly smiles for her as they passed her in the hall, and she had been an intimate observer of their lives for almost four weeks.

And soon Jessica herself would be the one giving the orders.

Paolo frowned once again at the results Crockett II had generated. At least this time the results were not wildly out of line with everything that had ever gone before. But the result was certainly speculative.

Looking at the patterns of corridors and rooms they had passed so far, extrapolating those patterns to a layout around the core of the ship, there was an anomaly. If the team went clockwise around the corridor one ring out from the old Gate location, and if they then turned right at the second opportunity, there should be something there that was . . . different.

Could it be the Hallelujah Gate?

Paolo feared that the only way to find out would be to go there, a very expensive proposition if he were wrong. He shrugged, and proceeded to post the forecast. He did not put a lot of money on it. Let someone else figure out what to do with the idea.

It had been a long time since Morgan had had a team this close to the goal with so little idea of what to do next. Should they just go to the old location, on the off chance that the Gate still stood there but had been sealed over, despite the doubts that this was the case? The 'cast gave them a dismal twenty-six percent chance of finding the entrance there.

Of course, there was a perfectly robust, sixty-three percent probability *Shiva* had set a trap at that location in the absence of a Gate.

Morgan sagged in his wheelchair. There really wasn't anything else to do, except wander around the corridors hoping for a break. Wandering down the corridors had been exactly his strategy when he had gotten to the heart of the center level on *Shiva I*. But there hadn't been any Destroyers looking for him that time, either. A rambling stroll would not suffice anymore.

A new forecast for a new Gate location showed up on the 'castpoint. Clockwise, two radial corridors away, someone predicted an "anomaly," possibly the Gate. Morgan watched almost idly as the odds in favor of this forecast improved slowly, then leveled off at twenty-one percent.

So the old location was still the better guess. But it was not much better, and still dismal. He clucked his tongue. Perhaps he should talk with CJ about this. She was, after all, at least as smart as he was.

CJ turned away from the scene of carnage, to look down the corridor she would soon start to run. Nothing remained here for her. She had no place to bury the dead. Their bodies would be consecrated in the nuclear fires of *Shiva*'s destruction. There were no dog tags to remove, or even any notices to send out; everyone who cared had watched the ending live.

Her most important task was to remember how to smile. Her team, after all, had set all kinds of records getting here. For the sake of the morale she must share with Axel and Lars, she had to remember how to smile.

She turned to her surviving teammates. She managed to bring forth an expression that wouldn't have looked out of place on the Mona Lisa. "Everybody ready?"

Lars and Axel nodded.

"Let's go."

CJ walked down the hall, back straight, head high. Axel limped beside her, using Roni's spike as a cane. Lars rode the bike a few feet behind them. The chest wound Lars had taken in the last battle was not quite as crippling as Axel's broken leg. But Lars, with the special harnesses on his oversized frame, was carrying their supplies. They saved more compressed air letting him ride and making Axel walk. As they rounded the gentle curve of the corridor, leaving the site of the battle behind, CJ began to feel her energy return. Her energy had changed, though. Now she could feel an edge to her strength, an edge born of hate.

Morgan came online. "CJ, it's time for a strategy session."

CJ's eyes opened wide. "Strategy! Why Morgan, I never thought you'd ask. Of course the answer is yes."

She listened as a long pause ended with a burst of laughter. The laughter ended as abruptly as it had begun. Morgan explained the situation, and the question: Should they go to the old Gate location, or the possible new one?

CJ trudged patiently along till Morgan had finished, then explained, "The answer is obvious, isn't it? I mean, even if they do put a trap at the old location, *Shiva* would surely put its biggest force in front of the real entrance, right?"

"Exactly right, CJ."

"So first we sneak up on the old location, recon to see how big the trap is. Then we trot on over to the new location to see how big a pile of guys *Shiva* has planted there. Whichever force is larger, that is the one we fight our way through."

She heard heavy, unhappy breathing at the far end of the commlink. At last Morgan replied, "I was hoping for something more elegant."

CJ laughed. "This *is* elegant, Morgan. It's just dangerous."

Morgan grunted. "Okay, that's the plan, then."

They came to the intersection where their current ring corridor met the radial corridor that led inward. CJ pointed down the hallway, into the center of the ship. "All right, everybody, let's go walk into the trap."

"Excellent," Lars proclaimed.

"Cool," Axel agreed. He waved the Destroyer gun he now carried. "Uh, before we continue, could I try this thing, just once before we get into a firefight? See how it feels when it hammers me into the wall?"

CJ nodded. "By all means, Axel."

Axel snapped the spike to his frame, aimed the weapon carefully down the hall they had just come up, and pressed the firing stud. Nothing happened. "Good thing we checked," he muttered. He automatically started a clearing cycle on the gun, the kind of cycle you'd perform as a matter of course on a jammed human weapon.

Jessica jerked back in her chair as the 'castpoint lit up like Vegas on New Year's. As Axel started to clear the breech, thousands of forecasts poured into the 'castpoint, all predicting that the gun would blow up in his hands. Mechanical engineers, retired soldiers, hopeful future Angels, and firearm specialists from around the world spoke as one. It was the Web equivalent of a scream of panic.

It would take less than fifteen seconds for a million trades to take place on the prediction. It would take much less time for Axel to die.

CJ idly watched Axel operate the gun.

"Freeze," Morgan said calmly.

CJ froze, and saw Axel do the same, in midoperation.

"Axel, do not clear the gun. Unfreeze."

CJ started to breathe again.

Morgan explained. "Repairing that thing is a little more complicated than fixing a Ruger, Axel. I'm getting instructions now."

Morgan relayed the plan, and Axel set to work. In a minute the weapon was ready for another try.

CJ heard Axel take a deep breath. "Here goes," he said as he pressed the stud once again.

This time a shot rang out. Axel staggered under the recoil.

"Wow," Axel exclaimed, "I see why you wanted the gun all for yourself, CJ."

CJ smiled cheerily. "That's right, Axel. You're the lucky one." CJ didn't have one of her own; magnificent as the monster guns were, the team needed one agile, able-bodied person who could move fast. Since she was the only able-bodied person left (the ache from her fractured arm didn't count), she was it. And the gun was just too big and clumsy for her role. It was a great shame. They'd left plenty of Destroyer weapons back by the slidechute. So many guns, so few people to carry them.

They walked slowly down the corridor toward the expected trap, staring at the blank wall with tense expectation. They came to the last intersection, where they would turn left to go clockwise to reach the anomaly. They stopped. CJ muttered, "Not a creature was stirring, not even a mouse." The corridor was empty of all save a deathly quiet.

Lars chimed in. "Well, at least it means old St. Nick has a chance to lay out some presents." He turned down the ring corridor, took five steps, and stopped. "Up you go, CJ." He held his hands out for her.

CJ accepted his help as she jumped lightly onto his shoulders. She started planting duodec charges on the ceiling. Axel knelt in the center of the intersection and carefully laid out a set of recon pyramids so that they could see the center of the trap from around the corner.

At last they were ready. Lars said, "I'm the strongest one, I get to throw it."

Axel stood on tip-toes and looked up balefully into Lars' eyes. "I was a baseball pitcher in high school. I get to throw it."

They both looked over at CJ. She threw up her hands. "It's the big decisions like this that leave me completely unable to make up my mind."

Morgan grunted. "Axel, you've got the pyramid in your hand. Throw it."

Axel grinned. He stepped to the center of the intersection, studied the far wall, brushed off a couple of signals from a hypothetical catcher, wound up, and threw the pyramid down the hall.

A massive clattering sound of mechanical movement came up the hall as the pyramid landed. Destroyers stepped out from around both the left and the right corners of the *Shiva*'s innermost intersection. Axel leaped to the cover of the ring corridor as gouts of fire washed the hallway.

CJ, already around the corner into the ring, smiled sweetly down at Axel as he lay where he landed. Her eyes were wide and fluttering. "Was that a strike, or a home run?" she asked.

"Damned if I know." Axel got up. "What next?"

CJ continued sweetly, "Why, Axel, don't you know? Now we run for our lives." Then she was moving. Then he was moving. Lars was already moving.

The sound of bad guys in hot pursuit surged up the hallway. CJ glanced back at the pyramids in the intersection, straining to see in the reflections the exact composition of the enemy force. "Mother Mary, I sure do hope we get to fight our way back through that mess."

Axel looked back. "Are you kidding? The armies of World War II were smaller than that."

"Yeah. But if we don't have to fight through those, it means we'll be fighting through something worse."

Axel grunted. "Hard to imagine."

They rounded the corner into the radial corridor that led to the anomaly. Axel half-screamed. "Okay, now I can imagine it." Halfway down the corridor, the place was packed wall to wall with mechanical creatures of every variety. A line of Destroyers opened fire as they jumped back around the corner from whence they'd come.

Lars just shook his head. "Extremely not good."

CJ's mind went almost blank. "Morgan, you have a plan?"

"No. But before we implement it, blow the roof."

Lars pressed the detonator. The charges in the ceiling let go, burying the first elements of the force following them from the trap.

❖   ❖   ❖

Morgan was not surprised by the wall of destruction they'd found barring the way to the anomaly. His expectation was not based on prescience or wisdom. It was based on statistics. *Shiva* had not yet dropped a really spectacular surprise on this assault, and *Shiva* always came up with one good stick to poke in his eye. It was a personal affront, that *Shiva* always put an obstacle like this in front of him.

For a moment, he forgot everything else, even CJ's place on the battlefield, in his concentration on the problem. He had the most dismal idea of his life. But, in a world barren of ideas, his dismal idea was also the best.

Solomon whistled for him: "Clowns to the left of me, jokers to the right, here I am, stuck in the middle with you."

Morgan scratched Sol's head. "Just what I was thinking. So you think it will work?"

Solomon whistled again, a passage from "Fanfare for the Common Man." Morgan noted that it was the ELP version, and decided not to ask whether that meant agreement or not.

Jessica sat forward in her chair. She'd done pretty well predicting what Morgan would do up to now. But this was the critical moment, the part of Morgan's responsibility that she had to match. If she could not figure out how to win in an impossible situation like this, Earth Defense needed someone else.

Clowns to the left of me, jokers to the right? Did that make any sense at all? Was there a clue here to some hope of victory? If so, Jessica would have to thank Solomon for the assist in figuring it out. But at first glance it didn't seem very relevant.

Were *Shiva's* robots really clowns? Of course not, they were lethal enough. But, Jessica realized, *Shiva* had never really had to control a close combat with firearms before—the Destroyers were the first firearm-capable machines to enter the field. Perhaps if you confused them . . . Jessica started scanning the Angels' equipment belts, to see if any smoke grenades had been salvaged. It was a slim chance, but it might work, against all odds.

CJ joined Axel and Lars in throwing a string of grenades behind them. Soon thick smoke blocked their view of the passage; the last thing they saw were Destroyers clambering over the rubble from the collapsed roof. As Morgan had told her, though the mini-tanks covered clean ground faster, the Destroyers were better at climbing obstacles.

CJ wheeled round and bounded across the intersecting passageway. A hail of Destroyer fire echoed down the hall at her passage, but CJ moved like the wind, and she had crossed the hall before the enemy could take aim. "They're just sitting there," she told her companions—her vidcam had already loaded that information down to Morgan and the Web, but Axel and Lars didn't share that feed.

Morgan spoke. "CJ. Personal damage assessment." Was there a thread of terror in his voice?

CJ spoke before even looking down at her armor. "I'm fine," she snapped, "I . . ." Her voice drifted off as she saw a line of blood from her right side. A bullet had just nicked her.

Seeing the gash, she could now feel it. She grunted. "Looks like I got scratched." She closed her eyes for a moment. "It still doesn't hurt as much as your blasted electroshocks."

The moments ticked by. As they'd hoped, the Destroyers approaching from behind did not fire blindly into the dense smoke. Eventually the Destroyers came close enough that the Angels could hear their heavy footfalls.

Morgan gave the order. "Go!"

CJ's arm whipped out and flung a smoke grenade as far as she could, while Lars did the same from the other side. CJ was right-handed, Lars was left-handed,

so neither exposed more than their forearm in the
endeavor. The twin grenades flew down the hall, arch-
ing over the first rows of minitanks. They threw another pair of grenades to join the first two. CJ yelled,
"Charge!"

All three Angels rounded the corners into the hallway leading to the anomaly, into the arms of the
waiting army.

Lars and Axel each let off a short burst from their
monster guns, turning large sections of the nearest rows
of minitanks into dead shells. Axel dropped another line
of smoke grenades behind them as Lars and CJ waded
into the now-disorganized minitanks before them. They
had a pattern: Lars would flip a tank, CJ would kill it.
Axel wheeled his bike up to the edge of the battlefield
and rolled off.

Morgan barked, "Shoot 'em now."

Lars dropped to his knees and fired blindly at the
Destroyers behind the smokescreen in front of them.

Axel lay on the ground and let go at the Destroyers
behind the smokescreen behind them.

CJ leaped into a small crevasse between the broken
armored shells of two of the dead minitanks and curled
in a ball.

As Axel and Lars fired, the Destroyers on all sides
finally responded, firing blindly from both directions.
Lars and Axel dived for cover near CJ. The floor shook
with the reverberations of the massed fire. Even the
minitanks seemed disoriented by the shaking and the
noise; hand-to-hand combat took a time out.

As before, as quickly as the sound had risen, so
quickly it faded out. As before, a handful of clicking
sounds informed CJ that the Destroyers were out of
ammo. The smoke began to dissipate, and through the
haze they could measure the extent of their victory, or
their defeat.

Only one Destroyer remained standing between them
and the anomaly. The Destroyers at the opposite end

of the hall had successfully wiped out all the others.
The Angels were back in business.

Axel lifted his weapon and, as a pair of minitanks
rushed him, he fired at the lone Destroyer down the
hall. "You're clear," he gasped.

"Axel," CJ cried out. She scrambled to her feet to go
help him, but Morgan interrupted. "CJ. Follow the plan."

Her feet responded to Morgan's orders, but her eyes
did not move till she saw the consequences of following the plan. Axel fired a second burst, killing one of
the minitanks before it got to him, but the second one
swarmed over him, swinging its blade with lethal precision and ferocity. "Go," Axel panted. "Remember, we
know why we're here, and they don't." Another minitank
piled onto Axel.

CJ's head spun forward. Had even a full minute
passed since she'd thrown the last smoke grenade? She
thought not, though it seemed like centuries.

The massed minitanks had hardly started to move
since being rocked by the blindfire of the Destroyers.
Packed so tight that they were almost wedged in place,
there was only one thing CJ could do with the enemy:
she leaped to the top of the nearest minitank and started
to hop. Skipping from one armored beetle-back to the
next, dancing away from the swinging blades that
reached up for her, she crossed the sea of enemy forces.

Reggie stood blinking at the oak frame of the entrance.
"Come on, Mercedes," he muttered to the disinterested
door that blocked his way, "Answer me."

The door flung open. Mercedes stood there, hands
on hips, her eyebrows drawn together in a storm. "I
ought to throw you out of the window," she growled.

Reggie held up his hands in a gesture of surrender. "Lead me to my doom, Mistress." He stood very
straight and still.

Mercedes laughed and spread her arms. "But I'm off-
shift now. And one way or the other, the fighting will

be over before I'm on again. So please come in." The dark anger on her face evaporated, and the sun came out, with rainbows shining and birds singing.

Reggie stepped into her open arms, squeezed her, and half-carried, half-dragged her through her own apartment. "However it comes out, I wanted to be with you for the ending," he explained.

"Me too." Mercedes pointed into her workroom. "There's the best view in the house."

"You've been doing a great job, by the way. I've been watching your forecasts."

"Thank you," she said distractedly. She looked back over her shoulder, hearing a sharp sound of battle from the other room.

"You're right, no chitchat till we've seen this through."

Arm in arm, they entered the work room to watch the outcome.

CJ reached the end of the carpet of minitanks and leaped lightly to the ground. She spun as she landed, to flip and kill the minitank she had just used as a stepping stone. She looked up to see Lars trying to duplicate her performance, leaping across the backs of the minitanks, but his progress was slow and painful. She could see his legs bleeding from a dozen cuts where blades had nicked him. Nevertheless, he was an Angel. He was still coming.

Morgan interrupted her observations. "Fly, CJ, fly."

She turned again and ran, ran for her life, ran for all the lives of all the people of Earth.

She reached the innermost ring corridor. A blank wall faced her. She gulped in air and said, "There's nothing here. Nothing." She looked to the left: it was just a hall. She looked to the right: a slidechute sank away into the floor. This chute was narrower than the corridors and the main chute—the academics back on Earth thought of them as being *Shiva's* equivalent of maintenance alleys. CJ pointed at the chute. Between gasps, she spluttered in dismay, "That's the anomaly."

Chapter Fifteen

The Anomaly

Paolo groaned. He knew the truth even before CJ said it: they'd never seen a maintenance chute like this at the ship core. Paolo did not doubt that this was the anomally *Crockett* had predicted.

Paolo and his team had done their best to find the Gate for the Angels. Instead, they had led the team to this stupid little chute, and to ruin. On the 'castpoint, the odds for finding the Gate here fell like a stone.

Paolo buried his face in his hands. Deaths uncountable would result from his folly.

CJ heard a burst of fire behind her. As she turned, Lars came running up. He slowed to a stop as he reached the smooth blank wall. CJ could see his shoulders slouch as he recognized defeat. They didn't have to look up to see the opposition, they could hear the march of minitanks bearing down on them.

Lars raised a his huge hand. "No!" he cried, and

slammed his fist against the wall with the force of a sledge hammer. The wall paid no attention.

Selpha watched Lars pound the wall and shared his despair, as did billions of others across the Web. Then she saw Peter sit up suddenly. "Cracks are interesting?" he asked.

Selpha knelt before him. "Yes, Peter, they are the most important thing in the world."

"There's a crack in this wall," he said confidently. "Eight meters right, eight meters down, from the point of impact."

"Thank you." She rushed to her keyboard, brushing tears of relief from her eyes.

Paolo's detectors generated a high-priority alert on Selpha's announcement. Brief though her statement was, Paolo was already keying the consequences back onto the Web before he finished reading it. "Yes!" he cried with a whoop of delight.

Sofia poked her head into the room. "You all right?"

"We found the Gate!" he exclaimed. Finished typing, he leaped across the room and swept her into his arms for a lingering kiss.

Sofia wrinkled her nose. "I guess that's a 'yes.'" She picked up the kiss where it had left off.

CJ stared up into Lars' sad face. "Let's take as many of them as we can," she said.

Lars nodded. They turned to face the enemy.

Morgan spoke. "We've found the Gate," he said. "It's halfway down the slide-chute."

CJ watched a gleam come into her last surviving partner's eyes. He lifted his weapon. Morgan spoke again. "Take the minitanks in front. Build a wall of corpses."

"Right," Lars replied. He fired. The leading rows of minitanks stopped cold, almost driven back by the hail of fire. Lars waited till the minitanks in back had partially clambered over the heap of dead fellows, and fired again. The pile of dead tanks grew deeper.

Lars knelt to begin the laborious task of reloading his gun. "I want replaceable magazines in the next version," he muttered.

"Pray *Shiva VI* doesn't think the same thing," CJ replied before turning to the chute. She looked for the Gate, but couldn't see anything.

Morgan had already guessed her next question. "They sealed it, CJ. But believe me, it's there. Use the ceramic acid to peel off the outer layers, to get past the weld. Finish with duodec." He paused. "I must confess, I'm not exactly sure how to get in position to use the acid, however."

CJ stared at the narrow slidechute, then smiled. "No problem." She held the spike across the chute just to make sure the chute wasn't too wide, then stretched herself out flat next to the slide. She inched over the edge onto the frictionless surface and started to slide. Her last sight of Lars was of him flipping an errant minitank that had broken through the wall he had built. More would follow, she knew. Along with the two Destroyers from the far end of the hall that had survived the shootout. "Hold 'em," she called out.

"Go," Lars replied calmly. "And this time don't stop for a malt."

CJ started to slide. As her speed picked up, she reached out with her feet against the outer wall, and reached up with her hands against the inner wall, the wall of the control room. Wedged there, she took control of her slide down the chute. "Let me know when I'm there," she asked Morgan.

"Check."

Moments later Morgan spoke again. "CJ, stop." She halted. Morgan continued, "Okay, it's on your left. Spray it."

Bracing herself with her right hand, she reached

around with her left, very carefully, knowing that if she broke her arch, she would slide away. No one had ever gotten back up a slidechute once they had gone down.

Success! She pulled the spray can off her frame and held it shakily up, aiming in the general direction of the wall. She started spraying.

The wall started to bubble. "This looks promising," she muttered, as much to encourage Lars as anything. A few droplets of the acid drifted in the air and settled on the arm of her frame, which enthusiastically started to bubble too. One droplet landed on her arm. "Good thing this stuff is only effective on ceramic," she muttered darkly. It hurt like fire, digging deeper and deeper into her flesh. She felt a pinprick in her shoulder as her suit responded to the agony with another injection of something whose name she didn't want to know.

A dark streak appeared in the wall, a hairline crack, but so straight, it couldn't be a random fracture. She screamed, "We have a Gate!"

A burst of fire from above ended suddenly with the desperate little click of an empty magazine. She heard a gasp of pain over the radio. "Hurry," Lars said weakly.

"Duodec," Morgan said.

CJ snapped the can back against her frame and pulled out a wad of explosive. Her right arm, she decided, might well have been fractured earlier. Despite having enough drugs in her bloodstream to supply a small pharmacy, her arm now throbbed like a Congo drum, and her whole body was shaking from the strain. She planted a detonator on the line of the door and started laying a line of duodec along the edge, as far as she could reach.

A loud clatter rang down from above, and a minitank, spinning out of control, hurtled into her. Her legs snapped away from the wall, and she was sliding, arm in arm with the minitank.

She pressed the button that blew the charges and shoved the minitank away from her. By the time she reached the next floor, she was up and ready. But so was the minitank. It swung its blade as if with relish, and at this time CJ did not quite block in time—the blade cut through her leg below the knee.

With a wild yell, CJ heaved up the minitank onto its back and gutted it. She fell over.

Lars spoke again, this time with a voice bubbling with blood. "Finish that malt," he ordered. He coughed, a retching sound from deep inside his chest.

Rising on her right leg, CJ looked up and groaned. The door had not yet blown open. Which did not matter, since she had no way of getting back up there, anyway.

Viktor spoke again, with uncharacteristic softness and patience. "Lou, you know there's only one way to get her back up there."

Lou practically screamed. "No, Viktor, no!"

Together, they listened as Lars coughed the last time. Viktor just looked at Lou with stern eyes.

Lou closed his eyes. "Okay, Viktor, we're posting now."

Morgan looked at the recommendation with eyes blank and drained of life. The idea would have made him sick inside an hour ago. But now it was their last, best hope. There wouldn't be much left of CJ afterwards . . . but still, he did have a plan.

Jessica huddled in a fetal position in her cocoon, gripping her legs with a strength that would leave her bruised for days. Then Granma's voice ran through her head—*What are you doing, girl? You have a job to do! Get on with it!* Jessica shook herself, and rose slowly till she sat straight in her chair. If CJ could do what she had to do, Jessica could do her own part. She clenched her teeth and watched, knowing what would follow.

CJ took a running leap at the chute—as much of a run as you can make with one leg—and leaped up the slide. She slid and slid, slower and slower, until at last she stopped and slid back down.

Reaching the floor, she shook her head wildly, throwing tears from her eyes. "I'll make it this time," she muttered.

"CJ," Morgan spoke her name softly.

CJ stopped in a crouched position.

Morgan's voice changed. It became the brisk, demanding voice that must be obeyed. She did as he said.

"CJ, pull off your compressed air bottle."

"Check."

"Stuff point-two-five centimeters of duodec into the mouth of the bottle. Put it against the wall."

"Check."

"Blow it."

Amidst the harsh sound of the blast, shards of the bottle flew past her, some bounding off her frame.

"Pick up the top half of the bottle." The top half was more or less intact.

"Jam two centimeters of duodec in the top of the bottle. Strap it to your left boot."

"Check."

"Lie on the slide, CJ."

Finally she understood what he was doing. She was about to become a one-time-only human rocket.

"Put one centimeter of duodec in your left hand. Hold the staff in your right." He paused. "CJ," he said tenderly, "you know what you're going to do?"

CJ smiled. "Yes, darling."

Morgan's voice became commanding again. "Then do it."

CJ took a deep breath, and lit the duodec beneath her foot.

As the explosive fired, CJ's right leg dissolved up to the knee. But it was okay; she was flying.

Up the chute she sailed. The distinctive crack of ceramic-on-ceramic winged off the wall next to her: a Destroyer was standing at the top of the slide, shooting.

It must have been a fresh reinforcement from some-where else in the ship—she knew they'd left the others running on empty.

Her velocity ebbed, but not before she reached the door. Taking in the whole scene, she could see that the acid had continued its work a long time before sub-siding. The door was completely visible now, almost free of the welding job *Shiva* had done. CJ knew how to finish the job. She raised her left hand and slapped it against the door.

The duodec in her palm exploded, throwing her against the far wall even as the Gate blew away, revealing the control room. With her right hand, her remaining hand, she heaved with the staff against the far wall and threw herself back to the opening.

But she could not quite reach it. As she started to slide away, she flung the tip of the spike up, and caught its hook on the lip of the entrance. She held on to the staff, dangling beneath the opening.

Another bullet splattered next to her. She looked up to see the Destroyer taking careful aim. There was nothing left to do.

Behind the Destroyer, a terrible burst of light shone forth, and another staggering explosion shook the walls and the slide. The vibration whipped CJ back and forth as she swung from her staff. Dimly she realized what had caused the blast: Lars, her protector, had blown all the duodec he carried. And he had carried a lot indeed.

The Destroyer bounced off the wall and slid spinning down the chute. CJ watched helplessly as the machine reached out to her with its right hand, to grab her shoulder. The machine tugged on her, but she held on, and looked at the Destroyer eye-to-eye.

Something else sailed past—another piece of a Destroyer. Looking back at the thing clutching her, she realized it was only a piece of a machine, even more broken than she was. She glared at the monster. "You're dead," she said. "Get the hell off me."

The ceramic fingers loosened, then slid away. A dull thud announced its arrival at the bottom of the slide.

CJ looked up at the Hallelujah Gate, just two feet away from her. Holding on with her right hand, she reached up with her left. "Ooops," she muttered. She'd forgotten. She didn't have a left hand anymore.

Reggie's eyes were locked on the screen, but still he could see Mercedes' open-mouthed stare from the corner of his eye.

In a peculiar twist of fate, Lars' camera was still functioning despite the incredible blast he had precipitated as his last act of desperation. The lens pointed over the ledge of the slide, and with proper computer compensation, the whole world watched CJ struggle at the end of her staff. She seemed so close, despite being so incredibly far away.

CJ's stub of a left arm waved futilely in the air.

Mercedes whispered, "Dear God, don't let go. Get up, get up." Her eyes glistened. Her shoulders sagged. "She can't make it."

Reggie watched for a moment and shook his head. Mercedes' eyes glistened with tears of despair. But, though he could feel the water welling in his own eyes as well, he felt no despair. His heart surged with pride. "Love, fear not. You have not yet seen the full strength that *Shiva* must fight. I have seen our CJ fight this battle before. It is not over."

CJ's arm stopped waving. She hung there for a timeless moment.

CJ shook her head violently again, this time to throw the sweat from her eyes. Her mind drifted, despite her determination, into a dreamlike state. She was in the Olympics again, and Sara Dubcek was just in front of her. CJ could see the finish line a few meters ahead. She could hear her father whisper to her, "Finish it, CJ." CJ breathed again, the biggest gulp of air of her life, and pushed. And Sara was behind her. And then the finish line was behind her too.

CJ blinked and once again she was dangling from her staff. Her palm was wet. Soon she would slip from the staff, and never return. She held.

Then a voice spoke to her. Whether it was Morgan, or her father, or herself, she knew she would never know. But the voice held her nonetheless. "Finish it, CJ," the voice said with a light, almost laughing confidence. She breathed, and heaved herself up with a power that must have belonged to someone else, for hers had long since fled.

Reggie watched the moment unfold as he had known it would. CJ was still. And then, somehow, she grew. And this new CJ, larger and stronger than before, pulled herself up, over the lip of the Gate, into the control room, with a single effortless motion.

"Well done, girl," he whispered to no one in particular. He spoke more loudly, this time for Mercedes. "Humans are so damned hard to kill," he said with a voice cracking with emotion. "Almost makes you feel sorry for the damned *Shiva.*"

CJ rolled across the floor of the control room, over and over; it was easy when you were missing so many pieces. She stopped as she came up against the vast, bulky elliptical panel in the middle of the room, covered with displays no one could read, with a large ceramic sphere rising from its center. She reached around her waist, unbuckled the football, and released the catch. A hissing sound followed as fuel-air explosive filled the room, preparing the place for a blast almost as devastating as that of a backpack nuke.

"Got you, you bastard," she cursed *Shiva.* Nothing could save *Shiva* now—if a robot came through the door, the football's proximity sensors would light up.

CJ grimaced as she noticed the pain from the remaining parts of her body. "Morgan, it still doesn't hurt as much as your blasted electroshocks," she ground out. Her body slumped as she passed out.

Jessica unwound her muscles slowly as she came out of the fetal position. Every limb in her body ached with released tension. Her arm and legs still tingled where she knew that CJ could no longer feel anything, but even that tingling was a pleasure of a sort. Being healthy and whole had never felt so miraculous and wonderful before.

All around the world, she knew, victory celebrations had begun even as CJ rolled across the floor of *Shiva*. The Hallelujah Gate had earned its name once more.

All in all, the idea of celebrating seemed obscene as she watched CJ lie there helplessly. At least the decent people would hold their celebrations until CJ's fate had been decided, inevitable though that fate might be.

But then she saw on her screens that MacBride was leaning forward in his chair, tense and determined. What was he doing now?

Feeling chagrin at not having expected this, Jessica sat up alertly. She had no idea what he was going to do. But clearly, he had a plan.

She heard her name being called. "CJ, CJ," the voice repeated insistently. Eventually she recognized the voice. It was Morgan, of course.

"Morgan," she whispered between short breaths, "looks like we made it. Sorry I'll miss the party."

"No!" Morgan barked. His voice once again commanded her. "Pull yourself to the door. Get out of there."

CJ shook her head. "Morgan—"

"Now!"

She pulled herself to the door.

"Keep going."

The shock of her injuries was wearing off. Through

the haze of pain-subduing chemicals in her bloodstream, she could tell that someone was in terrible agony. The person was far away, but she understood that it was probably herself.

"Go!"

She rolled out of the Gate, onto the chute, and slid down to the floor she had just recently tried so hard to leave.

"Get down the corridor. Faster."

She pulled herself along. She soon recognized another slidechute.

"Down."

Down she went. With no one chasing her, and nothing left that she needed to do, it was even more fun than the exercises and sims back at Powell. Even the distant person in egregious pain was enjoying herself.

She saw another slidechute and headed for it, but Morgan interrupted her game. "Go around this one."

Once again she did as she was told. In just a little way, she came to a hump in the corridor: the top half of a plasma beam tube. "Spray it, CJ. And set a ring."

CJ was amazed to find that she still had a bit of ceramic acid left. She used it, and set a ragged ring of duodec. "That's all I've got," she told the distant voice.

"It's enough. Roll back and blast."

CJ wondered how long it would be until the control room exploded. It should be happening just about now. Once the control room blew, she knew, only a couple of minutes would pass before the whole ship would light up, a veritable sun going nova. It would be a spectacular sight to see from a distance.

She squeezed the trigger and the ring of duodec exploded: she could feel the heat from the blast wash over her.

And as the sound of the blast died away, the sound of a whirlwind took its place. "Jump, CJ, into the tube! *Gogogo!*"

She barely heard the command, for she was helplessly unable to do anything except obey. The rush of air picked her up and swept her along with everything else it touched.

A deadly silence greeted her as she swirled down the tunnel: she was cut off from her comm to Earth, and in its absence she realized that the whole time she'd been on board *Shiva*, she'd been able to hear Morgan's breath, delicate as a snowflake, in the background. Now there was nothing. Even the whirlwind that carried her along made little sound, thinned by the vacuum that greeted it in the tube.

The air pressure fell, then steadied as air from the heart of *Shiva* continued to pour down the tube with her. She felt the emergency systems of her battered frame trying to wrap enough skinsuit material around her to keep her alive. She laughed weakly. What next?

Jessica stared at the blank screens that had once held views from the Angels' vidcams. She still had no clue as to MacBride's plan. Blast! If she were to be Mac-Bride's replacement, she would have to do better than this.

Of course, she realized with a little reflection, she shouldn't beat herself up too badly for missing this. She was sure that MacBride had spent the better part of the last two weeks mulling this problem over in his head: while she had been studying 'castpoints and dreaming about violent death, he had been studying *Shiva* and dreaming about paths for CJ's escape.

She did her best to figure it out. He'd gotten CJ into a plasma tube pointing straight down and out of the ship. Fine. The escaping air would carry her along. Also fine. But the plasma tubes had a series of blast shields in the outer section, much like the shields in the Alabaster Hall. He had to get those open somehow. Could MacBride trick *Shiva* into trying to fire the plasma beam, to open the shields of its own volition?

As she watched, Morgan punched a series of buttons. A new view of *Shiva* appeared, from a recon ship pacing it as it crossed the Moon's orbit. As the identical image lit up in her own cocoon, she understood Morgan's plan at last. Morgan hadn't dropped CJ down any old random plasma tube. CJ was hurtling down the plasma tube that had been hit twice with nuclear missiles from the fleet. Did Morgan think that the missiles had penetrated the whole course of shields, to actually penetrate the *Shiva*?

Even as she grasped Morgan's plan, confirmation appeared as one of her dead, empty windows came back to life—CJ's vidcam was back in operation, communicating with the recon ship. She could now see the view of the plasma tube from inside, via CJ's camera, at the same time that she watched from outside, from the ship.

CJ couldn't believe it. There was light at the end of the tunnel. Harsh yet beautiful sunlight reflected from the cracked and shattered surfaces of exposed rooms and chunks of armor. The wind whipping past her picked up chunks of debris larger than herself and flung them along in a tidal wave of jetsam. Beyond the wreckage, beyond the sunlight, she could see the stars in their icy splendor against the stark blackness of space.

The tube flared at the tip, where aiming magnets for the plasma beam operated. CJ was no longer bouncing off the sides of the tube with the frequency and vigor she had encountered earlier. Now she was flying along the route to escape and freedom. She started to laugh. She flew ever faster toward the mouth of the shattered tube.

A chunk of sandstone, a wall or a floor from some defunct section of *Shiva*, sailed in front of her, twisted in the wind, and jammed against two other chunks of material wedged into the wall fissures. CJ flung her arm in front of her as she slammed into the obstacle.

The swirling wind spun her and swept her around the blockage, but she'd lost her speed. Where she had been flying a moment ago, now she was floating gently.

She reached the mouth of the tube, then spun ever so slowly and gracefully away from *Shiva*, into the sunlight.

Morgan stared at the screen. Tears fell from his unblinking eyes. "CJ," he whispered.

"Morgan, Morgan, we did it." A quiet gasp followed as some minor twist caused a burst of pain. Morgan watched as CJ turned to look back at the ship she had just escaped. "It doesn't look so deadly now, does it? Kinda pretty, actually."

"I see something much more beautiful than any ship ever built," Morgan replied. His voice cracked.

CJ must have heard the crack in his voice. "What's wrong? Why are you upset?" She paused. He listened as she continued, as the truth dawned on her. "I'm too close, aren't I? I lost too much velocity." Morgan heard her take a deep breath. "Still, this is a record, darling. I'm the second person ever to get out of a *Shiva*. We've made the history books."

Morgan punched a button. "A rescue ship is on its way," he said with a voice that tried to sound matter-of-fact, but came out dull and muted.

"One miracle too many, darling. Good effort, though." She paused. "You know, it doesn't hurt at all anymore."

The camera view twisted, and Morgan saw a triple burst of light rising from *Shiva*.

"Morgan, it's firing," CJ said with alarm in her voice.

Morgan looked at his screens. "Everyone knows. It's taken care of. Promise."

"I'm glad I can count on—" White light flashed on Morgan's window and switched to black. He screamed at the darkness. He felt his heart thump with exquisite pain, and his eyes widened. The lights came up, and three paramedics burst into his cocoon. His last thought as he slipped into unconsciousness was, *Damn Samuels, anyway*.

Chapter Sixteen

T plus Two, The Cycle Begins

Reggie was, after all, a reporter. And Mercedes was, after all, one of five people on Earth who knew the Secret. And scooping the Secret was, after all, the heartfelt desire of any reporter after an Angel assault. Reggie could not help himself, he knew. He would take the story from her, no matter how hard she fought him off.

Curiously though, he did not care too much whether he won or lost. He realized that could spell the end of his true-blooded reporter credentials. That didn't bother him either. He felt he was winning anyway.

Mercedes lay at the end of the plush turquoise sofa overlooking L.A. No escape was possible for her.

Once again he nibbled lightly on her ear. He could feel her shiver at his touch; he reveled in it. "Tell me," he demanded in a hushed voice. "Tell me who won the prizes, or I'll torture you."

She shivered again and tried to get away. Her effort

was neither convincing nor successful. "You'd torture me anyway."

"Surrender," he commanded. "Or I will withdraw my torture."

"Uh," she said, surrendering.

A soft beep interrupted the proceedings. Reggie saw Mercedes open one eye, then the other. "Okay, I'll tell you who won." She smiled wickedly.

"No fair," Reggie protested as they both sat up. "They just published it, didn't they? Now I can just read for myself."

Mercedes giggled. "True enough. There they are." She pointed at the screen.

A list of brands and their contributions appeared on the screen. Reggie read them carefully.

The Grand Prize, five million Masterbucks for "Most Valuable Contribution to the Assault," had gone to the person who figured out how to modify the Destroyer gun for human operation. Reggie had no idea who had figured that out; clearly, this was a person he would have to track down for his next series on "Unsung Heroes," five years hence.

Second place, and four million Masterbucks, went to the person who'd found the cracks in the walls. Selpha, of course. He didn't need to see her brand to know she was the winner.

Third place had gone to the person who had forecast the presence of the anomaly, which had turned out to be the Gate. Reggie would have bet a lot of money he knew who stood behind that identity, but Mercedes would never take the bet, because she knew who it was just as well as he did.

Fourth had gone to the person who described the trap at the end of the Alabaster Hall. Reggie was pretty sure that that was Selpha and Peter as well. If so, they'd done very well indeed in this assault. He hoped the money could buy something wonderful for Peter, though frankly, he didn't have a clue what it might be.

Fifth place went to the person who'd designed the rocket that shot CJ up the slidechute for her last epic battle to reach the Gate. Another Unsung Hero story stood behind that one. Reggie could see he still had his work cut out for him. Which was just what he had hoped for: new winners every time, coming up with ever more novel solutions to the ever more deadly problems posed by the enemy.

A hundred prizes had been awarded in all, but he knew he did not have the time to study the rest. Reggie felt the delicate wet tip of a tongue tickle his ear. "Hey. Torturing the torturer is not allowed."

Mercedes paid no attention whatsoever. Reggie suddenly noticed he had no hope of escape, either.

Jessica's palmtop lay on the floor of her office where she'd dropped it. Neither she nor the General paid any attention. Jessica stared at the General in open-mouthed horror. "He can't be! He can't!"

General Samuels lowered his eyes. "We knew it would happen someday, Jessica. That's why we trained you."

"Morgan MacBride is not dead!" She just couldn't accept it. How dare that male chauvinist desert her now!

Samuels took a deep breath. "Well, for what it's worth, we've compared your scores with the predictions made by all the other people who have shadowed Morgan's performance. Jessica, you're the clear winner. You achieved an adjusted score of ninety-eight percent. Our closest alternate scored eighty-three percent. He is now catatonic, and therefore out of the running." He held out his hands. "You're our best hope, Jessica. *Shiva VI* will not wait for us to find someone better."

Jessica backed away. Then, reluctantly, she reached out and laid her hands in his. She knew the General well enough to know he had to be worried that she couldn't cut it. She shared the worry. Somehow, she would have to grow into Morgan's shoes, and she didn't have a clue how to do it. "I understand. What's next?"

"The next EarthDay Festival starts in three months. You'll control the team." He smiled wryly. "You start preparing tomorrow."

Jessica closed her eyes. She could see the office in which she stood, and Fort Powell itself. The memories associated with this place were too painful; she could not work here. She needed a place of solitude, a place so peaceful the land itself could drain the horror from her. Her eyes flew open. "Very well, General. But I have a condition. You *will* meet my condition." She felt the General tense as she explained. But she would brook no argument, and she made sure he understood.

Samuels chewed his lip. "Very well, Jessica. Whatever it takes, I shall make it happen." He paused. "I just hope you don't end up the way he did."

"But if I do, at least you'll have what you want. And Earth will have what it needs. Right, General?" She didn't mean to sound harsh, but it came out that way nonetheless.

His words came out in a whisper of agreement. "Right, Jessica."

Selpha worked the touchscreen with a tingle of joy; her fingers bounced off the screen as she completed her operations.

She heard the swish of a skirt behind her. Dorothie spun to a stop before her, practically dancing with delight. "I just saw the prize postings," Dorothie practically sang. "Magnificent, Selpha." Dorothie looked down at the computer. "You're taking the plunge?" she asked.

Selpha nodded. "Yes, yes, my sister. Peter's moment has come." She sat back from the screen. "I've posted the prize for a cure for his autism. And I've alerted the four research teams that have published the most promising results, just to make sure they know the prize is available." She looked up with a lightness of heart she could not ever remember feeling before. "I've also run links between the pieces of research that seem, at least to me, to hook together to form a solution." Her smile became too large for her to hold, and she came to her feet and hugged her sister. "Oh, Dorothie, I think we'll win through. Peter will know us, and be with us, soon."

Dorothie hugged her back. "He already knows you, Selpha. I know it's different, but he knows you, I'm sure. You're too wonderful a mother for him not to know, no matter what's been wrong with his mind."

For just a few moments, the sisters stood together, embracing the hopeful future.

Paolo looked out his office window. He saw Sofia picking her way through the broken concrete of the old driveway, no doubt planning her next round of renovation. She would not disturb him. "Luis, take me to Valhalla, please."

"As you wish."

The wallscreen opened into the Hall of Heroes, a virtual reality website of cunning detail wrought in cold stone and richly textured fabrics. The Norseman who had invented Valhalla thousands of years before would surely have been proud of this incarnation of his saga.

A new door led from the hall, as Paolo had known it would. He pointed, and his avatar walked down the hall, leaving behind an echo of footsteps. He entered the new room.

On his left, Axel leaned against the concrete wall of an old apartment building amidst a clutter of similar structures. His leering smile had softened. Here he had a charming, almost impish grin that reached even his dark eyes.

On his right, Lars stood at the lip of a sharp dropoff of pure powdered snow. A light wind whipped the sparkling white specks in a swirl about his burly frame. The wind stopped. Lars laughed, a bellow of bubbling mirth. The rich sound of his voice echoed down the slope, past the treeline, and on to the tiny town far below.

Next to Lars, Akira climbed to the crest of a jagged mountain. The sun fell behind him, outlining his small but graceful body at this moment of triumph as he conquered the mountain. Reaching the top, he bowed slightly to Paolo. The look in his eyes said that everything was as it should be.

Roni and CJ had not yet arrived. Two placeholders marked their future displays. Paolo would have to come back another day to see them.

Each scene was a portal through which Paolo could walk, and learn more about the person before him. Paolo started with Lars.

The Visual History Foundation had done a beautiful job, as usual. The stories of the men and women in this hall would live forever. Even the destruction of Earth could not dim the memory; the Foundation had mirror sites of Valhalla in orbit around Mars and Io.

"Paolo," Sofia yelled from somewhere in the house, "what are you doing?" He could tell by the tone of her voice, she wanted his help on her newest project.

Paolo laughed softly. "Just getting to know some people I never had the chance to meet," he whispered to himself. "Luis, close the window." He rose, and walked out quietly, as if trying not to disturb the Angels he left behind.

Sunlight streamed down through a break in the clouds. Chan Kam Yin examined the glistening surface of the Mustang from dozens of angles, weaving his head back and forth, seeking the slightest flaw in the wax finish.

Suddenly, for no visible reason, the Dealer laughed, filling the air with warm, melodious joy. His laughter came devoid of tension, of need, or of fear. For the first time in his long nineteen years of life, the Dealer laughed at himself.

He was rich now, a multimillionaire. Yet here he was, working for peanuts for other rich people. Well, it still qualified as a scam—others were paying him to have fun! Like, during two months of maintenance test drives he'd had more fun with the car than the fatuous owner had had since buying it. Sometimes rich people could be so foolish.

But the Dealer would not become one of *them*. Even with his five mil now diversified in a half-dozen mutuals, he was being careful with his money. He had already decided, not without some regret, to stick it out in his crummy closet of an apartment for a couple more years. Even several mil was not quite enough to live the way he wanted to live in Hong Kong—the place was outrageously expensive, almost as expensive as the diamonds its night sky suggested. Better, he figured, to save his money. Or rather, better still to invest, so he'd never *have* to do this kind of gig again.

His new truck, the one he'd invented for the trip up the Himalayas with its unorthodox ceramic hydrogen-powered engines, had been a huge success. He'd already gotten two more orders for trucks with similar specs, one for the Andes mountains and another for the Alps. There were other opportunities out there, too. He could already see that, to really exploit the potential he'd uncovered, he'd need working capital. That prize money was really going to come in handy; it would all go back into the business.

Well, not quite all of it. He turned away from the Mustang, to look with appreciative eyes once again upon the brand-new, screamingly silver Beechcraft by the landing pad. He would let other rich people keep and pay for the Mustangs for him. But he needed a skycar of his own. And gods be praised, he now had a beauty. Tonight he'd fly into Hong Kong with his new toy and return to the Cafe Deco. This time he would ask the hostess in her long metallic blue cheong-sam to dance with him. He would insist that she celebrate his hard-won victories with him. How could she say no? He was, after all, the Dealer.

Jessica's skycar landed behind her new house. She forced herself to remember that this was not a new house, though—it was a new home. She walked through the long shadows of twilight, out onto the porch that stretched beyond the edge of the hill. Behind her stood a simple white frame building. Before her she could see miles of high-desert forest; the stumpy trees spread to the edge of the world, and on into the Arizona sunset. No houses marred the view. Far to the right she could see the haze of the lights of Kingman.

For sixty years now, this place had been a sanctuary for people in pain. Jessica had no doubt she would need it more tomorrow than she did today, and even more the day after that.

A high whistling song wafted to her from within the house. She pulled out her palmtop, spoke briefly, and heard the latch of the door unlock. Calmly, quietly, she entered the world of Morgan MacBride.

Solomon spread her wings as she entered the room. "Boss gone," Solomon said mournfully.

"Boss gone," Jessica replied in soft agreement. She held out her hand to the bird, so Sol could step up onto her. "You're going to have to help me, make me better at being like the Boss. Okay?"

"Okay." Solomon bit her. "Ouch," Solomon said before Jessica could even withdraw her finger. A thin half-moon of blood formed on her finger; the blood looked black in the dusky light penetrating the bay window, and it hurt like hell.

Jessica narrowed one eye and stared at the bird with the other. "Bite me again, and you're cat food."

Solomon flapped her wings. "Sorry. Upset, upset."
Jessica nodded. "So am I. It's okay."
For a moment, Solomon's eyes pinpointed on Jessica,

then relaxed. "You new Boss," Solomon said with dawning understanding.

"I'm the new Boss," Jessica agreed. She offered her finger again.

Solomon walked across her finger, up her arm, onto her shoulder. She felt Sol start tugging at her hair, beginning to groom her. The bird dug down to the roots. Soon Sol was completely buried beneath her hair.

Lou stepped off the platform by the roton. Turning and holding up his hand, he offered a warning for his great-great-granddaughter. "Watch your step, Lanie."

"Okay, Pops," she answered without meaning it. He knew she didn't mean it, because not only did she not take his hand, but she also looked up, waved gleefully, and jumped the last three steps.

Viktor stood at the head of the line of people waiting to greet the visitors, his arms outstretched. "Welcome," he roared, "welcome to the vacation Mecca of Earth."

Melanie giggled as she ran into his arms. "Uncle Viktor!" she cried.

Lou squinted into the distance. The desolate sweeps of ice and snow threw back a blinding glare of sunlight. Even Melanie's fire-engine-red ski coat and fluorescent yellow snow bibs seemed dim in comparison.

Lou pulled his jacket tighter. "Mecca my foot," he grumbled. "Dante put better vacation spots than this in his *Inferno*." He followed the sound of a young girl's giggles playing a duet with an old man's bellows, into the drop port terminal.

"Another one." Reggie should have been astonished by the view on Mercedes' wallscreen. But there had already been so many astonishing things in the past few days, this was merely yet another astonishment.

"Another one what?" Mercedes lay stretched out on the sofa, her head resting on Reggie's shoulder, her eyes closed. Her voice had the sound of someone who didn't care about the topic, but cared very sincerely about the speaker who cared about the topic.

"Another *Shiva* attack on Earth."

As Reggie had hoped, that sounded just important enough to warrant the opening of one eye. He watched Mercedes as she watched the recording of two days earlier. *Shiva*, in its dying moments, launched three missiles against Earth, one Hydra and two Selks. A camera on an orbital sensor platform had spotted the missiles, and had followed the fast graceful shapes as a dozen countermissiles shot up from earth, from a spot in the Himalayas that just had to be the top of Everest.

"Look at those babies go," Reggie said, pointing at the long tiny streaks rising out of the atmosphere. "Those countermissiles are fast, much faster than anything I've ever seen."

Mercedes sat up. "They don't look any faster than the ones from *Shiva*."

"Sorry, you're right. Those countermissiles are faster than anything I've ever seen *us* shoot, almost as fast as the *Shiva* missiles they're trying to intercept. Now watch this."

The countermissiles took out the Selk missiles, but the Hydra had detected its own imminent demise and launched its six independent warheads. Another dozen countermissiles spouted forth from deep in the Himalayas, and the hydra submunitions flashed, one by one, into wisps of vapor.

"I've got to see how we launched those," Reggie muttered. He logged into a sensor satellite and bought some time with the high-resolution optics. It was a little expensive to rent satellite time just to satisfy his curiosity, but hey, he was a reporter. He directed the camera to zoom in on Everest, praying that the missile launcher was not buried in some cleverly camouflaged setup. If it was, he'd need to hire a specialist just to find the damn thing.

He need not have worried; a huge, ungainly machine sat on a flat space where once the peak of Everest had risen in transcendent glory.

Mercedes asked the obvious question. "What *is* that thing, anyway?"

"I have no idea." He leaned forward, as if three inches could make a difference in his view of an image thousands of miles away. Under his guidance, the satellite camera zoomed even closer while he studied the outline of the structure.

The launcher clearly had its own boron-hydrogen fusion plant. He could see a huge number of coils, probably for refrigeration . . . but that didn't make sense. Why would you need refrigeration amidst the glaciers of Everest? Meanwhile, some of those coils were almost certainly electromagnetic. . . . "It's a rail gun," he muttered.

Mercedes lay her head back on his shoulder and closed her eyes. "What exactly is a rail gun?"

"It's a device for accelerating bullets and missiles at very, very high speeds, using electromagnetism," he explained.

"Sort of a particle accelerator for really big particles?"

"Ummm, yeah, that's a fair analogy. Though as you can tell, our rail gun there still can't throw stuff as fast as a particle accelerator."

"Ummm." Mercedes nibbled on his ear. He supposed he deserved that, for what he had done to her earlier.

Reggie continued to look at the screen.

In a moment Mercedes sat up. "This really fascinates you, doesn't it?"

Reggie reached his hand behind her head, grabbed her hair, and pulled her close for a serious kiss. When they came up for air, he turned back to the screen. "I'm sorry, but it really is amazing, you know. It saved millions of lives." He zoomed the view back out, so they could see the entire Everest plateau.

Mercedes' laughter had a tinkling quality as she asked, "How did they ever get it up there?"

Reggie shook his head. "It just doesn't seem possible, does it?" He turned to face her, giving her his most serious, sincere look. "It must have been done by aliens."

Mercedes clapped. "The same ones that did the pyramids and the crop circles?"

"Of course." Reggie narrowed his eyes. "Don't you believe me?"

Mercedes reached slowly, carefully across his chest. Then, with a sudden lunge, she slapped the button on his palmtop. The screen shut down.

Reggie yelled, "Hey!" but Mercedes had already turned her attention to the nape of his neck. As the vampiress closed her lips upon him, he yelled again . . . but this time the cry was weak, too weak to summon help—even if he had really wanted it.

Mercedes pushed him back into the sofa. Reggie tried to complain again, but this time his response was muffled as Mercedes' mouth closed on his. He put his arms around her and stopped complaining.

Minitanks and Destroyers jammed the sandstone corridor. Jessica turned, ran down another hall, only to find the members of her team, dead at the dead end. She could not see any of their faces, but they all cried out to her. She ran again, and this time the corridor was empty, empty, and she was lost, no matter how she twisted and turned.

A voice echoed in the narrow halls. "Jessica, it's the General." The voice belonged to Trudy; at least Jessica had finally left the Boyfriend from Hell behind. She opened her eyes. "Okay, Trudy, put him on. But do not let him see me."

"Of course not." The wallscreen opposite her bed winked to life.

Jessica rubbed her eyes. "General. Thank God you woke me up."

The General's face on the wallscreen in her bedroom switched instantly from one of apology to one of satisfaction. "Anything to help you out, Jessica." He paused while she gathered her wits. "I just received some remarkable news. I thought you might want to share it. Join me at the Colorado Springs Burn Center in half an hour."

Jessica started to ask how she'd get to Colorado Springs from western Arizona in thirty minutes, when she heard the whine of a skycar descending.

The General continued. "I sent a rocket courier for you, it should be there any moment."

Jessica laughed despite herself. "Right, General."

The trip was a whirlwind. She forgot to bring Solomon, which left her chagrined because MacBride never would have left Sol behind. Her failure was probably just as well for the parrot, though—birds tended to get awfully cranky if they didn't get a full night's sleep.

The ship hurtled through the air faster than sound. Jessica barely had time to play the obvious guessing game with herself. What could be such good news at a hospital? How could any news compensate for the loss of Morgan MacBride? Had they somehow brought him back from the dead? And if not, why the fuss?

Yet when she landed on the roof of the burn center, the General greeted her with a smile that looked to burst like a ripe watermelon if he did not share the news soon. "This way." He pointed to an elevator.

The elevator stopped a few floors down. Together they walked down the bright white corridor; the General's hard leather shoes clicked with every step, and the sound echoed off the walls and the sterile metal equipment that gave a hospital its characteristic starkly cold feeling. He was in a hurry, and Jessica had trouble keeping up with him.

They came to a closed door. A soldier stood at attention. "Who ordered the guard posted?" the General asked.

The soldier saluted sharply. "General Neldner asked for volunteers, sir. We thought it only fitting."

The General nodded. "At ease, Lieutenant." He shook his head. He smiled once more at Jessica and opened the door.

Jessica stepped through timidly. A curtain obscured the patient's face, and the bedsheets draped most of the rest. All she could see at first was a strong yet delicate right arm.

Jessica walked slowly around the curtain. When she saw who occupied the bed, she stopped dead in her tracks. "CJ," she whispered in stark disbelief. She could see now that the rumpled sheets had hidden the missing legs.

"No need to whisper," the General said, probably in an effort to convince himself, since he was speaking very softly, too. "She's still in a coma."

Jessica turned to him with eyes of wonder, questioning.

The General explained. "The captain of the rescue ship knew they couldn't get to her in time—you know, a stealthed ship can't punch a lot of acceleration—so he launched all his life pods on a course to put them between her and *Shiva*. Think of it as a shield made of life pods." He shrugged. "It sort of worked. Didn't stop the radiation, of course, but it blocked most of the heat and light of the blast." He shook his head. "How she avoided getting hit by a fifty-ton meteor of *Shiva* armor as the ship came apart, we'll never know. The rescue ship did take a hit, wrecked it good." He laughed. "The captain and the crew all got medals of course." Another pause interrupted the story. "Anyway, the radiation wasn't as bad as it might have been. We used three radical experimental treatments on her, one to flush the radioactive isotopes, one to accelerate full cell replacement, and one to kill the secondary cancers caused by the accelerant." He shook his head. "It seems likely she'll survive."

Jessica looked at CJ again. There was something wrong . . . she walked around to the other side of the bed and gasped. She held her hands to her eyes.

"Like I said, the life pods only stopped most of the heat and light. But the pods vaporized in the blast. CJ still got a bit of the flash."

Jessica stared at the left side of CJ's face, then back at the General. "A little bit of the flash? The whole left side of her face is gone!" She continued the inspection. "Along with the whole left side of her body!"

The General came around the bed. He folded his hands on her shoulders. "Just the skin. Her left side is covered with synthaskin for the moment; the doctors assure me growing and grafting replacement skin will be straightforward compared to other measures already taken." A low guttural sound came from the General's chest. "We have no way of replacing her eye as yet, however."

Jessica frowned. "Missing both legs, an arm and an eye. She'd be better off dead."

Anger clouded the General's expression. "Oh, really, Jessica? You sure? Think CJ would agree?"

Jessica rocked back on her heels. She'd never heard the General angry before. He could be really scary when he wanted to be.

And to be fair, he was right. CJ wouldn't think of dying. CJ would not see the three-quarters-empty glass of her own body. She would pronounce it one-quarter full. "When's she going to be able to answer the question on her own, General?"

Another shrug accompanied the response. "The doctors say she's pretty much fixed now. The only thing she still needs is the will to fight it through."

"CJ? The will to fight?" Jessica howled in laughter. She laughed and laughed, until the tears ran down her cheeks. "I suppose I'd better stop in tomorrow. I expect she'll be up and around by then. If we don't put her to work right away, she'll drive the nurses crazy." She thought about all CJ's eccentricities, all the ways C. J. Kinsman would try to drive *her* crazy, and her laughter changed pitch. It was going to be a long five years till the next *Shiva*. "Do the people in this hospital know how to make a chocolate malt? They'd better get cracking."

Appendix

by Reggie Oxenford

First of all, I would like to thank the author of this historical work for the opportunity to set a few matters straight. With the experience of having been born long before me, the author has assured me that, even at the turn of the millennium, it was not clear to everyone that technology would lead us to the world in which we now live. So, for anyone who thinks that the emergence of our present-day life was always obvious, I thought I'd point out some of the early works that appeared on the Web back then, describing the first crude attempts to create the most commonplace aspects of our society. These pages should be easy to access through the historical Web archive of your choice.

The Skycar: The earliest work on the skycar was done by Moller International, described at: http://www.moller.com

The Roton: The earliest work on the roton was done

by HMX Inc. The roton can be found at: http://www.hmx.com/roton.html

Capability-Based Security: The author informs me that back in those days many writers based their stories on the idea that all the computers in the world would forever be easily compromised by hackers. Rubbish. As everyone knows today, the ubiquitous deployment of capability-based security abolished these concerns. A quaint introduction to these tenets is found at: http://www.communities.com/company/papers/security/

Early work on distributed, secure smart contracts and ecommerce using such security can be found at: http://www.erights.org

Idea Futures and 'castpoints: In the early days of the Web, the 'castpoints that today underpin much of the economy were considered to be forms of gambling and were outlawed. Incredible but true. To learn about the early ideas about idea futures, go to: http://hanson.berkeley.edu/ideafutures.html

To see one of the first Web implementations of an idea futures market (without money! It would have been gambling if people had used really money, right?! Such bloody foolishness), go to: http://www.ideosphere.com/fx-bin/ListClaims

Bidirectional links, link types, filters, detectors, and other standard Web features: In the first implementation of the Web, these standard features did not exist. I know, I know, it's almost incomprehensible to imagine using the Web without bidirectional links, but that really is how our ancestors worked. Imagine what remarkable people they must have been, to achieve so much with such crude and primitive tools. To see early ruminations about how hypertext might work with these standard features, go to: http://www.skyhunter.com/hyper.htm

To see some of the first experiments in upgrading the Web to support these features, go to: http://crit.org/index.html

If you have trouble finding any of these pages in your Web archive, to find other pointers go to: http://www.the-earthweb.com

EarthWeb's First PrizeBoard Prize!

You've read the book; you've even glanced at a couple of the URLs in the Appendix. There is, of course, one major episode of human history left undescribed in the novel, an event perhaps as big and important as the Crash: whatever happened to Microsoft and Windows?

If you have a personal favorite explanation of what happened to the Microsoft juggernaut in the future history of EarthWeb, go to

http://www.baen.com

to find out how to submit your explanation to the prizeboard.

The winning explanation will be selected based on the following 3 criteria:

1) Originality
2) Humor
3) Excellence as a forecast (i.e., the likelihood that this really will be what happens to Microsoft and Windows)

The winner of the prize will get to pick 50 books of his or her choice from Baen Books; several runners-up will qualify for five books each. Details as described at the Baen web site. Just type "baen.com" into the Location box of your Web browser (without quotes); participation is only available via the Web.

DAVID WEBER

The Honor Harrington series: *(cont.)*

Field of Dishonor

Honor goes home to Manticore—and fights for her life on a battlefield she never trained for, in a private war that offers just two choices: death—or a "victory" that can end only in dishonor and the loss of all she loves....

Flag in Exile

Hounded into retirement and disgrace by political enemies, Honor Harrington has retreated to planet Grayson, where powerful men plot to reverse the changes she has brought to their world. And for their plans to suceed, Honor Harrington must die!

Honor Among Enemies

Offered a chance to end her exile and again command a ship, Honor Harrington must use a crew drawn from the dregs of the service to stop pirates who are plundering commerce. Her enemies have chosen the mission carefully, thinking that either she will stop the raiders or they will kill her . . . and either way, her enemies will win....

In Enemy Hands

After being ambushed, Honor finds herself aboard an enemy cruiser, bound for her scheduled execution. But one lesson Honor has never learned is how to give up! One way or another, she and her crew are going home—even if they have to conquer Hell to get there!

continued ☞